W9-ARM-809

DEAD ELEVEN

DEAD ELEVEN

A Novel

JIMMY JULIANO

DUTTON

DUTTON

An imprint of Penguin Random House LLC
penguinrandomhouse.com

Copyright © 2023 by Jimmy Juliano
Penguin Random House supports copyright. Copyright fuels creativity, encourages
diverse voices, promotes free speech, and creates a vibrant culture. Thank you for buying
an authorized edition of this book and for complying with copyright laws by not
reproducing, scanning, or distributing any part of it in any form without permission.
You are supporting writers and allowing Penguin Random House to continue to
publish books for every reader.

DUTTON and the D colophon are registered trademarks of
Penguin Random House LLC.

LIBRARY OF CONGRESS CATALOGING-IN-PUBLICATION DATA
Names: Juliano, Jimmy, author.
Title: Dead eleven / Jimmy Juliano.
Other titles: Dead 11
Description: [New York] : Dutton, [2023]
Identifiers: LCCN 2022055489 (print) | LCCN 2022055490 (ebook) |
ISBN 9780593471920 (hardcover) | ISBN 9780593471937 (ebook)
Subjects: LCGFT: Novels.
Classification: LCC PS3610.U5348 D43 2023 (print) | LCC PS3610.U5348 (ebook) |
DDC 813/.6—dc23/eng/20230112
LC record available at https://lccn.loc.gov/2022055489
LC ebook record available at https://lccn.loc.gov/2022055490

Printed in the United States of America
1st Printing

Interior art: Forest © andreiuc88 / Shutterstock.com

BOOK DESIGN BY KRISTIN DEL ROSARIO

This is a work of fiction. Names, characters, places, and incidents either are
the product of the author's imagination or are used fictitiously, and any resemblance
to actual persons, living or dead, businesses, companies, events, or locales is entirely coincidental.

For Sheryl, Isla, and Nutmeg (the dog).
When we're together, everything's right.

DEAD ELEVEN

A NOTE TO THE READER

On December 14, my sister went missing. Her name was Willow. I suppose I could have written *her name* is *Willow*, because she's technically missing and not legally dead. But as much as it hurts to write about my sister in the past tense, it'd be disingenuous not to.

She's as dead as it gets.

The island where she vanished, a secluded place called Clifford Island but referred to as either *Clifford* or *the island* by the people who live there, is teeming with monsters—some figurative, some literal. It was one of those monsters that took the life of Willow Stone.

I know my sister is dead because I've been to Clifford, that tiny pinch of land in the waters of Lake Michigan in Northeast Wisconsin, mere miles off the coast of the narrow Door County peninsula. I investigated Willow's disappearance, and while her body has yet to be found, the only logical conclusion is that my sister's light was extinguished by the evil that dwells on Clifford. This evil had been slumbering before, but now it's definitely awake.

And it's hungry.

The story I'm about to tell will certainly sound unbelievable. I can assure you that what follows is the best reconstruction of what happened to my sister and how it ties into the, shall we say, checkered history of Clifford Island. And even if you choose to not believe a word of this, I implore you to keep an open mind about Clifford—even when it comes to the more fantastical elements of this story. You're welcome to do your own research on the island, and I encourage you to do so. But it won't be easy. Information about the island is scarce. I know; I've looked. Others have looked. The town's presence either online or in journals, newspapers, and books amounts to little more than blurbs here and there. It's as if the island just fell out of the sky one day in the not-too-distant past and few seemed to notice.

And this isn't some uncharted or seldom-visited region. Millions of tourists flock to the Door County peninsula every year; the coastline is brimming with idyllic beaches, historic lighthouses, and picturesque marinas—it's Cape Cod minus the sharks. The rugged islands surrounding the peninsula are a major draw for sightseers and adventurers; there are thirty-five named islands in total, and tour boats zig and zag between them during the summer months. Clifford is one of these islands, although the boats don't stop there. The island is nowhere to be found in Door County tourism pamphlets or magazines. Even the kind folks at the visitors' bureau in nearby Sister Bay on the peninsula didn't have much to say about it. One of them hadn't even *heard* of Clifford, though it's actually one of only two Door County islands (the other is Washington Island) that has a population north of five hundred residents. Washington Island has a daily ferry, tours of its lavender fields, a maritime museum, trolley rides, and dozens of hotels and restaurants. There is no Clifford Island ferry. No cutesy motels or pottery class retreats. The people don't want you there. The island is a whisper. The primary refrain I got from those who had actually heard of Clifford Island was:

They just want to be left alone.

But more and more people are now whispering about Clifford. Some islanders were ready to talk, and I listened. They told me things they probably shouldn't have. Things about my sister, and things about life on Clifford. About monsters. The toothpaste is out of the tube; it was just time. I know what happened to Willow. I know the evil that she discovered, and I know who was willing to shut her up to keep the world from discovering that evil, too. I know about the shadows that lurk on the island, the things that creep behind the trees and into the islanders' backyards late at night. Willow knew, too, and she paid with her life.

Now I'm the only one who can tell her story.

But the more I listened and the more I learned, the more I came to realize that this project of mine would be more than just the story of my sister. To fully understand Willow's disappearance, you need to know more about Clifford Island itself, and the people who live there. In the following pages, I'll tell you tales—some of them macabre and not for the squeamish—about some strange things that have happened on and off Clifford Island over the past three decades or so.

And how do I know these stories? Well, as the expression goes, I have the receipts. Before she left for Clifford, Willow wrote her estranged husband a letter outlining her intentions. She then wrote him numerous other letters during her short stint on the island. I read those letters, and now you'll get to read them. I was also shown text messages between a young islander, Lily Becker, and her mainland boyfriend, Connor Hudson, that shed light on secret and devious things happening on and around the island at the time. You'll read those, too. I also acquired copies of audio interviews recorded by Willow's high school youth group students from the island church. Those conversations were conducted at the behest of my sister right before she vanished, and the revelations in those recordings are alarming.

I've stitched the letters, text messages, and interviews, as well as *re-enactments*, for lack of a better word, of events that I uncovered during the course of my investigation into something of a unique and unortho-dox structure. Some of the events and artifacts are presented chrono-logically; other times I'll jump back in time to provide some valuable context that helps to illuminate the riddles of the island. This is all by design. The structure of this book takes you on the same journey of dis-covery that my sister and I both took. When you realize what's actually happening on Clifford—the true, sinister nature of the island—it's si-multaneously jarring and yet surprisingly plausible. Willow and I both felt it, but I came to my conclusions much quicker than she did. I firmly believe that's because I came to Clifford Island with my eyes open, while Willow's eyes were closed.

You'll see what I mean.

I wrote the reenactments as accurately as I could, and I'm of the opinion that they are more than simple estimations. It's a bona fide Clifford Island oral history, gathered, interpreted, and arranged by me. Yet, due to the content, people will no doubt accuse me of taking nar-rative license with the information. Of spinning yarns, sensationaliz-ing, trying to score a book and movie deal out of my sister's disappearance (I am a writer, after all). And look, I get it. It's understandable. When an author posits the existence of the supernatural, a reader has every right to raise an eyebrow. Much of this book's content will strike most as simply too crazy to believe. But you really should believe it.

It's all, unfortunately, true.

Lily Becker was the first person to read a completed draft. The girl grew up on Clifford and had become close to Willow over my sister's five weeks on the island, and I figured Lily would be a very accurate judge of its content. I worried what she would think of it. Did I go too far? Were my third-person reenactments way off base? Was I, simply, *wrong*? I emailed a copy to Lily, asking her to pay particular attention to her chapters—she loomed large in the narrative, and I felt an obliga-tion to really nail her role in the story. I even attempted to get inside her head as a character and relay her inner thoughts to the reader, which at times felt presumptuous and intrusive on my end. After all, Lily isn't just some character in a book; she is a real person who has been through some serious hell.

I nervously waited two days, then three, then four. Maybe I'd misrepresented her, or maybe she just didn't want to relive any of it. I couldn't blame her.

On the fifth day, a reply from Lily appeared in my inbox. It read simply:

Close enough.

1

THE OLD WOMAN
AND THE CORPSE

Esther and Gloria had a routine.

Every day at 1:12 p.m., the elderly neighbors would shuffle to their mailboxes—Esther on one side of the gravel road, Gloria on the other—and they'd wave to each other. The widows owned the only two houses on a rural, one-mile stretch of road on Clifford Island. Their properties had been cut into the forest a half century ago, their homes engulfed by pine trees, with hidden driveways peeking through thin gaps in the sweet and earthy-smelling woods. Not many cars went that way; some days it was only the mail truck. The fog was a bit heavier at this particular spot, and despite the lack of island traffic, more deer seemed to dart out and get obliterated there than any other place on the island. The stench of rotting flesh lingered for days. Something to remind the women that death could sneak up at any moment.

They were a superstitious pair, after all.

The women's routine went like this: Esther walked down her driveway wearing blue slippers, gray cotton pants, and a red cardigan. She reached her mailbox and raised her right hand to Gloria, who would be wearing a faded white nightgown. Gloria waved back. The women checked for mail and then doddered back up their driveways.

It went like that every day, rain or shine, sleet or snow, for twenty-five years.

Many days there was no mail delivered. Christmas, the Fourth of July, Sundays, of course. But sometimes there was just no mail. No letters, no bills, no JCPenney catalog. The mail truck drove right by, or simply didn't come at all. The women checked their mailboxes anyway, always at 1:12 p.m. If it was colder outside—and it certainly got very cold this far north, especially in the clutches of a Wisconsin winter—Esther and Gloria bundled up in jackets and mittens. But Esther always wore the gray pants and cardigan underneath, and Gloria always wore the nightgown. It was tradition.

The two women lived alone for decades, but they were far from bored. Esther played cribbage at the small community center on Thursday nights. Both women sang in the church choir on Wednesdays, Saturdays, and Sundays. Gloria enjoyed tending to her garden; Esther had a chicken coop. They often exchanged pleasantries at the café downtown, usually commiserating about the runny eggs and burnt coffee. Esther and Gloria were friendly, but they weren't friends. Some islanders wondered why they weren't friends, as if being old and alone meant you had to be friends with your neighbor, who was also old and alone. They'd even get asked that question from time to time. *Why don't you drive together to church? You live across the street.* But both women felt that they couldn't be friends. They knew their bond ran deeper than friendship.

The 1:12 ceremony was their purpose. It started one afternoon, and then they found that they needed to do it every day. The routine was all they needed and all they wanted from each other, and both women would be damned if they'd be the one to break the streak. It gave a sense of structure to their lives, a sense of balance to their little corner of the universe. It made Esther and Gloria feel that the things they did mattered, that someone else depended on them. No one else had depended on them for a really long time.

Check time. Open door. Walk down driveway. Wave. Open mailbox. Walk up driveway.

Every day.

Twenty-five years.

But then, one unseasonably warm October afternoon, Gloria wasn't at her mailbox. The moment Esther stepped outside her front door, she knew something was wrong. The world felt different, and she couldn't explain it. Esther walked past her mailbox, across the road, and up Gloria's driveway. She hadn't been to Gloria's house in years, and she felt like she was trespassing. Her chest tightened, and her pace quickened. She knew she had to do this, and she wanted to get it over with quickly.

The front door was unlocked. Esther clasped the handle and gave the door a gentle push, thinking how strange it was to open a front door that wasn't her own. The weight, the squeak. It felt so utterly foreign to her.

"Gloria?" Esther called out. Nothing. She felt the dread spread throughout her belly. She had a feeling about what she was about to find, and she just hoped it wasn't gruesome and that it wouldn't cause her to heave her small lunch of an English muffin and cottage cheese onto Gloria's floor. Esther rounded the corner into the living room, and there it was: Gloria's body slumped in a brown recliner.

"Oh, Gloria," Esther whispered.

Gloria was dead. Esther knew that immediately, and her first thought was relief—it was not a gruesome sight at all, and her lunch stayed put right where she'd left it. There was no putrid smell, no blood, and the body wasn't bent or twisted in any unholy directions. Gloria's right arm dangled off the armrest, and her mouth hung open. Esther had found her husband's dead body in much the same position many decades ago, and she had known immediately then, too. Gloria, like Esther's late husband, appeared to have died of natural causes. A heart attack, maybe a stroke.

Or perhaps her body just finally gave up while taking a nap—Esther hoped that was the case. Something totally painless and without fear.

We all deserve to go that way, Esther thought.

Esther kept right on staring at Gloria's dead body, waiting for something to happen. She didn't know exactly what that something would *be*, but she waited all the same. The dead woman stayed right where she was, sunk into the recliner, properly dressed in that white nightgown—the one she wore to check the mail every day. Esther had never seen it this closely before. It had been patched up dozens of times. Little pieces of stitching jutted out here and there, and the bottom six inches had more wear and tear, no doubt the result of countless days trudging to the mailbox in snow or mud. Esther was surprised the nightgown had lasted this long.

She looked around the room. The furniture was dated and worn, just like her own. *Just another solitary old bird like me*, Esther thought. She caught her reflection in the rectangular, chunky Zenith TV that sat in the corner. It made her look older and tinier than she was, and for a moment she pondered the idea of mortality and wondered if her own date had already been circled on Death's calendar and she just didn't realize it yet. A large grandfather clock ticked loudly. Esther read the clockface: 1:19 p.m.

Reality crashed in. They weren't supposed to be here. Gloria wasn't supposed to be dead. The two women were supposed to be outside, puttering down their driveways in their daily uniforms, checking their mail. Actually, that was supposed to have happened seven minutes ago.

They were seven minutes late.

They were breaking their routine.

The old woman's body stiffened with panic. Esther didn't know what to do. All she knew was that their routine was all they had. Actually, there was no *they* anymore. It was *she*, and only she. It was the first time she'd been truly alone in, how long was it now, almost thirty years? The exact amount of time didn't matter. In that moment, the only thing that mattered anymore was the mail routine. Her purpose, *their* shared purpose, the one Esther shared with the dead person in the living room.

She had nothing else but the routine, so she had to act quickly.

The old woman gripped Gloria by the wrist and then dropped it immediately, recoiling at the body's coldness. It had caught her off guard. She had picked up a dead cat once before, and it felt nothing like this. Steeling herself, Esther reached forward and gripped the wrist again, this time dragging Gloria's corpse off the easy chair. The body fell limply to the shag carpet. Gloria's open eyes pointed blankly toward the ceiling, and Esther had a passing, terrible thought that those dead eyes might snap sideways and seize upon her—*Oh, you thought I was dead, missy? I'll show you dead*—but Gloria's body stayed very much lifeless, her eyes trained on absolutely nothing at all. Esther gripped Gloria by the right ankle and started pulling. It was slow, painful work. Gloria couldn't have weighed more than ninety pounds, but Esther wasn't much bigger herself. She hauled the body inch by inch to the front door, and when she reached the foyer, Esther dropped Gloria's leg to the floor. The dead woman's foot thumped on the linoleum. Esther put her hands on her knees, her ancient lungs pounding, her pulse racing.

She couldn't drag her any farther. Esther needed another way.

She found a wheelbarrow next to the garage, steered it awkwardly to the front door, and, even though she was sure she'd never lifted anything so heavy in her entire life, heaved the frail body inside. As Esther guided the rickety wheelbarrow down the driveway, there were a few times where it almost rammed into a tree trunk or tipped over. She was certain if it tipped, that would be it. She'd used up all the energy she had, played her trump card, and the corpse would just remain on the gravel driveway until she could convince someone else to help her with her morbid task. But Esther's steering was sound, the wheelbarrow level and true, and she made it all the way to the end of the driveway right next to the white mailbox with the red flag, one of the sacred locations of the women's routine. Her arms were wobbly by this point, and she couldn't have made it much farther. She released the wooden handles and the wheelbarrow tipped over, Gloria's body sliding onto the road like a pile of dirt.

Esther gathered her strength, and she looked up and down the road. No cars in sight, and she didn't hear any in the distance, which wasn't an odd thing in the slightest. Anyone driving in her neck of the woods was always a surprise to her anyway. She looked down at her wrist to check the time, but her gold watch with the champagne dial—the one gifted to her by her late husband, seemingly a lifetime ago—wasn't there. It wasn't part of the mail-checking ensemble. Regardless, she knew she was woefully behind.

If I'm an hour late, will it still count? she thought. *What about two hours? Three hours?*

She looked across the road toward her own house, thinking it looked quite different from this angle, like she was looking at it through Gloria's eyes for the first time. But there was no time for nostalgia or taking a moment to truly appreciate the world from someone else's perspective. She needed something to tie and fasten the body, and she needed it quickly. Her heart pounding, she briskly walked back to her own place, retrieved her husband's old belts and some zip ties, and then went back to the corpse and got to work.

Did she wave with her right hand or her left hand? Esther wondered. She couldn't believe that she couldn't remember such a simple detail, and she blamed it on the adrenaline. Esther settled on Gloria reaching inside the mailbox with her right hand and waving with her left, so that's how she propped up the body. It took six belts and three zip ties, and in the end, it didn't look convincing at all. To make it all work, she had to shove half of Gloria's arm inside the mailbox, and her body then swung out awkwardly with the other arm above her head and zip-tied to the wooden post. It didn't resemble someone checking their mail. It looked exactly like what it was: a dead body clumsily tied to a mailbox.

Satisfied, Esther walked back to her house and went inside. She looked at her clock: 2:22 p.m. They'd missed their routine by more than an hour, but Esther decided that was okay. The fact that she was doing it at all was what mattered. She tried not to think about what would happen the next day or the day after that. She'd come up with something, she reasoned. Something to keep it all going, something to keep the trains running on time. For now, she had to hold up her end of the bargain.

Esther opened the front door and, trembling only a little, strolled as casually as she could down her driveway through the pinewoods. She got to her mailbox and raised her right hand to Gloria, who, of course, was dead and tethered to her own mailbox. Esther popped open the little black door and reached inside. No mail today. The old woman closed the door and turned to walk away, the ritual complete, all right with the world. But then she hesitated.

She looked back at the corpse. Her dead neighbor hadn't moved an inch, thankfully. But that wasn't what Esther was thinking about. She was thinking about that *nightgown*, about what would happen to it after all this madness.

It was old, sure. Just like her and Gloria.

But it had a few good years left in it.

Maybe more.

Especially if Esther fixed it up.

This might be Gloria's last time checking for mail, Esther thought, *but that doesn't mean the nightgown can't still be a part of the routine.*

I won't let anyone take that away from me.

Esther hustled up her driveway to grab a pair of scissors from her sewing kit.

There was one more thing that needed to be done.

Larry Chambers, a carpenter in town, spotted the body a few hours later. He didn't usually drive out that way, but he had just gotten his 1991 Dodge Ram jumped, and he remembered reading that you should drive your car around for twenty minutes after a jump to juice up the battery. So Larry decided to drive aimlessly around the island for a while, and that's how he found himself in Gloria and Esther's neck of the woods on an autumn afternoon.

From a distance, he thought it was a person stretching. He got a little closer, and he thought it was a scarecrow. Then Larry slammed on the brakes, and the beer bottles he'd drained that morning rolled and clanged together on the passenger-side floor of his truck. He adjusted his rearview mirror and looked at the body again, just to make sure his eyes weren't deceiving him.

The man turned off his car and sat in silence for a few moments, his gaze not leaving what he had now determined to be a fresh corpse, strung up like a marionette. He patted his jeans, but he did not have a cell phone. He turned the key, but the engine wouldn't turn over.

The truck would not start.

Larry looked at this watch. It hadn't been twenty minutes yet.

"Sonofabitch," he muttered.

He wasn't quite sure what to do, only that he had no intention of dealing with this problem by himself. Larry turned his head toward the house opposite the dead woman—surely someone else had to be wise to this debacle on the side of the road—and through the trees he spotted another old woman, this one very much alive, peering out cautiously from behind a curtain in her front room. He hopped out of his truck and made his way to the woman's front door. He rapped three times and Esther answered, looking exceptionally calm and composed. Larry recognized her. It was a small island, after all.

"You, uh," Larry stammered, "you do know there's a naked woman tied to a mailbox out there, right?"

Sheriff Donovan and two deputies arrived not long after that. Donovan made the deputies do all the dirty work. The men cut down Gloria's corpse, put her naked body into a bag they dug out of the trunk of their cruiser, and placed the body in the back seat. No pictures, no prints, no ambulance, no evidence bag. They even gave the belts back to Esther; the broken zip ties they tossed onto the back-seat floor of the cruiser.

Donovan stayed with Esther for a while. They sat next to each other on a beige love seat in the old woman's sitting room. The big-bellied Donovan outweighed Esther by nearly two hundred pounds, and his end of the love seat sank a bit. Esther told the sheriff everything—well, almost everything; she left out one very important detail—and that's when the tears finally came. Donovan put his large arm around the elderly woman, and she collapsed into him. The old woman sobbed, and her tears stained Donovan's light blue uniform. The sheriff scanned the room, admiring the fine craftsmanship of the armoire with the slightly ajar lower drawer in the corner, and his nose twitched from the Scotchgard smell that seemed to pervade the entire house.

"What's going to happen now?" Esther asked Donovan.

Donovan honestly didn't know. Esther's words just sort of hung there. He considered trying to come up with something comforting, imagining what Pastor Rita might say—she always had a way about these kinds of things—but he elected not to go down that road. The pastor had the magic touch; Donovan did not. He'd call Rita in a bit, though, to be sure, because she had to be informed about things like this.

She probably knows already, the sheriff thought.

She seems to know everything that happens round here, even before it happens.

Donovan just told Esther that she'd be okay and that his office would handle all the details. Call the right people, things like that. Cop stuff. Donovan mumbled something about getting started on the paperwork, and the hefty man grunted a bit as he climbed to his feet. His armpits felt sticky. The house was old and stuffy—it was too damn warm for late October, and he wanted some fresh air. The sheriff went outside and found Larry sitting on the ground next to his truck, his back against the left rear wheel, a lit cigarette dangling between his fingers.

"Mind if I get a jump, Sheriff?" Larry asked.

Donovan didn't mind. Clifford Island was the kind of place where the sheriff would jump your car. It was the most action the sheriff might see all week, dead and naked women tethered to mailboxes notwithstanding. Donovan pulled his cruiser next to Larry's truck, popped his hood, and attached the jumper cables to both cars. Larry turned his engine over a few times, and it roared to life. The truck had logged more than 250,000 miles, but she still had some sass about her.

Donovan reached into his pocket, pulled out a dirty handkerchief, and wiped the sweat from his temples. Larry hovered behind Donovan, and the sheriff sensed the man's presence, his uneasiness. Without turning back, Donovan knew that Larry was shifting ever so slightly from foot to foot, and he heard the *thwwwwk* of Larry's fingers as the man flicked the cigarette butt to the ground. Donovan had great instincts, impeccable intuition. It's what set him apart from other cops, the sheriff thought.

"What is it, Larry?" Donovan asked, his tone sharp. He was irritated, and he didn't care if Larry noticed.

"My old lady does that same thing," Larry said.

Donovan raised an eyebrow. "Your missus does what, now?"

"That *Groundhog Day* stuff. And I'll tell you the same thing I've been tellin' her for years. It ain't necessary."

Donovan said nothing. The sheriff just stared across the road, letting his own thoughts bounce around his head. He still didn't know what to make of everything.

Larry nodded over at Esther's house. "Just what in the hell was that old broad thinkin'? Why would anyone in their right mind think they should do something like that?"

"She had her reasons," Donovan replied, finally turning to face Larry. Larry chuckled. "Yeah, they all do. I'm just sayin', it ain't necessary."

"You said that already."

"Why would she—"

"For Pete's sake," Donovan said, the anger rising in his voice. "She probably thought she was helping, giving herself a little peace. You're a doggone broken record." Donovan removed the jumper cables and walked to the back of the cruiser. He tossed the cables in the trunk, slamming it harder than necessary when he was done. If he was trying to prove a point, Larry wasn't having it. Donovan climbed into his squad car and was about to slam the door to really get in the last word, but Larry put his hand on the door, gripping it tight.

"This ain't sittin' too well with me, Sheriff," Larry said.

"How's that?"

"Did you see how she was tied there? Belts and the likes? I've never seen anything like that in my whole life. Makes me think funny things are happenin' around here. I dunno, I just don't want anyone else gettin' strange ideas, is all."

"I haven't got all day." Donovan sighed. "If you're looking to ask me something, do it fast." Larry's truck rumbled in an almost hypnotic pattern near the two men.

Rrrrrrom, rrrrrrom, rrrrrom.

"I s'pose, I'm just askin', should we be concerned about this?" Larry's tone was firmer than it should be when speaking to a man of the law.

"Not your problem, Larry," Donovan said. "But if you happen across any more funny business, just call the office. Now, get your sweaty hand off my cruiser. Just waxed the damn thing this morning."

With that, Donovan closed the door and sped off. Larry left minutes later, but not before studying the two houses on that rural stretch of road very carefully. He was looking for more funny business.

He didn't see any.

———————

Esther lay awake for some time that night in her bedroom upstairs. The wind outside picked up; the shutters banged against the siding of the old woman's house. A rooster crowed from the backyard, then another. A storm was brewing, and Esther wondered if she was the reason for it, if her actions had disrupted the universe in some way.

Her routine, the ritual. Expired.

The universe knew.

She swung her legs out of bed and stood up—she noticed the creaking and cracking of her knees as she did so—then tiptoed over to the window. The shutter clapped against the house faster and faster.

A storm. Just a regular old storm. Right?

Esther clasped one side of the heavy green curtains with her left hand and pulled them open a few inches, cautiously peeking into her backyard. She didn't know what she expected to see outside, only what she wanted to see. She hoped to see an empty backyard, the chickens sequestered safely in their coop—their usual drill when a storm was about to roll across the island. The chickens knew; they always knew. Esther longed for this familiar sight, a sight she'd seen hundreds of times before. Then maybe, just maybe, this would be a regular old October rainstorm—nothing ominous, nothing of her doing.

The chickens were not in their coop.

They were scampering around the yard, frantic and anxious, bouncing around like pinballs. Something had them spooked. Esther had never seen them like this before. The rain began, gently at first, but it quickly fell faster and harder. The chickens still did not retreat to their shelter. They remained outside in the developing thunderstorm, scuttling and squawking, flapping wings that were now wet and slick.

They were not themselves.

Esther shuddered, and she released the curtain.

She backpedaled slowly and bumped into her bed frame, falling backward onto the king-size mattress. Esther sat there like that, staring at the curtains, and she whispered a short prayer. She thought how hollow the words sounded, for even though she sang in the church choir and attended every service as sure as the sun rises, she didn't *really* believe in that sort of thing. Esther believed in other things. She believed in order, in equilibrium. She believed in the universe, and she was now quite certain it was some physical manifestation of *that* gathering outside, coming for revenge. Things were out of whack. Unbalanced. Gloria's death was the cause. Poor, poor Gloria. She and Esther had held together their little corner of the cosmos, and that was now broken.

Esther would be punished.

A low rumbling shook the house. It wasn't enough to knock the old woman over, but Esther instinctively grabbed her bedspread with both hands. The bed rattled, and a framed photo of Esther's late husband wobbled and then fell off the nightstand and onto the wooden floor. Esther heard the glass inside the frame shatter.

And then it was still.

Esther couldn't quite believe it had happened at all. She had never felt anything like that on Clifford Island. Not ever.

An earthquake, all the way up here?

She bent down and picked up the ornate silver picture frame, and the remaining shards of glass fell out onto the floor to join the others. Her eyes met those of her dead husband, and she longed for that old photograph to speak, to tell her that everything would be okay. When those assurances did not arrive, Esther simply clutched the frame to her chest, and she lay down in her bed, closing her eyes.

Something terrible was coming for her, and she decided she wouldn't open her eyes when it came.

The rain subsided to something of a soft patter, and there was a rapping on Esther's front door. Esther sat up in bed and listened closely, making sure her ears weren't deceiving her. She placed the picture frame on the bedspread next to her, and she heard it again.

Another rapping.

Louder, faster, more impatient this time.

Esther had a feeling about who would be standing on her porch, and her intuition was sound. When she ventured downstairs and pulled open the front door, Esther was met by the concerned face of Rita Higgins. The island pastor was wearing a black slicker, beads of water dripping off the hood as it hung down over her forehead, partially obscuring the woman's ordinarily warm blue eyes.

"Where is it?" Rita asked. Her tone was agitated, and Esther was taken aback.

"Where's what, Pastor?"

Rita ignored Esther's reply and simply brushed past her into the house. She walked purposefully into the sitting room, disappeared from Esther's view, and reemerged seconds later.

In a blur, the pastor was out the door.

The old woman was, again, alone.

2

WILLOW

Forty-Nine Days until Her Disappearance

Two hundred sixty miles away, in Wildwood, Illinois, Willow Stone had her own routine. Every Tuesday and Saturday, she cleaned her son's room. It wasn't the most exciting routine, but Willow enjoyed it. So many things in her life seemed abstract or simply endless, but tidying up Jacob's bedroom was a task she could start, seeing the finish line, and complete in an hour or so. It was nice to draw a checkbox and immediately fill it in.

Mark it down. Check.

It was a Saturday night, and the routine continued. Willow picked up one of her son's many baseball trophies and wiped it with a dustrag. The rag picked up next to nothing. Willow had cleaned the same trophy four days ago, after all. She stripped the bed and put on a fresh mattress cover, sheets, and comforter. Willow tucked the comforter underneath the mattress and pulled each corner taut, running her hand over it when she was done, admiring the smoothness. Then she wrinkled it, just a smidge. The kiddo liked it that way. She filled the mop bucket with water and soap and got to work on the hardwood. When Willow did a good job, her son liked to say it gleamed like the United Center floor before the Chicago Bulls took the court. Willow assessed her work.

Yep, she thought, *definitely United Center–worthy.*

She caught her reflection on the shiny floor, which was a bit like looking into a funhouse mirror. The angles were somewhat skewed, Willow's thin frame bending this way and that. Her wavy auburn hair looked almost black. She couldn't make out her green eyes, and this disappointed her, a bit.

Jacob had those same green eyes.

She lay in bed that night next to her husband. Dominic was sleeping soundly, but Willow's mind was racing. She was thinking about teaching and about the lesson plans she needed to create. Only, she wasn't a teacher anymore. She'd quit five months ago. Willow wondered when she would finally lose her teacher brain, that part of her that kept wanting to connect everything back to school, but she hadn't lost it yet. It might never leave her, she realized.

Willow heard a noise out in the hallway. Light footsteps.

It's just Jacob getting some water, she thought.

She thought back to her last few months in the classroom. Willow had always been one of the good ones, but she'd felt herself slipping. Showing up just as the first bell rang, playing more and more movies. She'd even let students sleep in class, which was something she'd never done before. Willow swore she would never do it, become one of those teachers she remembered from her youth who walked into the classroom, took that day's lesson plan out of the file cabinet, and slapped a transparency overflowing with old marker scribbles onto the overhead projector. *Here you go, you bloodsucking kids. Hasn't changed in fourteen years. It's good enough.* Willow never quite got to that point, but she saw how quickly she could spiral, and it alarmed her. So she quit.

Her principal, an exceptionally friendly woman who used to teach middle school science, offered Willow a temporary leave to get her head right. *You're one of our best, and we don't want to lose you*, the principal told her over strong coffee from the faculty lounge. Willow turned her down. She didn't want to feel the weight of the job anymore, and so she submitted her resignation.

Another noise out in the hallway caught Willow's attention, and it made her raise her head. The creak of Jacob's bedroom door. Willow turned toward Dominic, whose back was to his wife. The man was snoring softly. Willow couldn't help but think her husband looked tiny lying next to her. He'd always been a slender guy, but Dominic was down twenty pounds over the past year and a half. His hair was graying, too, though she would certainly never bring it up. She wasn't sure how he'd react.

Willow heard the soft click of Jacob's door closing.

Always so restless, Willow thought.

She gazed at the clock on the nightstand: 11:46 p.m. Willow laid her head back down on the pillow and tried to stop thinking about school. Anything else would do. A book she'd read, perhaps, or a movie she'd recently seen. Willow came up empty. She had tried to watch TV that night but couldn't make it more than five minutes into a program before losing interest completely. And it wasn't even her mind wandering: she hadn't been thinking about anything else in particular, but she realized she'd still retained nothing about what she'd been watching. A blankness had taken hold of her, and yet somehow, she sat on the couch for nearly an hour and a half flipping through channels.

Jacob's bedroom door opened again.

What is going on tonight? Willow thought.

She again heard footsteps treading lightly on the cherry hardwood flooring. They stopped in the hallway, next to the Gustav Klimt painting, Willow guessed, based on the creak of the floor in that spot. Her thoughts flashed to her own childhood, of getting into mischief with her older brother, Harper, and their mother punishing them by not

letting them speak to each other. She remembered bypassing this punishment by passing notes back and forth with Harper, using a framed
photograph of an Italian bridge on the staircase wall as their communication mechanism. Willow would write her brother a note, slip it behind the frame, and tilt the frame *ever so slightly* to let him know that
the package had been delivered. Harper would read the note and write
back in kind; the two felt like secret agents.

Willow smiled at this memory, but then her heart sank a bit when
she realized Jacob had no brother or sister to play secret agent with—
the boy was her only child.

The footsteps continued, until they reached Willow's bedroom door
and stopped. The doorway was open about six inches, and Willow lifted
her head. She stared into the darkness at the crack between the open
door and the frame. Willow felt—no, saw; she certainly saw it—an
outline of a figure standing there in the hallway, watching her and
Dominic.

"Honey?" Willow said, sitting up in bed. "What's wrong?"

The figure did not move. Willow heard light breathing from the
hallway, and the figure shifted a bit.

When Jacob was a toddler, he once scared the hell out of Willow by
climbing out of his crib in the middle of the night. He'd never done it
before. Willow awoke to a hand on her foot and she screamed bloody
murder, sending the poor kid into a crying fit. She and Dominic had
a good laugh about it after everyone settled down. That was seven
years ago.

"Baby?" Willow called out. "Is everything all right?"

The jiggle of a hand on the doorknob. Her bedroom door squeaked
open another inch, which made Willow reflexively reach over and shake
her husband awake. A groggy Dominic sat up in bed, rubbing his eyes.

"What is it?" he said.

"Jacob is— There's someone there," Willow said.

Dominic just sighed and lay back down.

"You have to stop this," he said sharply, turning his back to Willow and pulling the covers over his shoulders.

Willow looked toward the doorway, and the figure was gone. She listened closely and thought she heard footsteps descending the staircase, but she wasn't sure. Dominic's words echoed in her head.

You have to stop this.

It wasn't the first time he'd said those words to her. Dominic had grown more and more impatient with her over the last few months, especially after she'd quit her job. He was seeing too much of her, Willow thought. No more after-school badminton practices with the kids, no more happy hours with teacher friends. She used to sit at the kitchen table grading essays for hours to the soundtrack of laughter and chatter as Dominic and Jacob enjoyed a baseball game on TV. Now she had nothing but time. Time to dwell.

He's right, Willow thought. *I have to stop this.*

But it just feels so good.

Willow stepped out of bed and walked to Jacob's bedroom. She quietly pushed his door open and switched on the light. The room was exactly as she'd left it that night. Clean as a whistle, floor glimmering. Of course, Jacob's bed was empty. The boy wasn't there.

He had died eighteen months ago.

Wait, is that . . . ?

No, that's not right.

Willow left to retrieve glass cleaner from underneath the bathroom sink, then went to work cleaning the windows in her dead son's bedroom. She'd already cleaned them an hour ago, but she spotted a smudge. Besides, it couldn't hurt to clean them again.

Mark it down.

Check.

3

HARPER

I arrived on Clifford Island by what seemed like a secret entrance. It was a rickety brown dock on the south side of the island. The small pier led to a staircase carved into the trees—the wooden railings dangerously close to rotting away and falling to the ground, the gnarled steps swallowed into the thicket above. The main pier was on the north side of the island, but the angler I'd hitched a ride with wouldn't take me there. I wasn't really sure why, and I didn't press her.

I'd noticed as we approached Clifford that her head turned away from it, as if she couldn't bear to look at it for too long. There was nothing odd about the island at first glance. One edge rose to form a cliff that looked about one hundred feet high; from there it gently sloped down and leveled off, making the rest of the island appear to be nothing more than a dense forest of trees poking out of a giant flattened rock on the water. I couldn't see any buildings peeking through the heavy woods near the shore, at least not from our approach. If there were, in fact, five hundred people currently residing on Clifford Island, they hid themselves very well.

The angler did not offer any words of wisdom about where I was headed; she didn't even say goodbye. Her boat sped away as soon as my second boot hit the dock. Waves crashed into the stony shores behind me, and my body shuddered in the brisk December wind.

The fishing boat receded into the distance, and I turned to face the island that didn't want to be found.

You moron, I thought to myself, waving my phone around in the air. I'd emerged from the staircase onto a gravel road, and I had no idea where to go. Of course my phone had no reception. I swore under my breath and clicked on Google Maps anyway, hoping that an offline version of the area had been saved. The app launched, and I pinched and zoomed my way to where Clifford Island should have been located in Lake Michigan.

No dice.

There was nothing but gray and blue polygons.

I shoved my phone back into my pocket, looking left and right. The road was cut into the forest, both ends winding out of sight. I chose right for no particular reason, and I headed that way, duffel bag bouncing over my shoulder, the bottoms of my blue jeans already wet with snow and slush. There were no homes set back into the thick woods that surrounded me, no utility poles lining the road. I had a sinking feeling that there simply wasn't even a town here at all, or that the island had been recently abandoned. They were uncomfortable thoughts, and I hoped neither was true.

All I needed was for one person to be on Clifford with me—my sister, Willow, who had journeyed here last month and had not returned. Or, if she had indeed come back, I had no clue of her current whereabouts. I still didn't know the full story. Actually, I barely knew the preface to that story.

All I knew was that Willow had been to this island.

And I was trying to track her down.

I heard the rumbling of an engine behind me—I was not alone, after all—and I turned to face the approaching car. I waved my hand, and the brakes screeched as a sedan stopped beside me. The windshield was so fogged up that I could barely make out the driver; the entire vehicle was a clunker in the worst way. My heart leapt in my chest a bit, thinking that my sister might be behind the wheel.

I wasn't that lucky. The driver cranked down the passenger window of the boxy gray Buick, revealing a bearded man in his late sixties. He sported a Buffalo-plaid hunting cap and matching flannel jacket, and puffs of his breath escaped like cigarette smoke into the cold air.

"Where'd you come from?" he asked, his tone more inquisitive than accusatory. You'd think I'd materialized out of thin air right in front of him.

"I got dropped off on the pier down there," I said, pointing vaguely in the opposite direction. "I'm just looking for my sister. I think she's here somewhere, or was here."

The man considered this, and I could almost see the wheels in his head spinning.

"She came here in November," I continued. "A few weeks before Thanksgiving, I'm pretty sure. I haven't been able to get ahold of her."

"You heading into town?"

"I hope so, yeah."

The man hesitated, and then he reached across the passenger seat and pushed the door open. I plopped into the seat beside him and attempted to close the door, failing miserably. The door bounced back open, and I tried again, failing once more. My third attempt did the trick, and the door finally clicked into place. The car was at least thirty years old by my estimation.

"It's my wife's," the man said, wiping the condensation off his windshield in a circular motion, making a viewing area no larger than ten inches in diameter. "Door works about as well as the defroster. Tires balder than I am." He cackled at his own joke, slipping the car into drive.

He must've noticed the nervous look on my face, because he added, "Oh, don't worry. I can drive these roads blindfolded."

The interior of the car wasn't much warmer than the air outside, but it was a welcome reprieve all the same. The old Buick chugged along, and the islander's eyes flickered between me and the road.

"Your sister, huh?" he asked.

"Yeah, Willow. Fortyish, reddish hair. Do you know her?"

He shook his head. "Willow. Willow. Can't say that I do."

"How many people live here?"

"Not as many as there used to be."

I was confident he was making an old-man joke, but it still seemed a bit grim, considering the circumstances. *Circumstances.* Is that how I would describe what had led me this far north, a stone's throw from the Canadian border?

"You sure she's on this island?" he added. "We don't get many strangers."

I didn't know what to tell him, because I wasn't even sure myself. All I knew was that Willow had definitely been to Clifford Island, at least, in the recent past.

I had discovered that information solely by chance.

It was Willow's next-door neighbor who'd tipped me off just a few days ago. He tracked me down online—me, the brother one state over—concerning a tree that had fallen onto his property, alerting me that my sister and her husband had left their house to rot. They both just packed up and left one day, never to come back.

I honestly had no idea.

According to the neighbor, Willow and her husband, Dominic, had separated in October—Dominic immediately left for Florida, and Willow traveled to someplace up north called Clifford Island a few weeks after that. I knew my sister and her husband were having problems, but splitting up and abandoning their house just didn't sit right with me.

I initially tried calling them both, but I had no luck. Dominic's phone was disconnected, and Willow's went straight to voicemail, which was full. I checked social media, but Willow hadn't posted anything since Jacob passed nearly two years ago. The most recent posts on her Facebook wall were messages from her friends, wishing her well and sending thoughts and prayers. Links and memes, motivational sayings. Willow hadn't commented on any of those. Never even pressed the Like button. Dominic didn't have a social media presence.

The whole thing felt *off*.

So here I was, performing something of a wellness check on my sister, for lack of a better term.

If she was still on the island at all.

"She was here," I insisted to the islander in the Buffalo-plaid hat. We emerged from the forest, and the landscape was dotted with farmhouses and snowy fields. We still hadn't passed another car, but seeing actual structures with smoke rising from chimneys provided me with a small sense of comfort.

"She tell ya she was here?" he asked.

"Not exactly," I said, which made the old man chuckle.

It was true—Willow hadn't let me know outright she was coming to Clifford. Her neighbor had done that. Apparently, Willow had told the curious neighbor her travel plans as she was shoving bags into her station wagon in her driveway on some November morning. And it wasn't that I was disbelieving of the guy who'd pestered me to pay to remove a tree from his property, but I had to know for certain.

Two days before I traveled to Clifford Island, I first made the four-hour drive to Willow and Dominic's house north of Chicago, just to see for myself. I arrived in the early evening, and the neighbor was right: the house looked abandoned, or, at the very least, Willow and Dominic had become snowbirds. No lights were on inside. Snow had piled up in the driveway; a large recycling bin was tipped over next to the garage. The in-ground basketball hoop just off the driveway leaned forward a bit. A shutter hung crookedly from the second floor, perhaps the victim of a windstorm. I remembered Willow's garage code from the last time I'd visited—0403, Jacob's birthday—and, thankfully, the door rumbled open. The inside of the home was damp, cold. Knowing that a happy family once lived here made my heart sink. In the study upstairs, I made a particularly startling discovery.

Willow's *collection*, for lack of a better word.

Scattered around the room—pinned to walls, arranged on the floor, spilling out of manila folders—were printouts, maps, and pictures all having to do with one place: Clifford Island. I recognized instances of Willow's handwriting on the pages, notes and underlines here and there. From my cursory glances at the content, many of the printouts contained only a single mention of the island—often Clifford was just a name on a list of other islands, nothing more. There were dozens of Clifford-related documents in the office; there just wasn't a lot of meat on those bones.

The neighbor was right, I thought.

I studied the materials again, and I contemplated whether Willow might have been simply planning for a trip or a weekend retreat. That didn't seem likely. This was not vacation planning. No way.

This was obsessive.

Thorough.

It was like Willow had been looking for something, trying to put together the pieces of some puzzle.

Why was she so interested in this place?

I again pondered that very question as I sat in the passenger seat of a Clifford Island four-wheeled death trap, simultaneously praying that the old guy next to me wouldn't drive us off the road and into a ditch. I noticed him side-eyeing the duffel bag at my feet, which did little to instill confidence in his road alertness.

"I know, I didn't bring much," I said, kicking at the bag a bit. "I was thinking it'd be a short trip."

He smirked, his eyes returning to the road. "I hope you brought your long johns."

I hadn't. Didn't own any. I'd merely packed a couple of changes of clothes and some toiletries, not having much of a game plan besides checking out the island, which was five hours from Willow's house; eight hours from my place in Noblesville. Not quite day trip material, but not far off. Not that I was in any hurry to get back to Indiana—I typically didn't work between Christmas and New Year's, and this year was no different. Still, I would've gladly dodged work for a few days to make sure Willow was okay. The fine folks at *The Noblesville Gazette* could have docked my pay for all I cared.

This was worth it.

"You want me to take you someplace in particular?" the old man asked, looking over at me. "Told the missus I'd be home soon to fix the kitchen sink. Darn thing sprung a leak this morning."

Our conversation going nowhere helpful, I elected for a different approach with the man in the driver's seat.

"Do you know Lily Becker?" I asked.

It was a sneak attack on my part, and it seemed to throw him. His neck stiffened a bit, and he sat up straighter in his seat. I'd named one of his own.

The islander's head turned forward, and he cleared his throat before speaking. "Everyone knows everyone round here."

"Do you know where she lives?"

"I do, but she won't be there right now, I'm guessing."

"Where is she?"

He chuckled. "Where the kid always is."

The school seemed to be on the outskirts of town—everything seemed to be on the outskirts of town—I still wasn't sure if Clifford had a downtown. We crested a small hill and there it was, the only structure along a country road, looking lonesome nudged up to the desolate fields of white that surrounded it.

The building itself was long and single-story; it reminded me of the elementary school from my youth. Built with cinder blocks, looking suspiciously like a prison. The snow-speckled, changeable-letter sign out front—apparently untouched for some time—read: HAVE A SAFE AND HEALTHY SUMMER! There were only two cars in the parking lot, which didn't surprise me. It was December twenty-eighth, after all. Winter break. We pulled up to the entrance of the gymnasium, and the brakes held up at least one more time. I moved to exit the car, but the old man reached across the center console, clasping the sleeve of my jacket.

"You take care of yourself, okay?" he said. His eyes were warm but also looked almost pleading. I tried not to read into it too much.

I thanked him for the ride, and he released my coat. I stepped into the parking lot, managing to close the door on the first try, which I took as a good sign. The islander sped off into the gloomy sky, and I realized that we'd never introduced ourselves. An odd thing.

Maybe he doesn't know how to talk to strangers, I reasoned. He did say they didn't get many of them on Clifford.

But I knew they had gotten at least *one* other stranger very recently. My sister.

I'd seen a picture of Willow and a high school basketball player named Lily Becker, chatting on the sidelines after a game right here on Clifford Island, snapped just six weeks ago.

I don't think I was ever supposed to see that picture, but I saw it just the same. And if Lily Becker was indeed inside this gymnasium right now, I was dying to learn what she had to say about it.

And what she had to say about my sister.

Maybe she knew why Willow came to this place.

4

WILLOW

Forty-Five Days until Her Disappearance

Dear Dominic,

You think I'm crazy. I know that. But I had no other choice but to write you a letter. An email I wrote to you bounced back, and I don't have your brother's number. You've blocked my phone number, too, I'm pretty sure. I have things I need to tell you, and short of me driving down to Florida, this letter is the only way.

What follows are the things I tried to tell you the day you left. There was obviously a gap in our communication (that's the understatement of the century), and now that a few days have passed and things have cooled off, maybe I can tell you the things I wanted to say . . . but calmly and with a bit more clarity. More has happened since our fight, too, but I'll get to that.

First off, I'm sorry. I came at you pretty hard that morning, especially when you kept saying that you didn't see what I saw. I've had time to really reflect on this, and I get it. We are both still grieving in our own ways right now, and our minds are in different places. So, I apologize for calling you a liar and using other types of colorful words. You weren't "lying." What you saw just looked different than what I saw.

I'll be honest with you: that morning, when you said you didn't even *see* those words on Jacob's bedroom floor at all—that you didn't know what I was talking about—I felt . . . delusional. Like some lunatic. But the more I think about it, the more I forgive you for it, because I get it. You've been lost, Dom. We both have been. For a really long time. I apologize for psychoanalyzing you (the tables are really turned now), but to me, it's like you have blind spots and can't come to grips with what happened to our son. Those words under Jacob's toy chest really were your last straw, I guess. Like, you refuse to believe Jacob is gone—and I do, as well, in my own way—but you also refuse to believe those words might mean something. And then there's your old career, and . . . I know you don't want anything to do with that stuff anymore. I get that.

But as messed up as all of this is, I'm not deranged. Those words were right there on the floor. They still are. And they *do* mean something. It's not some freakish coincidence. That's what I was trying to tell you that morning, but there were tears and screaming and . . . I know it wasn't my best moment. And I'm sorry for that. I truly am. I just want to rationally explain where I was coming from that morning.

Will you hear me out?

The night before I found the words written in Jacob's bedroom—so, your last night in our home—I had that nightmare for the first time in decades. Yes, the same one you interviewed me about the day we met. I know that interview seems like a thousand years ago now, and we don't talk about it anymore. You know the one.

That nightmare.

I dreamed that the *thing* was back. And in my dream, I'm in Jacob's room. I'm alone. Our son isn't there. It's just me lying in his bed underneath his sheets. I hear it coming up the stairs, and I jump out of bed and quickly shove Jacob's toy box against the door. Just like I used to do when I was a little girl and it was my toy chest. Then I'm just waiting for the doorknob to jiggle. I'm waiting for it to find me again.

I woke up, thank God, before anything terrible happened. You were still sleeping like a stone. I sat up in bed, sort of overcome by this tsunami of relief, but then I felt that shame again, that feeling of abject humiliation I felt as a kid. That I'd done something wrong. That I'd brought evil into the world and someone else was going to get hurt by it, that I was putting the people I love most in danger, again. The dream felt so real that I actually went to our window and looked outside, worried that it might be there. There was nothing, of course.

But the dream didn't leave me. It gnawed away at me, and I just had this hunch that the nightmare returned for a reason. So I went to our boy's bedroom, got down next to Jacob's toy chest, and I slid it over a few feet, just like in my dream, just like I did when I was a girl. It felt like I was *supposed* to do it, like something was guiding my hands against the chest, helping me push. Then I saw the words on Jacob's floor.

Clifford Island.

I don't know how long they've been there. I haven't moved that chest in ages, Dom. Certainly not since Jacob's accident. And I've really studied those words. They look like it could be Jacob's handwriting. I know the way our boy writes the letter *a*, and the *a* in *Island* looks like it was written by our kiddo. God, I wish we could've spent more time studying them together, but then we fought and you were out the door and . . . well, you know. But I did my part. I tore the house apart looking for anything else, other words scribbled under furniture or even in that dank crawl space of ours. I found nothing.

Those words—Clifford Island—have done nothing but eat away at me.

I googled it, and there's not much out there. There's hardly an internet presence at all, which is just strange. The Wikipedia page is so small there isn't even a scroll bar. I couldn't find much. Only that Clifford Island is an island in Wisconsin near the Door County peninsula, you know, that tourist spot? So, maybe four or five hours northeast of here.

I've never been to Clifford. Never heard of it. It's small, hardly anyone lives there. There's a school, and I saw some basketball scores from the last couple years sprinkled online here and there, but that was mainly it. If Jacob wrote those words on his floor, how had he heard of Clifford Island?

I called a few of his old teachers. They never studied Clifford Island in school. There's no books about the island in the library. I spoke with the parents of Jacob's friends, and none of them have been there. Do you remember Jacob's friend Will? And his father, Steve? He's never heard of Clifford, even though he knows Door County pretty well. His parents have a place up in Ephraim. But it exists, Dom. It's so small it could be a crumb, but I'm looking at Clifford Island on a map right now. It doesn't make any sense.

I think this is a sign. It's all too connected. My childhood, the toy chest, the dream, everything. There's a reason we stayed in this house after the accident. There's a reason those things happened to me as a kid. There's a reason I had that nightmare again. I'm supposed—*we're* supposed—to do something about this, I just don't know what. But it's more than this cosmic hunch.

I guess . . . I'm feeling like a bad mom. What if I didn't really know our boy? I tried so hard. *We* tried so hard. I thought I knew everything about Jacob, but what if I didn't? Was Jacob keeping a secret from us? Did that horror I experienced as a kid get passed down to our son somehow? It sounds so stupid and far-fetched, but what if some evil found Jacob, too?

It's a stretch, I know. But the idea won't leave me. It's kept me up the last few nights, this nagging worry that I just can't shake. I need to yank it out, root and stem.

I'm going to Clifford Island. There, I said it. I just have this feeling that this has something to do with our boy. I know Jacob got hit by that car, and there's nothing mysterious about that. We saw it, and I'll never be able to unsee it. But what if there's more? Things we don't know? We've been keeping Jacob alive by staying in this house and honoring his memory. Maybe this is the next step in my journey, or in his journey.

Anyway, I just wanted you to know all this. To tell you that I'm not crazy, and to apologize for my part in everything. I'm not asking you to do anything, because I want to give you the time and space you need right now. I love you, Dom. So incredibly much. And when you're ready, let me know. If you just want to talk about anything, please call me. I'll be on Clifford Island.

Later, bucko.
Willow

P.S. Jacob's baseball mitt is missing. Did you take it with you? He always kept it on the workbench in the garage. I was planning on treating it with some leather conditioner I found in the laundry room. I watched a video on how to apply the oil and everything and, well, I feel like Jacob would've liked that, you know? But the glove wasn't in the garage. And I'm positive that's where he kept it. Just putting a bug in your ear about it. I understand if you took it with you. Baseball was a part of your thing with him, I know. Anyway. Love ya.

5

HARPER

I lingered outside the gymnasium entrance.

What if Willow is inside, right now, with this Lily Becker kid?

What would I say to her?

My throat felt thick, and my hand trembled as I reached toward the door handle. I pulled back before I grabbed it.

Does Willow even want to see me?

Was she hoping someone would come looking for her?

For the first time since I'd hit the road for Door County, I felt ashamed. That I hadn't done enough to maintain my relationship with my sister. That I'd let Willow down. It pained me to accept the truth about my part in all this.

I hadn't spoken with my sister in three months.

In fact, I'd spoken with Willow only a handful of times since her son died almost two years ago. And the few times I did, I got the impression that she didn't want to be talking to me. That she didn't want to be talking to anyone, actually. She was distant, short. Broken. I could've pushed harder, but I didn't. I chose to give her space, time to grieve. She had Dominic, after all. I assumed they were figuring things out together, navigating those god-awful circumstances the best they could, and they didn't need the brother from Indiana cutting in.

I remembered the last time Willow and I spoke quite vividly.

It was last September, and I was covering a high school football game outside Indianapolis. The halftime score was 49–3, and I'd already banged out most of the article on my laptop in the press box. The back-ups were on the field before the second quarter ended. The outcome of the game certainly wasn't going to change, and all I needed was the fi-nal horn to sound, so I could snatch the official stat sheet and grab a few boilerplate quotes from the coaches. Sometimes a prep sports reporter's job was easy; sometimes it was hard. That was one of the easy nights.

Figuring I could zone out for the second half, I thought to check in with Willow. I rang her up, and we chatted. It was all very surface level, and I never brought up Jacob. But I felt like we danced around him constantly, as I worried that a simple question like *How are things?* im-plied that I was asking, *How are things now that the best thing in your life is gone and never coming back?*

I wondered if our conversations were as torturous for Willow as they were for me.

Before we hung up that night under the stadium lights, I told her:

"You know, you can rely on me for anything. I don't know what you need, but if you ever do need anything, just say the word."

There was a short pause on her end, and she simply said, "Okay." It wasn't an important-sounding *okay*; I didn't pick up on any meaningful subtext. It sounded the same as everything else Willow had said to me since Jacob died.

Aloof, at arm's length. Like it didn't really matter.

Like she was just making conversation.

So we didn't have any more conversations.

That was the last one.

Now, here I was, about to enter a school gymnasium on some isolated island where Willow could conceivably be *at this very moment*, and I had no clue what I would say to her.

I decided it didn't matter, that the physical act of being here was enough. If she was here, some brotherly instincts would kick in and I would say the exact right thing without even thinking about it.

I swung the door open and strode inside. I heard the unmistakable sound of a single basketball being dribbled in the gymnasium—for my money, there wasn't a more distinct sound than that; I sometimes dreamed that very sound—and I went to go check it out.

There was a girl inside. Just one solitary girl, dressed in baggy shorts and a mesh practice jersey, brown hair tied back in a ponytail, shooting free throws at the far hoop. One of the gym lights buzzed and flickered above her. The orange basketball rose from the girl's fingers and—*clang*—it bounced off the rim. She hustled after it and snatched it before it made it to the sideline, then performed a few exaggerated, angry dribbles before heading back to the free-throw line. She hoisted another shot into the air and—*brick*—this time off the heel of the rim. The girl grabbed the ball before it hit the floor and slapped one palm loudly onto the side.

This is her, I thought. *The kid from the photo.*

Lily Becker.

It had taken some sleuthing to figure that out. I was never meant to see the photo of Lily and Willow chatting amiably in front of the scorer's table after a Clifford Island basketball game. No one was. It had been deleted from the internet, but I'd tracked it down.

Before I left for Clifford Island, I did some research of my own. Willow had done hers, and I did mine. Initially, my internet scouring was about as productive as my sister's. Which is to say, not very. Online information about Clifford was scarce, at best. Just bread crumbs, here and there. I did stumble across a few phone numbers—the police station, city hall—and I tried my luck with those. They were out of service.

Then I found something that really gave me pause: an article on a rinky-dink newspaper website. It was a recap of a November girls' basketball game between the Clifford Island Mudhens and the Gibraltar Bulldogs. The game took place on Clifford, and in between the paragraphs detailing the action *should* have been photos of the game. But they were gone. Only blank squares and rectangles remained with *X*'s that denoted errors. The files had been deleted from their host site.

Finding it strange, I plugged the article URL into the Internet Archive Wayback Machine, but the article hadn't been archived by the service. I was just about to give up before remembering, *You dolt, you're a sports reporter, you have connections.* I made a few calls, and I was quickly able to track down the photographer.

"It was the strangest thing," he told me. "The article was up for a day or two, and then I was told to remove the photos. People on Clifford Island weren't happy about them, I guess. I have no idea why. I didn't want to make a stink about it, so I took them down."

He still had the original files, and he emailed them to me as a zip file. I unzipped the collection on my laptop, and after sifting through hundreds of photos of in-game action, I came across the picture of Willow and a Clifford Island player. A cross-check of the box score informed me that this player was Lily Becker.

She and my sister weren't the focus of the photo. That would be the Gibraltar coach chatting to a few of her players after the game, the team all smiles after a blowout victory. Willow and Lily were off to the left in the photograph, and my sister was unmistakable. Knowing what I knew about my sister's obsessive research about Clifford, seeing Willow in the picture sent goose bumps up and down my body. Maybe it was the recent distance in our relationship, but it felt, in some weird way, like seeing a ghost.

I sent the photograph to my phone and left for Clifford not long after that.

Another *clang* inside the cozy Clifford Island gymnasium shook me from my thoughts.

Lily Becker had just hoisted another brick, and this one really did the trick. The girl caught the ball off the bounce, leaned back, and drop-kicked it high into the bleachers.

Lingering in the doorway of the gymnasium, I felt like I was intruding on some really personal, soul-searching moment. If I'd been profiling the kid for a local prep sports exposé, I'd have a helluva way to start my story, but this was no profile. I contemplated how to approach her, but it was then that Lily seemed to instinctively sense my presence. She looked over at me, and I didn't know what to do, so I walked inside the gymnasium, climbed the bleachers, and retrieved the basketball from the third row from the top.

"Here you go," I said, throwing her a bounce pass while descending the bleacher steps.

"Thanks," she said. "I'm not usually a head case, I swear. It's a little embarrassing."

I waved it off, meeting Lily at the left baseline a few feet from the three-point line. "It's cool, really. I'm sorry for watching. You've got a nice shot." I mimicked shooting a free throw as I said this, and the kid sheepishly laughed.

"But the ball is supposed to go in, right?" she said. The girl looked at me cross-eyed, no doubt reaching the point of realization that she didn't know whom she was talking to. "Are you a new teacher here?" She gestured at my bag. "Or a hitchhiker or something?"

Kind of, I thought. "I'm a reporter. A sports reporter, actually."

She rolled her eyes. "Oh God. Did my dad call you?"

"Your dad? I don't—"

"Ugh." She sighed, turning away from me, her hair flipping up and down. "I knew he would do this! I tell him I'm quitting, and he tells someone, and they tell someone, and pretty soon there's a reporter here stalking me in the freaking gym." The girl threw her hands up in the air and the ball bounced on the floor a couple of times. She seized it with two hands and spun around to face me. "Seriously, this isn't even *that* big of a deal. So what if I quit? My dad has wanted me to quit since, like, forever, anyway. Are you from Sturgeon Bay?"

"What? No, I'm from Indiana."

She stared at me, confused. "Indiana knows about me? Why do they care?"

"They don't—I mean, yes, I'm a sports reporter, but that's not why I'm here. It literally has nothing to do with why I'm here right now, actually."

"Oh," she said, her eyes softening. She looked at the floor a little embarrassed. "My bad. I'm, like, freak-show central today."

"No, no, no, it's fine. And I'm sorry for, I guess, sneaking up on you. I just got to the island, and I'm looking for someone . . ." I trailed off, pulling my phone from my pocket. A few swipes of my finger and the photo of Lily and Willow appeared. I held the screen out toward Lily's face, and her cheeks went flush. The basketball didn't fall from her hands, but I wouldn't have been surprised if it had.

I feared the absolute worst.

"Oh God," I said, mortified. "Did something happen to her?"

Lily's posture instantly relaxed. "What—no. I'm sorry if I was being weird—it's just, I miss her, is all. I didn't expect to be accosted with some random picture today. You caught me by surprise, like, whoa, there's me and Ms. Stone."

I realized I'd come across as some weird mix of a stalker and a movie detective, and I made a deliberate decision to steady my voice. "You miss her?" I asked. "When did she leave?"

"A few weeks ago, I think."

"Where did she go?"

Lily shrugged. "I think home. I can't really remember. God, I suck, right? She probably told me."

She's definitely not at home, I thought. *That place hadn't seen another person in months.*

"What was she doing here?" I asked. "Sorry, I'm just firing questions at you left and right. And I haven't even introduced myself."

I extended my hand, and Lily moved the basketball to one side and gave me a sweaty handshake. Her eyes squinted, studying my face. "You're related, aren't you?"

"I'm Willow's brother. Harper."

I detected a hint of recognition in her eyes, even though we'd never met. At the very least, I felt like she knew who I was.

"Lily," she said. "But I'm thinking you already knew that."

I smiled timidly. "I did, yeah."

Lily began dribbling the ball with her left hand, her eyes looking past me across the gymnasium. "I'm not sure what to tell you. Ms. Stone worked at the church for, like, about a month, I think? She was the youth ministry director. You know, youth group? But then she left. I didn't find it too weird."

"Why was she here?"

"She . . . needed a fresh start, is what she said. She was still . . . struggling, you know?"

"You know about her son?"

Lily nodded solemnly, not breaking concentration from her dribbling. Jacob was always the elephant in the room, and any mention of him always ground conversations to a halt. My interaction with Lily was no different.

"Willow did a lot of research about the island before coming here," I told her. "Almost like she was looking for something."

"Research?" Her tone was almost absent. "What did she find?"

Dribble. Dribble. Dribble.

"Didn't look like much," I replied.

Lily smirked. "That doesn't surprise me."

"Why not?"

"No one cares about this place," she said. "We're, like, nobodies up here."

"Do you have any idea what Willow could've been looking for?"

"Beats me."

I couldn't help but continue to press her. "She didn't mention anything?"

Bounce. Bounce. Bounce.

Lily shrugged. She crossed the ball over to her right hand and stooped lower to the court. Her eyes still looked past me, and I thought back to the study in Willow's home. The printouts, the research. It seemed so excessive. She wouldn't just come here for a fresh start. No, there was a specific reason.

"Is it a common thing to get strangers all the way up here?" I asked.

"You're here, right? It's not *that* uncommon."

I wasn't sure what to make of the kid. She seemed smart, pleasant—if not a bit sardonic—but it felt like she was playing games with me. All at once Lily seemed to decide that she was done with our conversation, and she picked up her dribble and let loose a long jump shot. It banged wildly off the rim and ricocheted off the first row of the bleachers. Lily said nothing and walked after it, leaving me alone a few feet from the three-point line.

I didn't know what to think. The girl had a shell that was difficult to crack. Or was it just avoidance? I thought back to what she'd told me moments before about Willow.

I miss her.

Whoever this kid was, my sister seemed to have had an impact on her. Lily might have played an important role in Willow's story up here.

Lily grabbed the ball and hoisted another potential triple, this time from the far corner. Again, her shot had a feather touch—I'd seen hundreds of players over the years, and Lily's mechanics absolutely *screamed* Division I prospect—but the ball caromed off the rim. The girl swore loudly, and the expletive echoed around the walls of the gym. She angrily untucked her jersey and stormed out.

The wheels in my sports reporter head spun faster, and I saw a two-thousand-word piece develop before my eyes. Lost island, promising athlete. And she'd just quit the team? Is that what she told me when I walked inside? I wasn't here for inspiration for a writing project, but I couldn't help myself.

I wondered, *What's Lily's story?*

LILY

The Previous Summer

Why is he looking at me like that?

It was the third quarter, and the game was tied. There were more people in the stands than Lily was used to seeing. Parents, brothers, sisters. Small children sprinting up and down the sidelines. A few other teams had taken over sizable areas of the bleachers, most of the players wearing sweatpants and headphones, nodding along and lost in music. The fans were dressed casually, lots of khaki shorts and T-shirts. The aroma of hot dogs and buttered popcorn wafted into the gymnasium, and Lily could smell it while she was situating herself at the lower block underneath the basket, waiting for number 15 on the opposing Jacksonport Raiders to shoot her first free throw.

Lily had her hands on her knees as she gathered her breath. She'd played every minute so far, and her contributions were keeping the Clifford Island Mudhens in the game. Lily wasn't sure how many points or rebounds she had. She never kept track of those things, at least not during the game. After the final buzzer sounded, she was always pleased to learn her stat line, but only if they'd won. Which wasn't often.

Seriously, what is he looking at?

The first free throw swished through the basket, and the referee grabbed it after one bounce. Lily was only peripherally aware of the ball going in. Her attention had shifted to a boy who sat with a few of his teammates in the bleachers behind the baseline, about twenty feet away from her. They were dressed in Sturgeon Bay practice gear and had wandered into the gym like they owned the place about fifteen minutes prior. Two of the boys lounged in the bleachers, joking and laughing about something. But the other boy—the third boy—kept sneaking glances at Lily. She'd noticed it the last time she was down the court during an inbounds play. The boy wasn't really watching the game. He was interested in Lily, in particular.

The referee bounced the basketball back to number 15, and the girl dribbled the ball a few times, sizing up her second free throw. Lily turned her head and made quick eye contact with the boy. He was her age, she guessed, a junior or senior. His brown hair was cropped close to his head, the classic high school athlete haircut. He was cute, Lily thought, but the way he had been watching her just pissed her off a bit. She was a little flattered, too, but mainly pissed. There was a game to win; she didn't have time for this.

What are you looking at? Lily mouthed to the boy. He sheepishly looked away, and Lily noticed his right knee quickly bobbing up and down, like he couldn't stop himself from doing it. She couldn't help but smirk at his embarrassment.

That three-second moment of distraction threw Lily off her game. She didn't notice number 15 launching her second free throw, and Lily was just a hair late in boxing out her opponent. The ball careened off the rim, and the Jacksonport power forward behind Lily was able to reach above her and snare the rebound out of the air.

And this *really* pissed Lily off.

The power forward kicked the ball out to a guard standing near the three-point line, and the Raiders reset their offense. That rebound should have been hers. Lily knew it. She *never* failed to execute a simple box-out. That was Basketball 101, something they teach seven-year-olds at summer basketball camp.

A stupid boy? Lily thought. *I missed the rebound because I was looking at a stupid boy?*

The Jacksonport power forward stuck her hips into Lily and backed her down a bit near the block. She outweighed Lily by about twenty pounds, and Lily was forced to backpedal two feet. Lily bent her knees and shoved her forearm into the power forward's lower back. Depending on the referee, this was oftentimes a foul. Especially during the regular season. But this was a summer basketball tournament, and people had barbecues and pool parties to get to, so the referees usually let this type of thing slide to keep the clock moving.

The guard fed the ball to the power forward, and the girl caught it with two hands. She was nearly all the way on the block now, and a barrage of scenarios raced through Lily's head: a left-handed hook shot, a quick turn-and-face jump shot, maybe a short fadeaway. The girl could have pounded a few dribbles and backed in Lily another foot, but that close to the basket it was a bad idea. A sneaky guard was liable to cruise in from the far side of the court and steal the ball away, so Lily didn't expect the girl to do that. No, she knew her opponent's tendencies by this point in the game. She'd guarded the girl for most of her twenty minutes on the court. Lily knew exactly what the girl was going to do, and she goaded her into it.

She was ready.

The power forward gripped the ball with two hands, her back to the basket, and Lily draped herself all over her. Lily inched to her right, giving her opponent just a little bit of space and making her think that a leftward spinning right-handed baby hook shot would be met with little resistance. And the power forward played right into Lily's trap. She swung her arms to the right—her elbow nearly colliding with Lily's chest—and then quickly spun back in the other direction and leaned in for a baby hook off the glass.

But Lily was already standing there. It was too late for the power forward to change course, so she had to hope that muscling it up over Lily would work.

It didn't.

Lily ascended high above the Jacksonport power forward, and her hand met the ball mere inches after it left the opponent's fingertips. Lily was so geared up—so ready, so excited to swat this feeble shot attempt out of bounds—that she was able to position her body perfectly and really get her money's worth out of it. She was able to aim the block *exactly* where she wanted it to go, and her aim was true.

The basketball rocketed off Lily's hand into the bleachers behind the baseline, and it smacked the boy in the Sturgeon Bay practice gear who'd been checking her out directly in the face.

The crowd gasped.

Someone from across the gymnasium yelled, "Oh shiiiiiiiiiiiit!" which elicited a few laughs from the crowd.

The boy's hands went up to his face. Lily took a step toward the baseline, her hands on her hips, a huge smile crossing her face. The boy dropped his hands, his forehead red from where the ball had smashed into him.

He smiled back at Lily.

Lily didn't return to the island that night. She could've—it was less than an hour's drive to the pier and then a short jaunt on the boat back to Clifford. But then she would've had to do it all over again the next morning. It was a two-day tournament, so she and her father stayed at a family friend's house in Sturgeon Bay. Her father was early to bed—nine thirty every night, like clockwork—and Lily snuck out the back door at nine forty-five.

She was going to meet the boy.

The boy, Connor Hudson, was a senior, like Lily. He stuck around in the hallway outside the gymnasium to talk to Lily after her game. The red mark on his face wasn't quite gone yet, and he joked that he'd be suing Clifford Island for facial-reconstruction surgery. He sort of tilted his head just a little bit when he said this—and whenever he made any sort of joke or humorous offhand remark—a physical tic that Lily picked up on right away. She found it immediately endearing, and she wasn't quite sure why. She just wanted to hear more jokes, more anecdotes, corny or not corny. Connor invited her to a bonfire at his friend's house later that night, and Lily happily accepted.

She met him two streets over from the family friend's house a little before 10:00 p.m., and then they drove another ten minutes to pick up Lily's friend and teammate Kayla. They found her sitting on a curb, a very worried look on her face. The rail-thin girl quickly slid open the side door to Connor's dad's minivan and jumped inside.

"I can't believe we're doing this," Kayla said, slamming the door shut.

"We aren't breaking any laws." Lily shrugged. "What's the worst that could happen?"

"Um, we could get into serious trouble?" Kayla replied.

Kayla was right, but Lily didn't much care. She could count on one hand the number of times she'd slept off Clifford Island in her entire life, and each time she'd been accompanied by her father. Clifford kids weren't allowed to leave the island without an adult; it was one of the island rules. She knew her father would disapprove of what she was doing—she did sneak out, after all—but really, what was the worst thing that would happen? A disapproving glance? The *I'm just really disappointed in you* talk? Nah. This was worth it.

Connor hesitated for a second and then put the van in drive. He kept his foot on the brake. "Are you sure this is cool?" He looked at Kayla, then at Lily. "I feel like I'm a bad influence on you guys, like I'm your drug dealer or something."

The slight head tilt. *I wonder if he knows he does it*, Lily thought.

"It's fine, it's fine," Lily insisted. She looked back at Kayla. "Right?"

"Just," Kayla said, before sighing. "It's fine. Let's go."

Connor took his foot off the brake and stepped on the gas. "Newcomers have to do more coke than anyone at the party, just a heads-up. It's like *Scarface* all the time around here. Do you guys know that movie?"

Another head tilt. Kayla rolled her eyes. Lily smiled, bit her lower lip, and looked out the window.

Why do I find this geeky mainlander boy so cute?

There were no mountains of cocaine at the party—the head tilt kind of gave away the joke—but there was lawbreaking. Underage drinking, mainly. One of the high school kids showed up with a case of lukewarm beer that had been sitting in his parents' garage, and the twelve or so kids standing around the bonfire passed them around. Lily and Kayla politely refused; Kayla because she was simply too nervous to do such an audacious thing as drink a beer, and Lily because it could threaten her chance at a Division I basketball scholarship. Sure, this was just a silly bonfire in someone's backyard that probably no one cared about. But one loud song on the speakers outside could precipitate a phone call; one phone call could bring an overzealous deputy to the house; the deputy might write the kids drinking tickets to prove a point; the admissions department at Michigan or Iowa State or wherever might find out, and . . . no. It was quite the Rube Goldberg chain of events, but basketball was Lily's one-way ticket away from the strange islanders and the control they kept over the kids—dictating what they wore, the types of music they could listen to, not letting them leave the island unsupervised. Basketball was her escape, and she could not, would not, jeopardize her future.

Besides, that room-temperature beer looks like crap anyway, Lily thought.

The party host invited Connor and the two Clifford girls to hang out in the walkout basement, and the group headed that way. Lily immediately noticed that Connor left his beer outside on the ground—

he'd cracked it open, but he hadn't taken a sip. Lily wondered if it was because he was their driver or because he saw that she wasn't drinking and wanted to follow her lead. Whatever the reason, it didn't matter. Connor was simply attentive to her, and she liked it.

The kids plopped down on one of those oversize L-shaped sofas, and the host—a boy named Zack, Lily learned—turned on the television and grabbed a video-game controller. He clicked a few buttons, launched a streaming-service app on the TV, and began endlessly scrolling. His breath reeked of alcohol, and his gray Sturgeon Bay Eagles T-shirt was sprinkled with spots of beer.

Connor sat directly next to Lily, and their thighs were touching. It was a pretty innocent thing. Everyone's thighs were practically touching at that point, but to Lily it felt simply electric. She should have been in bed at the house of that family friend she'd met twice before or, even more depressing, in her own bed on Clifford Island, only miles away from the mainland but feeling like a million more. Boys like Connor didn't exist on Clifford Island; moments like these didn't exist. Lily and the friends she'd known since they were in diapers were like one collective old married couple—finding joy but also always putting up with one another, warts and all.

"How do you guys even have a team?" Zack asked, his eyes not leaving the TV.

"What do you mean?" Lily said.

"Aren't there, like, twenty kids at your whole school?" Zack said.

Lily laughed. "I mean, some years we don't have a team. We've been lucky the last few years. Next year, not so much."

"Really?" *Scroll, scroll, scroll.*

"Me and Kayla are graduating," Lily said. "There will be only four players left."

"I'll find you some players," Connor chimed in. "A couple of ringers who have boats. Shouldn't be too hard."

Like they'd let anyone move to our little island, Lily thought.

She pressed her leg into Connor's a little more, and he pressed his into hers. He tilted his head a bit—Lily thought he was about to make another joke—but he didn't. He just blushed, and Lily liked him even more.

Zack kept scrolling and scrolling before dropping the controller in Kayla's lap.

"I don't know," Zack said, burping a little and standing up. "Let one of the newbies decide."

Lily noticed the uncomfortable look on Kayla's face. She *knew* her friend, and she guessed Kayla wouldn't do well in this moment. Kayla hesitated a bit, then she lifted her hands and held the controller aloft with two hands on the extreme edges, like she was sitting behind the wheel in driver's ed class for the first time. The girl poked at a few buttons with her thumbs, and Zack burst out laughing.

"Oh my God," he said. "It's upside down, you know? How much have you been drinking?"

Kayla, what are you doing? Lily thought. *Just put it down.*

Zack grabbed the controller and flipped it right side up. He placed it back in Kayla's hands and guided it down to her lap. "Pick anything you want. Anyone want another beer?" He looked at Connor and the girls, who all shook their heads.

"I'll take one," a voice called out from across the basement. Lily looked over toward the voice and saw a boy chalking up a pool cue. He looked somewhat older than the rest of the party crew, lacking that wiry high school athlete look. His hair stuck out from underneath a backward hat, and his midsection was softened with a few too many late-night pizza orders. A college kid, for sure.

Zack simply pointed at him and loped back outside. The trio were now alone with the college kid. Lily watched him slide the pool cue through his fingers, and the balls smacked together on the table. He admired his break before looking up toward the high schoolers on the sofa.

"Are you guys from Clifford?" He seemed a little too excited to ask this question, like the girls were celebrities or something.

Lily nodded, and the kid put down the cue. A huge grin crossed his face.

"I knew it!" he exclaimed.

"So what?" Lily said, not caring if the kid picked up on the irritation in her voice.

He kind of smirked and made his way over to them. He certainly had the strut of a university kid home on summer vacation. "I'm not trying to be weird or anything, but it's kind of a big deal to see one of you out in the wild. The mysterious *Clifford Island*!" He wiggled his fingers in front of his face when he said this, like he was about to introduce a magic trick.

Lily's stomach sank. She turned to Connor and Kayla and gave her best *let's get the hell out of here right now* look. It worked, because the pair immediately stood up.

"Wait, wait, wait," the boy said, "you guys aren't leaving, are you?"

"We were planning on it," Lily said.

"I just want to talk a bit!" he said. "Or get a picture or something." He was only a few feet away from the group at this point, and his breath smelled more potent than Zack's.

"Seriously, you want a picture?" Connor said. He sounded more confused than anything. If he was going to get tough with the guy at some point, it wasn't happening yet.

"Not with *you*," the boy said. "I mean, you clearly aren't an islander. You are dressed far too normal to be from Clifford." Connor instinctively looked down at his clothes and then glanced between Kayla and Lily.

Crap, Lily thought. She had considered packing a different outfit before she left Clifford, but how was she supposed to know she'd be out and about, carousing at a bonfire? That hadn't even crossed her mind. If it had, she would've brought along one of her more innocuous outfits, something a bit more modern—whatever she had in her closet that was the *closest* thing to modern, actually. Instead, she was dressed in one of her usual getups: faded denim overalls with one strap hanging down, a neon green cropped shirt, and white Keds shoes. She guessed Kayla didn't stick out as much: Airwalk low-tops, jean shorts, and a vintage black PLANET HOLLYWOOD WASHINGTON, D.C. sweatshirt, the logo wrinkling and fading. Perhaps separately they'd have gone unnoticed, but together they made quite the pair.

"I'm not really in a picture mood," Lily said, pushing past the college boy and heading toward the sliding door.

"Hold up," he said, grabbing Lily by the shoulder and spinning her around.

"Did you seriously just do that?" Lily remarked.

"Hey, man," Connor said, walking over next to Lily. "Cool it, okay? She doesn't want her picture taken. Just leave it alone."

The college guy put both his hands up in a mock-surrender fashion and backed up a few steps. "It's cool, it's cool," he said. "I won't take the picture." He removed his phone from his pocket and tossed it to Kayla, who was still frozen in place by the sofa. She caught the phone awkwardly.

"You take it," he said.

Kayla stared at the phone in her hands like she was holding a ticking nuclear device. Her mouth was agape, and she locked eyes with Lily. Kayla looked like she was trying to say something, but no words were coming.

"I saw you with the controller a minute ago," the college boy said, motioning over to the couch. "I thought, really? The stories are true? These kids really haven't touched anything made in the last twenty years? So, let's put it to the test. If you can figure out how to take a picture with my phone—and it could be a picture of anything, like, the mantel or whatever, I really don't care—I'll leave you guys alone. Cool?"

"Kayla, this is stupid," Lily interjected. "Put it down and let's get out of here."

"Just take the stupid picture," the college boy said, sounding exasperated. "Jesus, this isn't complicated."

Lily wasn't quite sure what point this guy was trying to prove, but he was drunk and surly, and maybe that *was* the point. Lily's eyes moved to Connor, and he looked like he was sizing the guy up. Connor was athletic, sure, but this guy appeared to have thirty pounds on him, and a few beer muscles to boot.

Kayla fidgeted with the phone in her hands, and Lily knew just how uncomfortable the girl was. She was pretty certain Kayla had never touched a cell phone in her entire life. Lily *did* have a cell phone—it definitely skirted the rules of Clifford Island—and on more than a few occasions she'd offered it to Kayla to play a game or check out some photos.

Kayla always refused.

I feel like I'd be disappointing everyone, Kayla had once told Lily. And now, here she was, holding a stranger's phone seemingly against her will. Her streak was broken. First the video-game controller, and now this. Lily's heart broke for her lifelong friend, and she wondered how upset she'd be when they finally got out of this, and how much she'd blame Lily for it.

"Ugh," the college guy blurted out, snatching the phone from Kayla's hands. "You guys are so freakin' weird. Seriously. What is wrong with you? You dress like . . . time travelers or something, and I try to have one basic conversation with you and it's all . . . uh . . . uh . . . like you've never talked to another person your entire life. For real, what are you guys doing up there in that commune of yours? Like . . . worshipping King Kong or something?"

He pushed past Lily and Connor and whipped open the sliding door.

"We're saving your life," Kayla blurted.

Oh, Kayla, Lily thought. *No, no, no. Don't say that.*

The college guy turned around and stifled his laughter. "Wait, what?"

Don't do this.

You can't.

Not you.

"What we're doing up there," Kayla said softly, "is saving your life."

Stop, Kayla. No one is supposed to know about this.

The college guy was, finally, speechless. Connor appeared similarly perplexed. Everyone looked at Kayla, who now had a spark of defiance in her eyes that Lily had never seen before. Growing up on Clifford Island, Lily had always just kind of played along with everything. She hated the rules, despised the oppressiveness—and she thought that all the other kids did, too. They all said as much. *We dress like this because we have to dress like this. We'd love a cell phone, but our parents won't let us.* But maybe she was wrong. What if her friends were placating her and telling her what she wanted to hear? Or, deep down, they were just torn? Maybe Kayla wasn't worried about breaking the rules because of getting in trouble or disappointing her parents; maybe she *actually* believed in the things the adult islanders believed in.

No, it wasn't possible.

Was it?

Kayla leered at the college kid. It was in that moment that Lily decided she'd finally had it. If Clifford Island could make a believer out of her best friend, then the island had really gone too far. She wasn't sure when, and she wasn't sure how.

But she was sure.

One day, Lily resolved, standing there, *I'm going to blow the whistle on the whole goddamn thing.*

7

CLIFFORD ISLAND

EXCERPT OF LILY BECKER INTERVIEW WITH PETER ELLIOT

LILY: Tell me about the island.

PETER: What is this for again?

LILY: It's an oral history project for Ms. Stone.

PETER: This isn't your project?

LILY: No. It was Ms. Stone's idea. It's for the church.

PETER: And Pastor Rita gave this her blessing? To record me?

LILY: I'm sure she did. Everyone in the youth group is doing the project.

PETER: Huh.

LILY: What's that?

PETER: Oh, I'm not trying to turn this into a problem, but I find it odd that Kayla didn't say anything about this. Or that she didn't want to interview me.

LILY: Are you offended?

PETER: A little, yeah.

LILY: Maybe interviewing your own dad is awkward? I don't know.

PETER: Who is she interviewing?

LILY: I'm not sure. But it's okay if I interview you, right?

PETER: I suppose, but why did you choose me?

LILY: Honestly? I have a free period, and I was walking by your office and saw you inside. You looked kind of bored, actually. Guidance counselors on this island don't have much to do, I guess.

PETER: You've made an inspired choice.

LILY: Thanks.

PETER: What are you doing with the recordings?

LILY: We're just collecting stories for the islanders. Something for everyone to listen to and enjoy. To build fellowship, you know?

PETER: And you're sure that it's okay that we're—

LILY: It's for the church, Mr. Elliot. It's fine. You can ask Ms. Stone if you want.

PETER: No, no. I'm sure it's fine.

LILY: Okay, so, I'm here with Mr. Peter Elliot, local high school guidance counselor on Clifford Island. And we are talking about, um, Clifford Island. Mr. Elliot, what's your relationship with the island?

PETER: My relationship, let's see.

LILY: Are you originally from here? Or, born here, whatever.

PETER: No, I actually moved here in 1992. Maybe the last island transplant, now that I think about it. Except for Ms. Stone, that is.

LILY: How old were you?

PETER: I was twenty-two. Felt old at the time, but looking back, still a kid. My aunt lived here, and I visited a few times growing up. I always liked it. It just felt simple. The kind of place where everyone knew everyone. Very friendly. But you know that already, right?

LILY: It's nice. The people, I guess.

PETER: Salt of the earth. Anyway, around the turn of the decade—so, 1990—I was kind of bouncing around, no real plans or direction. Kind of couch surfed for a while, worked job after job. Flipped burgers, poured coffee. Ran a bike shop for a little bit. Wagon trained around with buddies, followed some bands. Worked as a roadie for a hot minute.

LILY: That sounds cool.

PETER: Long hours, low pay. Hung around a lot of hollow people, if that makes sense. Made mistakes. Spiritually, I was lost. Then one day I spoke with my aunt on the phone, and she told me that the school up in Clifford was looking for a guidance counselor. Sounded different. A nice change of pace. I applied and got the job. And it changed me. This island . . . it healed me. Met my wife up here. Had children. This place is what I needed all along.

LILY: How did you meet Mrs. Elliot? I mean, she wasn't Mrs. Elliot when you met her.

PETER: There was an island hoedown under the pavilion at the rec center. I knew within five minutes of meeting Darcy that I wanted to spend my life with her. It's sappy, I know, but it really felt like it was meant to be. There's just something about this island, Lily. I'm telling you. Is this the kind of stuff you want for your interview?

LILY: Sure, I guess. So you guys had kids and lived happily ever after?

PETER: Well, children were a bit of a struggle for us. For a long time, we didn't think it was in the cards. And then we eventually had Kayla, and then Kyle a few years after that, and, well, here we are.

LILY: You've never had an urge to leave?

PETER: How do you mean?

LILY: I mean, you guys don't want to explore the world or something? I mean, Mrs. Elliot is a lifer, right?

PETER: She is.

LILY: That's just crazy to live your whole life in one place. No offense, I'm just saying.

PETER: Clifford Island is in Darcy's blood, I think. She's third generation.

LILY: Kayla said her great-grandmother was here during the Clifford Sickness back in the early 1900s, right?

PETER: Yep, great-grandmother. She was here for the sickness. Horrible time, I'm sure.

LILY: I mean, between that and, well, other stuff that's happened here, it's just surprising that people stay. You guys, too, you know?

PETER: How's that?

LILY: Well, there's the obvious stuff with the entire island, but you know, the accident with Kayla's grandmother must have been hard for you guys. I'm sorry, that's, like, really personal.

PETER: Kayla told you about that, huh?

LILY: I mean, we're friends. I know a little, not a lot. I don't mean to pry.

PETER: It's okay, it's . . . it was hard. You're right. Kayla doesn't remember it, thank God for that. She was so little. The accident was a terrible time for our family, but it only solidified our love for Clifford. The amount of support we received from the community was overwhelming. I think that's when I really knew I'd never go anywhere else. I knew I truly belonged, and I would do anything to help the children, to help the island heal and grow, to overcome its demons, so to speak. It certainly has its fair share. I've seen them.

LILY: Not that I'm counting terrible things that have happened here, but there was the Clifford Sickness, the accident with Kayla's grandmother, and then there was, well, you know. Were you here when it happened?

PETER: It?

LILY: Well, you know. The thing from, well. *It.*

PETER: Is this what this project is about? *It?*

LILY: Is it a part of your story, I guess? If it isn't, then we don't have to talk about it.

PETER: Technically I wasn't here when *it* happened. I was on the mainland that night.

LILY: What were you doing?

PETER: I was in Milwaukee at the . . . now, what is that called? The Eagles Ballroom. That's right. Seeing a band.

LILY: Anyone I'd know?

PETER: Nah. I'd heard a few tapes, and I found out they were coming to my neck of the woods. Wanted to check them out. Great show that night. One for the books. Got my hands on a recording of it not long after. Still listen to that show all the time.

LILY: Really?

PETER: Every night.

LILY: Wow. Superfan. You're . . . devoted.

PETER: I think it helps.

LILY: I guess that's what people would want you to do.

PETER: There's an official release of it now, real crisp soundboard, not that you care about those types of things. I still prefer the audience recording. I'm rambling about music now, I'm sorry. Where were we?

LILY: And then you came back that night? The night it happened?

PETER: The next day, I think. Yeah, the next afternoon. Hitched a ride back up north. You could do things like that back then.

LILY: What was it like coming back? Was it just like, whoa?

PETER: Do you really want to know?

LILY: I . . . I don't know what I want to know? It's just, you grow up hearing some things, and some people say that they see this or that, and no one really talks about this thing, but it's always there hovering all around everyone. It smothers you.

PETER: It's been that way for a long time here. I think I felt the same thing when I visited as a kid.

LILY: The smothering?

PETER: The stories, the myths. Just the feeling that there is something else here with us. Even before it happened, I think everyone here knew it was coming, but we tricked ourselves into believing it wasn't possible. Even though in our hearts, we knew it was. Does that make sense?

LILY: Not really, no.

PETER: That's okay. It's certainly real. Everyone knows it now.

LILY: If you say so.

PETER: What do you think?

LILY: About what?

PETER: About the evil. About the things people say.

LILY: I don't believe it. I think it's all bullshit.

PETER: As your guidance counselor, I'd officially advise against swearing in front of adults, especially while you're at school.

LILY: Well, I'm graduating in six months, so I figured I'd start practicing. It will be a nonstop swearathon when I get out of here. I can't wait.

PETER: So, you've decided on leaving?

LILY: I'm planning on it. I just don't think this place is for me.

PETER: Nothing is compelling you to stay?

LILY: I don't think so.

PETER: Not even the earthquakes?

LILY: I didn't feel those.

PETER: Or Mr. Gordon?

LILY: His brother got sick. Or maybe he just bailed. Being a teacher here must really suck. I mean, teaching the same stuff, year after year—

PETER: Lily, after all of this—

LILY: I just want to leave, Mr. Elliot. Is there anything wrong with that?

PETER: Where are you headed? School?

LILY: Isn't that your job? To guide me?

PETER: Most people don't leave, you know.

LILY: I guess I'm not most people. I'm hoping to play basketball somewhere. Anywhere that will take me.

PETER: Let me ask you this. Hoop dreams aside for a moment. You said people here see things, and people talk about things. Have you ever seen anything, or felt anything?

LILY: Zilch.

PETER: And why not?

LILY: Because I just haven't? It's like, you grow up hearing stories and fairy tales, and you believe them because you're young and stupid and haven't seen the world yet. But then you get older and you're like, well, if Santa is real, how come I've never heard him on my roof? If there's a monster in the woods, how come it's not in my backyard? I think the world is actually really, really ordinary. Bad things happen, and good things happen. But it's people that do these things.

PETER: And your dad. What does he believe?

LILY: You don't want to talk about my dad, Mr. Elliot.

PETER: He's here, you're here. Why doesn't he leave?

LILY: My dad has a job?

PETER: It's more than that. Much, much more than that.

LILY: Well, he's the city clerk. He's important. He has responsibilities. We can't just up and leave.

PETER: You could. It's your choice, your family's choice. I just think there's something compelling your father to stay other than being the city clerk on some sleepy island the rest of the world couldn't care less about.

LILY: Okay, I'll bite. Do you want to know about my dad? What he believes?

PETER: Sure.

LILY: Let me tell you a story. I know this is supposed to be your story, but I'll grab the mic for a bit.

PETER: It's okay. I want to hear this.

LILY: The cell phone thing. I have one, and my dad trusts me with it at home. I'm old enough now, I guess. But he only trusts me with it during the day. At night he locks it up in a safe downstairs. He puts both of our phones in there. It's just different at night, he thinks.

PETER: Can't say I blame him for that.

LILY: So, this is back in the summer. In July. I had a tournament in Sturgeon Bay, and I met this boy. Connor. He plays basketball, too. He watched one of our games.

PETER: How did you do?

LILY: Lost by eleven. Don't really want to talk about that one.

PETER: Fair enough.

LILY: So, Connor is really nice. We text a lot.

PETER: Text?

LILY: My house gets reception. Like, one bar, but we get it.

PETER: You better be careful about that.

LILY: I am. I don't do it very often.

PETER: So, dating a mainlander, huh? That must be challenging.

LILY: It is. We make it work somehow. He's really nice, Mr. Elliot.

PETER: How much does he know?

LILY: I know the rules, Mr. Elliot.

PETER: Are you sure about that?

LILY: Well, if you think I'm this amazing rule follower, I've got some bad news for you.

PETER: Oh, Lily, what did you do this time?

LILY: It's not that bad.

PETER: Just tell me.

LILY: So, like I said, Connor and I mainly just text. And this is last summer, it was late and I wanted to talk to him. Well, type, whatever. But my phone was locked up. So I snuck into my dad's room, and I took the key to the safe. He keeps it in the nightstand. I went downstairs and took my phone out of the safe, and I went back up to my room. And I'm always really, really good about all of the rules. My curtains are always closed at night. I usually cinch them with those, God, what are they called? Those construction things?

PETER: Clamps?

LILY: Yeah, clamps. The plastic ones. My dad makes me use them. But that night, I didn't. I was distracted. And I guess there was this gap in the curtains. Like, six or eight inches. If you were outside, you could see into my bedroom. See me, I guess. But I didn't notice because I was lying on my bed texting with Connor. And I don't know how long the curtains were like that, how long I was laying there. Twenty minutes? I'm not sure. But all of the sudden my door swings open, and I'm so freaked out the phone kind of jumps out of my hand and lands on the bed.

PETER: Your dad?

LILY: Yeah.

PETER: He was worried about you. Fatherly senses.

LILY: Fatherly anger, yeah. He must've seen the open safe, because he barges into my room, grabs the phone, and shoves it under my pillow.

PETER: I think it's more than that. He must have sensed something outside your window.

LILY: I didn't, that's for sure.

PETER: Did you clamp the curtains after that?

LILY: He did, yeah. Then he grabbed me and hugged me, and we just sat there like that for a long time. And he was holding me really, really tight. He doesn't usually hug me like that.

PETER: Lily, he was protecting you. Something was after you, and your dad felt its presence. You just couldn't see it, that's all.

LILY: I don't think so. I think he was lying.

PETER: Now, why on earth would he do that?

LILY: I don't know. To keep the myth alive. To make me believe.

PETER: You don't?

LILY: No. I don't. Is that bad?

PETER: It's something you probably shouldn't tell people. But you're telling me right now, and we're recording it.

LILY: Are you going to take the tape?

PETER: I think that's up to you. Like you said, my job is to guide you. It's literally in the title of my position, kiddo.

LILY: You won't make me delete it?

PETER: No, I won't. You do what you feel is right.

LILY: It's just . . . I don't think I'm the only one who feels this way, Mr. Elliot. About believing. About this way of life. Kids are talking. Whispering, I guess.

PETER: Is Kayla doing some of this whispering?

LILY: She does. Well, kind of.

PETER: So, yes or no?

LILY: She mainly listens to me whisper. But she's a good listener.

PETER: She's a good kid. And a trustworthy kid.

LILY: I know. It's just . . . the thing is, if Clifford is not an open secret yet, it will be soon. Our generation is just different. We ask questions. I'm sure it used to be a lot easier around here without cell phones and the internet. It's only a matter of time, you know? Before everyone in the outside world finds out about us.

PETER: We'll just have to make sure that doesn't happen, right?

LILY: I guess.

PETER: Is there anything else you want to know? About me?

LILY: I'm curious about a lot of things.

PETER: Okay. Have I ever told you that I've seen one?

LILY: One of what?

PETER: What was outside your window.

LILY: Get out of here. Stop pulling my leg, Mr. Elliot.

PETER: It's true. Turn that tape off, and I'll tell you all about it.

LILY: Okay, fine. Go ahead and tell me.

PETER: I thought you said you didn't believe.

8

WILLOW

Thirty-Four Days until Her Disappearance

Dear Dominic,

I'm writing to you from picturesque Clifford Island, where the scenery is nice and the people are not so nice. Okay, I haven't met that many people yet. Only a few. To be fair, one older guy doing repair work *was* ridiculously nice—just, a gentle soul. But I had a run-in with another islander this afternoon who clearly had some anger-management issues. Allow me to explain.

I'm strolling through downtown Clifford, and I take out my cell phone to snap a photo. Then, out of nowhere, WHACK. This old guy creeps up behind me and swats my phone right out of my hand. The screen shatters on the pavement, and this nutcase is hooting and hollering and says something like, "I don't know who you are, but you never, ever take that thing out around here again, you hear me?" Then he storms off, and I'm just standing there tongue-tied holding a phone with a spiderwebbed screen.

Charming fella, right? Maybe something was just wrong with him, like, he wasn't well? That story was just an extremely long-winded way of telling you that my phone is now basically unusable. It kind of feels freeing, in a way. Not that there's any service up here, anyway. I'm truly off the edges of the map up here.

Well, as promised, I'm here. Clifford Island. I'm sitting in a small clapboard cottage that is surrounded by northern hardwoods and a whole lot of silence, and I'm just feeling like this is a new reality. A new chapter for me. I'm still taking it all in. I was kind of hoping I'd step foot on the island and there'd be some immediate revelation. Like, some painfully obvious aha moment that answered all of my questions immediately. No such luck. That would've been far too easy. I've just been getting a feel for this place. Here's my observations so far:

1. The island is small. Has a one-horse-town kind of feel. I could probably walk end to end in a few hours.

2. If I wasn't on something of a mission, I could just relax and enjoy the peacefulness of it all. It's absolutely picture-perfect. Rich forests. Rocky shores. Farms and lavender fields. Crisscrossing country roads. Zero stoplights. Porch-lined Victorian farmhouses tucked away down hidden gravel paths. It's like something out of a novel.

3. Downtown is quite charming. Café, general store, grocer, mom-and-pop pharmacy, barbershop, the obligatory watering hole, post office (with a portrait of Bill Clinton hanging inside. I know, weird). Everything is very "hometown pride," if that makes sense. The café has this bulletin board with dozens upon dozens of photos of local children and science-fair-type ribbons and certificates pinned up to it—it's all very sweet.

4. Every car I've seen so far is either a beater, old as dirt, or both. Seriously. Nothing from after the Berlin Wall coming down. Clunker after clunker, brown rust flakes sprinkling the ground, one of those

conversion vans with a retro orange stripe and a "Bush/Quayle '88" sticker slapped on the bumper (what is it with love for old presidents on Clifford?). It's just so weird to not see one Tesla or soccer mom SUV prowling the streets.

5. There's a phone booth here. An honest-to-God phone booth!

6. The technology in my cottage is, how should I put this, preindustrial? No cable, no internet. Just one of those tube TVs with the rabbit ears antenna. And that antenna doesn't do a darn thing. I clicked around the dial, adjusting the ears this way and that, but I got nothing but wavy and scrambled pictures. Maybe the signal doesn't reach this far? Oh, and I have a VCR, which is the first one I've seen in ages. I can pick between *Kramer vs. Kramer*, *Splash*, *Jaws*, *Close Encounters of the Third Kind*, and three episodes of *M*A*S*H*.

7. The phone is of the rotary variety. Remember, you spin the wheel? Kind of neat, actually.

8. Did I mention no internet? Right, no internet. So my laptop is basically an eight-hundred-dollar word processor at this point.

9. I do love my cottage. It's simply darling. That's where I met the gentle soul—he was fixing my gutter, just getting the place all set for me. Clarence. He's the custodian for the school and volunteers his time to do odd jobs around the island. I talked his ear off with questions about the island—and Clarence indulged every single one. Very friendly guy, I hope to see more of him.

I only just arrived on Clifford Island yesterday, but I think I've got this place figured out already. They are going for that "simple living" kind of life. Old-fashioned. It's almost like, stepping onto the dock for the first time, I'd traveled back in time. I mean it. But what does this place have to do with our son? I don't know yet. I haven't got the first clue, actually. And I can't be an investigative reporter about this, running around and shoving a microphone in people's faces. The islanders will think I'm a nutcase (maybe I am, but still). I'm going to play it smart. I need to acclimate myself. Integrate myself into the community first, and then I'll find the answers I'm looking for. Only, I'm not sure I even know the questions. I need time, you know? And a reason to be up here, at least for appearance's sake. I think I figured it out.

I got a job. Like, a *job* job, on the island. I know, I know, I buried the lede. Sorry about that. I'm now the official youth ministries director at Prince of Peace Lutheran Church. That's right, the woman who hasn't been to church since college is now the spiritual mentor for a group of impressionable high school youth. This wasn't my plan, but targeted ads got me. It must've been all of my googling about Clifford before I left. The job just kind of popped up as one of those ads at the top of my inbox. I'd already been thinking about *maybe* finding work up here, and there it was. Serendipitous.

I didn't think I'd have a chance at getting it. No way. But my teaching experience must've been impressive, and maybe that's all I needed? I certainly didn't mention my agnosticism (we'll leave that between you and me). I exchanged a few messages with a Pastor Rita Higgins, and here I am. Crisp new Bible in hand, and rent-free accommodations in a not-un-Hemingway-like bungalow on church grounds. That sealed the deal for me. The pay is surprisingly high (well, on a youth director scale), and I can still afford the mortgage on our place back home. I don't mind doing that, by the way. I'm not sure what your plans are in Florida or when you are coming back, but I'll take care of it.

I'm just . . . not ready to let go of our home. We have too many memories there. All of us. It feels nice to know that I can go back anytime and Jacob's room will be just as it was. I don't know—it's just comforting. That bedroom is a warm blanket to me.

We could go back there, you know. One day, together. When I find the answers I need up here, and you get whatever you need to get out of your system. That could be a pipe dream, though, one that I'll table for the time being. I think we both just need time. For right now, I have other immediate goals. Three of them, actually.

First, I need to figure out what this place has to do with our son.

Second, I need to learn how to be a youth ministry director. Or learn how to fake it. It can't be *that* different from teaching. Besides, it might be nice to feel like I'm helping kids again. Not to toot my own horn, but do you remember how good at that I was?

And third, perhaps most pressing, I need to trim one of the tree branches outside my cottage. It's been scratching and banging intermittently against the wall for hours. I swear it sounds like someone is outside, asking to be let in.

I'm not going to get a lick of sleep up here.

Later, bucko.
Willow

WILDWOOD HIGH SCHOOL STUDENT NEWSPAPER

THE WILD TIMES

October 2015 edition

We're back with a special spooky edition of *The Friday Five*, temporarily renamed *The Frightful Five* in honor of Halloween! Today's guest is everyone's favorite English teacher, Mrs. Willow Stone. She has been a valuable member of the English department for seven years, and she's also coached the badminton team to consecutive conference championships. Way to go, Mrs. Stone! Check out her sometimes-terrifying answers to your questions, and don't forget to stop by Mrs. Stone's classroom after school on Halloween to pick up a special treat. You may be the lucky recipient of a full-size candy bar—wow!

QUESTION: **Hi, Mrs. Stone! Thanks so much for sitting down with us today. Our first question is, why did you decide to get into teaching?**

ANSWER: Thanks for having me! I guess I was always one of those kids who wanted to be a teacher. I had really amazing teachers growing up, and they kept pushing me to be whatever I wanted to be. The funny thing is, teachers don't really push you to be teachers. It's always other careers—you know, if you like animals, maybe you should work in a zoo or be a veterinarian. But I always enjoyed school and helping people, and teaching seemed like a natural fit. There's also just something special about a school community. It feels bigger than you, and you feel like you are contributing something to the greater good. There's a real sense of belonging. Oh, and I was always the kid staying after class to clean the chalkboard, so maybe I just wanted to keep doing that!

QUESTION: **Ha! That's really great. Our next question comes from one of our readers. Jude wants to know, "Mrs. Stone, do you have a favorite Halloween?"**

ANSWER: I'm assuming Jude is asking about a specific year? I'd have to say my most recent Halloween, last year. My son, Jacob, was old enough to realize what was going on, you know, he finally grasped the concept of going to a house and getting free candy. So he was really, really excited and we were just out there for hours and hours. And I'd made him this little *Ghostbusters* brown jumpsuit and proton pack— it was so cute. It took me forever to make it, and he's already out-grown it! I'm not sure if he'll remember it, but I took probably a hundred photos so it's definitely well-documented!

QUESTION: **It sure is! Do you have a favorite book you like to teach?**

ANSWER: We do a collaboration with the social studies department, and we use a book called *Hard Times: An Oral History of the Great Depression.* I think that getting the story from the people who lived during that time, in their own words, really helps you get a richer understanding of history and makes the past truly come alive.

QUESTION: **We have another question from one of our readers. Riley asks, "Do you have any favorite scary movies?"**

ANSWER: I'm not the biggest fan of scary movies. I'd rather watch a comedy with my husband or something animated with my son. If you become a parent one day, you might find that your kid's tastes become your tastes, and that's totally okay. I've seen *Frozen* so many times I feel like I could transcribe the script, right now, without the movie even playing! But to go back to Riley's question, the original *Halloween* movie is really scary. I think it's from the seventies? My older brother showed it to me when I was a kid, and it really freaked me out! So if you're looking for a movie to watch to get you into the spirit of the season, that's a good one.

QUESTION: **That's so cool that your son likes *Frozen*! Okay, one last question, do you believe in ghosts?**

ANSWER: That's a really interesting question. Not necessarily ghosts, but I definitely had some experiences as a kid where I thought that monsters were real. But I will say that my husband used to be a psychologist, and he delved into things like sleep paralysis and nightmares. He never told me anything specific about his patients, but I got the impression that there might be more to the world than just what we see.

QUESTION: **Wow, spooky stuff! Thanks so much for being our guest today!**

ANSWER: Thanks for having me!

10

HARPER

The church was empty when I walked inside, save one person in the third row of pews on the right-hand side, head bowed in silence. I wondered if it was Pastor Rita Higgins—the person I was seeking—but I didn't dare to disturb someone lost in prayer.

Or was it my sister?

It was an overly optimistic thought, and a stupid one. I walked down the center aisle toward the altar and examined the woman out of the side of my eye. Older, mid-sixties, I estimated. Her eyes were closed, and her cheeks appeared to be stained with tears.

"My girl," the woman whispered to herself, or to God.

I sheepishly looked away.

Lily had given me directions to the church grounds—which was a few miles from the school, not that anyplace on this island could be much farther—and suggested I speak with the pastor, Willow's boss on Clifford.

The queen bee, Lily called her.

The person praying could've been the pastor, I supposed, but I didn't stop for introductions. I instead reached the altar and turned around, admiring the small cathedral. It was unpretentious and impressive all the same. The wooden pews looked handcrafted; the eight stained-glass windows adorning the side walls were sparkling and meticulously designed, each depicting a different scene from the Bible. I hadn't been to church in ages, but the things I had learned in Sunday school stuck with me—I'd seen these images before. Jesus holding a shepherd's crook flanked by a flock of sheep; Mother Mary cradling Jesus's limp, rag-dressed body after the Crucifixion. One of the windows appeared to be newer than the rest—the colors brighter, the images sharper, the clothing more modern. The children weren't dressed in robes or tunics, as I expected them to be. The artist had instead adorned them in less biblical-era items: things like shorts, hooded sweatshirts, and flower-printed dresses. One child wore a red basketball jersey. It all seemed very specific, and I wondered if they were residents of the island. The dozen or so children stood on a small hill, holding hands behind the Lord—his arms held aloft—the sun dipping into an orange-and-violet sky.

Jesus and the little children, or a version of it. Another familiar image etched into my brain thirty years ago.

Those Sunday school teachers did a helluva job, I thought.

The rear doorway opened and a figure appeared dressed in black pastoral robes. She held her finger up to her mouth and then waved her hand, motioning for me to come over. I made my way back down the aisle, passing the praying woman in the third pew again.

She didn't so much as flinch.

"My girl," she whispered again.

I wasn't sure if she'd even noticed me at all.

I thought I'd be able to sense my sister's presence when I stepped inside her island cottage, but I couldn't. Instead, I smelled some intense combination of bleach and Lysol. I looked over at my tour guide, the island pastor, who looked similarly perturbed by the aroma.

"Heavens to Betsy," she said, rushing to a window. "Let's get a little fresh air in here before we pass out and fall right on our keisters, no?"

Pastor Rita Higgins was older, but she moved like all-conference running backs I'd covered over the years—picking her spots and heading there with purpose. It was clear immediately upon meeting her that she could command a room, if solely by her physicality. There was simply a *swagger* to her movements. The petite woman filled out her navy-blue parka well, and she appeared to be built solidly—I imagined countryfolk like Rita always getting their hands dirty, tossing bales of hay and chopping wood. She slid open a window and flashed the same comforting smile that I'd seen a dozen times since we'd met thirty minutes ago, the ends of her fur-trimmed hood bristling slightly in the soft, welcoming breeze that entered the cottage.

"Well, this is it," she said. "I don't think she left anything behind, but you're welcome to have a look around. This whole thing doesn't make a lick of sense; I hope you find something here."

The pastor had been surprised I couldn't locate Willow. Rita was certain Willow had left two weeks ago—just as Lily had told me—and Rita insisted I take a look at the cottage, just in case Willow had left something that would key me to her whereabouts. I quickly agreed to the impromptu tour.

The cottage wasn't far from the church itself—down a few narrow paths in the forest, a couple of clearings over. The first clearing was home to a boarded-up mansion, which the pastor explained was an island historical landmark. Lots of damage inside, she said, due for a real makeover one day. She'd led me past the antebellum home and down another path, and we arrived at my sister's cottage, private and isolated.

Willow's former place was cozy and dated. One bedroom, tiny kitchen. The light-oak cabinets looked like they hadn't been updated since the '80s. A beige Dustbuster was mounted near a wall outlet; a white toaster and microwave flanked the stove. I ran my hand across the counter for no real reason. It was spotless.

"She didn't say she was going anywhere else?" I asked.

Rita shook her head. "Ready to go home, was all she said."

"How did she leave?"

"That I don't know. I can ask around for you, honey. Not many ways to get off this rock, I'll tell you that much."

You were her boss and worked with her every day, and you don't know how she left?

I kept that thought to myself and moved into the living room. An old rotary phone was placed directly in the center of an end table, perfectly perpendicular to the wooden edges, which was indicative of the entire cottage—everything seemed to be placed precisely where it was supposed to be, and not an inch off. I sensed the pastor behind me in a way that almost felt like she was closing in on me, but then she drifted toward the couch.

"We don't get many newcomers around here, but your sister, she fit right in," Rita said. "The kids really took to her. Real bright light, that one. I was sad to see her go."

Yeah, so where is she?

I stooped down and sifted through some VHS tapes in a drawer below the television stand. The TV itself looked to be an antique. I stood up and walked into the bedroom, where I found only a twin-size bed with a green comforter next to a nightstand. A Bible was inside the wooden drawer. I flipped through the pages.

"Anything?" Rita called out.

"Don't think so," I called back to her. I opened the double closet doors—a few metal hangers hung on a bar, and nothing else. I returned to the living room and plopped down on the sofa, a hideous thing with an orange-and-red floral design. Rita sat down beside me.

"How certain are you that Willow is missing?" Rita asked. Her eyebrows drew together, and for a moment I thought she was going to put her hand on my shoulder.

"I'm not," I said. "At all, actually. It's just—it doesn't make any sense. She and her husband go their separate ways, I can't get ahold of either of them—"

"Is it possible she's with Dominic?"

"I guess, but why is his number disconnected? Why did Willow shut off her phone? It's not like them."

"Could she be with a friend? A relative?"

I was embarrassed to tell her I didn't know the names of any of Willow's friends. "I don't know. I guess? But our parents passed away a long time ago, and—no one comes to mind. Not a one."

"When was the last time you spoke to her?"

I clammed up, and I took a breath before speaking. "Three months." I stood and walked to the television. My fingers jostled the antenna back and forth, and I saw Rita's reflection in the TV screen. She leaned forward, watching me closely. "I know, some brother, huh?"

Rita's fingers danced along her chin. "Sweetheart, time has a way of moving quickly. Before you know it, months or even years have gone by." The pastor paused. Even from the reflection I could tell she was continuing to study me, determining something I was unsure about. I decided to change the subject.

"Do you know about Willow's son?" I turned to face her, and her eyes met mine.

"I do," Rita said. "Just a tragic, terrible thing. Were you and the boy close?"

It wasn't meant to, but the question cut right through me. Maybe because I was never really that close with the kid, even though things appeared fine on the surface. We shared common interests: video games, sports, things like that. Nothing earth-shattering, but Jacob always seemed to enjoy talking to me. I took him to see a movie once, and we shot hoops in his driveway whenever I came to visit. I didn't attend as many of his baseball games as I should've—I could've hopped in my car and made the drive so many other times; I know that now—but when I *was* sitting in the metal bleachers at the baseball diamond, I made sure to hoot and holler and clap and really let the kid know I was there.

Maybe Jacob thought it was insincere. The cheering, any of the other things we did together. His death made me question everything.

What's an uncle-nephew relationship supposed to look like?

I never really knew.

Like in my relationship with Willow, I simply could've done more.

Not that I didn't try. I always splurged on Christmas and birthday gifts for him, although oftentimes those splurges came via a mail carrier in a blue uniform. I was always at least one state away from Willow and her small family, but I did my best to keep in touch. Phone calls, video chats, texts. Things like that. But that was all *before*. Before the speeding car and the scooter and the helmet that flew off Jacob's head—I never could bear to even picture it. I suspect Willow didn't think about the accident much, either. I had the distinct feeling that, in some ways, she pretended it never even happened.

The last time I visited Willow's home—about a year after Jacob's death—it *felt* like the boy was alive, and that was very much by design. On that day, I'd found myself upstairs looking for a bathroom, and I accidentally wandered into Jacob's bedroom. It looked like he'd been there that morning. The *Star Wars* comforter on the bed was folded, but it was an imperfect fold, like Jacob had hastily done it because Willow made him do it. The posters on the walls—a sneering red Chicago Bulls logo; a few Marvel superheroes; the *Pirates of the Caribbean* attraction at Disney World—were hung just slightly unleveled, which gave the appearance that a ten-year-old kid had hung them up himself and the parents left them that way, because that's just the way those posters are supposed to be hung. At least a dozen sports trophies and a few knickknacks sat on shelves, but again, they looked like they'd been placed there by a kid.

Standing in my dead nephew's bedroom, the god-awful realization hit me that Willow and Dominic had deliberately left the bedroom exactly as it was following Jacob's death. It was a time warp, like something people would pay admission to see at some founding father's childhood home off the interstate. A light wind came in through an open window, the drapes fluttered a bit, and I half expected Jacob to be hiding behind those drapes, the decisive winner of a yearlong game of hide-and-seek.

Surprise! I'm not dead! I've been right here the whole time!

The idea of it was enough to make me retreat to the hallway. I pressed my back against the wall, bringing my hand up to my mouth. I knew I would never go inside that bedroom ever again.

I never wanted to go near that house again.

And now, here I was, in another house that Willow had called home, and the guilt was absolutely ripping through me. I'd never considered myself a bad uncle, a bad brother—but maybe I had been all along. How are adult siblings supposed to stay in touch? Is there some manual that I should've followed? I had friends and coworkers who never mentioned their siblings—I was fairly certain some of them merely saw brothers and sisters around the holidays, and no more than that. One fellow reporter hadn't spoken with his brother in twenty years. *But Willow and I should've been different*, I thought. We were close as children, but then what happened? Life? Careers? Our lack of proximity didn't help, but I could've done more, should've kept pushing, especially after Jacob died.

But Willow didn't want that. She stopped communicating just as much as I did—it takes two to tango, after all. That doesn't mean we didn't care about each other.

And I'm here right now, aren't I?

Exploring some strange island on some hunch that something's wrong?

That has to say something about our relationship, that I was willing to make things right.

If I could learn why Willow had come to Clifford Island and why she obsessed over this place, then maybe our relationship could begin anew. I could be the brother Willow deserved, the one she hopefully remembered from her childhood. The one who played dinosaurs and Barbies; who showed her slasher flicks and shoot-'em-up R-rated movies when our mother was asleep; who smiled while she and her giggling friends smeared lipstick and eyeliner on my face at a slumber party; who shoved over in bed and comforted her when she was utterly convinced that there was a monster roaming our house.

Alone with the pastor in Willow's old place, I felt the urge to lay everything out for her, to confess my sins, in a way. The moment felt right; the location felt right—Willow came to this very place, perhaps seeking solace—and maybe she achieved it right here in this dingy and outdated little bungalow. Perhaps I could do the same. My gaze darted around the cottage—it was comforting to know that Willow had looked upon the same sofa, the same thin walls—and again, I thought everything seemed a little too perfect.

A little too staged, like someone wanted me to see it this way.

The vibe suddenly felt insincere, Rita's demeanor fake, her smile plastered on.

It was just an instinct, but the feelings of suspicion swelled inside me, growing stronger by the second. I wondered if the pastor could sense the wariness in my gaze. It wasn't a real estate showing, so why did the cottage resemble one, but with ancient technology and furniture from a 1985 garage sale? I zeroed in on a framed painting on the wall to Rita's left—nothing fancy, just a sunset over a lake, a flock of white birds gliding in the sky—but it gave me pause.

Something seemed off.

The way the frame hung there.

The slight crookedness.

It seemed *familiar*.

The urge to confess my sins dissipated. My thoughts were no longer on Rita's fairly innocuous question to me—*Were you and the boy close?*—but instead traveled back to my childhood.

Me and Willow.

Secret agents.

It felt like it was happening again.

"Jacob was a good boy," I said to Rita, attempting to play it cool and hoping she couldn't sense my perhaps wild hypothesizing. "No family should go through that. It's not fair, you know?"

"Willow was still torn up about it, you can be darn sure about that," Rita said. "I think that's why she came all the way up to our little community. For peace, for comfort. I did my best to comfort her, for my part." She smiled at me warmly, and the wrinkles in her face seemed to increase threefold.

"Can we look at her office in the church?" I asked. "Maybe there's something there. A phone number she wrote down, an address. I don't know. Anything. I'm desperate."

Rita nodded and rose to her feet. "Of course, dear. Whatever you think would help."

I followed the pastor out the door, and we walked about ten feet from the cottage before I abruptly stopped, patting my pockets.

"Shoot," I said. "I think I left my phone inside."

Rita furrowed her eyebrows and was about to speak, but I didn't give her the chance.

"One second!" I stammered, rushing back inside the cottage.

I beelined toward the painting, the one that was hung crookedly by about a half inch. It was the only thing in that entire cottage that was not exactly where it was supposed to be. Maybe someone had bumped into it, but I didn't think so. I grabbed it with two hands and lifted it off the nail on the wall. I knew something would be there. It felt like more than a hunch.

I flipped the painting over, and there it was.

An envelope was wedged between the picture frame and the backing, and I instantly recognized my sister's handwriting.

She had written a name on the outside of the envelope.

Mine.

11

BERGENDOFF DEPARTMENT OF PSYCHOLOGY

Student Study:

Thematic Examination of Nightmares and Bad Dreams

Interview Subject #4—Willow Coates

November 12, 2003

DOMINIC: All righty, please state your name.

WILLOW: Willow Coates. Senior, Bergendoff College.

DOMINIC: Thank you, Ms. Coates. I'm Dominic Stone, also a senior here. This interview is part of my senior thesis project exploring the psychology of nightmares and bad dreams, and the emotional impact they have on the dreamer. Your participation is entirely voluntary, and the information you share today is confidential and will be used for the sole purpose—sorry, I lost my place here . . .

WILLOW: That's okay.

DOMINIC: Okay. Let's see, blah, blah, blah . . . used for the sole purpose of identifying themes and the emotional impacts of nightmares and bad dreams. You will not be identified by name in the study, nor will any personally identifying information be included.

WILLOW: And I get fifty dollars.

DOMINIC: It doesn't say it here . . . but, yes, you get fifty dollars.

WILLOW: That's why I'm here.

DOMINIC: My goal as the interviewer is to stay as neutral as possible. Any follow-up questions I ask are for clarification purposes and are not meant to influence your words or emotions in any way. Does everything I stated sound acceptable to you?

WILLOW: It does, yes.

DOMINIC: All righty. Ms. Coates, do you ever experience nightmares or bad dreams?

WILLOW: Sometimes, I guess.

DOMINIC: Can you describe one of these instances?

WILLOW: Well, a few weeks ago, I dreamed that it was the end of the semester, and in my dream, I hadn't gone to any of my classes. I'd just blown them off all term, finals were coming up, and my attendance was zero.

DOMINIC: How did that make you feel?

WILLOW: Panicked? And then, relief, I guess, when I woke up.

DOMINIC: The day that you woke up from this dream, did it affect you in any way?

WILLOW: What do you mean?

DOMINIC: Did it influence your behavior in any way that day or moving forward?

WILLOW: I mean, I think I might've studied more that night. Or, gosh, I went out with my friends? I'm sorry, I can't remember.

DOMINIC: That's okay.

WILLOW: I'm really sorry. I'm, like, the worst subject imaginable for this. I don't think I could tell you what I had for breakfast this morning. You'll probably take my fifty dollars away.

DOMINIC: You'll get your fifty dollars, trust me.

WILLOW: Sorry, I'll try and do better. I want to make sure you're not wasting your money on me.

DOMINIC: Technically, it's the psychology department's money, but—

WILLOW: I'll try and come up with some really hard-hitting stuff for your thesis, I promise.

DOMINIC: So, what did you have for breakfast today?

WILLOW: A yogurt parfait . . . and orange juice.

DOMINIC: See, you're getting better already. You nailed that one.

WILLOW: Nope, check that. *Strawberry* orange juice.

DOMINIC: Ah, we were so close. That's my favorite, by the way.

WILLOW: That doesn't seem very neutral of you.

DOMINIC: I'm sorry, you're right.

WILLOW: I'm just kidding. And if I keep being terrible at this I'll give you—the department—its money back, or buy you some strawberry orange juice or something.

DOMINIC: I might take you up on th— Okay, let's get back to the interview.

WILLOW: Okay.

DOMINIC: Ms. Coates, can you think of another time you've had a nightmare or bad dream?

WILLOW: Can it be any time?

DOMINIC: Sure. Recently or in the past. Anything you can think of.

WILLOW: I want to give you something good . . . Let's see, well, there was this thing when I was a little girl.

DOMINIC: How old were you?

WILLOW: I must've been six or seven? That's when it started. I'm sorry, I haven't thought about this in a really long time.

DOMINIC: Was it a nightmare?

WILLOW: Yes. I mean, it didn't start as a nightmare. Like, there was a real thing that happened that triggered the nightmares. But, again, it was so long ago that I'm not sure what's actually real and what my mind sort of twists around. Do you know what I mean?

DOMINIC: I think so, yeah. What was the thing that happened? Or might've happened?

WILLOW: I was at the grocery store with my mom, and I wandered off. Looking for cereal or something. But I got lost and I couldn't find my way back to her, and there's just this sea of people in the store, at least that's how it is in my head. And this guy, this *man*, grabs my shoulder and turns me around to face him, and he's just . . . warped. Like, stretchy? Too long, like his arms and neck and head had been rolled out. Like Play-Doh.

DOMINIC: This isn't the nightmare, right? This is what happened at the store?

WILLOW: This is my actual memory of the guy. But it's through a kid lens, you know? I'm sure he didn't really look like that, but . . . that's how I remember it. Really skinny with this scraggly, long red hair and breath that smells absolutely rancid. Just, horrible. And he leans down and whispers into my ear, *"Run to your mother."*

DOMINIC: My God, that must've been— What did you do next?

WILLOW: Ran. Ran like hell. Finally found my mom. I was crying and all that. Hysterical, probably.

DOMINIC: Did they find the man?

WILLOW: I don't think so. I remember my mother talking to a clerk, but I mean, who knows what I actually saw. And I wasn't technically threatened, so it wasn't a police matter or anything like that. It was just some creepy guy, but again, I was so young. I'm sure everything about it has been twisted in my head.

DOMINIC: But you had nightmares? From this?

WILLOW: Wouldn't you? *Run to your mother.* I mean, come on.

DOMINIC: It would probably give me nightmares, yes. That sounds . . . Wow.

WILLOW: Yep, wow. I had nightmares for years and years. Off and on. I can't . . . I'm sorry, I haven't thought about this in so long.

DOMINIC: We don't have to— I mean, you don't have to keep— I can give you the fifty dollars and we can end the interview.

WILLOW: Oh, no. Really, I'm fine. I'm just trying to remember it all. I had nightmares of the guy, the warped guy, basically replays of the incident. For years and years, but not like every night or anything. They came and went. It wasn't some constant thing.

DOMINIC: Did it— Do you remember it having an impact on your life?

WILLOW: Kind of? I wasn't— Well, I guess one of the dreams was one of those waking dreams? I was caught in between my dream and being awake, and I thought I saw the warped man outside my window. On my lawn. He'd . . . grown. Or changed. Like, his torso and legs were gone. He had, just, really long arms connected to his head. And that was it. Kind of spidery, I guess.

DOMINIC: Uh-huh.

WILLOW: It . . . scuttled, across the lawn, and I heard it open the back door downstairs and come inside.

DOMINIC: But this was your dream?

WILLOW: Well, it's not real, so yeah.

DOMINIC: Right.

WILLOW: But I thought it was real at the time. I was probably nine years old or something? But I remember hearing it coming up the stairs. And I . . . bend down and peek through the crack at the bottom of my door, and I see it. I see the long arms balancing in the hallway, and its hair brushing along the floor as it kind of glides toward my room. Then its head leans down and spots me. It looks right at me. This is all possible, right? Like, there's a scientific explanation for this? I'm calling it a waking dream, but you might know more about it.

DOMINIC: Well, like you said, you were either still dreaming, or hallucinations can occur in that semiconscious state between waking and sleeping.

WILLOW: Uh-huh.

DOMINIC: That's the sciencey way of saying you're not crazy.

WILLOW: That's comforting. Whatever the reason, I shoved this toy chest I had in my room against the door, and I sat there, leaning against it. And I kept hearing the guy whisper, *"Run to your mother,"* over and over again from behind the door. I think I woke up in my bed? Yeah, that's right. But the chest had been moved. So I had *actually* slid it against the door at some point, for real. Crazy, right?

DOMINIC: Did that specific nightmare—

WILLOW: Have an impact on my life?

DOMINIC: Sorry, I'm a broken record. I'm trying to remain—

WILLOW: Neutral, I got it. And it's fine. I mean, it was fine. I was just so . . . ashamed about everything? Does that make sense?

DOMINIC: Can you explain why?

WILLOW: I was young, but I still knew it was silly, you know? Monsters aren't real. There was this one part of me that was, I guess, embarrassed that I believed it actually happened. That something came into my house.

DOMINIC: So, you did believe it was real?

WILLOW: At the time? I think so. Yeah.

DOMINIC: And the other part?

WILLOW: I'm sorry?

DOMINIC: You said, part of you was embarrassed that you believed in monsters. What else were you feeling?

WILLOW: Fear. But it was less for me and more for my family. I was scared that I'd somehow invited something evil into the world, and my family would suffer from it. Like, what if that thing in my yard came for me and got my mom instead? Or my brother? That's where the shame really came from, I think. That it was all my fault.

DOMINIC: Did you tell your family how you felt? About your dreams?

WILLOW: I told Harper, I think. We were close. I'm pretty sure I slept in his bed a few times.

DOMINIC: That's your brother?

WILLOW: Yeah. And I'm sure my mother knew. How could she not know?

DOMINIC: Do you still have the nightmares?

WILLOW: I don't, thank God. They just stopped one day. A long time ago. I just outgrew them. That was it, I guess.

DOMINIC: I'm glad everything worked out.

WILLOW: You're serious about not attributing my name to this, right? People will think I'm nuts. They'll probably take my name off of the graduation list.

DOMINIC: You can trust me.

WILLOW: Can I?

DOMINIC: I'm feeling a little bad right now. Like I've coaxed you into resurfacing a horrible memory. How about you and I go get a strawberry orange juice right now? Full fifty bucks and a strawberry orange juice. My treat.

WILLOW: You don't seem very neutral at all right now.

DOMINIC: I know. I'm not.

WILLOW: And I'm fine, really. This isn't something that has affected my life for, like, ten years. It doesn't—I moved past it. A long time ago. You can quote me on that.

DOMINIC: Okay, I will.

WILLOW: So, strawberry orange juice?

DOMINIC: On the house. It'll be our secret.

WILLOW: I hope so.

DOMINIC: No one will ever find out about this. I promise.

12

WILLOW

Thirty Days until Her Disappearance

Dear Dominic,

I'm not sure if you're particularly interested in what I'm doing up here, but I'm going to keep sending these. I thought about you the other day. I was downtown, and this guy was blasting "Livin' on the Edge" from a boombox on his shoulder. (And this wasn't a kid, either. Guy was mid-fifties?) Anyway, it reminded me of us winning that trivia contest at that indoor-water-park restaurant years ago. You remember, the tiki bar that reeked of chlorine? The last question was something about Aerosmith, you knew the answer, and then we found a twenty-four-hour Walmart and spent our entire winnings on six bags of Tapatío Doritos because you knew I'd been craving them for weeks. We cranked up "Livin' on the Edge" in the car, windows down, me howling, and crumbs blowing everywhere. Simpler times, right?

Up here in the land that time forgot, my investigation continues. I've got a few Clifford Island oddities to tell you about. I'll start with:

The house.

I got weird vibes from this place my first day here, and a few mornings ago those vibes were confirmed. This was Tuesday. I headed to the church pretty early after a morning hike. I'm passing by this building on the church grounds called Seminary House, and there's Pastor Rita and like six or seven older folks outside the house, holding hands and praying. I heard some light chanting, I think? I'm not sure. But I had the immediate sense that I was intruding. I don't know what they were praying about, but it felt like they were praying to the house. A few of them looked up, and I kind of scurried away with my tail between my legs.

It's hard to explain why it was so uncomfortable. Maybe it was because it was so early in the morning and I felt like I'd surprised these people, or maybe because the house itself is an oddity. It's this huge, gorgeous antebellum house with a wraparound porch just sitting in the forest near the church. Four columns in front extend up to the second story, and the white siding looks brand-new. Absolutely immaculate. Straight out of *Gone with the Wind*.

Here's the really bizarre part: all of the windows and doors are boarded up. You can't get in. No one goes in there. But I've seen that nice old guy Clarence and other islanders doing work on the outside of it. They upkeep the hell out of this thing.

I see the house every day. It's probably like fifty or sixty yards from my cottage down a windy, weed-choked path in a small clearing. It kind of looms there, just, very striking but very out of place, if that makes sense?

I asked around a bit, and I guess Seminary House is a historical landmark. Rita showed me this article about it from some Wisconsin history digest. One of the island founders lived in the house way back when, so it's registered with the state or the island or something. Not long ago it had real bad water damage, and I guess the whole place was practically gutted. Tons of black mold, stuff like that. Unsalvageable. But because it's a town icon they left it standing and do routine upkeep on the outside. I've gotten a closer look a few times, checked out the boards on the doors. Those suckers are nailed on there tight. The whole thing makes me feel slightly uneasy whenever I pass by. The place just radiates with these weird vibes.

No one else seems to think so. I brought it up to my youth group kids and they practically oozed with, "Meh, whatever." Classic teenager response.

Okay, so maybe nothing, right? But here's the other weird oddity:

O. J. Simpson.

This is just straight-up bizarre. I've now seen *three* different people watching the O. J. Simpson white Bronco car chase on TV. Once was when I was at the pub, and I just assumed it was an O. J. documentary. Some lonely old guy was sipping beers and watching the boob tube at the bar. Sports fan, true-crime enthusiast, cool. Nothing to see here. Flash forward to last night. I'm taking a hike and I'm passing by a house, and I can see right inside. An entire family is sitting in the living room watching the O.J. chase like it's must-see TV. A lot of O.J. fans around these parts?

Then, I'm leaving the church the other night, and a few parishioners are gathered around a rolling TV cart in the foyer, watching the helicopter footage of the O.J. chase like it was happening live.

What gives?

I dunno, maybe I'm grasping at straws with this stuff. Maybe I'm mistaking weird houses and strange coincidences for some brooding mystery that needs solving. I don't know. But it's just eccentricity after eccentricity piling up on this island, and I can't really explain any of it.

What did Jacob know about this island? Anything at all? Because the more I try to learn about Clifford, the more dead ends I hit. I fished through church records, looking for anything that might connect to Jacob or our family. Again, nothing. There's a plaque near downtown commemorating a handful of people who died of something called the "Clifford Sickness" like one hundred years ago, but none of those names rang familiar. I just have to keep talking to people, and hope that some connection to Jacob will pop out like a jack-in-the-box.

Honestly. Am I looking in the right places?

Later, bucko.
Willow

13

WILLOW

Twenty-Eight Days until Her Disappearance

Her visit to the old schoolhouse spurred a new strategy.

The structure was a cherished Clifford landmark, Willow had heard, just a ramshackle wood-frame schoolhouse on the island's southeast side, not far from the rocky shore. *Decorated in graffiti with the names of the kids*, a person at the diner told her. The second she saw the graffiti covering the wooden siding, Willow felt reinvigorated by the spirit and creativity of youth. She made a point to walk around the entirety of the schoolhouse and really admire it—the structure was tagged with a dozen or so names drawn in a variety of eclectic styles, no doubt the artsy island kids, Willow thought. Cursive and stenciled, zigzagged and straight, pinks and blues and greens and purples.

Olivia.

Shane.

Kimberly.

There were others. She looked for her son's name, and her gaze traveled up the modest bell tower piercing the murky autumn sky. Willow's eyes locked on the iron bell that hung within, and she couldn't help but wonder when it last might have been rung. She pictured a small horde of nineteenth-century schoolchildren rushing inside, the girls in long dresses and the boys in flannel shirts and corduroy trousers. Willow imagined the sound of the bell traveling across the entire island, perhaps waking a tardy student from his slumber, his mother pushing him out the door while he pulled on his knickers.

Willow cracked a smile. She missed being a teacher, she realized, but the moment passed, and she again searched the schoolhouse siding for Jacob's name. She came up empty. And then her thoughts leapt back to Jacob's bedroom, to the words *he'd* written on the floor.

Clifford Island.

And so, she decided that if Jacob had chosen to write something on the floor that was meaningful to him in some way, then maybe she should write something meaningful *about* him. Maybe a list of things the boy loved, or things she loved about him. Perhaps that would unlock something and help her journey on this island, she reasoned. It was worth a shot. She didn't know where to begin, and her pen incessantly tapped the yellow notebook paper as she sat at the small kitchen table in her cottage.

There was just so much.

The kiddo loved animals. One of his favorite things was dinosaur documentaries. He enjoyed making his parents cards around the holidays, even when it wasn't assigned in class.

She wrote those things down. They seemed kind of surface level to her, so she dug a little deeper.

What's something more unique to him?

Jacob apologized profusely all the time. Even when there was no need to apologize, like when he stubbed his toe. *Sorry*, he'd instinctively say. Willow thought it came from her and Dominic's politeness to each other. Jacob grew up hearing it all the time. *Please. Thanks, hon. I'm sorry.* Willow used to think his apologetic behavior wasn't healthy, that it was a sign of low self-esteem. She read parenting articles, the ones littered with personal anecdotes giving advice that probably wouldn't work with your own kid and just made you feel like an awful parent. Willow eventually resorted to telling Jacob to stop saying it, to stop apologizing all the time. *Sorry*, Jacob reflexively responded.

Willow never told Jacob or Dominic, but she eventually grew to adore it.

It was just so *him*.

She wrote that down—*serial apologizer*—and stared out the window and into the trees. The pen blurred up and down.

Tap, tap, tap.

Why was this so hard?

She drew another column next to Jacob's and wrote *Willow* at the top.

What am I good at?

Her thoughts instinctively went to the time when she'd lost Jacob, because they had a tendency to go there. That week, she existed in a perpetual state of shock, but she was still on her game. There was simply so much to do. Choosing a coffin. A cemetery. Flowers. Food. A mountain of sympathy cards to read. It wasn't exhausting. Willow was always a natural at getting things done. She enjoyed a to-do list, and everyone seemed impressed by how well she held herself together during that horrendous time.

Really? I'm going to write down that I was good at arranging my son's funeral?

She instead wrote:

My job.

Willow stared at the words on the page. She hadn't planned on writing them—they'd just come, almost subconsciously.

It had only been one week, but Willow impressed herself at how good she was at being a young adult ministries director. She had no formal job training, no experience working for a church. People asked, and the lying came easy.

Oh yes, I was a weekly churchgoer back in Illinois. I have a personal relationship with Jesus Christ.

Willow hoped no one would check up on that. But really, why would they? How could they? *People can't even google me up here. It's simply not possible.* The new youth ministry director wasn't a believer, but she acted like one. That was all that mattered. That, and the job, of course. But that part was surprisingly easy. Different tasks slid across her desk, and Willow got them done. Church newsletter: written, printed, and copied. A fundraiser to support Doctors Without Borders: the wheels were in motion. The job felt nearly as satisfying as cleaning Jacob's room back home.

Do this, check. That's done, check.

But the main part of the job was the people. Godly values must be displayed whether you're standing in line for Communion or buying a can of soup at the tiny grocer downtown. You're on a team—the Lord's team—and that jersey meant something. So Willow attended her first church services in decades, poured Folgers coffee out in the church lobby, ate pastries, and mingled.

Oh, the damn *mingling.* She'd attended three services, but church already seemed more like a social destination than a place to worship and plead for forgiveness. Willow considered herself blessed with the gift of gab, and each conversation was a chance to show off, to win a conversation competition.

I am new here, but you'll like me. I will win you over.

But the person Willow was winning over the most?

Herself.

It had only been seven days since she'd arrived on Clifford, but Willow found her grief dissipating. That burning sensation in her chest that once glued her to the couch was fading. She'd begun to eat normally again. Vegetables and fruit, not just stale cereal and whatever hadn't expired in the fridge. She was exercising. She was reading a book, an actual *novel.* No mindless internet scrolling, no cell phone tethered to her hand. In the early mornings, Willow hiked to Huntington Beach and watched the waves roll into the shore. The beach was something of a local icon. Its shores were covered with small white limestone pebbles. It was illegal to take them as souvenirs, but Willow still snagged a few for herself.

She glanced over at the rocks sitting on the coffee table.

I like them because they remind me of Jacob, right?

The smoothness reminds me of a fresh comforter in his bedroom.

Or maybe he would've enjoyed collecting them?

Willow couldn't bring herself to like something just for *her*—it had to be about Jacob, no bones about it—and she angrily tore the piece of paper off the notepad and tossed it onto the floor.

The heck is wrong with me?

Willow stood up from the table and grabbed her coat. She needed some air, needed to do something else. There was a basketball game at the school, and that sounded like a good idea. Besides, Lily had invited her.

Another chance to win people over and support the kids from youth group.

She could grieve later.

The Clifford Island K–12 school gymnasium was small. It reminded Willow of the "second gym" from her high school growing up. The dark and dingy one, the one usually reserved for the freshman basketball team. The one with the leaky roof and flickering lights.

Here, it was the main gymnasium—the only gymnasium—and Willow was one of about sixty fans watching the Clifford Island Mudhens girls' varsity basketball team square off against the Gibraltar Bulldogs. It was the third quarter, and the Mudhens were losing by twenty-four points. The girls looked dog-tired, and Willow couldn't blame them. They had only six players compared to Gibraltar's roster of thirteen players. It didn't seem fair.

Lily Becker caught a pass on the right wing, and she shot-faked.

Her defender leapt in the air, and Lily dribbled right around her and cruised into the lane for an uncontested lay-up. The small crowd cheered mightily. You wouldn't know it was a blowout. A Bulldog lazily inbounded the ball, and Lily pounced. She smacked the ball out of the Bulldog point guard's waiting hands, grabbed it, and went up with a shot. She was fouled, and the ball rolled across the rim, sat there for a moment, then fell into the hoop. The hometown referee empathetically signaled that the shot counted. Lily made the free throw, her three-point play complete. It was now a nineteen-point game.

It was as close as the Mudhens would get the rest of the night. They lost 59–32.

Willow hung around for a bit after the final buzzer sounded. She wanted to talk to Lily, to let her know she'd played well, to continue building that bond. Willow had met Lily at the first youth group a few days prior, and she immediately took a liking to the girl. She reminded Willow of herself when she was in high school. Smart, athletic, outgoing. She was one of those kids who had a bright future ahead of her. Willow could just tell.

The eight or so kids who had come to watch filed out of the gym. During the game, Willow hadn't been able to stop glancing over at them. She was trying to pinpoint their fashion sense. Early '90s? Mid-'90s? Willow had never considered herself the hippest person, but she always tried to stay aware of trends. When she was a teacher, she enjoyed studying how the kids dressed, what was in and what was out. She'd seen it all, and things usually went round and round. Cargo shorts and pants were once fashionable with the boys; her last year teaching it was above-the-knee shorts and khakis. The girls once wore low-cut jeans with exposed belly buttons. Now jeans were high-waisted, with ragged, frayed hems. The early '90s were already kind of back, but these Clifford Island kids took it to the next level.

One boy sported a puffy Green Bay Packers Starter-brand jacket. Willow remembered those from her middle school days. A redheaded girl wore distressed overalls over a striped T-shirt. Steven, a senior who had come to her youth group meeting that week, was dressed in a colorful sweater with dozens of dissonant patterns. The girls' jeans were looser around the thighs, the guys' jeans acid-washed. It was like a group of extras from *Saved by the Bell* had been marooned on the island.

It made Willow smile.

Kids are always on point with their fashion. They know what's cool.

Still, this seemed a little over-the-top. Willow had never seen anything like this. She tried to imagine a pack of her former students dressing like this, but she couldn't. Maybe for Halloween; perhaps for decades day during spirit week. Was this all the islanders had to wear? Hand-me-downs from older siblings? It was all so extreme. Willow glanced at her own outfit. Yoga pants, purple long-sleeve tee, scarf. Pretty ordinary stuff.

But Willow felt like she was the one who stood out.

The postgame music blared throughout the gymnasium. "Whoomp! (There It Is)." Willow laughed to herself. A funny choice after getting walloped on your home court. She walked down to the scorer's bench and locked eyes with Lily. The girl wiped the sweat from her brow with a towel, and she untucked her white jersey from her shorts. Lily gave Willow a little wave before walking over. Willow couldn't help but notice that Lily looked a bit disappointed. They had just taken a pretty good beating, after all.

"Thanks for coming, Ms. Stone," Lily said. "That was cool of you."

"Thanks for inviting me," Willow replied. "It was fun watching you play."

"I'm glad someone had fun." The sweat trickled down Lily's temples, and she wiped it away. Her ponytailed hair was soaked. The girl was still a little out of breath.

"Can't win 'em all, right?" Willow reasoned.

"We didn't win a single game last year, so it'd be nice to win eventually."

Willow politely laughed. She assumed Lily was being sarcastic, but she wasn't sure.

"Seems like a good turnout, right?" Willow asked, looking around the gymnasium.

"It's okay." The girl shrugged. Lily's head turned, and she suddenly looked irritated. Lily exaggeratedly waved to a group of adults about fifteen rows up in the bleachers and called out to them over the music. "Yes, Dad, I see you! I'll be there in a second!" She turned back to Willow. "Jesus, can I get one moment?"

"Oh, I'm sorry," Willow said. "I can just—"

"No, no," Lily interrupted. "That came out wrong. It's cool talking to you. I just don't want to talk to him right now. He will somehow turn this into a lecture about me quitting basketball. Like us getting blown out was a sign or something."

"Are you serious?" Willow couldn't believe it. Lily was the star of the team, the only bright spot on an otherwise ragtag roster of players. And her dad wanted her to quit?

"He thinks it's kind of dumb," Lily said. "That sounds bad. He'd prefer for me to focus on school, or whatever. He comes to all my games, but I swear to God he's hoping I will tear my ACL or something. Fingers crossed, right?"

Willow smiled. She enjoyed the kid's cynical wit.

"I think I spotted a crowbar back at my cottage," Willow replied. "Just let me know and I can, you know, *whack*. A little Tonya Harding special."

Lily busted out laughing. "Jesus, Ms. Stone. Nice reference, by the way. You'll fit in well around here."

"You coming to youth group tomorrow?"

"I'll be there," Lily said. "Anything to get out of the house." She looked up at her dad again. Willow glanced that way, too. The group of six adults looked far too serious, like they didn't want Lily talking to

Willow. Hands in pockets, very square and stiff postures. Willow's brow furrowed a bit, and she felt a hand smack her shoulder. It was Lily's.

"Boomers, right?" Lily joked. Willow liked this. True, she was twenty years older than this kid, but she couldn't help but feel an instant connection.

Yeah, lame adults.

She hadn't been expecting to bond this quickly with one of the youth group kids, but here she was. It made her feel like a teacher again, like back in her heyday. Before her son's accident. Before the burnout. She quickly remembered that connecting with kids was a pretty satisfying feeling, and she relished the moment.

"Anyway, I gotta go," Lily said. She waved at her dad before turning to Willow and saying under her breath, "Only nine more months. I can do this."

Willow quickly did the math.

Nine months. Freshman year of college. This kid can't wait to hit the bricks.

Lily trudged up the bleachers toward the adults, her untucked jersey swaying behind her. Willow considered following her. Thought maybe she should, with her new role in the church and all. She had seen Lily's dad at services collecting the offerings, and she hadn't introduced herself then, either. There was something intimidating about the guy, and she couldn't quite figure out why.

Willow turned and walked to the exit instead. She passed a boy lurking on the baseline, someone she hadn't noticed at the game. He looked to be a high schooler, but he was dressed differently from the other kids she'd seen tonight. Not a Clifford Island kid. He looked, well, less trendy. More normal. Blue jeans, New Balance shoes, Patagonia jacket. Like one of her old students from her teaching days. The boy paced the baseline near the visitors' bench, rubbing the back of his neck and biting his lip. He looked like he was waiting for someone, and Willow thought that person might be Lily.

How cute, Willow thought. *Lily has a boyfriend.*

She understood why the boy would be taken with her. Willow had only spent a small amount of time with Lily, but she already admired her. She had that spunk and youthful spirit that Willow once had. Lily was ready to move forward and leave this place. She had motivation; she had drive. But as much as Willow admired this in Lily, it wasn't what she wanted for herself. She was still struggling to admit it, but she *liked* it on Clifford Island. The place was like a time machine. Willow felt like she'd stepped backward into a simpler age, where modern problems simply didn't exist.

In that moment, standing in the Clifford Island K–12 school gymnasium, Willow pictured herself staying on the island for a long, long time. She knew that she would soon solve the mystery of why those words were written on her son's floor. It was only a matter of time. Then she'd have the closure about Jacob she so desperately sought. Happiness for herself couldn't be far behind.

She could have everything, and it was in this place.

Before exiting, Willow looked back into the gymnasium. She spotted a few islanders having what looked like a tense conversation with a photographer. The photographer raised his hands and pointed this way and that, the strapped camera bouncing around his neck. He seemed to be explaining himself, but the islanders weren't having it. Willow sheepishly looked away and walked through the door. Public confrontations always made her antsy.

She remembered her own confrontation with the man who had broken her cell phone when she arrived on the island, and Willow instinctively patted her pockets. In the end, it didn't matter. There was no need for her phone up here.

She smiled to herself and mouthed along with the song.

"Whoomp! (There It Is)!"

Willow took a stroll through the dark school, just because she was curious. The eighth-grade classroom was only a few doors down from the kindergarten classroom, which was strange to her. She entered the kindergarten room, and she was immediately transported back to when Jacob was six years old and starting elementary school. Colorful bins. Art supplies. Rainbows on the wall.

These rooms just never change, she thought.

Willow spotted a book on a desk and she picked it up. *Mary and Patches*, the title read. On the cover, a little girl clutched a teddy bear. Willow turned to the first page and began reading.

A long time ago a little girl named Mary had a teddy bear named Patches. Mary loved Patches. They played together. They slept together. They did everything together.

But, as Mary grew older, Patches grew more ragged. He lost buttons. His stitching ripped. The stuffing poked through his arms and legs. This happened to Mary's friends' stuffed animals, too. The other kids threw out their stuffed animals and got new ones. But Mary kept Patches. She knew Patches was the most important stuffed animal of all. So Mary never got a new stuffed animal. She kept Patches.

Mary grew older. She got married and had kids of her own. And Patches stayed by her side. He was dirty and flimsy, but Mary didn't mind. She loved Patches.

Mary became an old woman. And all of her childhood friends, the ones who discarded their old stuffed animals, were now gone. They didn't live as long as Mary and Patches. Mary went to their funerals, and she brought Patches along. And although it was very sad, Mary understood why her friends had died. They didn't know the meaning of loyalty and love. But Mary did. So she lived longer than her friends.

Mary and Patches will be together forever.

Willow flipped over the book. *Who published this?* she thought. There was no publisher listed. No UPC symbol. It looked like a local print job.

Jesus, what a morbid freaking book.

She put it back on the desk and continued her exploration of the school. The computers in the media lab looked like they could only handle a few rounds of *The Oregon Trail*. A few of the walls seemed in danger of crumbling into a heap. The whole building was in dire need of refurbishment. Willow spotted a few of those celebrity READ posters she remembered from when she was a kid. A *Fugitive*-era Harrison Ford. Bette Midler. Michael Chang. Bo Jackson. She wondered if the kids had even *heard* of Bo Jackson.

She rounded a corner and heard the squeak of a mop on tile. The man doing the mopping was Clarence, the repairman she'd met her first day on the island.

"Nice to see you again, Ms. Stone," he said, his lips curling into a smile. Willow was impressed he'd remembered her name, but then again, everyone knew everyone's name around here. "What are you up to walking around an empty school this late at night?"

"Just caught a game, and now I'm doing some exploring," she said.

"That gutter hold up okay?"

"Best gutter I've ever seen in my life."

Clarence chuckled. "You remind me of my daughter," he said, a twinkle in his eye.

Willow blushed. "Is she my age?"

"Oh, no. She passed a long, long time ago. Just think she might've grown up like you, is all."

Willow was touched by the old man's sincerity, and she told him as much before going on her way. She passed Clarence's office as she left; it was basically just a converted broom closet. It did have a TV, though, and on the tiny screen Willow saw that familiar white Bronco slowly cruising down a Los Angeles freeway, tailed by a gaggle of police cars.

She stopped for a moment, and her head tilted a bit as she gawked at the television. It was the fourth time she'd seen the O.J. chase on TV since arriving on Clifford Island, and she was trying to determine if this was somehow meaningful or merely a coincidence. Clarence noticed the confusion on Willow's face.

"Everything okay?" he asked.

Willow snapped out of it. "Oh, it's fine. Just thinking."

She decided it was just too strange to be anything *but* a coincidence, and she strode down the school hallway. *Besides, why exactly would everybody be watching that, of all things, over and over again?* Willow questioned how many times she'd actually seen the O.J. chase since arriving on the island, and she decided maybe she was mistaken.

Islanders watching the white Bronco chase on a perpetual loop?

Willow laughed to herself. It was too preposterous.

She shook the thoughts from her head, bundled up in her coat and gloves, and headed out the side door of the building.

It was a three-mile hike home. Willow enjoyed walking everywhere; she liked living simply. She did this even though she had been given a car by the church. It was from the twentieth century, of course, like every other car Willow had seen on the island. A 1992 Chevy Corsica with 192,000 miles. She'd fired it up exactly one time.

Snow flurries whipped by her as Willow trekked along a country road. The moon lit Willow's way, and the woman's breath rose and fell in the northern air. Then Willow heard a sound. From the woods to her right, she heard twigs cracking, branches rustling. It didn't sound like an animal plodding through the forest; the steps seemed too careful and deliberate. They sounded like they were pacing her.

Willow stopped, and the sounds stopped right along with her. The woods sprouted about ten yards off the road, and Willow strained to look through the trees. The forest was thick. All she could see was trunks and branches and leaves, seemingly an infinite number.

She considered calling out but didn't. Willow didn't know exactly who was in those woods, but she didn't want to draw any attention to herself. *A woman, alone at night, with nothing but her cottage keys to defend herself?* Whereas twenty minutes ago Willow had felt like she belonged, now she felt like an outsider. A female outsider walking alone at night, at that.

Willow started up the road again, and her pace quickened. The sounds from the forest returned, matching her step for step. Willow moved faster, hoping against hope for a Good Samaritan to appear. The headlights of a passing car she could flag down, or maybe a fellow islander out for a late-night walk. But there was nothing. She was alone on a road in a forgotten place, and there was something in the woods, following her.

She began to run.

Her cottage was close now; Willow could see it in the distance. Her lungs burned and her legs ached. She'd fallen down twice while running for her life, and each time she did, Willow imagined a hand grabbing her ankle and pulling her into the black depths of the forest, her fruitless screams dissipating into the night. But both times she'd managed to scramble to her feet, slipping only slightly as her thighs began pumping once again, her mind longing for the relative safety of her cottage on church grounds.

And now it was *right there*, maybe forty, fifty yards away. She could barely make it out in the whirling snow. Willow considered this a blessing—maybe whoever it was in the woods couldn't see her, either. Between her own footsteps and panting breath, Willow hadn't heard anything from the forest since she began sprinting. But she wasn't taking any chances.

She ran even harder, and she had the terrible thought that someone wasn't pacing her from the side anymore but instead was directly behind her. Willow wasn't sure; she hadn't looked back, not once. When she'd begun her sprint a few miles back, her mind flashed to middle school track and something her coach had told her: *Never, ever turn your head to look back. It will only slow you down.*

And so, she didn't.

She slipped once more ten yards from her front door, frantically clambering to her feet with one hand while pulling out her keys with the other. Willow slammed into her front door, jamming the key into the lock on the third try, and she threw herself inside the cottage. She landed on her belly on the floor, kicking the door shut and lunging toward the dead bolt. Willow felt her body relax with the click of the lock, and she sat against the door, her breath finally slowing, the adrenaline fading, her calves and hamstrings aflame.

"Thanks, Coach," she muttered to herself between breaths.

Willow sat like that for a few minutes, and when no one came barging into her cottage and the only sound she heard was the wind whistling through the trees, she decided she was finally safe. As more time passed, she began to doubt everything she thought she'd heard. She chalked it up to nerves, to the dark, to being in a new place. It was an animal; it had to be. Or nothing at all. There aren't things in the woods that follow people. That was the stuff of dark fairy tales.

Good Lord, am I Little Red Riding Hood or something? Willow thought.

Five inches of snow fell during the night. In the morning, looking out the front window of her cottage, Willow couldn't make out any of her frantic footprints. They'd all been covered by a shimmering carpet of fresh powder. Still, she was curious. Willow threw on some boots and her coat, and she ventured outside and looked around.

Behind her cottage, she found a fresh set of footprints that certainly weren't hers. The tracks led from the woods directly to Willow's bedroom window, where they abruptly stopped, turned around, and retreated back into the forest.

Willow quickly went back inside.

The dead bolt clicked, but it didn't do the trick this time.

She no longer felt safe.

14

LILY AND KAYLA

Twenty-Five Days until Willow's Disappearance

Lily was trying to zone out, but the baby screaming to her right was making it difficult to do so. Sitting at her desk, Kayla was doing her best to calm the baby down—she tried burping him, as the home economics teacher had instructed, and was rocking him back and forth, but that wasn't working. The infant simulator continued to wail.

Kayla, take the stupid doll out in the hallway, Lily thought.

Or, you know, just stick it under your shirt.

The simulator technology was a bit too modern for Clifford's standards, but the islanders decided to make an exception. Lily's doll was jammed in her backpack. Her baby had started crying during fourth period, and Lily simply smothered the doll with a sweatshirt. That seemed to do the trick. The simulator would track that Lily never tended to the doll's needs, but Lily didn't care. Fourth period was her free period, and she wanted to shoot hoops.

Priorities are priorities.

Kayla's doll continued to bawl—the tinny, robotic nature of the wail made it so much worse to the ears than a real human baby—and Lily looked to her history teacher, a doughy, balding man in his mid-fifties named Randy Gordon, for support. But Mr. Gordon wasn't interested in doing Lily or any of the other eight students in the classroom a solid. His sole interest seemed to be in reading directly from the textbook at the front of the room. Situated behind a podium, the teacher droned on.

"Terrorism truly became a national issue at the beginning of the last decade," Mr. Gordon read. He looked up at the students. "Can anyone define terrorism to the class?"

Steven raised his hand, and Mr. Gordon nodded at the boy.

"It's when people, or groups," Steven said, "attack other people and use violence and stuff to, like, make a point about something."

"Very good," Mr. Gordon said mindlessly over the cries of the baby.

Really, Teach? Lily thought. *You aren't going to have him clarify that a bit more?*

She looked over at Steven, and the boy shrugged and smiled. He was wearing a white T-shirt that read, COED NAKED LACROSSE: ROUGH, TOUGH, AND IN THE BUFF, which was pretty inappropriate for school, and Mr. Gordon was letting *that* slide, so why wouldn't he also let some half-assed answer from the same kid slide as well?

Lily rolled her eyes. As far as autopilot education went, it could have been worse. The fact that Mr. Gordon had stopped to engage the students at all was a bit of a surprise. Lily's gaze drifted to the walls of the classroom, and she grew even more annoyed at her situation. Sports posters seemingly covered every square inch of the classroom—Lily loved sports, of course—but they had nothing to with the American history curriculum, so what were they doing there? Plus, these posters were *old*. Like, minutes from disintegration. Lily had no idea what a "steel curtain" defense was, but given the sun-faded colors of the posters, she assumed it must've been around the birth of the NFL.

Kayla shushed the baby and continued to rock the doll, and the simulator finally calmed down, the crying diminishing to a sputter. Mr. Gordon's eyes returned to the textbook on the podium.

"'On February 26, 1993, a truck bomb exploded in a parking garage at the World Trade Center in New York City,'" Mr. Gordon read. The doll's crying ceased completely, and the classroom was quiet, save for the voice of the teacher. "'This terrorist attack resulted in the deaths of six people and injured over one thousand more,'" Mr. Gordon read.

Lily scanned the faces around her. The students had their textbooks open on their desks—the really thick kind of textbooks, the kind that give you spinal problems if you carry too many in your backpack—and those who could were following along. Some of the textbooks had lost pages over the years. For better or worse, Lily's was still intact. The girl skipped ahead a few lines to see what was coming.

Oh no, Lily thought.

He wouldn't.

Would he?

"'The World Trade Center attack was planned by . . .'"

Mr. Gordon read on. He was almost there. So close to saying it.

"'Terrorism was brought to the forefront of the American conscious-ness. . . .'"

Here it comes.

"'The goal of the terrorists was to completely topple the World Trade Center towers. . . .'"

Don't sound like an idiot, Mr. Gordon.

Just don't.

The teacher cleared his throat. "'The truck bombing is the deadliest terrorist attack to occur on American soil. The World Trade Center towers remain standing.'"

Lily waited for a moment for Mr. Gordon to clarify. Something like, *This is clearly outdated information*, or, *We all know this isn't true anymore*. But the teacher was silent. When Mr. Gordon turned the page and continued reading, Lily had finally had enough.

"Oh, COME ON!" she blurted.

Mr. Gordon looked up, startled. Every head in the classroom turned toward Lily.

"We are actually going to pretend that . . . you know," Lily said, flabbergasted. "That the truck bombing, in 1993—yes, it was bad—but that it was the *worst* thing to happen, that something else didn't . . . I mean, do I even need to say it?"

Mr. Gordon narrowed his eyes. "I'm merely reading from the textbook," he said slowly. "This is what the textbook says."

Lily threw her hands in the air. "Give me a freaking break!" she blurted. At that moment, as if sensing the tension in the classroom, Kayla's infant simulator began to wail again. Lily reached wildly across the aisle toward Kayla and yanked the doll from her friend's hands, shoving the infant into the backpack at her feet in one fluid motion. "And can this doll shut up for one freaking second?!"

Kayla gaped at her friend.

Mr. Gordon calmly closed the textbook on the podium.

"Ms. Becker," he said, "please see me after class."

Lily slouched lower in her chair. She wouldn't even make eye contact with Mr. Gordon; the man didn't deserve as much. They'd sat in silence for at least thirty seconds, on either side of the teacher's desk, each seemingly daring the other to speak first. All the other students had moved on to eighth period; it was just Lily and her teacher, playing the silent game. It was Mr. Gordon who finally broke.

"Ms. Becker, you know why we do what we do," he said.

Lily still wouldn't look at him.

"There are certain things we all know, but we don't talk about them, because there's no reason to talk about them. We just know."

Nope. Still not looking.

Mr. Gordon leaned forward, and the teacher's voice dropped to just above a whisper. "Of course I know about 9/11. Of course I do. Don't take me for a fool."

That's a little better, Lily thought. *But still not quite.*

"I know things are hard for kids around here," Mr. Gordon said, leaning back, his voice taking on more of a conversational tone. "Being a kid is tough under any circumstances. I get you."

You get me?

No, you don't.

Lily stared at her lap, biting her lower lip.

"Now," he said, "I know your grades are slipping a bit. My class, Mrs. Andersen's class. And you have plenty of time to catch up, so I'm not gravely concerned, but grabbing the doll, Lily, shoving it in your bookbag . . . that was a little excessive."

"It's just a doll." Lily shrugged.

There, she thought. *I'm communicating. You can't say I didn't talk to you.*

Mr. Gordon sighed. "Look, you can space out in my classroom. That's fine. You can blow off your science homework. But home economics? That's important. Maybe the most important class of them all."

"Wait, what?" Lily said. The sheer audacity of Mr. Gordon's statement made the girl straighten up in her chair.

"I'm just saying," said Mr. Gordon, "that raising a family, learning how to be a good parent, a good mother—these may be the most important lessons you learn in school."

Lily was stunned.

Her silence before had been her choice. Now, for the first time in this conversation, she was physically incapable of speaking.

Lily slid back down in her chair. She was definitely done communicating.

And Mr. Gordon was definitely going to pay for that last remark.

The kids stooped behind the bushes. There were three of them crouched in the front yard of Mr. Gordon's house mere feet from the picture window, and the night seemed exceptionally dark. The few streetlights that existed on Clifford Island lined the Podunk downtown, and sometimes those weren't even switched on.

It was next to impossible to be a hermit on Clifford Island, but Mr. Gordon was the closest thing to it—when he wasn't teaching, of course. The teacher's house was on the east side of the island, buried in a thicket of trees down a lonely dirt road. Even in the daytime, his house was difficult to find. But the kids knew where it was.

Steven slowly stood up and peeked inside the house and then popped back down. Lily noticed the excitement in his eyes.

"No movement," Steven said.

"We're still early," Lily said. "He won't be there until eight."

"Seven fifty-eight," he replied.

Lily rolled her eyes. "Whatever."

Kayla said nothing.

Lily clutched the VHS tape in her hand, savoring the moment. She'd thought of this a long time ago—just a simple, harmless prank to get under everyone's skin—but she hadn't had the gall to actually do it until tonight. Her conversation with Mr. Gordon had pushed her over the edge.

Mr. Gordon deserves a little lesson of his own, Lily thought.

For his blatant sexism.

For him always teaching the same stupid stuff over and over and over again.

God, this was a long time coming.

That alone made this feel like the right time to Lily. Well, that and Kayla. In the past few months, she'd felt her friend slipping away from her, felt her shifting ever so slightly to the islanders' side. Lily loved to complain about Clifford Island, and for their entire lives Kayla had commiserated with her. But that was changing. It was subtle, but Lily noticed the difference. Kayla was no longer piling on when Lily grumbled; now the girl said fairly indifferent and noncommittal things like "uh-huh" or "yeah." Sometimes she just nodded, and other times she looked away. Lily knew her friend well enough to tell that something had changed. And then there was the incident on the mainland over the summer—the video game controller, the cell phone, the *we're saving your lives* nonsense. Lily hadn't brought herself to even discuss that night with Kayla. The two pretended like it never happened and carried on with their lives on Clifford. But Lily hadn't forgotten, and she was quite certain that Kayla hadn't, either. But instead of hashing it out, Lily decided it was simply time to show Kayla how stupid it all was. To prove that their way of life on Clifford Island was pointless and that nothing would happen if people broke the rules.

And tonight was the night.

"I have the first season of *Friends* if you guys wanna come over later," Lily said.

"Finally," Steven replied. "I've been wanting to see that."

"Kayla?" Lily asked.

Kayla didn't respond. By the look on her face since the trio had arrived, Lily thought her friend might throw up.

"They are VHS, if that helps," Lily clarified. "Connor scored them at a Goodwill."

Kayla smiled uneasily.

"Two minutes," Steven said, looking at his watch. "This is gonna be good."

"What do you think he'll do?" Lily asked.

"Smash the TV?" Steven guessed. He looked over at Kayla, and the girl shrugged.

Lily noticed Kayla shivering a bit, and she hoped it was because of the chill in the air. *Just wait, Kayla*, Lily thought. *You'll see.*

Steven looked down to his wrist. "It's go time," he said, and right on cue, their teacher emerged from the kitchen into his living room. The kids got a good look at him through the large picture window—the curtains were open and unclamped, and Lily could not believe their good fortune. It was almost as if their teacher was asking for it. Mr. Gordon sauntered over to the entertainment unit, stooped down, and slid open the drawer on the bottom. He rose, slightly winded from this task, holding a VHS tape.

"He's gotta be able to tell," Steven said giddily. "Do you think he'll notice?"

"I doubt he even looks at it," Lily said. She still held Mr. Gordon's tape in her hand, the one the man *thought* he was holding. Lily had crept inside his home through an unlocked side door about an hour earlier and switched out Mr. Gordon's tape with a different one.

"Oh my God," Steven exclaimed. "He is gonna lose it."

Mr. Gordon popped the tape into the VCR resting on top of the television set and lurched over to the easy chair near the window. He didn't know it, but he was ten feet away from the kids behind the bushes in his front yard, two of them grinning and one of them biting her lip nervously. The teacher sank a good four inches into the easy chair and began fiddling with the remote controls.

Lily glanced over at Kayla. Her friend wasn't even watching the balding man in the chair—she was looking out toward the garage, then down Mr. Gordon's driveway, then down the dirt road through the trees. Her eyes scanned their surroundings, looking for movement.

Jesus, Kayla, there's nothing out there, Lily thought. *Absolutely nothing is going to materialize from the trees. That stuff doesn't exist.*

Mr. Gordon suddenly straightened up in his chair. Something was wrong. On the television, Michael Jordan passed the ball to Scottie Pippen, who held the ball near the top of the key. *Defense, defense, defense*, the Phoenix Suns fans chanted.

This wasn't right. MJ and Pip weren't supposed to be on the screen. Mr. Gordon should have seen Patrick Ewing, Hakeem Olajuwon, Robert Horry.

Madison Square Garden.

Knicks and Rockets, not Bulls and Suns.

Lily grinned mischievously. She'd gone as far as to change the label on her dad's VHS tape—the tape containing the entirety of game six of the 1993 NBA Finals—to match what had been hastily scribbled on Mr. Gordon's tape years ago. *Knicks Rockets* was all it read, and in the thirty or so seconds Lily had crouched like a thief in the teacher's living room she had managed to draw a near facsimile of that chicken scratch on a new label she'd stuck on her dad's tape. Not that it mattered. The man hadn't even looked; the guy had been on autopilot.

Not anymore. He shot out of his chair with surprising speed and agility, and he smashed the eject button on the VCR just as Jordan rose up for a fadeaway jumper. Lily almost erupted with laughter and had to cover her mouth with her hand. Steven was nearly bouncing up and down, and Kayla couldn't even watch. She'd spun all the way around to get a better look at her surroundings.

"Now? You think now?" Steven whispered excitedly.

"Do it now," Lily said, her hand still over her mouth.

Steven reached into the waist pocket of his pullover jacket and whipped out a black cloak—a Grim Reaper–inspired getup he'd picked up at a thrift store years ago on the mainland. The boy slipped the robe over his head, and then he pulled on a rubber zombie mask—jaw partially ripped open, cheek muscles exposed, flesh decaying. The boy pulled up the black hood so that it covered his eyes almost completely. The drape sleeves hanging from the underarms scraped the ground. Steven giggled a delicious laugh through the latex mask.

"I'm going in," he muttered.

He quickly scampered around the bushes. Wedging himself between the shrubs and the side of the house, Steven shuffled along the picture window until he stood directly in the center, staring at Mr. Gordon. The teacher had now dropped the imposter VHS tape and was on his knees, frantically digging through his collection of movies and TV shows he'd amassed over the years. He tossed them left and right, and Lily could hear the plastic items clacking together. Steven turned his head around toward Lily.

"Yeah?" he asked.

Lily nodded excitedly, and Steven swung back toward the window. He banged on the window a few times, and even though her view of Mr. Gordon was now obscured, Lily could see their startled teacher's shoulders jerk upward. Steven raised both his arms in a menacing pose and let out a guttural *growl*. Lily had never heard him make such a sound, and she was impressed at the authenticity. To her, it sounded like a mixture of a wild animal and a semitruck. She couldn't imagine what it sounded like behind plate glass, but it must not have been pleasant, because Mr. Gordon clamored backward against the entertainment unit, and the man just screamed. It was a gut-wrenching, terrible sound, and it made Lily instantaneously regret everything. All at once she wished she'd never thought up this idea, hadn't dragged her friends along, hadn't switched the tapes.

Steven dropped below the picture window onto the ground—maybe he'd doubled over with laugher, maybe he was hiding, Lily wasn't sure. But now she got a real good look at Mr. Gordon through the window. The man was still screaming, one shrill yell after another, and Lily guessed he couldn't help it. It was just his body reacting, something his mind had prepared for all these years.

He had broken the rules. He was supposed to be watching the Knicks and the Rockets, and he wasn't. It was a different basketball game. Now he was paying the price.

Mr. Gordon scrambled to his feet, and Lily noticed the dark stain emerging from below the teacher's belt on his khaki pants.

He'd wet himself.

Remorse gripped Lily; she felt the pang in her gut. It wasn't supposed to be this way. Mr. Gordon was supposed to be scared for a moment, then realize there was a student outside his window in a stupid Halloween costume, and the three laughing kids would run off and head home, all right with the world, nothing awful emerging from the forests of the island. Then Kayla would understand.

See? People can break the rules and nothing bad happens. They could've changed their ways a long time ago, but they choose to do things this way just to control everyone. It's all one giant scam.

It certainly wasn't a scam to Mr. Gordon.

Lily had never seen someone look so pitiful—she momentarily forgot about the sexism and Mr. Gordon's straight-from-the-outdated-textbook, reality-be-damned method of teaching—and her heart just shattered for the man who was now collapsed on the floor and sobbing.

Steven finally stood and faced Lily. He must've noticed the shock on the girl's face, and he spun to face Mr. Gordon. Steven pulled the mask off his head and put his hand on the glass. Their teacher peered up for a second, his cries replaced by a look of sheer confusion. He looked right at Steven, Lily thought, but there was no recognition in their teacher's face. He simply appeared lost and embarrassed, the stain of urine now running below his knee. Lily wanted to run inside and hug him, but her legs were rooted to the ground. Mr. Gordon's head dropped back down, and the tears returned.

Lily tried to say something, but no words came. She didn't know what to say, anyway. She looked to Kayla, to try to make sense of everything. But Lily wasn't even sure if Kayla had seen any of it.

The girl still had her back to the window.

She was intently watching the forest.

Her bedroom curtains were clamped tight. Kayla lay in her bed staring at the wall, hugging her stuffed animal against her chest. The girl replayed the events of the evening over and over again.

The tape.

The costume.

The screaming.

Oh my God, the screaming.

She'd never actually heard someone scream like that before. Sprawled out on her bed with the rest of the island asleep, Kayla thought she could still hear the sound echoing in the distance. Maybe it was Mr. Gordon screaming again, or maybe it was something else.

No, it's him, or it's my imagination. Because the thing I've seen try to scream like that can't actually do it. It isn't capable.

Or maybe . . .

Crap. Mr. Gordon broke the rules tonight. Maybe the evil knew.

Maybe it came for him.

Kayla pulled up the covers closer to her chin. She focused in on what she thought were the screams, and then she decided that she couldn't hear anything. There was nothing but silence outside her window. No breeze, no rustling of trees. And this filled the girl with dread, because now there was nothing to mask other sounds from reaching her bedroom, things that might come from the forest.

She pulled open the drawer of her nightstand, removing a yellow Discman and headphones. The girl slid the headphones over her head and hit Play.

The compact disc began to spin. "Round Here" by Counting Crows filled Kayla's ears. She was usually fast asleep by "Rain King," seven tracks deep into the album.

Kayla closed her eyes, and she thought of Lily. She wanted to tell her friend what she really thought about the island—about the things she'd seen—but she didn't think Lily would believe her. *Stubborn* was putting it lightly.

Maybe our teacher wetting himself will do the trick, the girl thought. *Lily's perspective might change.*

It was an optimistic thought, one that Kayla didn't think would actually come to fruition. *If Mr. Gordon gets out of this*, Kayla considered, *then maybe tonight was all for the best*. Lily needed to see what people on this island were capable of, to witness real fear. True *belief*. People don't just scream like mad and piss themselves for no reason at all. Maybe Lily would consider another viewpoint, for once in her life.

Kayla doubted it.

She didn't quite understand her friend. There was *so much* out there, but Lily dismissed it all. It didn't matter that the islanders told macabre stories about monsters in the woods, things that preferred to come out at night when the moon was at its highest point. Lily found that ridiculous. It didn't matter that many islanders insisted there was a "dark shadow" that had materialized on the island, a shadow that fishermen and settlers had claimed they'd also encountered hundreds of years ago on nearby islands in Lake Michigan. *They were smoking something*, Lily scoffed. They learned in school about a sinkhole that had emerged on nearby Shilling Island, and that the evil had supposedly crawled out of this hole almost three hundred years ago, heralding the beginning of this awful mess they were all caught up in. *Yeah, show me the evidence*, Lily said. And then there were the bone-chilling cold spots that had emerged two separate times throughout Clifford's history, spots that forewarned that the evil was about to strike. *Wouldn't there be some barometric record of this?* Lily wondered.

The only thing that would convince Lily was seeing something for herself, Kayla decided. That or one of the believers potentially wetting their pants. And then a terrible thought appeared in Kayla's head, one that made goose bumps run up and down the girl's arms.

If Mr. Gordon is killed tonight, maybe, somehow, it would help everyone on Clifford. Not just make Lily believe—maybe it would stop the evil in its tracks.

Maybe the evil could finally sleep forever.

She couldn't believe she would think such an awful thing, and she tried to bury it away. But it wouldn't go away—the idea stuck there, and Kayla played around with it for a bit, bending it this way and that. She knew the rules of the island, but she didn't really know the consequences if the rules were broken. How could anyone? The future was so uncertain; maybe if Mr. Gordon *did* die, this could all be over.

And then more thoughts reared their ugly heads.

What if something evil came while we were still outside Mr. Gordon's house?

What if that evil thing had killed Steven?

And what if, somehow, Steven's death stopped this whole thing?

Again, Kayla felt dreadful, and she shoved the thoughts way down. She hoped she would never think them ever again.

"Mr. Jones" carried on between Kayla's ears, and the girl was now almost out. Her body relaxed, her grip on her stuffed animal loosened. The pillow felt exceptionally cool and comfortable.

The last thing she considered was how lucky she was that the night had gone their way. Something truly terrible could've happened, but it hadn't. Not yet, anyway, and Kayla muttered a little prayer, asking for everything to work out okay. They'd go to school Monday, Mr. Gordon would say hello, and everyone would carry on with their lives like the teacher hadn't suffered a complete emotional breakdown in front of three of his students.

Yes, this will all be totally and completely fine.

Hunky-dory, as Pastor Rita liked to say.

The girl drifted into sleep. As she did, she thought she felt her bed shake, only a little.

She decided it was just a dream.

15

HARPER

The smell of cigarettes pervaded my senses, but it didn't really bother me. My thoughts and attention were elsewhere.

Night had fallen on Clifford Island, and I'd retreated to a pub—the only pub on the island, as far as I knew—where I'd been met with a light haze of tobacco smoke as I pushed open the door. It seemed to permanently linger in the air, a thin mist floating just above the heads of the dozen or so patrons milling at the bar and in various booths circling the establishment, and the scent immediately took me back to my pub-hopping early twenties, when indoor smoking was not only legal in bars but also seemingly encouraged.

Clifford Island apparently never got the memo that that had changed.

Still, I had other, more pressing matters to ponder. Like where I was going to sleep that night—I hadn't seen a single motel since I'd arrived, nor had I received any invitations from the islanders with whom I'd interacted.

Not that I'd accept.

Not after I'd read my sister's note.

I hunched forward a little farther in my corner booth, my sister's letter in my hands, wary of being watched by the pubgoers. I reread the contents of the envelope again and again. There wasn't much there, but that didn't make it any easier to digest. I simply hoped that perhaps by the eighty-seventh time my eyes moved down the page it would all make sense.

Dear Harper, the letter from my sister began.

There are things I need to tell you about

Willow's words abruptly stopped. Underneath that unfinished sentence, Willow wrote:

Don't follow them.

Run to your mother.

My sister's words appeared to be written in haste, like she was in a rush to get them on paper. The way she'd written *Harper* on the exterior of the envelope was similarly off-kilter.

I couldn't stop my thoughts from running away with me.

Why was she so pressed for time?

Was Willow running from something?

Was she in some kind of trouble?

The significance of Willow leaving a letter for her brother and not her husband was not lost on me. Perhaps things with Dominic were icier than I imagined. But Willow wanted me to find that letter, and she'd placed it in a location that she knew only I would look.

Behind a picture frame.

Like when we were kids, playing secret agents.

I tried to make heads or tails of Willow's message to me.

Don't follow them.

Run to your mother.

The latter phrase struck a chord. It wasn't a literal command or suggestion, I knew—our mother was long dead. No, it was in reference to *that thing* from when we were kids.

Something about a monster.

And Willow's nightmares.

My memories of those nightmares were foggy. I remembered a young Willow snuggling up to me in my bed, her tears wetting my pillowcase, my arm around her trembling shoulders.

Those words had haunted her back then, had permeated her dreams.

Run to your mother.

On the nights when the dreams took hold, Willow would sometimes repeat that phrase in a whispered hush as she struggled through sleep. They came out like a gasp, over and over again, and I'd lie next to her, holding her close, willing the words to stop, praying for the nightmares to cease.

And now, Willow had written those same words thirty years later, in what seemed like some dire warning.

My God, she doesn't still believe in monsters, does she?

It felt like such an odd thing to write, and I worried about Willow's mental health. She hadn't been doing well, clearly, since Jacob died. But monsters and evil and all that? It was possible she'd gone down that road, but that would be a surprise to me. She hadn't mentioned the things since we were kids.

And what actually did happen back then?

I tried to remember.

Something about a long-haired monster in the yard?

And it came from . . . God, where was it?

A department store or something?

Something with our mom?

It was all muddled in my memory, which suggested that it was never a very big deal. It was just a kid thing, and then she outgrew it all. It was over.

Willow isn't into this sort of thing again, is she?

I tried to conjure up a rational reason for her to have left this message for me to find, and I came up empty. Perhaps she wrote that exact phrase because she knew that I was the only one who'd recognize it. Willow wanted me to know that, yes, she'd been to this island. It was a code of sorts. A cipher.

Only, I was at a loss for what it actually meant.

And then, of course, there was the other part.

Don't follow them.

Don't follow who?

Monsters?

What were you trying to tell me, Willow?

The macabre mystery of it all was making my head ache, and I took a long swill of the mug of beer that sat before me. The dose of alcohol provided no more clarity. I placed the drink back on the table and again examined my surroundings. Neon beer signs, jukebox blasting the Allman Brothers' "Whipping Post," O. J. Simpson documentary buzzing on the tube television hanging above the bar. The islanders drank and chatted among themselves. Outside of the expected *Evening, stranger,* and *Where you from?* the islanders had mainly left me alone since I'd arrived.

Except for one guy.

He didn't flash the stink eye, but I could tell he was interested in me. The man was older—early fifties, I guessed—and he had an amiable look. Nice jeans, black fisherman's sweater. There was an air of importance about him. A town official, perhaps. But he hadn't introduced himself, so I couldn't be sure.

But his gaze kept returning to my corner of the pub, almost like he was keeping tabs on my whereabouts.

I tried to ignore him, chalking it up to my heightened sense of paranoia since finding Willow's letter. Buried in my darkened booth, I considered my options.

Ask more questions about my sister?

No, she might have been in trouble. Why else would she write me a cryptic note and stash it in a place that only I'd think to look? And that cottage was scrubbed clean, and maybe it was because—no. I wouldn't allow those dark thoughts to take hold. But it certainly appeared that Willow might have been in danger, and one of these islanders swigging beers might have been the reason. Don't want to ruffle any of those feathers.

Act like I just randomly found myself on Clifford?

Good luck, friendo. You already made your intentions clear to three people on the island, including the queen bee. These people know who you are and why you are here. I'd bet dollars to doughnuts that word traveled extremely fast on an island this small.

Call someone back home?

Maybe. I'd have to sneak a phone call on a landline for that—I still didn't have a single bar of reception on my cell phone. But I didn't have any evidence of foul play; it seemed like a rush to judgment to alert authorities. What would they do? Send in a chopper? Please. And what would I tell them? Something about a hurried letter that alluded to monsters and nightmares?

Nothing sounded good at the moment, so my solution was to play it cool and have a few drinks at the local tavern. Nothing suspicious about that. If I needed to search Willow's cottage again later, I could. Heck, I could even crash there for the night, too. Maybe I could find the kid again, that Lily Becker. She had to know more. And if I needed to swipe a boat and get the hell outta Dodge, well, I'd cross that bridge when I got there.

A blast of cold wind made me shudder, and my hand shot down to the letter to keep it from blowing off the table. Pastor Rita strolled through the open door, kicking snow off her boots.

"Heya, Ernie," she called out to the bartender, pulling the stocking cap off her head and smacking it against her thigh. A few snowflakes fell to the floor. "How we doin' tonight?"

The bartender—a husky guy with tired eyes—just kind of nodded, barely looking up from the glasses he was cleaning. I slid the letter off the table and jammed it into my front pocket. Rita walked straight to the bar, not noticing me in the corner booth off to the side. She sat down next to the guy in the fisherman's sweater, and the two began chatting.

I wondered, *Did fisherman's sweater see the letter and alert the pastor?*

No, that was just my imagination running away with me.

To anyone else it was just a random piece of paper and nothing more.

Did Rita know it was behind the painting the whole time?

Is this a setup?

Rita grabbed a drink and made her way in my direction. She *had* noticed me, or had been tipped off that I was here. My muscles tensed; my heart raced. I started absent-mindedly scratching at my leg over the letter, and I snatched my hand back once I realized what I was doing.

"It's nice to see you again, Mr. Coates," Rita said, raising her voice above the classic rock soundtrack blaring throughout the pub. She slid into the vinyl-upholstered booth with me, and I shoved over, pulling my duffel bag aside to make space. "I know what you're thinking: What's the town pastor doing at the local watering hole?"

"Oh, no, I didn't think that at all," I said, feigning a smile.

"Honey, if you're the babysitter, you can't spend all night gabbin' on the phone and raidin' the fridge. Sometimes you need to check on the kiddos." She winked at me and took a sip from her glass, which was filled with a red liquid. "It's just cranberry juice, don't get your undies in a bunch."

I laughed nervously and took a swill of beer.

"Although I certainly can't abide by all the smoking," Rita continued, waving her hand around in the air, scrunching her nose. "I keep tellin' anyone that'll listen, those things will kill ya."

"I guess laws don't apply this far north," I joked.

Rita chuckled. "We're off the radar, darling. Clifford's got its own laws, own values, in a matter of speaking. We're good people. Just living our lives, doing the best we can." I nodded, and Rita's eyes narrowed. She was sizing me up again. "I can tell you're thinking something. Come on, out with it. I'm not gonna bite ya."

"I guess," I started awkwardly, "I didn't expect there to be a bar up here."

"What did you expect?"

I looked around the pub. "Not this."

"We live awfully simple, but we're not cavemen, that's for sure." She tipped her drink back before resting it on the table. "Find anything else this afternoon?"

Oh, nothing much, just a hidden letter to me from Willow, I thought. "Went to a few places, talked to a few people. Just a bunch of dead ends."

That was a lie. I hadn't talked to anyone else. It seemed too risky. I'd merely walked the island until locating downtown, then settled on having a few spirits in someplace warm while I decided my next move.

"I'm sorry to hear that," Rita said. "I told you before, I'm going to make some calls, talk to some people. We'll find your sister. She's probably safe and sound, and you just don't know it." She smiled at me affectionately, and despite everything I still felt oddly comforted. Rita was a damn good pastor. "So, what do you do, Mr. Coates? What makes you tick?"

"I'm a writer," I said, polishing off my beer.

"How fancy! We talkin' books?"

"Maybe one day."

"Any ideas knockin' around in there?"

I shrugged. "A few."

"Well, what do you write about?"

"Sports, right now. High school sports." Calling oneself a *writer* of high school sports was a tad disingenuous, but I decided to go with it.

"Keep chasing your dreams, honey," Rita said. "Writing is no easy thing."

"Do you write?"

The pastor laughed. "Pen the sermon every week, although it's really just notes and scribbles. Chicken scratch is being generous. Most of it is right up here." She tapped her temple with her finger a few times. "I let the good Lord guide me. Hasn't steered me wrong yet. If there's something I haven't quite figured out, he always leads me right to it."

I smiled politely, picking up my empty mug and turning it in my hands.

Rita's eyes narrowed, and I couldn't shake the feeling she was studying me. Interrogating me. Fishing for information. Her questions to me seemed calculated, her responses meant to elicit something specific, something she wanted to know.

Or to *let me know* that she knew something.

Is she coyly suggesting that she's wise to Willow's note?

No, that was just me being fearful. My mind was out of sorts. My sister's letter had made me edgy; my anxiety was calling the shots.

Only . . .

What was the last thing Rita said?

Something about the Lord guiding her?

And she will always figure things out?

It was a very pastoral thing to say, nothing surprising. And yet, I felt like there was subtext there. A message.

A threat, practically.

She wanted me to know that she was on to me.

That anything I discovered about my sister would be known to her soon enough.

That she was in control.

I'm not sure how long I sat there with my mouth agape, but thankfully someone from the bar called over to Rita, and the pastor excused herself from my booth. She sidled up to the man in the fisherman's sweater, and the pair chatted quietly.

I realized I was breathing quickly, and I gathered myself. I again absentmindedly rubbed my pants over my thigh, confirming that the letter from Willow was still safe and sound.

But I just couldn't shake the thought:

Rita is in control.

The pastor and a few others made their way to the exit not long after that. I froze when they did, half expecting to be muscled out of the booth by the group, the letter ripped from my pocket. Thankfully, that didn't happen. Rita and the men merely bundled back up in their winter gear and ventured out into the frigid evening.

I felt my entire body relax the moment the door closed.

Maybe she doesn't know about the letter.

Or she's dragging this out just to make me suffer.

The night marched on. An older couple arrived and shared a couple of drinks, alone, in a booth on the opposite side of the pub. I couldn't help but notice they were sporting matching blue T-shirts that read, HAPPY HEAVENLY BIRTHDAY CODY! THIS ONE'S FOR YOU! The bittersweetness of their celebration didn't escape me, and it made me wonder how Willow celebrated Jacob's birthday after the boy's accident. I pictured Willow and Dominic decorating their house, decided that was too morbid a thing to do, before remembering the kid's bedroom remained untouched.

They already pretended Jacob was still there, just a bit, right?

Maybe they did throw a celebration.

Balloons, cake, the whole works.

The thought of Willow in a paper hat singing "Happy Birthday" to her deceased son sent a quiver through my stomach.

I shoved the thoughts away.

The mourning woman in the Clifford pub started hysterically sobbing—a visceral, violent wail—and the couple exited, the man's arm wrapped tightly around the woman. They disappeared into the night, as did a few other islanders after that.

I decided to stay as long as possible and simply leave when they kicked me out. Then I'd head to the cottage under the cover of darkness while the island slept. It was all I could think to do.

And after that?

Until then?

I strode to the jukebox. If I was going to close the place down, I might as well choose a few tunes. I was buzzing a bit from the beers. Not much—but enough to impart my musical tastes on the locals. It seemed less suspicious than hunkering down in the corner all night long, anyway. I scanned the selections.

Sir Elton, of course. Aerosmith. Led Zeppelin. AC/DC. Pink Floyd.

"What do you think?" a voice called out to me. I spun around and faced the man in the fisherman's sweater. His tone was casual, his face genial.

"Oldies," I replied, playing it cool. "I dig it."

Fisherman's sweater looked over at the bartender, who was still cleaning glasses. I wasn't sure if he'd stopped all night. The man in the sweater then reached into his pocket and pulled out his phone.

"This okay, Ernie?" he asked the bartender.

The white rag in Ernie's hand finally ceased moving, and a few other patrons noticed the phone, too. Everything just kind of stopped. A real-life record-scratch moment. The bartender looked at the man a bit cross-eyed, his eyes dancing between him and the phone in his hand.

The hell is happening here? I thought.

"Everyone here is on the level," the man insisted. "It'll be fine. Nothing will happen."

The bartender raised his eyebrows. *Really, pal?*

"Just a few songs," the man continued. "No one will know. We'll be careful, just like last time."

A few of the other patrons chirped up.

"Come on, Ernie."

"Let us have a little fun."

"It'll be fine."

"No one will find out."

The bartender looked over at me. His eyes seemed to announce to everyone, *You do realize that this stranger is here right now, right?* No one seemed to care. The bartender dropped his shoulders, relenting.

"Just a few songs, Vincent." He sighed. "Okay?"

The bartender's caginess was impossible to miss. Whatever the guy in the sweater wanted to do, it seemed to be a risky idea. My earlier thoughts about him seemed to have been confirmed: maybe he did hold some sway around the island. Vincent grinned, and Ernie walked to the front of the pub. He tested the wands hanging from the window blinds—ensuring the slats were closed tight—and then he pulled out a set of keys and locked the door, pulling on it a few times just to make sure. Nice and secure.

My adrenaline spiked. Fight or flight.

Am I going to get whacked right now?

Vincent stepped behind the bar and opened a small cabinet door, and I craned my head to see what he was doing. I braced myself for anything. A gun, perhaps. Maybe something slower and more painful. A hunting knife, pliers.

This is it.

They know about the letter.

They did something to my sister, and I'm next.

My mouth felt exceptionally dry, my knees shaky. If I needed to run, I had nowhere to go. Vincent continued to dig inside the cabinet. All I saw was a mess of cables, a VCR, and an audio receiver. Vincent fiddled with everything for a few seconds before looking back at me.

"You mind?" he said, pantomiming a yanking gesture. "The jukebox?"

Hold up.

They aren't going to snuff me?

Vincent pantomimed some more. I caught his drift, and I fumbled with the small plug for a few moments before managing to pull it from the wall. Elton John's piano fell silent. Vincent leaned down and fiddled some more, and the O.J. documentary—which I suddenly realized had been playing all night—zapped out on the tube TV.

"God, I'm so sick of that shit," Vincent grumbled. He hit a few buttons on his phone, and different music filled the pub. A synth bass riff. Kick drum. It was poppy, dancy. The lyrics kicked in, accompanied by finger snaps. It took me a few seconds for my classic rock–accosted brain to pinpoint the tune.

"Bad Guy."

Billie Eilish.

"Now we're talking," Vincent said, walking out to the center of the pub and bopping his head. "Something different."

The other patrons all started bopping along, too; heads nodding, toes tapping the floor, hands drumming the tables. Vincent held out his beer in one hand and strutted a bit, moving his hips to the rhythm, head down, eyes closed, locked into some sort of personal dance zone, oblivious to everyone around him. Even Ernie the bartender got into the action—I noticed him nodding along, mouthing the lyrics, and when the synth riff dropped he actually turned the volume dial *up*, and this pub that had been musically locked into the 1960s and '70s now felt akin to a dance club.

There was simply this *feeling* in the air.

A euphoric release.

But then everything changed.

It started slowly. One guy stopped singing; another stopped drumming the table. Their heads turned toward the bar, and they were looking at something, jaws dropped. I turned as well, and there was Vincent, back against the bar, a look of utter fear crossing his face. His jaw quivered, and he stared at the pub door. His hands balled up into fists as if anticipating some kind of an altercation.

Ernie finally noticed, and he darted behind the bar, yanking Vincent's phone out of the wall. Billie Eilish was cut off mid-lyric. The pub went quiet, and everyone stared at the door along with Vincent.

"What is it, Vinnie?" someone asked.

"She's . . ." Vincent sputtered. "She's . . . here. She's outside."

I felt an undercurrent of understanding in the room. Nothing more needed to be said. Everyone in the bar knew who *she* was. I opened my mouth to speak, but I thought against it.

Vincent slid down until he was sitting on the grimy floor against the bar. He covered his ears with his hands, seemingly stopping himself from hearing sounds that no one else in the pub could hear. He curled up into a ball, resting his chin on his knees, eyes upturned and watching the door. I also noted a look of determination that wasn't there before, almost like he was daring whatever was outside to come on inside and have a go at him.

I still didn't hear a thing. The place was as silent as a tomb. Outside, too. Heads turned between Vincent and the pub door. The guy with the gnarly beard gripped the table and slowly rose, as if bracing for something to come barging inside. Others did the same.

"Did we do this?" someone whispered.

"Shut up," Ernie said harshly.

"Can anyone else hear it?" someone else blurted out, his voice shaky.

"Jesus, shut the *hell* up," Ernie growled.

No one said a word now.

We just waited.

A booming *crash* at the door made me jump. The entire door seemed to pulse inward before resettling—it was almost like someone had barged into it at a full sprint, but not quite. No, it was more akin to a blast of wind hitting the door, nearly knocking it completely off its hinges. I was slightly crouching now, as were other bar patrons, instinctively assuming defensive positions.

I just didn't know what we'd be defending ourselves against.

Then the entire pub shook.

Not enough for me or anyone else to fall over—it seemed to barely register—but the bar certainly vibrated enough that we all looked at one another with the same expression, our eyes all asking the same question:

Did you feel that?

I'm not sure how long we stood like that. Thirty seconds, maybe a minute. Eventually, Vincent's took his hands from his ears; his posture relaxed. He stood up and took a few deep breaths.

"She gone?" Ernie asked.

Vincent nodded, and his head turned in my direction. Our eyes met, and we held each other's gaze. I tried to read the man's eyes. They seemed to say, *You get all that? That was all for you, stranger.*

I looked away.

Ernie fired up the O.J. documentary, and the white Ford Bronco again raced down the California freeway on the television. Vincent plugged in the jukebox, and the Rolling Stones boomed throughout the pub. Ernie again began cleaning glasses, and everyone carried on as if nothing had happened. Beers were raised; conversations were had.

I thought to myself, *What is this place?*

16

MR. GORDON

Twenty-Five Days until Willow's Disappearance

The only thing Randy Gordon had done since it happened was change his pants. He hadn't even cleaned up the small puddle of urine that had dripped out of his khakis and accumulated on the floor. Mr. Gordon had merely stripped off his trousers, thrown on a dirty pair of sweatpants he'd fished out of the bottom of the hamper, and returned to his easy chair.

Now he was waiting.

Waiting for *what*, the man wasn't quite certain, but he knew something was coming, all the same.

How could it not? he thought.

I've never broken my routine, not since the town meeting.

I deserve this.

He wasn't angry with the children. He couldn't tell exactly who had been outside his house; he thought he recognized Steven in that black robe, but he wasn't certain about that. He assumed Lily was with them, but again, there was no way of knowing. But he wasn't angry. There were no vengeful feelings coursing through his veins, no urge to call parents or run to Pastor Rita.

Mr. Gordon just felt ready. He decided that the kids had done him a favor. There was no point anymore. That's why he hadn't closed and clamped his curtains, the man thought, why he hadn't done it in months. Let whatever happens, happen.

He was just so tired.

That damn *basketball game.* He knew every rebound, every outlet pass, every back screen, every crossover—hell, every single *dribble*—and each night he slipped the tape into his VCR, he didn't think he'd be able to make it all the way through without cracking completely, but each night he somehow mustered the strength to keep his sanity through the final horn. His persistence surprised him every single night. Mr. Gordon had secretly hoped for years that something would happen to the tape. A house fire, or simply the tape itself becoming twisted, or perhaps ripping in half. But that dang videocassette miraculously stayed intact, and his VCR still hummed like the day he'd bought it. So, the man kept right on trucking. It was the least he could do for Clifford, he thought.

Still, the game wore him down, he decided. Made other parts of his life unimportant. He had no social life, few relationships. He was a very bad teacher—he knew that, and he was okay with that, because teaching history didn't really matter. Not on Clifford. He could've been the world's greatest educator—individualized activities, alternative assessments, all that new age, twenty-first-century buzzword stuff—but it wouldn't make a lick of difference. So why even try? Just read the textbook, shove some worksheets in their hands, and call it a day. All that mattered were the rituals, and making sure that these kids stuck around and had babies of their own. Fight the fight.

The *fight.*

His was ending, and that was just fine and dandy with Mr. Gordon. Sitting in his easy chair, staring out the window into the forest, he smiled thinking of his body's instinctual reaction to the wrong tape playing on his television.

The frantic digging.

The pissing.

Mr. Gordon laughed so hard he actually snorted.

The fact I impulsively pissed myself in front of my students is funny? Wow, this island has really done a number on me.

Replaying the incident in his head, he felt no regrets, no fears about walking into class and facing his young tormentors. He simply yearned to see the results of the madness he'd lived through on Clifford, to see just how accurate all the legends and stories were.

He desperately wanted to know before he went.

And now I might get the chance.

Then he saw them. It wasn't children this time, not some teenager in a cheap Halloween getup. No, it was a pair of yellow eyes watching him from the forest. Something was peering into his house from behind a tree, and Mr. Gordon stared fiercely right back into those eyes, island rules be damned.

He knew them well, like everyone on Clifford.

Don't look at them.

Don't follow them.

They were simple enough, but Randy Gordon was ready to do some rule breaking. He squinted hard at those yellow eyes, daring whatever was behind them to come closer, to show himself, to show herself, or *itself.* He didn't have the first clue. There were many stories, surely, and the dead thing was usually someone close to you. Family, probably, maybe a friend. He'd never heard of a dead thing *stranger* before, although he supposed that anything that came back from the dead was something of a stranger, even if you'd known that person for sixty years. They couldn't be the same; no way.

Whatever the case, he'd been a believer before, and he sure as spitfire was a believer right now.

The figure behind the tree moved slightly, just a slight sway of the head—*it's thinking about coming closer,* Mr. Gordon thought—and the man stared back something fierce, goading it to come closer. He tried to make out the form of the figure, but it was just so dark. It seemed a bit on the taller side—wait, did it? It might've been his father, Mr. Gordon guessed, and if the figure was wearing his signature brown flannel overshirt and blue jeans, he'd know for sure. His old man had always worn that, from the day Mr. Gordon was a baby bouncing on his knee, to the times he was slapped with a belt on the rear for talking back, to when the colon cancer ripped through him and left him a withered husk of a person.

Mr. Gordon rose from his easy chair and strode toward the picture window, putting his face on the glass and cupping his hands around his eyes. He wondered if he was the first islander to ever do this, to actively study one of these dead things, and he felt a measure of pride. The figure moved behind the tree and emerged from the other side, and Mr. Gordon thought he saw a hand move up and down the trunk, slowly grazing the rigid bark. The man studied the movements, searching his mind for a hint of familiarity.

Did my mother move like that? he thought.

Or my sister?

Or my second-grade teacher, Mrs. Terosi?

His inventory of dead family and friends was growing by the second, and Mr. Gordon had never felt more alone. A sadness and an emptiness overtook him, and he was acutely aware that he'd been a loner—no, a recluse, outside of his job he was definitely a recluse—for the past fifteen years, ever since his sister gave up the ghost, leaving Mr. Gordon alone in a house in the woods.

And maybe it was that ghost outside, that dead thing, his *sister*, coming to take him somewhere, to teach Mr. Gordon what really happens when you break the rules.

His head felt spacey. A swirling he'd never felt before—much different from tying a few on before hitting the hay—and then an urge swelled in his belly, rising to his chest, reminding him of when he had been a middle school boy and really noticed girls for the first time. It was a welcome feeling and he craved more of it, his entire body now pressing against the window, fighting more and more for a look at what was hiding in the forest. The dead thing with the yellow eyes turned and crept away, and Randy exhaled, a release he hadn't felt since making love for the first time at the age of twenty-four, which also turned out to be the last time. That made him wonder if the dead thing was Fern Wallace, *that* girl, the girl from when he was twenty-four, but she'd moved away from the island decades ago. He'd never spoken to her again, and he wasn't sure if she was now dead or alive, but this could be her, Mr. Gordon thought.

His breath quickened. He knew it made no sense, but if he followed her, he could make things right. Mr. Gordon had never married, never had children. Outside of his ritual, he hadn't done his part for the island.

Maybe he and Fern could . . .

He smiled then, a big, droopy, stupid smile. Mr. Gordon was going to follow this dead thing, and he knew that two things were impossibly true at the same time: he and Fern could live long, happy lives together and make half a dozen babies for Clifford Island, and he was about to die.

His body moved without him realizing what was happening. His brain was not directing his movements at all. Mr. Gordon felt like a fish navigating a current, the stream guiding him between rocks and around downed logs. He was vaguely aware of the earth shifting below his feet as he exited the front door. It was a weak shake, but it was there all the same.

Mr. Gordon walked into the forest, barefoot and without a jacket. The snow and the brisk winter air meant nothing to him. The only thing he was aware of was where this dead thing was leading him. When he saw the house, forty minutes later, he thought, *Huh. Of course it's this place.*

Moments later, the teacher was dead.

17

WILLOW

Twenty-Four Days until Her Disappearance

The door to Pastor Rita's office was closed. It was certainly uncommon for that to be the case—Rita often worked with the door open to encourage visitors, always welcoming them with a smile and a folksy greeting. The pastor *loved* to chitchat, Willow had quickly learned during her time working for the church. But right now, the door was closed, and through the window Willow spotted Rita talking with two men, their postures tense, their faces serious. Rita sat leaning forward in her chair, her hand on her chin, listening intently to what the men had to say.

Willow quickly walked past the office, hoping she wasn't noticed.

On an island as small as Clifford, faces became familiar quickly. Willow recognized both of the men in the office with Rita—they were parents of two of her youth group kids. One of them worked at the school; the other was Lily's father. She remembered the latter from the basketball game, glaring hard at her and Lily from the stands as the two chatted near the scorer's bench. She'd also seen both of them at the church before, often staying to chat with Rita following a service.

Right-hand men, they seemed like.

Willow had the pressing thought that they were discussing her, something about her being followed the other night, as if they were the ones who'd arranged it.

They wouldn't have this conversation while I was in the building with them, would they? she thought.

She dismissed the idea as neurotic, although she still stuck her hand in her pocket anyway, slipping the key to her cottage between her fingers to use as a potential weapon. It was something she'd been taught in high school health class, and she'd never forgotten it.

Willow turned two corners and descended a dark and dingy staircase toward the church archive room. Rita had promised to show Willow around, but the pastor was, well, *busy*, Willow determined. That was a conversation Willow had no intention of barging in on, so she chose to explore the archive herself.

When Willow learned of the existence of the archive, she knew immediately that it was a place she'd need to check out. The history of Clifford Island was still something of a mystery to Willow—her internet sleuthing before journeying to the island had produced barren results, and her search so far in the time she'd actually been here had been similarly frustrating. There was no library, no town newspaper. The church archive room was the best she could do. She wasn't sure exactly what she would find down there, but the church felt like an important place on the island. Something of a guidepost, it seemed, for the islanders. Maybe it would produce something that connected to Jacob and the peculiar words written on his floor.

It was worth a shot.

Willow reached the bottom of the staircase and pushed open a heavy wooden door. For a parish on a small island, the archive room was about as big as Willow expected it to be. The room was around twenty by twenty feet, entirely lined with bookshelves. Black, red, and brown leather-bound books were crammed into every available space. In one corner of the room sat a large mahogany writing desk with long, narrow drawers and brass handles.

She was immediately disappointed. At first glance, much of the collection looked to be old hymnals or different editions of Bibles. Willow examined the books more closely. Most of them were old and thick, appearing to not have been touched in years: *Expository Thoughts on the Gospels*, volumes I–IV; *The Bruised Reed*; *The Confessions*, by Augustine; *Institutes of the Christian Religion*. Nothing about Clifford Island immediately jumped out at her.

Willow moved to the desk, and she spotted a large leather portfolio with a golden clasp. She opened it, and inside was a collection of yellowed newspaper articles, all pertaining to an event called "The Clifford Sickness." The articles were clipped out of their original newspapers, and Willow was hesitant to even touch them—she was worried they would fall apart in her hands. She scanned one of the articles:

9 dead.

Hallucinations.

Presumed drowning.

"That's our little reminder folder," a voice behind Willow said. Willow was so startled she yelped and jumped a bit, and she turned to face the voice.

"Oh my God, you scared me," Willow said. She was relieved to see Pastor Rita standing on the other side of the room. "I'm so sorry."

"What are you sorry for?" The pastor smiled, but Willow thought it looked a bit different than usual. It seemed more forced. Willow thought that Rita looked a bit rattled—it was the first time the pastor's innate chipperness wasn't lighting up the room, and Willow assumed it was due to her conversation upstairs.

Just what were they discussing in that office? Willow thought.

"I know you were supposed to show me the archive," Willow told Rita, "but I guess I wandered down here on my own."

"Oh, it's fine, honey. I'm glad you found that."

Willow motioned toward the articles. "You said it was a reminder folder?"

Rita moved to Willow. "That's what we call it. Whenever anyone needs a little reminder about how life can be snatched away from you at any moment, we take a look at the folder. It's just a reminder, that's all. Of how lucky we all are to be here, of how quickly things can turn." The pastor's gaze was unfocused, her tone a bit somber.

"What happened?" Willow asked.

"Hard to say, it was so long ago. All we know is that back in 1921 a few people got sick here on the island. No one really knows what it was. But folks started having hallucinations, fevers, things of that nature. People were worried it would spread like wildfire and take the whole island, but that didn't happen."

"What did happen?"

"One morning the island woke up, and the sick people were gone."

"Gone?"

Rita nodded and took one of the articles in her hand, holding it gently. "Nine souls, may they rest in peace. It's reckoned they drowned. Hallucinated themselves right out of bed, and no one ever found 'em. Probably walked right off a cliff into the water. Riptide took them away."

"Oh my God," Willow muttered.

"Well, let's just hope God found a special place for those islanders," Rita said. "I'm sure he did." Rita gently placed the article back into the portfolio and closed it, softly patting it a few times. "And like I said, if anyone needs a reminder of how precious and fleeting life can be, well, we mosey on down here."

Willow looked to the floor. She wondered if it was possible Jacob had heard about this somehow, this *Clifford Sickness*, but she hadn't come across it in her days of internet searching. How would Jacob have known? She had the idea that maybe *Clifford Island* simply meant appreciating what you have and living in the moment, and maybe her son wanted her to know that before he died, and somehow, he'd stumbled across it somewhere—but that didn't make a lick of sense.

Rita noticed the confusion on Willow's face. "Everything okay, dear?"

"Oh yeah, everything's fine. Sorry, I was just thinking."

Rita smiled, her features softening, the brightness returning to her face. "You sure do apologize a lot."

"Sorry, I—" Willow caught herself, and she laughed. "Wow, I'll try to stop doing that so much. It's something that runs in my family. The apology thing."

"Well, to turn the tables a bit, I've got an apology for you."

Willow furrowed her brow. "What do you mean?"

"Oh, I'm not sure he'd want me telling you this, but Lionel Ebelhack accidentally caught a glimpse of you sleeping the other day."

"Who—what?"

Rita laughed. "It wasn't on purpose, honey. You might've noticed some footprints in the snow the other morning leading up to your little place. Did you happen to see them?"

Memories of the night of the basketball game flickered in Willow's head. The noises in the forest, her sprinting to the cottage, the footprints in the snow outside her window. She could feel her stomach begin to turn.

"Yes?" Willow said nervously.

"Well, that was poor Lionel. He was out tracking deer early in the morning, and he came by the cottage. He wasn't sure if anyone was living there and didn't want to startle anybody if, you know, *kablooey*." Rita mimed a shotgun firing with her hands. "So he walked up to the window, and there was this *itsy bitsy* little crack in your bedroom drapes, and Lionel saw you snoozing there."

Willow felt her skin crawl. "Oh my God."

"Oh, don't you worry. He didn't mean to do it, and I assure you he's all tied up in knots about it." Rita shook her head back and forth. "Poor Lionel. You should've seen the look on his face when he told me. Man's embarrassed looking at his own naked rear end in the mirror; I can't imagine what he felt seeing you sleeping there. Either way, he's too sheepish to apologize to your face, so here I am doing Lionel's dirty work. Hope it's all fair and square between you two now."

It all seemed a little too convenient for Willow to believe, but she went along with the explanation anyway. Still, she had questions.

Isn't it poor form to hunt that close to public buildings, like churches?

Do hunters usually track deer during snowstorms?

The finer points of hunting culture and etiquette were lost on her, but Rita's story seemed entirely reasonable. Besides, the alternative was far, far worse. Willow hadn't even told Rita about her sprinting home from the basketball game—the fact that the pastor had brought up Lionel's story and apology independently made it unlikely to be a quick cover on her end for something more nefarious, Willow thought.

"Was that Lionel in your office a bit ago?" Willow asked Rita.

She thought perhaps Lionel was a father of a youth group kid—she still wasn't sure of the men's names.

Rita waved off the question. "Oh, no, that was just boring church business, nothing you'd be interested in, sweetie. Quite the stodgy pair of fellas I have to deal with sometimes."

The two left the archives moments after that, their steps echoing in the stairwell. Willow couldn't help but think that, as stodgy as those guys were, the pastor had seemed extremely concerned with what they were telling her. She braced herself to see the two men as she arrived back on the ground level, but they were already gone. Again, she wondered if this was all about her.

Willow was already to her office before she realized that her hand was in her pocket, balled up in a fist, the key to her cottage pointing outward, ready to strike.

CLIFFORD ISLAND

Twenty-Three Days until Willow's Disappearance

TEXT MESSAGES BETWEEN LILY BECKER AND CONNOR HUDSON

CONNOR: I need your help

LILY: Yes you definitely need help

Haha

CONNOR: Sick burn

For real though

I've come to you for sage advice

Well sage information I guess

LILY: Okayyyyyyyy

CONNOR: I'm writing this thing for the school
paper

An urban legend piece

So I need some local stories

For the article

I'm kinda on a deadline here

LILY: Like scary stories?

CONNOR: Legends yeah

Stories rooted in legend

You know what I mean

But local ones

I have some but need a few more to round out the article

LILY: Hmmm

CONNOR: This sounds promising

Like maybe you are thinking

LILY: Yeah I'm thinking

CONNOR: Clifford is just too weird right

You probably have dozens of legends

LILY: Hmmmmmm

Well

CONNOR: . . .

Yeah?

You've typed then stopped like 3 times

LILY: Sorry

Okay

I have a good one for you

I think

CONNOR: Oh yyyyyyyyyyyyes

Lay it on me

LILY: You're far too excited about this

CONNOR: This better not be one of those things where I get cursed

Like I need to pass it on or I die

That would ruin my night

LILY: Nope

Just a standard kid ghost story

We had a bunch of these growing up

This is the best one for sure

CONNOR: Fire away

LILY: Okay well

Here goes

When we were kids there was a story about this woman

Mother Oga

CONNOR: Okay

LILY: And the deal was

We all have toys when we are kids

Stuffed animals and things like that

Teddy bears

You know

CONNOR: Sure yeah

LILY: And when stuffed animals get old we throw them out

Get new ones

Old ones go in the garbage

CONNOR: Right right

I'm tracking

LILY: Well the Clifford legend was

We should never throw out old stuffed animals

Never ever ever

We should keep them forever and ever

If you didn't Mother Oga would be angry

And she'd find you

CONNOR: Ooooooooooooh

Continue

LILY: If you ever heard someone say her name out loud

Mother Oga

You had three nights to make her happy

You had to put your old stuffed animals in every corner

Of your room

To prove to her that you still had them

That you never threw them away

It was a presentation in a way

To show you were a good girl

Or a good boy

You know what I mean?

CONNOR: Weird

And if you weren't a good girl

?

LILY: She'd appear the first night in an empty corner of your room

She'd be angry

And that was like a warning to you

Find an old toy for every corner

Or the second night she'd be on your ceiling

Staring down at you

CONNOR: SWEET MARIA

This is goooooooood

And what about the third night?

If you don't find old toys

LILY: She takes you

You're gone

CONNOR: Intense

!!!

LILY: Yeah it creeped us out

Oh

And Oga was a taxidermist in the story

Or something

So after she took you she'd stuff you

Take you to her creepy old house

Now you're one of her toys

Mother Oga's toys

CONNOR: Dang

You've done quite a service today

We here on the mainland salute you

LILY: Okay good haha

Happy to help

CONNOR: So this was a thing?

For real?

LILY: Oh yeah

No one wanted to say her name

It was kind of a big deal as kids

And a pain in the ass haha

You know to put out the toys

Borrow them from a friend if you threw

yours out

CONNOR: You remember doing it

LILY: A few times sure

My old stuffed animal

Cindry?

Ah the memories

CONNOR: And you put the toys out?

Like you believed she'd come?

LILY: I was ten

So yeah this stuff freaked me out

You grow up though

CONNOR: What about the house?

LILY: The Oga house?

CONNOR: Yeah

Was it a real place?

LILY: Well Oga wasn't real

So no

CONNOR: You know what I mean

Was there a house that was supposed to be hers?

LILY: Oh yeah

It's all boarded up

Still is

I think our parents just wanted us to stay out of there

Hence the stories

CONNOR: We should check it out!

Find the stuffed bodies!

LILY: You need to relax about this haha

Stupid kids stuff

There's nothing there anyway

Just a regular old house

CONNOR: Fine fine

You have more to tell?

LILY: More stories?

CONNOR: Yeah

LILY: Maybe another time I guess

It's really not a big deal

Oga

One story out of dozens up here

Or maybe . . .

CONNOR: Maybe what

LILY: Connor

CONNOR: Lily

LILY: Connnnnnnnnnnnor

CONNOR: LILLLLLLLLLLY

LILY: I just said her name

Out loud

Mother

Oga

CONNOR: Wow this is happening

LILY: Thadda

Nnnnyhnnnnnnnnn

Drddaa

CONNOR: Um

What?

LILY: Corner

Here

She's here

CONNOR: Lol

SPOOOOOKY

LILY: Help

Please help me

It's

Help

CONNOR: Lily

For real

Lily?

Hey are you there

Ummmmmm

Lily seriously

Hey what happened are you there?

Lily?

I'm going to call your dad

Seriously I am

Stop fooling around are you okay?

LILY: BOO!

Text message jump scare

Haha

CONNOR: I don't like you anymore

LILY: Yes you do

CONNOR: Yes I do you're right

God forbid I'm concerned for your safety!

Some of us take the supernatural more serious than others

LILY: Well thanks for your concern

It's noted

Hey

CONNOR: Yes?

LILY: You're going to publish this thing?

The Mother Oga story

CONNOR: I mean yeah

That's what we do

I need to submit tonight

So it should be posted tomorrow

LILY: Where does it go?

The article

CONNOR: School website

We don't do print anymore

Relic of a bygone era

LILY: Hmm

CONNOR: Is that cool?

LILY: Well . . .

You know what?

Sure

Go for it

CONNOR: You really had to think about that one

I didn't think it'd be that big a deal

Is it?

LILY: It kind of is

CONNOR: Why?

LILY: I'll tell you about it sometime

Just not yet

CONNOR: Well that's very mysterious

LILY: If only you knew

19

WILLOW

Twenty-Three Days until Her Disappearance

Dear Dominic,

I might have something. A lead. I spent some time at the pub tonight, nose buried in a book and having a few drinks. This guy Larry shows up and has a few too many. A lot too many, actually. Guy was pretty blitzed. Eventually he stumbles over to my booth, and he's chatting me up a bit. Asking me what I'm doing here, what's my story, things like that. His eyes are slits and he's slurring his words. I'm being out-of-town nice, and I ask him if he has any advice for a newbie in the area. He leans down and says, "Better be watching where you step. Strange things are happening around here. Don't want to wind up like, uh . . . who was that, oh yeah, poor Gloria!" He's tipping his beer and spilling it all over the floor as he talks, mind you. I'm like, what are you talking about? Then he says:

"You don't know about poor Gloria? All dead and naked like a scarecrow! Craziest thing I've ever seen! People are saying—"

But he can't finish, because this goateed guy who I think was eavesdropping on us the entire time sidles up to Larry and throws his arm around him. Says something like "You've had a few too many tonight" and "Maybe you should hit the road." But it was definitely in an *I'm telling you, not asking you* sort of way. He and the bartender guide Larry outside, and the poor guy nearly trips over the curb pulling out his car keys. Larry hands them over to the goateed guy willingly—I'm pretty sure it wasn't his first time—and the two peel rubber in Larry's truck. Of course, the truck is a million years old, like everything else around here. Had this peeling and faded bumper sticker that says, FIGHTING FOR PEACE! COME HOME SOON. OPERATION DESERT STORM. I'm assuming Larry is a war veteran and maybe saw some things overseas. Maybe it messed him up pretty bad. I don't know. Is any of this a lead? Maybe. Maybe not.

But after Larry was escorted out, I got the side-eye the rest of the night from people at the bar. People just seemed, how do I explain this, *careful* when they spoke to me? Every conversation at the pub seemed just a little too hushed, a bit too careful. There was this odd cloud of *concern* hanging over the entire place. I don't think I can adequately give it justice.

The whole night was just a microcosm of the social experience up here. People are nice, but there's something just a bit off. Their smiles are a bit too stiff, their pleasantries a bit too practiced. I talk to people as much as I can, and sometimes it feels like I'm speaking with preprogrammed robots. I ask questions, get to know people, try to find some connection to Jacob. *Ever been to Wildwood, Illinois? Do you have family anywhere else? Boy, this place is a little old-fashioned, huh?* Their eyes quiver, like they're choosing the appropriate response from a list. I tried to talk music with a woman my age, and I think I mentioned Lady Gaga or something, and she gave me this *look*. Almost like she was malfunctioning. *Command not found.*

I'm not trying to sound crass or like I'm better than these people. Really, I'm not. I suppose I'm just different than them, and I do *try*. Like,

I met this nice, older guy outside the post office—and within, like, two minutes, he just started telling me all about his boy, Shane, and how much he loved trains, and how for years he dreamed of taking him to the mainland to ride the Amtrak from Green Bay to Chicago. Only, Shane died a long, long time ago. But the way this guy spoke—the wistfulness, the longing—you would've thought his son died last week. He obviously knew that I'm mourning our son and was trying to relate, and he was just so sweet and I did my best to connect with him—but it was just tough, you know?

It's just really hard with these people, but I suppose I get it. The islanders probably aren't used to socializing with anyone outside their tribe, so to speak. I'm like some alien species to them. We're really far north, isolated from mainland society. People go fishing, boating, stuff like that. I've seen some supplies delivered at the docks and what I assumed was a boat carrying the island mail. But there's no regular ferry to and from the island. No one really leaves. They absolutely want to stay here, away from the world and the world's problems. It's their choice.

Anyway, I'm going to look into the Gloria thing. This guy Larry was a drunken mess, sure, but I feel like it means something. He has information I'm not supposed to have, and I'm going to find it. And, I'm not sure about this at all, but it might be related to this really intense conversation the pastor was having with these church guys a few days ago. It could've been a misread on my part, but I just had a bad feeling about the whole thing, And now with tonight and Larry . . . it could all fit together. Maybe it's a reach, but it's all I've got, you know?

Oh, I didn't tell you this one yet: The other night I walked home from a basketball game, and I was convinced someone was following me. I then literally ran home in the snow. It wasn't my best look. I feel a bit better about it now, but you should have seen me. Your wife, running for her life on some random island in Wisconsin, all because she thought she heard something in the woods. Then there was a Peeping Tom situation and . . . it's a long story. I'll tell you next time we're together.

This is a lot. I know it is. And I think I'll be okay, I really do. But I've just been scared sometimes up here, is all. Never more so than tonight. These people muscled Larry out of the bar, and he was one of their own.

If I track him down, what will they do to me?

Later, bucko.
Willow

20

HARPER

I left the pub not long after the Billie Eilish dance party, hiking through the frigid air back to Willow's cottage near the church. I looked behind me every two minutes, wary of being followed. I saw not a soul.

The cottage was locked when I arrived, which I found strange— Clifford didn't feel like the kind of place where anyone would lock anything. I considered breaking a window to get inside, but I quickly determined that would be too aggressive. After the events at the pub, I was cautious of doing anything that would draw attention to myself. Heck, I was cautious of doing *anything* at all.

These people here are a bit off, I thought.

The locking of the doors, the forbidden music.

The thing outside that only Vincent could hear before it rammed the door. She.

And, of course, there was the pub *physically shaking*; I wasn't sure whether it was a geological tremor or the building settling into the ground.

I wasn't sure about anything.

I tried to make sense of it all during my trek back to Willow's place.

The song and door ramming could have been one giant ruse by the islanders—the put-on of the century, for my money—but a performance of that scale at the pub would be pretty hard to achieve. And that would have been some *damn fine* acting going on. No, there was real fear in Vincent's eyes, real tenacity and steadfastness in his belief that there was *something* outside, something, perhaps, that was otherworldly in nature.

The man wasn't pretending.

And he wanted me to see.

Then the entire event was capped off by the shaking of the pub—the timing of it too perfect, the physical logistics capable only in a theme park attraction, not in a tiny bar on some secluded island.

The whole thing seemed supernatural in nature.

Only, I wasn't a believer in that sort of thing. Never had been, not even when Willow was spooked as a child. But now, Willow's letter in my pocket, and knowing that my sister's intentions on Clifford may have involved something with monsters and evil . . . well, I was intrigued. Not certain enough to believe that there was really some paranormal conspiracy, but enough that I was definitely rattled.

I checked the cottage windows. All locked tight. I spun around, examining my surroundings, planning my next move. The woods were quiet, the sky clear. I shifted my duffel bag to my other arm and exhaled, the self-awareness settling in.

I really think something happened to my sister, don't I?

And I've really gone too far to turn back now, haven't I?

The church was close by; I'd been there earlier in the day—*my God, have I really only been here less than a day?*—and I knew that was my best bet to find something. Keys to the cottage. Heck, maybe even Willow herself was there. After what I'd just witnessed at the pub, it wouldn't be the strangest thing to have happened to me all night.

I headed up the path, weaving through the trees, and I found myself at the edge of a small clearing. The boarded-up antebellum house I'd passed by earlier in the day with Pastor Rita came into sight, about twenty-five yards ahead. *Something House* . . . I couldn't quite recall what Rita had told me it was called, but at the time I'd found the shuttered yet upkept mansion to be somewhat peculiar.

A flash of light near the peculiarity made me gasp, and I ducked behind a tree trunk, squinting my eyes to get a better view through the darkness, trying to determine what was ahead of me in the clearing.

It was a person holding a flashlight.

One arm around the trunk, I gently placed my duffel bag to my side, slowly lowering one knee then the other to the wet and snowy ground. I closed my mouth, focusing on breathing through my nose, mindful of being heard. The figure—a man or a woman, I couldn't tell—paced around the front of the house, the thin beam of light pointing all around the general vicinity. After a few back-and-forths retreading the same ground, the figure sat down on the front stoop, and the flashlight extinguished.

If I didn't know any better, I'd say the person appeared to be patrolling the area, their actions similar to those of a security guard or soldier.

But why the antebellum house?

It was boarded up.

Just what exactly is inside?

The flashlight reactivated, the beam moving away to the opposite end of the clearing, the figure again performing another round of patrols. Worried I was the reason for all this—*they'd surely examine the area around the cottage next, right?*—I took the opportunity to scoop up my duffel bag and backpedaled down the path. After covering about fifteen feet of ground, I took a hard right into the forest, planning to circle the clearing within the safety of the woods and emerge on the opposite side. My original plan was still in play: find keys to the cottage and go from there.

It was all I had.

I moved slowly and carefully, gently clasping low-hanging tree branches and moving them aside, my attention split between not making a single sound and the brooding nature of the shuttered mansion. I could still see its dark outline through the trees and in the clearing, and my gaze traveled there every few feet—I looked for light emanating from behind one of the window boards; I had a ghastly thought that Willow was shuttered inside and under watchful guard, but all I saw was blackness. Halfway around the clearing, I noticed the flashlight coming closer—the guard had elected to explore my location. I froze among the trees, one hand covering my mouth, lest the light pick up my breath in the icy air. The beam traveled through the clearing, scanning the woods a few times, thankfully gliding right past my position. The guard sauntered away and disappeared around a corner of the home. I finally exhaled, realizing how desperate my situation was becoming.

Buried in the forest.

Middle of the night.

Temperature dropping.

Nowhere to go.

No one to trust.

I continued onward, inching through the woods, dropping my toe first on each step to evaluate my footing before lowering my heel, sometimes hugging my duffel to my chest to prevent the bag from getting caught on an errant branch. It took some time, maybe ten or fifteen minutes, and then I arrived at the path on the opposite end of the clearing. Emerging from the trees, I turned my head and peered behind me—the patroller was again perched on the front stoop of the house—and I quickly moved ahead along the path, completely out of their view. No sooner had I relaxed when I realized what I'd come face-to-face with.

The church.

I knew it would be there, but it was striking all the same. It must have been my eyes playing tricks on me in the night, but the chapel seemed to materialize in the dark like some unavoidable beacon. It seemed taller than in the daylight, thinner, more ominous, the front doors its mouth and the two windows halfway up the front its eyes. I was reminded of being a boy and entering my middle school after hours to retrieve a textbook—all sense of familiarity was erased; the school simply felt foreboding and dangerous, like no one was supposed to be there at that time. Just like this place.

But I knew I had to go inside.

It was all I could think to do.

There was a single car in the parking lot—a blue Clifford Island police cruiser—and I assumed it belonged to the guard I'd nearly crossed paths with earlier. The sheriff, perhaps a deputy. Hopefully, there was just one cop on the premises.

I studied the church windows again, looking for a flashlight bouncing around behind the glass, but I saw nothing.

I knew what I had to do, but I froze.

Am I really about to do this?

Break into a church?

My arms shivered from the cold, and my knees were knocking. My cheeks felt stiff, my hands numb. I considered trekking onward past the church, finding a barn or shed and crashing there for the night. But my time felt short, my opportunities few. If I'd really stirred things up on Clifford Island with my arrival, I knew I had to act quickly—besides, the darkness was my ally. Exploring the church at the witching hour was my best option.

Find the keys to the cottage.

Then figure out what's in the abandoned house.

Maybe find a way in there, too.

That place has to be important.

I calmed my nerves, planning on walking toward the church, but I hesitated yet again. A nagging feeling was digging away at me, one that I couldn't shake.

What if the pastor is inside, waiting for me?

For some reason, I was less frightened by backwoods cops than I was of the local island pastor. I thought back to our conversation at the cottage, our interaction at the bar. She seemed to steer my every word with a friendly menace and calculated precision.

I thought it again.

Rita is in control.

I shook off the idea the best I could. The church beckoned, and I pressed forward.

If there were any clues about my sister's whereabouts inside, I sure as hell was going to find them.

21

RITA

Twenty-Two Days until Willow's Disappearance

Rita paced back and forth in the small room behind the chancel. She'd never felt this nervous before—she hadn't even been nervous at that fateful town meeting decades ago. Back then, she'd felt she had answers. Now she didn't.

It was a totally different story.

The pastor walked past the rolling hanger rack—her arm brushed against the collection of long white vestments the children wore when they lit the altar candles—and she poked her head out the door, examining the crowd.

The sanctuary was jam-packed. Standing room only. She was used to a full house during Sunday services, but the pews were never filled like this, and never for a Friday service. The parishioners were shoulder to shoulder, quietly murmuring to one another. A sense of unease pervaded the air. Rita certainly felt it, and she was confident that every person in the sanctuary felt it, too.

They want me to tell them everything will be all right, Rita thought.

But I can't tell them that.

I just don't know.

There had been the situation with Esther not too long ago. But that felt like a blip, an outlier. It was the first time something had really gone wrong on Clifford in a long time. Sure, people had seen dead things before. Their existence dated back at least one hundred years. Their presence was nothing new. But lately, it seemed, their sightings were more common, even when people kept their curtains closed at night, which was a suggestion most islanders followed to a tee.

Their behavior recently was more . . .

Unstable, erratic.

They were *antsy*, Rita had decided. They were looking for any opening they could find, any crack in the facade.

And lately, there seemed to have been more and more.

There was the earthquake, localized on Esther's property. Rita had felt that. She'd been awake, sipping tea, and Rita had felt just the tiniest quiver of her house. If she'd been sleeping, she wouldn't have noticed at all, she'd decided.

Then, there was another, over at Randy Gordon's place. Out of anyone on the island, Randy lived the farthest from his closest neighbor. It was a wonder anyone else had felt it. These quakes didn't shake the whole island—they were just small rumbles, confined to the places where people were breaking the rules of Clifford. Others nearby might just feel the smallest of trembles, or maybe nothing at all.

And now Randy was gone.

His closest neighbor had felt the tremor and went to check on Randy. Finding an empty house, he'd immediately notified the pastor.

And now, people wondered. Did Randy break the rules? His curtains were open, after all.

Was he taken?

But people have surely broken rules before, Rita thought.

Nobody's perfect, save for the Lord, of course.

Good grief, why is this all happening now?

Maybe it's finally our time.

She didn't want to believe that. The people of Clifford had fought so hard for so long; there had to be a way to keep this going. They just had to double down, work even harder, follow every rule to the letter of the law, so to speak. Then those dead things would retreat to their dark places, wherever those places might be.

The evil would continue to rest.

Rita studied the people in the crowd, and she didn't like what she saw. It reminded her of the big town meeting from decades ago.

Faces looked ashen, pallid. Shoulders were tight, eyes puffy. Handkerchiefs rose and fell as sweat was wiped from foreheads and temples.

She couldn't help but notice the injuries in the crowd. Herbert Mahoney's right arm was in a sling; Sue Blackwood had bruising around her neck. The pastor knew where these injuries originated, and she hoped it wouldn't become a disturbing trend. The dead things had only ever tried to lure islanders away before—or *did* lure them away, like Randy Gordon, everyone assumed—or they simply tormented people with their words, threatening the islanders. But they had never been capable of actually *physically* coming into contact with the living.

But that seemed to be changing.

Rita was concerned these things were *evolving*, for lack of a better word. The more time that passed, the more the danger increased. Or maybe their new ability to injure the islanders was just a hiccup, not a trend. Maybe the earthquakes would cease.

She could only hope that was the case.

The pastor wiggled her fingers and cracked her knuckles.

It was almost time now. She didn't have many prepared words; she was just going to wing it, going to give a rah-rah sermon of sorts.

She just needed to rally the troops, she decided.

Of course these dead things are more erratic now. Of course the ground is shaking. It has been so long; this island was so overdue; it was only a matter of time before the evil that dwelled on Clifford was going to fight back.

We just need to be strong, was what she would tell them.

That, and they needed more offerings. More gifts to the evil, something to satiate its desires. Rita wasn't convinced they worked, but they might help, she reasoned.

Anything to give these poor souls hope, Rita thought.

She scanned the crowd one more time, looking for Willow. She'd sent the woman on a fool's errand, instructing her to wait for a delivery at the docks that wasn't actually supposed to arrive. Peter Elliot was stationed outside the doors by the lobby to intercept her, just in case she came back.

Willow couldn't hear this. It wasn't her time yet.

It would be soon, Rita hoped, but not yet.

She continued to search the faces for Willow, and she thought she spotted a cowboy hat among the crowd. For a moment she thought it was her father—the dead-thing version of him, of course. The man had been dead some forty years, but he'd always worn a Stetson hat while working on the farm where Rita had grown up. The pastor looked closer, but she didn't see the hat anymore. It had just been her mind playing tricks on her. Still, it filled her with confidence and love—love for islanders long gone, and love for islanders still kicking.

She intended to keep them kicking as long as God would allow it.

It's his call, but it's my duty, she thought.

The pastor took a deep breath and ran her hands over her own black vestment, smoothing out any wrinkles.

She stepped out into the chancel.

22

WILLOW

Twenty-One Days until Her Disappearance

A youth group meeting was in full swing. They met in a room that used to be the church nursery—there weren't many young children on the island anymore, and the nursery was no longer needed. The toddler toys and play mats had been replaced with sofas, a Berber throw rug, and an entertainment unit complete with a tube television, boombox, and Super Nintendo game system—but still, the youth group kids weren't the biggest fans of the space. They thought it smelled funny—*I'm catching a whiff of old diapers*, Lily said—and Willow didn't disagree.

Willow sensed some weird vibes from the get-go of their meeting. The kids weren't really engaging with one another, and each of them was doing their own thing. Willow wondered if something had happened among the three of them. *Love triangle problems? Just a run-of-the-mill teenager spat?* She'd been young once, too, of course. These types of tiffs usually resolved on their own. Willow decided to let it play out.

Kayla was sitting cross-legged on the floor playing a game of solitaire, alternating between making a move and fiddling with the neon slap bracelets lining her left wrist. The kid just seemed a bit edgy; Willow had noticed how Kayla wandered the room when she first arrived, stopping at each window and fidgeting with the closed curtains. She had barely acknowledged Lily, who was lounging on a couch flipping through photos on her phone. It was strange for Willow to see a cell phone; she'd practically forgotten they existed. But without cell phone service, what was the point? Willow thought about it for a moment, and she realized that Lily was the only person she'd seen using one on the island. They were almost like contraband on Clifford.

Can't keep kids away from them, she thought.

Steven was nodding along to the Guns N' Roses *Appetite for Destruction* album on compact disc while spinning small circular items on a table. Willow first thought they were silver dollars before recognizing the items as the plastic, milk cap–esque collectibles from her own youth. She gaped at them for a moment.

Are those Pogs?

They certainly were. She took a closer look, recognizing a few of the Pogs as ones she had perhaps owned when she was a kid: the yin-yang symbol, the No Fear clothing brand logo, the Pink Ranger from Mighty Morphin Power Rangers.

Did they outfit this place solely from a thrift store?

Steven moved to the boombox and clicked a few buttons, and the first notes of "Sweet Child o' Mine" filled the room. Steven did a little air guitar lick before exploring the other CDs stacked next to the boombox. Mainly classic rock. Steely Dan. The Beatles. The Eagles. Dire Straits. Willow spotted Nirvana and Weezer albums tucked away in there, too. Steven spun the volume dial a couple notches louder and then flopped onto the sofa, snatching a Game Boy from the end table in one swift motion.

Willow still didn't know exactly what to do at these youth group meetings. This was the third gathering, and the previous week there had been six kids. Tonight, there were only three.

Have I scared them off already? she thought.

At their first meeting, Willow cut out a few choice Bible passages and threw them into a hat. Each kid picked one out and had to draw a modern-day parallel. They seemed to enjoy the randomness of this, especially when Willow dropped in more obscure passages like, "Then Samson went out and caught three hundred foxes. And he took torches, turned the foxes tail-to-tail, and fastened a torch between each pair of tails. Then he lit the torches and released the foxes into the standing grain of the Philistines, burning up the piles of grain and the standing grain, as well as the vineyards and olive groves." Lily pulled that one. She joked that the group should head out on a fox hunt and torch the whole island, you know, just for fun. It's what God would want, she said. The kids snickered at this, but Willow could only wonder if Clifford Island could handle even the smallest of fires. The town's Podunk fire department looked like it operated out of someone's shed.

When it was Willow's turn, she lied. She pulled a quote about God's plan, and she hid her disdain pretty well. Willow told the kids that she'd known God had a plan for her ever since she was a girl. That his divine plan had led her to this place, to this small island, to preach his word.

This was, of course, a lie.

Willow was never supposed to be here. Willow's son's death had driven her here, the message on his floor practically packing her bags for her. Her son was never supposed to die. Jacob was supposed to be sprinting around the basepaths of a Little League baseball diamond, eating way too many cupcakes at a birthday party, starring in a school play, getting frustrated with homework, having his first kiss, wearing a mortarboard, going to college, meeting someone who made him happy, wearing another mortarboard, weeping when his own child was born. He was never supposed to die. That wasn't a plan. It was a travesty.

Willow didn't tell the kids how she really felt, of course. That wasn't why the church had hired her. She still wasn't sure *why* they'd hired her, why they paid her a salary that far exceeded what youth ministry directors in the Midwest made on average. She'd googled it before she left, and her jaw about hit the keyboard.

Sitting there with the kids during her third meeting as Prince of Peace youth ministry director, it only made Willow feel more like a fraud.

They are paying me a stupid amount of money to babysit teenagers?

She decided to own it—at least for the night—so she challenged the kids to a few rounds of a racing game on the Super Nintendo. Willow won ten out of twelve races—she'd owned the game growing up and had always given her brother a sound whupping; picking up the controller again was like riding a bike. It was a nice distraction, and it helped Willow forget about her problems, if only for an hour or so. She found herself not dwelling on the events at the pub—the hushed conversations, the way those islanders had forced out Larry for talking to her. Willow had still gotten nowhere with that; she was too afraid to ask anyone about it. She had hoped to perhaps gain a little insight at the previous day's worship service—it seemed like the whole island came out for church; she was bound to hear a little chatter about this Gloria person—but Rita had sent Willow to wait at the main docks for a delivery of Communion wafers and other "essential" church items. Willow waited in her car at the pier for more than an hour, but no boats arrived. She missed the entire service.

Their impromptu video game tournament completed, it was time to call it a night. As she was switching off the game console, Willow realized that the kids had never loosened up. She'd been laughing and playfully trash-talking while her race car zipped around the different tracks on the screen, and the kids had only cracked smiles. Kayla had barely said a word, Willow realized.

I just can't win with this crew, she thought.

As Steven and Lily zipped up their jackets, Willow noticed Kayla taking her time—the girl was holding her coat and playing with the zipper. It was immediately obvious what Kayla was doing: She didn't want to leave with them. Or she wanted to stay and talk to Willow, alone. Willow wasn't sure, but she decided to give Kayla the out.

"Kayla, can you stick around for a minute?" Willow asked. Willow spotted the relief on Kayla's face as the girl dropped her jacket back on the sofa.

"I'll catch up with you guys tomorrow," Kayla told her friends. Lily furrowed her brow a bit, then announced her goodbyes, and she and Steven headed out. Willow took a seat on the sofa, and Kayla followed suit. It wasn't until they saw Lily and Steven descend into the darkness outside that Willow decided to speak.

"Is everything all right?" she asked.

Kayla shrugged. She picked up her coat again and toyed with the zipper some more, pulling it up and down. "Can I . . ." Kayla said. "Can you keep a secret?"

Willow felt a measure of surprise. Here she thought she'd been bombing her first two weeks as youth group director, and now one of the kids already wanted to confide in her?

"Of course," Willow said. "That's what I'm here for."

"It's just . . . you're an adult, right?" Kayla laughed to herself. "I mean, you *are* an adult. I just needed to talk to one of the adults here about something, and the other adults here . . . I can trust you, right?"

Willow didn't know what was coming. Something about sex, she guessed. Is that why the kids were so weird tonight?

"You can absolutely trust me, Kayla."

"Okay, well, did you hear about our history teacher?"

Willow cocked her head. "No, I didn't."

"Well, he, Mr. Gordon, he went missing."

"Missing?" Willow said. "What do you mean?"

"I mean that he hasn't been at school, and no one has seen him in a few days, and I'm worried that it's my fault."

Willow felt a knot form in her stomach. Out of all the ways this conversation could've gone, she would never have predicted this.

"Your teacher is *missing* missing? When did this happen?" Willow asked.

Kayla relaxed just a little. "He might not *actually* be missing. He just might have left the island without telling anyone. But a few nights ago, we played a prank on him, and he got, like, really freaked out. And no one has seen him since."

"You played a *prank*?"

Willow put a little extra mustard on the word *prank*. She wasn't trying to sound judgy; she was honestly confused.

"But that's the part you can't tell anyone about, okay?" Kayla replied. "No one knows that we did it. I guess I'm just worried that we freaked him out really bad. You know, that it's our fault."

Willow wasn't sure what to say to the kid. A prank gone wrong? What did these kids do?

"Kayla, I . . ." Willow tried her best to form the words. "Did you guys hurt your teacher, this— What's his name?"

"Mr. Gordon."

"Did you physically hurt Mr. Gordon in some way?"

"No." Kayla shook her head. "We didn't. Steven just dressed up in this creepy costume and . . ." Willow studied the girl as she sorted through things in her head. "We just scared him. That's all. I guess I just wanted someone to tell me it was all going to be okay."

Kayla put her head on Willow's shoulder, and Willow put her arm around her. The girl was whimpering a bit, and Willow had no idea what to do. She shushed and cooed to Kayla like she was a little girl who just skinned her knee, while also wondering exactly what Kayla's life was like if she needed reassurance from someone she'd met only a few times in her life. What about her parents? Pastor Rita? A family friend? Surely there must be some adult in her life whom she could trust.

Why me? Willow thought.

"It's going to be okay," Willow said without really meaning it. How would she know? She had no idea what happened, what *was* happening.

Kayla lifted her head and wiped away her tears. "You mean it?"

"Of course I do."

"And you can't tell anyone I told you, okay?" Kayla insisted. "Not Lily, not Steven, not my parents, not anyone."

Willow held up her middle three fingers in the air. "Scout's honor."

Kayla laughed at this, and the girl rose from the sofa. She zipped her jacket up and moved to the door. "Promise?" she said, turning around to face Willow.

Willow nodded and smiled. Kayla turned to leave, but then spun back toward Willow again.

"Ms. Stone, did you feel an earthquake the other night?"

The words caught in Willow's throat. "I'm sorry, what? An earthquake?"

Kayla nodded. "A few nights ago. Did you feel something? It might've been small, and it would've happened on the other side of the island."

"Um, no, I didn't."

Kayla smiled, reassured. "Neither did I."

The girl left, and Willow sat on the sofa in the room that still smelled like old diapers, absolutely dumbfounded.

Willow couldn't stop thinking about it. The conversation with Kayla had left her with a deep sense of unease. Quite frankly, she was spooked. Kayla's emotional state seemed to go much, much further than run-of-the-mill teenage angst.

Did something happen to this Mr. Gordon guy? Willow thought.

Promise or no promise, Willow couldn't help herself. She stopped by Rita's place after youth group, a small ranch house not far from the church. Rita answered the door in her nightgown, nursing a cup of tea.

"Willow? What on earth are you doing here at this hour?"

"I'm sorry," Willow said, "it's just that the kids were concerned tonight. Something about their teacher being gone from school. I think his name is Mr. Gordon. Is he okay?"

She wasn't breaking her promise to Kayla, not really. Maybe it was a technicality, but Willow had promised she wouldn't mention the prank, and she had no intention of doing so. This was just a simple inquiry, that was all.

She just *had* to know.

Willow studied the pastor's reaction to her question, and she detected the slightest change in Rita's face, like someone keeping their poker face but letting it slip for a millisecond.

"Oh, Randy?" Rita replied. "He's doing fine, far as I know. He left for the mainland a few days ago to take care of his brother in Minneapolis. Man's very sick, is what we hear. That's nice the kids are so concerned about ol' Gordo. Maybe the substitute teacher is driving them up the wall, seems the likely case."

Willow smiled. "Thanks. Again, I'm sorry to show up like this out of the blue."

"Oh, think nothing of it, honey. I've knocked on your door a few times; it's about time you returned the favor." Rita winked at Willow, bringing the cup of tea up to her mouth and taking a sip.

Willow turned to leave, but then she pulled a page right out of Kayla's handbook. She turned back toward the pastor and said, "This may be an even weirder question, but I swear I felt an earthquake here the other night. Did you feel something?"

"An earthquake up here?" Rita snorted. "That'd be a first. The US Geological Department of Something or Other would be here with measuring sticks and science rods, testing the soil and making us famous if that were the case."

Willow laughed. "I must've been dreaming, I guess."

"Sounds like an exciting dream! Lay off the sugar after nine o'clock, Ms. Stone, that'll help."

The two exchanged goodbyes, and Willow headed back to her cottage, two thoughts racing back and forth through her head.

The first was that Rita's response to her earthquake question flowed just a bit too quickly off the tongue, almost like it was prepared in advance for an occasion like this.

And second, she desperately hoped she had not betrayed Kayla.

She was quite certain the kid would never forgive her.

CLIFFORD ISLAND

Nineteen Days until Willow's Disappearance

TEXT MESSAGES BETWEEN LILY BECKER AND CONNOR HUDSON

CONNOR: New letters?

LILY: ?

CONNOR: Recruitment letters

From scouts

LILY: Oh

No nothing new

Just Marquette and Whitewater

CONNOR: That's still awesome

Like super-duper awesome

LILY: Thanks

We'll see

Christmas tournament is when they're coming

That's the big one

My ticket out of here

It's literally everything

I'm counting the days

CONNOR: Pulling for you

Gonna find some rabbit's feet

Maybe make voodoo dolls of the other teams

Whatever it takes!

LILY: Haha

Thanks

CONNOR: Oh speaking of voodoo

My urban legend piece

It won an award!

LILY: Wow

Really?

Good for you

CONNOR: Thanks

It was just a monthly award thing

From our website hosts

They host a bunch of school paper sites

There's a lot of awards

Lol

LILY: I think it's cool!

CONNOR: Well thanks

Got it in right before the deadline

It all happened like really fast

Won't let fame go to my head

LILY: So what happens?

CONNOR: Not much

The article got pushed out and promoted

On the host platform

I get a digital badge or something

I get flair Lily

FLAIR!

LILY: Neato

Wait

Pushed out?

CONNOR: Yeah

Boosted or whatever

More eyes on it

Lily?

LILY: Yeah

CONNOR: I want to do a follow-up piece

More stories more legends

I like this stuff

LILY: I can tell

CONNOR: Do you have any more?

LILY: You think I'm some bank of weird legends?

CONNOR: Well

LILY: Well what

CONNOR: You do live on Clifford

LILY: And

?

CONNOR: Weird place

You know that

LILY: No kidding

CONNOR: And I've been there

So I know that too

LILY: I mean

Nothing around here is true

They are just stories

CONNOR: Exactly!

That's what I'm looking for

Legends

What about the house?

LILY: What house?

CONNOR: Seminary House

LILY: How do you know about that?

CONNOR: Went down the rabbit hole one night

Found some really obscure message board

Creepy place

I'm probably being hacked as I type

Weirdos

LILY: What did they say?

CONNOR: About Seminary?

LILY: Yeah

CONNOR: That it's haunted

You know

The usual stuff

LILY: Oh

Well

There are stories I guess

CONNOR: So it's true!

LILY: None of what you hear about Clifford is true

CONNOR: I read a bunch of people died there once

Like murdered

A long time ago

And the house is still there

LILY: And you believe that?

CONNOR: Well

It's plausible

LILY: Connor

Don't you think we would have torn the house down?

Like we would just leave a murder house standing

Come on

CONNOR: Fair point

Wait

Is Seminary House

The same as the Mother Oga House?

The place she was supposed to live

LILY: Bingo

CONNOR: I probably should have realized that sooner

Lol

LILY: Is it starting to make sense now?

These are just rando scary stories about an old creepy house

That's it

Every town has one

CONNOR: Well do you have more stories?

Stories about your island

For my new article

LILY: I guess

Look

How many people read the last article?

You said it was boosted

Or whatever

CONNOR: Oh

I mean like three thousand or something

It's not as many as you think

LILY: Huh

CONNOR: Hold on I can pull it up

One sec

2849 views

No Gangnam Style but not bad

LILY: Did you attribute the Mother Oga story to me?

CONNOR: Sure did

Did you not want me to?

LILY: I mean

I didn't say don't do that

CONNOR: Wait

LILY: What?

CONNOR: This is weird

LILY: What's that?

CONNOR: The article is here

But the stuff about Clifford is deleted

LILY: Really?

CONNOR: The hell?

Hold on

LILY: What are you doing

CONNOR: Logging into the admin side

Wait what?

It says my teacher edited the article

This morning

Why would he do that?

And delete just the Clifford stuff?

I don't get it

LILY: Hmm

I think

Connor?

CONNOR: Sorry I'm just kinda pissed I guess

Censorship or something?

Lame

LILY: Connor

I've heard of this happening before

CONNOR: What?

At my school?

LILY: No

Stuff about Clifford on the internet disappearing

Dangit

I shouldn't have told you that stuff

CONNOR: Lily

What are you talking about?

LILY: Actually

You know what

No

Screw them

I'm so sick of this place

So over it

CONNOR: Uhhhhhhh

Lily?

LILY: The one time I open my mouth

I get busted in like two seconds

Honestly this is such BS

CONNOR: You've really lost me

LILY: Will you find out what happened?

Now I want to know

Find out if it was your teacher who deleted it

CONNOR: This is weird

LILY: Will you please ask?

I'm just fed up with this

CONNOR: Okay

I'll talk to him

But if he did delete it

And only your part

Why would he do that?

HARPER

I pushed open the doors of the church—the fact that these doors weren't locked wasn't lost on me; that cottage had clearly been locked for a reason—and I entered the darkened lobby. The sanctuary was straight ahead, and I could dimly see the pews and altar in the moonlight streaming in through the skylights. But I wasn't heading that way. Off the lobby to the left was a hallway that wrapped around the nave, and that's where the offices were located.

I stepped slowly and carefully, moving past a set of folding tables and an array of potted plants. The smell of stale coffee permeated the air, and the furnace clicked and turned on, which startled me a bit.

Is someone here?

No, that's automatic.

Keep going.

The door to Pastor Rita's office was slightly ajar, and I pushed it open, the hinges squeaking. I headed straight toward the desk and pulled on the main, long drawer—this, unfortunately, was locked. The other drawers were locked as well. I swung around and faced the bookshelf, running my hands along the edges and in the gaps above the books, thinking it might be a good place to stash a set of keys.

Nothing.

Hesitant to turn on the office light, I dug my phone out of my pocket and switched on the flashlight. The beam traveled around the room. More books, a sitting table, a few religious knickknacks on the desk. I pulled on some file cabinets in the corner, but those drawers wouldn't budge.

I dropped the phone to my waist, the beam now pointing to the carpet. I was out of ideas. Not that my original idea was particularly sterling to begin with.

I was plotting my next move when I heard it.

The doors to the church shutting in the foyer.

Someone else was inside.

Panicked, I switched off the flashlight on my phone and spun around, looking for a place to hide. My options were limited. Running crossed my mind, but this person could be close. It was no more than a thirty-second walk from the foyer to Rita's office, and I'd wasted, what, ten, fifteen seconds contemplating my move? This person could already be rounding the corner.

Or *people*.

There was no way of knowing.

I opted to duck down and hide under Rita's desk. I jammed myself under the desk overhang, at the last second sticking my arm out and scrounging around Rita's pen holder on the desk's surface. The metal cup toppled over and I swore quietly to myself.

Someone must've heard that, I thought.

I grabbed blindly at the spilled items, finally clasping the letter opener I'd been seeking.

An even trade for the ruckus I just caused.

I waited, crouched under the desk, head on my knees, duffel bag poking out, gripping the letter holder like a knife.

Then I didn't so much hear someone as sensed someone.

I just knew someone was in the office with me.

I *felt it*.

The guard from Seminary House, maybe another flatfoot from the Clifford Island PD.

Maybe Pastor Rita herself.

My hand shook from fear, but also from self-doubt. Any confidence I had that I was doing the right thing was completely shot, if it was even there to begin with.

Am I really going to use a letter opener as a weapon?

Am I actually going to stab someone?

I'd never been in a fight in my life—never taken a punch, never even felt like someone *might* punch me—and here I was, ready to pounce like a jungle cat.

I steadied the letter opener in my hand.

The floor creaked on the opposite side of the desk.

I certainly wasn't crazy.

There was definitely someone in this office with me.

I shifted a bit, searching for the best squat position to leap out, but I didn't get the chance.

"Get up," a voice called out.

It was a man's voice, and it sounded familiar.

I didn't move.

"I know you're down there," he continued, sounding a bit exasperated. "Just take it easy and stand up."

I wiggled out from underneath the desk—it was somewhat of a struggle; my pouncing plan certainly wouldn't have gone very well—and I slowly rose to face the man, still brandishing the letter opener like a buck knife.

It was Vincent.

The man from the bar.

The man who'd, maybe ninety minutes earlier, been terrified out of his gourd by something outside the pub.

She.

"Put that thing down," Vincent said. "I'm not going to hurt you."

"You swear?"

"You have my word. Just take it easy, okay?"

I lowered my hand and placed the letter opener on the desk. "Just what the hell is going on around here?" I asked. Even through the darkness of the office I could see Vincent smirk.

"Was that you?" I continued. "Guarding the house out there with the flashlight?"

"No." He shook his head. "I had a different job."

"What was that?"

"Following you."

I'd suspected something was amiss on this island, but Vincent's words confirmed it: I was in a world of trouble, and I was pretty sure Willow had been as well.

"Vincent," I said, "who is *she*?"

He cocked his head, meeting my gaze.

"She?" he asked.

"Outside the pub. Earlier tonight."

Again, Vincent smiled.

"My wife," he said.

VINCENT AND LEOTA

2005

Vincent shoved a pair of socks into a gym bag, then another. He riffled through the drawer, searching for the best-fitting pairs but quickly decided it didn't matter. He could always buy new ones off the island. Vincent grabbed one last pair of argyles and slammed the drawer closed.

He heard a cry from Lily's room, and he went to go check on his daughter.

Please be asleep, he thought. He didn't have time to console her right now. He had to pack, and fast.

Vincent poked his head inside Lily's bedroom, and the toddler stirred for a moment. She turned over onto her left side and settled into the mattress under her blanket. Vincent exhaled. He knew she would keep sleeping. The kid always slept well, ever since she was a newborn. A damn miracle, that one.

He returned to his bedroom and flung open a suitcase. He dumped some shirts and pants inside, then hastily grabbed a few belts off a rack and tossed them in as well. He turned to his wife's side of the closet, and he paused. He had never thought this far ahead. The past week had been such a whirlwind—casket, flowers, wake, funeral, so many casseroles he'd need an extra freezer just to store them all—he'd never considered which of his dead wife's things he'd actually take with him when he fled.

He liked the fact that her clothes hadn't been touched since the last time his wife had been in the closet—and this made him think of Rita and her vision for the island. God's plan, this and that. The pastor probably thought his wife's death might convince him to stay on Clifford Island forever, and here he was doing the opposite, skipping Dodge in the wee hours of the night.

"Vinnie?"

Vincent spun around to face the voice. It couldn't be, but it was.

"Hi, sweetie," his wife said.

There are no words for something that shouldn't be possible, so Vincent just stood silent, mouth agape, staring at the woman he'd helped bury three days ago. He about lost his balance, and he grabbed on to his wife's collection of sundresses for support. Words finally came, although they sounded like a skipping record. The first syllable of *Leota* sputtered out of Vincent's mouth three times, and on the fourth try he managed to speak his wife's entire name. Leota blushed and smiled, brushing her hair behind her right ear. She was dressed in navy sweatpants and a fleece pullover, the same outfit she'd been wearing when her car careened off the cliff on the east side of the island one week ago.

"How is this— It's not," Vincent said. He cautiously approached his wife, reaching out to her with his right hand. "This is a dream, or—"

Vincent almost touched Leota's face, but his wife took a step backward. She moved gracefully, almost like she was floating. Vincent's hand dropped back to his side, and he gawked at the dead person in their bedroom.

"Come with me," Leota said gently. She motioned to the empty doorway and smiled. Leota turned and walked out of the room.

Vincent hesitated. He'd heard the stories, of course. He knew them far too well. He was one of the keepers of the faith on Clifford Island, one of the believers, even though he'd never actually seen one himself. Now here was one—one of those dead things that roamed the island—imploring him to follow her. He cursed to himself. If he'd just started packing an hour earlier, hell, even thirty minutes earlier, none of this would have happened. He and Lily would've been speeding away on a boat, never to return to Clifford. They could've left all this madness behind them.

But it wasn't madness. The stories were real.

Vincent moved to the doorway and out into the hallway. He had a feeling about where Leota might be, and his gut instinct was true. He stepped into Lily's room, and there was Leota, standing over their daughter's crib.

"She's so peaceful," Leota whispered, staring at Lily.

Vincent froze. He and Lily were in danger. That much he knew for certain. These dead things were unstable, and no one knew what they actually wanted. A few parishioners at the church had had encounters, so they claimed, but Vincent was never sure what to believe. One woman swore up and down that her late husband vacantly roamed their home at night, whispering her name—she refused to acknowledge the dead thing's presence, and it eventually threatened to pummel her skull with a shovel; another insisted her dead son simply rocked in a chair in her bedroom with a satisfied smile on its face. That was before the thing began *screaming* all night long, the woman insisted. It was so bad she wanted to kill herself, and she had tried and failed on one occasion.

These dead things were unpredictable, all right. Leota was calm right now, but Vincent knew she could turn at any moment.

Leota started humming a lullaby, and Vincent choked up. Despite the fact that his wife was dead, there was nothing inherently frightening happening. On the contrary, Vincent's heart broke. He'd never expected to hear his wife sing a lullaby to their daughter ever again. All he wanted to do was embrace this dead thing, scoop up their daughter, and stand there like that, forever.

The lullaby stopped. Leota looked toward Vincent, and now the thing stared at her husband. Vincent didn't know what to say, so he blurted out, "We should've left a long time ago. All of us."

This didn't seem to register with his dead wife in the bedroom.

She just blankly stared.

Vincent swallowed hard. Wondering if they should have fled Clifford years ago had consumed his thoughts over the past week. There was no doubt about it—Vincent felt responsible for his wife's demise. He was an island lifer, and Leota was not. They'd met in college during Vincent's "Island Rumspringa," as he liked to call it. University was the first time in Vincent's life he'd been off the island for more than a day, and he met Leota during freshman orientation. They fell for each other fast and hard, and that was it. After graduation, he convinced her to settle on Clifford Island—his home—with him. Leota had never really had a home—she grew up an army brat, and all her life she'd craved someplace to lay actual roots, to feel a connection and a sense of belonging. Because she loved Vince, Leota had hoped Clifford Island would be that place. And despite all the strange island rules, all the nutty people and their traditions, Leota had settled into playing the role of dutiful wife and eventual mother, and she played it well.

But there was always this gap they could never bridge. For years, Vincent worried that something might happen to Leota or Lily on Clifford Island. Something natural or supernatural—he'd grown up knowing it was a place where evil skulked about, after all, even if Leota chalked it all up to silly superstitions.

Locking eyes with his recently deceased wife, he felt his worst fears were now realized.

The dead thing still said nothing.

"We're leaving, Lee," Vincent stammered. "She can't stay here. Lily can't stay here."

Leota looked back down toward Lily, and she reached into the crib. From his vantage point, Vincent couldn't actually tell if Leota was touching their daughter. He didn't know how the rules worked, how these dead things actually interacted with the physical world. All he had were the stories he had heard, and now he had a story of his own.

The thing finally spoke.

"Do you know how I wound up at the bottom of that cliff, Vinnie?" Leota asked softly.

Vincent had his theories, and none of them involved negligent driving. He considered that Leota had maybe seen one of those things, the same thing she was right now. Maybe it had been slowly walking along the side of the road, arms to its sides, like one of those phantom hitchhiker legends that circled the world. Maybe it had jumped out; perhaps its face had elongated as it screamed something *terrible* at Leota, and the startled woman had swung the wheel, careening off a cliff.

The irony of that, Vincent thought.

A nonbeliever seeing one of those things?

The one person who wanted to get away from this island more than anyone?

He had another theory but couldn't think about it for too long.

He wouldn't.

The people on this island. They were his friends, his brothers and sisters, in a manner of speaking. Everyone looked out for everyone on Clifford.

There was no way that they would . . .

No.

"It doesn't matter," Vincent told the dead thing.

"They killed me," Leota said.

It had to be a lie. These dead things had a bit of a reputation. For tormenting, for going for the jugular, whether it was true or not.

Only . . .

Leota had been a threat to the islanders' way of life when she was alive. Most of the islanders never left Clifford, but Leota traveled to the mainland quite frequently. Concerts, shopping, travel. She'd felt like a caged bird on Clifford, though even when she escaped, she always flew back. But everyone knew of Leota's skepticism. That undercurrent was always there, and it seemed to permeate every single interaction Vincent and Leota had with others on the island—at every social gathering, at every Sunday church service. Leota never announced her feelings out loud with a megaphone, but she didn't really need to. Everyone knew how the woman felt.

She did not believe in dead things.

She did not believe in Clifford's mission.

She thought her fellow islanders were crazy.

Leota was, and always would be, an outsider.

None of this ever sat well with some of the islanders. Vincent knew that.

But murder?

They wouldn't do that to her, Vincent thought. To *him*. To *Lily*. There had to have been another way. The islanders could have sat down with Leota, explained to her how much their mission mattered, how much *she* mattered. They could have made her swear up and down that she'd keep her silence, that she'd never let spill the awful things that had happened on Clifford.

No, it was negligent driving. A simple accident. Those types of things happened all the time. Or Leota saw a dead thing. That was plausible. Ironic, but plausible. Yes, Leota had seen something in the middle of the road. Maybe she swerved to avoid it, her car plunged off that cliff, and—

She would have kept the secret, Vincent thought.

All they had to do was ask.

My God, why didn't anyone just ask her?

He was starting to believe it.

Murder.

The dead thing moved a few steps closer, and Vincent moved a few steps back. He noted her posture changing—she was moving with purpose now, with aggression. It was just like the stories he'd heard.

These dead things start out peaceful enough.

But then something happens.

They *turn*.

Vincent found himself against the wall in the hallway, and he closed his eyes.

"Go away, Lee," Vincent growled, keeping his eyes pinched shut.

"I'm staying right here," Leota said, her voice turning almost sultry. Vincent swore he could feel his wife's breath on his face. "And so will you. You will never, ever take my daughter away from me."

Vincent refused to open his eyes; they were closed so tightly he thought they might be welded shut. Then the voice got right next to his left ear and whispered lusciously, "I'll see you soon." Vincent felt a compelling surge run throughout his body, and he fought the temptation to wrap his arms around his wife and feel her body one more time.

The surge faded, and he knew then the thing was gone.

Vincent immediately rushed into his daughter's bedroom and put his hand on her chest. Lily was still sound asleep. He felt the gentle rise and fall of her breath, and his body slumped with relief. He hadn't been certain she'd be alive—again, Vincent just wasn't quite so sure how any of this dead-thing stuff worked.

But he knew now it was real. Everything the islanders said was real. He hadn't been fighting a lost cause for the past ten years. There was vindication here. And now he knew, deep down in his soul, that no matter how terrible it might be for Lily to grow up in this place, they had to stay and fight. It was the noble thing to do.

Wait, the man thought.

No. These people murdered my wife.

And I'm just supposed to take that one on the chin and say thank you?

Stick around and fight alongside them?

These murderers?

Vincent looked around his daughter's bedroom. He saw the framed unicorn pictures he and Leota had hung a few years ago, the same nightlight that he'd used as a boy, the stitched sign from Lily's baptism. That one was a gift from the church.

Maybe stitched by the same person who ran Leota off the road.

He silently left Lily's bedroom and pulled the door closed. He shuddered as he did so, feeling the gooseflesh travel up and down his arms. He was thinking of something, and it wasn't a revenge plot against the people of Clifford, or throwing Rita against a wall and demanding answers. He wasn't thinking of when or how Leota might come back to him again, or what type of Leota she'd be when she did.

No, it was something else.

Vincent was still too terrified to admit it, but he *wanted* his wife to come back again.

Seeing her again—the tiny dimples in her cheeks, the bridge of her nose, the freckles where her neck met her shoulder, the way her hips sashayed a bit when she walked.

Her voice when it turned breathy and gravelly.

I'll see you soon.

He liked it.

26

WILLOW

Seventeen Days until Her Disappearance

Dominic,

I'm freaking out right now. I can't sleep.

It all stems from this afternoon. I clocked out just after lunch, a little early Thanksgiving gift from Rita (she invited me to her place for the holiday, but I lied and told her I was busy. I don't know, felt weird). I used my extra few hours to go exploring. It was another cold and wet day, and I was bundled up, hitting trails, wandering down gravel roads, and I stumbled across this little ranch house buried in the woods. Kind of run-down, sagging front porch. I immediately recognized the truck in the driveway. Rust bucket, Desert Storm bumper sticker. It was Larry's truck from the bar. I'm thinking, what good fortune! I can talk to him and find out more about this Gloria thing.

I knocked on the screen door. No answer, but the interior door was open, and I took a look inside. Spotted yet another tube TV. Also spied a vintage typewriter and one of those triple-decker stereos with the cassette decks and record player. I think a Bon Jovi 45 was spinning up top.

From my vantage point, I saw a woman go out the back door and walk outside. Larry's wife, I assumed. Slightly older, a cordless phone the size of a hair dryer pinched between her shoulder and ear, carrying a basket of laundry. I walked around back and did this little wave as she's hanging laundry on a clothesline. She puts the phone down, looking extremely irritated. Almost like I'd interrupted something really important. The woman had these very deep-set eyes, and they bored a hole right through me.

"Is Larry around?" I asked.

"Who wants to know?" she said.

"Oh, I just met him at the bar the other night. I'm Willow. I'm new in town."

"Well, he's gone. Left the island. Not coming back for a while."

"Oh," I told her. "I'm sorry to bother you."

"Well, you should be," she said. She walked back inside and gave the back door a good *slammo* in the process. I was the unwanted visitor, and I got the hell out of there.

You want to know one of the strangest things about that encounter? It was thirty degrees outside and drizzling. Who hangs up laundry to dry when it's freezing and rainy? Just an odd bird all around. I didn't trust her. I had this sinking feeling that whatever Larry was about to tell me in the pub was REALLY off-limits to people like me, and the dude caught some serious flak for it. Like he got thrown in the town brig or something.

Flash forward to the evening. I'm sleeping, and I have this absolutely macabre dream. That monster from my past is outside my cottage, milling about, balancing on one arm and testing the doors and windows with the other. That intensely red hair kind of shimmers in the moonlight. Larry appears from the woods, and he approaches the creature, almost like he's hypnotized and can't help himself. I'm inside the cottage, pounding on the window, begging for him to not get any closer. But he does, and the monster's hair grows and slithers toward Larry, and it ensnares him. Wraps him up like a spider catching its prey. It pulls Larry in close, and the monster's face is now just one giant mouth, and it shoves Larry inside. And I'm frozen at the window as this poor, helpless man is simply engulfed by this nightmare creature. He's just screaming and screaming.

I shoot up in bed, absolutely drenched in sweat. And, like from when I was a kid, I'm in that weird post-dream haze again. What's real, what's not real? I swear, absolutely swear, that I still heard Larry screaming. It's echoing outside my cottage in the night, and I jump out of bed and go to the window. I think it's coming from Seminary House, that boarded-up place through the trees.

I felt this urge to go check it out. But then another urge hit in my stomach. I run to the bathroom, drop to my knees, stick my head in the porcelain, and just unload my dinner into the toilet. I hadn't puked like that since around the time of Jacob's accident. I think . . . those screams I heard reminded me of your screams. When it happened, when that Jeep came around the bend and, well, you know the rest.

Ugh. I can still taste the vomit, and that was hours ago. I've swished mouthwash probably six times. It's still there.

Why are these things happening to me? It feels like not that long ago I was getting better, and now that *dream* is back again. It's almost like the island is doing this. I'm poking around; I'm asking questions. It knows I'm inching closer to something, and it's warning me. *Here's a god-awful nightmare for you to chew on where a poor man is viciously inhaled by a beast. Now, back off, or I'll really make it hurt.*

God, I sound absolutely unhinged. I'm fully aware of that. Just toss me in the padded cell. There's absolutely nothing happening at that house right now.

But.

I just have to know.

I have to go look at that Seminary House.

I just have to be sure.

This poor man could be inside, screaming for help, and I'm the only one who can hear him.

That's it. I've made a decision.

I'm checking it out.

Willow

27

WILLOW

Seventeen Days until Her Disappearance

Willow gazed up at Seminary House. The angles never seemed sharper, the shadows never deeper. She'd half expected to see a light flickering from inside and behind the heavy boards that covered the windows—as if its nerve endings were firing—signaling to Willow that, yes, it was alive, someone had just paid it a visit, and now it was *feeling things*. Willow wondered if this light would be red or yellow or perhaps green, an impossible light, and she wondered if it would be meant for her, like how those words, *Clifford Island*, on the floor of her son's bedroom, were also meant for her.

The wind picked up and kicked up some of the powdery snow that covered the shrubs near the front porch, creating something that resembled mist circling the entrance, as if the elements were conspiring to pave the way for Willow's entrance.

Come inside, I've been waiting for you.

The home seemed to stretch forward into something of a canopy— *did it always stretch out this far?* Willow wondered—and she felt the sides of the house creeping forward as well, as if positioning itself to give the woman a welcoming embrace. Her gaze wandered toward the chimney and she looked for a puff of smoke, maybe evidence of someone inside, stoking a fire, or maybe something the house itself could conjure on its own.

Or that thing—that nightmare creature—took care of poor Larry, licked the flesh and muscle and fat off his bones, and was now burning what was left of him.

Willow thought these horrible things standing there, wearing only jogging shorts and a hooded sweatshirt, arms wrapped around herself, her body shivering and her teeth chattering. She walked the perimeter of the house and checked every possible entrance, pulled on every single board on every single window, and even put her ear up to the plywood that covered the front door.

Willow listened intently, waiting for Larry's screams to again erupt from the interior of the house—she waited and waited, and then she thought she heard a *heartbeat*, a pulsing and throbbing sound, a surefire sign that this house had actually come alive before her, and all the dreadful things she'd imagined would surely come to pass.

She jumped back, realizing it was her own heart in her throat.

Willow turned away from the home, retreating to her cottage, not looking back.

Once inside and the dead bolt secure, Willow lay down and closed her eyes. Her thoughts traveled back to her childhood and to how powerful a nightmare could be, to just how *real* it could make everything seem. She had convinced herself that a man was being killed, that a house was coming alive.

These were not rational thoughts, Willow knew, not in the slightest.

She thought back to Harper, to crawling into his bed when they were kids, to when she'd unburdened herself to him, terrified that an evil creature would devour not only her but their entire family. As these memories played in her mind, Willow could almost *feel* her brother's arm around her, could almost *hear* her own nine-year-old voice whisper the words she'd heard that god-awful monster mutter from outside her bedroom door:

Run to your mother.

These memories made her wistful, in a way, for her youth—for a time long before Jacob, long before she met Dominic in college. Willow found herself wishing for the simplicity of childhood, and she'd even go right back to the times when she'd been convinced a monster was stalking her home. As horrifying as it was, life was uncomplicated back then, and she'd had her brother to comfort her, to protect her.

Now she had no one.

Everything seemed so much more complicated, and in that moment, she missed Harper and her mother terribly. Her mother was dead, of course, but Harper was not. He'd lived only one state away, and Willow regretted her role in their slipping relationship.

We both stopped trying, she thought.

But after what happened to my life, could anyone really blame either of us?

Sprawled out on her bed in that tiny cottage, she resolved to make it right with her brother, after she found whatever it was she was looking for on Clifford. And deciding that, Willow realized that maybe her life right now wasn't *that* different from when she was a child. It felt like everything was coming full circle.

Nightmares. Monsters. Connect with Harper.

Willow buried herself under her covers, pulling the blanket over her head.

She slept a dreamless sleep.

CLIFFORD ISLAND

Sixteen Days until Willow's Disappearance

TEXT MESSAGES BETWEEN LILY BECKER AND CONNOR HUDSON

CONNOR: You up?

LILY: Yep

CONNOR: Here's what I found

Sorry it took a few days

My teacher was out of town or something

He just emailed me

LILY: Wow emailed on Thanksgiving?

What a dear

What did you find out?

CONNOR: My teacher is really cool

Like it never made sense to me that he'd delete something

And not tell me

He always talks to us about edits

Always

LILY: So he didn't do it?

CONNOR: It was him

But the principal made him

LILY: Why?

CONNOR: The principal said he got phone calls

Complaints or something

That the article was spreading false information

LILY: I mean

They are URBAN LEGENDS

They aren't supposed to be true

CONNOR: I know

But why just the Clifford stuff?

There were like five other stories

From different places

LILY: I'm sorry if you're in trouble

Are you?

CONNOR: I don't think so

Just irritated

Why didn't he tell me?

My teacher

He just did it hoping I wouldn't notice

I don't get it

LILY: I get it

It's what I said before

Stuff about Clifford online just disappears

There are people on the outside

Pulling the strings

That's what I hear

CONNOR: Wait what?

Like my principal is a bad guy or something?

Or my teacher?

Lily

What is going on

LILY: Look

I'm going to tell you some things

Okay?

CONNOR: Okay

LILY: I've never done this before

Told anyone about what goes on here

Just bear with me

CONNOR: Okayyyyyyy

LILY: I know you know Clifford is weird

You've been here

CONNOR: I mean

It is weird

Like super weird

LILY: We have rules that we live by

1 No modern technology

2 No current fashion

3 Keep your mouth shut about everything

That's a simplification but yeah

That's the gist

And I'm breaking that third rule really bad right now

But there's more to it than just the rules

A lot more

CONNOR: Is this a joke?

LILY: There are all sorts of myths and legends about Clifford

And the wackos here believe them

It's insanity

We even freaked out our teacher so bad that
he's gone

Peaced out of here

CONNOR: Wait what?

LILY: Hold on

Can I call you?

CONNOR: Sure

LILY: Okay

One sec

CONNOR: You're probably sleeping

I'm not

I'm just thinking about everything

I guess I just wanted to say thanks

Thanks for trusting me

I won't tell anyone

I promise

You can trust me

But some of those things you said

I guess I'm worried

Are you sure you haven't seen one of those things

The dead things?

WILLOW

Sixteen Days until Her Disappearance

Dear Dominic,

I saw him. I saw our son. He is here.

You'll need context for this. Trust me, it makes more sense this way. Here goes.

It started earlier tonight. Pastor Rita came over for tea—I think she didn't want me to be alone on Thanksgiving. She's been dropping by most evenings, and we chat. She must think she is my counselor or something. Of course the subject turned to Jacob, because of course it would. I'm not hiding it. There's not a flashing sign on my forehead, but people are aware that I'm grieving. They don't know I'm looking for some connection between our son and this place, but I'm definitely the newbie in town "who lost her son." I've heard the whispers, noticed the *that's that woman* stares. Word got around.

Anyway, Rita is a bit of a local icon up here. Islanders stop just short of tossing rose petals in her path. She gives these fiery sermons on Sunday, spit is flying from her mouth, and people are literally weeping in the pews. It's the real deal, and everyone gobbles it up. She's a Clifford lifer, like everyone else. Grew up on a farm and took care of her father after he was injured in some sort of an accident. Maybe that's why she seems so taken with me—family members and tragedies, you know. It all tracks with how the islanders seem to view her: She's a motherly figure, almost like a protector. A shepherd. And for a woman pushing seventy, she has energy for days. I swear, she doesn't sleep, which means I don't sleep, because she'll wander over to my cottage at all hours of the night just to talk. And we will sit here for hours, ruminating on life and faith and sharing stories. She's friendly but intimidating. I'm terrified beyond belief every time that she'll figure out that I'm a total fraud. You know, when I pray in church, I'm actually thinking about Jacob, or you, or what I had for breakfast. Anything but speaking to God, actually. Some youth ministry director, huh?

Well, tonight she got to me. Wore me down. I started blubbering about "being this close to cracking" and "not being strong enough." Pitiful stuff like that. God, I can't imagine what I looked like. I truly broke when Rita told me that Jacob passing was part of my journey. I didn't want to hear that crap. Who would? Then she hugged me, and she whispered, "What is it that you want, child?" And I'm crying on the shoulder of someone I've known for a few weeks, and I say:

"I just want my boy back."

Now, I think that all the time, but I've never said those words. Not like that, never so concisely. And maybe, just maybe, there is something mystical about Clifford Island. Maybe I uttered the magic words or something. Like Rita was some human wishing well. I don't know yet. But earlier tonight, after Rita had gone home, Jacob came back.

The Jacob. Our son. In the flesh.

It wasn't a dream. It wasn't a nightmare with a monster with red hair. I was 100% awake, in my bed. I sensed something and opened the drapes, and there he was. Our Jacob. Outside, standing in the fresh snow.

I'm trembling as I write this, but I'll get through it.

It was our boy, Dom. Our collective *life* was staring inside my cottage window, looking exactly how he did before the accident. Unblemished, absolutely perfect. How he looked every single damn day before we lost him. I was too stiff with shock for my heart to crumble, because it should have. Then Jacob put his hand on the glass, like he was reaching out to me. Begging me to help him.

I didn't know what to do. I think I just got kind of lost in his eyes. To have it be so long and then to look into your child's eyes again? It was absolutely intoxicating. My hand floated up to the glass, and Jacob started whispering something. I couldn't hear him, but I could read his lips. The movement of his lips and jaw were immediately familiar to me.

He was apologizing. *I'm sorry, I'm sorry.*

It was absolute blunt-force trauma to me. I'm thinking, *What are you sorry for? We shouldn't have let you scooter in the street. We should've made sure your helmet was properly secured. We should've double-, triple-checked the strap.*

Kneeling on my bed with my hand on the window, inches from our son, it finally hit me what he was doing, *why* he was saying that phrase. I'd temporarily forgotten that defining trait of his. He must've said the words *I'm sorry* ten thousand times growing up. He wasn't apologizing for the accident. This was just Jacob being Jacob. We'd tried to kick him of that habit for years, but in that moment, I wanted him to say those words forever. That phrase was so unmistakably him, and for a second, I let go of my guilt and sorrow and just crouched there in a trance, relishing each syllable.

He abruptly stopped. More words came, different ones. I couldn't make them out, but he was saying another phrase over and over again, and I'm just cursing myself. *Hear him, damn it, just hear him.* He raised a finger, bringing it to his lips.

Shhhhhhhhh, he seemed to say.

Then he turned and walked away into the darkness.

I sprinted outside, kicking up snow and screaming his name. I made it to the back of the cottage, but he was gone.

I must've searched the forest for an hour, calling his name.

Nothing.

It's the darnedest thing. I'm shaking with adrenaline, but also with new resolve. New purpose. He is here, on Clifford Island. Our son is somewhere on this island, right now, in some form. I was right. That voice in my head telling me that Clifford had something to do with Jacob was telling me the truth.

I just don't have the answers yet. I don't know how Jacob is wrapped up in all of this, why *Clifford Island* was written on his bedroom floor. Why every piece of technology in this corner of the world is carbon-dated. Why people dress like late-twentieth-century time travelers. Why a conversation with a woman of God seemingly willed our boy into existence. And why all the O.J. stuff, lest I forget.

Can you help me? I think it could all have something to do with this Gloria person who is supposedly dead, but I have no clue who she is. I called a couple of nearby newspapers on the peninsula, and neither of them have any Clifford Island obituaries from the last ten years. I even called the Door County medical examiner's office, and while they can't divulge any information to me, they told me I can put in a death certificate request through the Wisconsin Department of Health Services. But that's no help, because I'm not a family member, nor do I even have a full name of who I'm looking for.

I'm too afraid to ask anyone on the island about this, because it will seem like I'm poking around. You should've seen the way they escorted poor Larry out of the bar. The anger and concern in their eyes as they did it. I know his wife told me he left the island, but she was so short with me, and just so . . . I don't know, cagey? Did he actually leave Clifford, or did these people do something to him? I've been back to the pub, and Larry hasn't—at least, not when I'm there, and there's no real other place to drink around here. I saw him at church before all this, too, and he hasn't been back around. What gives? I can't look interested in him or Gloria. What might they do to me? This may be just paranoia, but I can't take any chances.

I need you to do some research. There are things I need to google, and I'm convinced I'd solve the mystery of Clifford Island in twelve seconds flat. But I'd have to go to the mainland to do that. But I can't. I can't leave. What if Jacob comes back and I'm not here? And then he never returns? Can you imagine?

I tried your number again, but it's been disconnected. And I refuse to tell anyone about this but you. Not my brother, not your mother. You have every right to know, because he is your son, too. But other people . . . I just don't think Jacob wants me to open my mouth.

The way he *shushed* me.

I think he was letting me know, this is our secret.

Don't tell a soul.

I hope I'm not doing anything wrong by telling you. I just wish we could talk about this, about the last thing Jacob said to me. About what Jacob was whispering to me outside my window—the second phrase, after he'd stopped apologizing to me, after he implored me to keep his secret.

I *did* hear him, Dom. Right before he vanished into the darkness.

He was saying, *Run to your mother.*

Willow

30

WILLOW

Fifteen Days until Her Disappearance

It was a particularly dreary and blustery morning on Clifford Island, and Willow turned her face away from the wind. She was moments away from dropping her most recent letter to Dominic in the blue government collection box, the one just off the curb outside the Clifford Island Post Office. The letter was in her left hand, and she pulled open the collection door with her right. She reached inside to release the envelope—the first step on its journey to Florida—but then she pulled back.

She wasn't sure why she did that.

She just felt *funny*.

Like she shouldn't mail this one.

And it wasn't merely because Jacob had *shushed* her, imploring her to keep his presence a secret—although that thought had crossed her mind; she'd simply been sharing so much with Dominic about Clifford, about spirits and being followed and potential abductions—but right now, putting information out into the world was starting to feel . . . was it . . . dangerous?

Weird?

Wrong?

Willow couldn't quite pinpoint it.

She looked up from the collection box toward the post office. A worker was inside, adjusting a sign on the interior of the window. His eyes met Willow's, and he immediately looked away.

Willow found his reaction odd, the man's posture rigid. She realized that perhaps this was the reason she'd hesitated in dropping the letter into the collection box.

Did I sense this guy earlier? she thought.

She looked down at the box and extended her hand inside, and then she pulled back, her gaze returning to the post office window.

She again met the eyes of the worker, and he looked away, focusing on his task.

But it wasn't much of a task, Willow thought. The sign was already taped to the window. The man wasn't applying new tape or moving the paper; he was merely smoothing it out, picking at the edges but not actually removing the tape, not moving the sign in the slightest.

Is he just faking this? Willow thought.

Is he watching me?

Willow now felt very uneasy, and a shudder traveled up and down her body.

She shoved the letter into her coat pocket and walked briskly down the street. After she'd walked about fifty paces, Willow looked back. The man had come outside, and he was standing on the post office steps, peering down the road in Willow's direction. When he saw Willow looking behind her, he immediately went back inside.

Willow zipped up her coat to the very top, and she tucked her chin and mouth inside her jacket. Her pace quickened, and she began the hike back to her cottage, the suspicious thoughts not leaving her.

When she got inside, she jammed the letter in the drawer next to her bed.

And again, like when she had hustled home after the basketball game, Willow wondered if it was all in her head.

There was a pretty innocuous reason why those footprints were there that morning outside her cottage, right? she thought.

Just a confused hunter.

And I've met weird islanders before.

Maybe the guy at the post office is just another one of those weirdos.

Still, the suspicion remained, and she made a decision right then, sitting on her pink-and-green floral-patterned bedspread.

She wouldn't send any more letters.

31

CLIFFORD ISLAND

Thirteen Days until Willow's Disappearance

TEXT MESSAGES BETWEEN LILY BECKER AND CONNOR HUDSON

LILY: I can't even anymore

It was the pastor at my church who called your school

Pastor Rita Higgins

You there?

She found out about your article and had it removed

Talked to me all about it

Very disappointed that I broke the island rules

Remember what I told you?

Keep your mouth shut about everything?

I broke the rule

And now I'm paying the price

Then she bombarded me with questions about my teacher

Apparently, the guy is still missing

I held strong

I mean, what was I supposed to say?

Or think?

That some evil creature got him?

Good Lord

The brainwashing around here

These people are nuts

Want to know my punishment for all this?

We aren't going to the tournament

The Christmas tournament

The official word was "a mixup with registration"

And now we're too late

The brackets are drawn up and we can't play

I know that Rita pulled strings to make us drop out

Just to punish me

Just so scouts can't see me play

Just in case I got offered a scholarship and left Clifford

She wants me here forever

It was her Connor

Are you there?

I just

I can't

That was my one shot

The big one

I can't believe this happened

Connor

You there?

I have an idea

I've thought about doing this for awhile

But now with the basketball thing

I'm fired up again

I'm ready

I'm just done here

I want to take this place down

Expose all of the secrets of this island

Unmask the nutjobs for the world to see

Break every single rule imaginable

And I need your help

Find out anything you can online

About Clifford and the islands around here

Maybe people have missed something

I'll gather what I can too

My dad has stuff

Documents and things like that

We can create an exposé or website or something

"The Secrets of Clifford Island Revealed"

You can write an article about it

Send it everywhere

It's just time

We'll talk soon

Don't tell anyone about this

This is just me and you

Our secret

No one can know what we're doing

Okay?

But just know

In case you want out now

If we burn this thing down

There may be trouble

Lots of it

HARPER

"I'm sure you think I'm a lunatic," Vincent said, taking another drag off his cigarette. He held out the pack toward me, and I shook my head. It was the second time he'd offered me a smoke, and I wondered if he even remembered that he'd offered me one the first time.

"I don't think you're a lunatic," I said, swirling the coffee in my mug. "But you got some good taste in music."

He smirked.

We were sitting at Vincent's kitchen table having a debrief of sorts. I'd trusted the guy enough to accompany him to his house, even though he'd been tasked with following me home from the bar.

Pastor's orders, he'd said.

Now it was the middle of the night, and we were sipping coffee, sorting things through. Lily was asleep upstairs, and Vincent had already told me to keep my voice down a few times. I was edgy, apparently.

"Look," I said, trying my best to speak softly, "I'm just looking for my sister. And there was the stuff at the bar, and then I almost shivved you with a letter opener, but still . . . I've got nothing except some hasty letter from Willow I found behind a picture frame. I need your help is all I'm saying. And I'm thinking you *will* help me, because you wouldn't have invited me here otherwise."

"I shouldn't be talking to you," he said. "You've got people's attention."

"I hadn't noticed," I lied.

"I'm only saying, this island isn't good for your health."

"And it's good for yours?"

This made Vincent grin, and his smile filled me with dread. Vincent was right—this island didn't seem good for my health, or anyone's health, for that matter. I knew that something had freaked the man out so bad that he'd collapsed on the floor of the pub, something that the rest of us couldn't even hear.

She.

His wife.

He told me Leota's story on the walk to his house. How she'd always been an outsider, and he thought that she might have been murdered by their fellow islanders. Heck, the manifestation of his wife *told him* as much, he'd said.

It was obviously hard for me to fathom, the dead-wife-coming-back-as-a-ghost part, but also the fact that a guy could live and fraternize and go to church alongside people he suspected actually murdered his spouse. I expressed those very sentiments on our walk through the crunching snow to his house, and Vincent merely nodded, his gaze looking off somewhere in the distance.

"It was either get revenge or help fight this thing," he eventually told me. "Sometimes you have to put your grudges aside for the greater good."

"That's a helluva lot bigger than just a grudge," I replied.

He snickered at that, and no more was said about the matter. The point was made.

This man really believes in his role of fighting evil.

I'd gone from skeptic to somewhat evenhanded listener over the course of a day. The thing outside the pub, the tremor, and Vincent's story—his absolute, stone-faced conviction—combined with Willow's words had me wondering if my cynicism about the existence of the supernatural had been woefully misguided. I wasn't convinced yet, but I'd become open to the possibility. I suddenly grew very nervous sitting there with Vincent, as if that thing could be with us, *right now.*

Am I actually believing that this guy's dead wife could materialize out of thin air?

My eyes quickly scanned the kitchen.

Vincent noticed my uneasiness. "She's not here. Trust me, I'd know."

"But do you know where my sister is?" I was growing impatient. All this talk of ghosts and fighting evil seemed to be burying the primary reason I'd come to the island.

"It's complicated," Vincent replied.

"Then make it simple."

He sighed and looked me dead in the eye. "She went inside the house, is what I heard."

"The one being guarded by the cop?"

Vincent nodded. "Seminary House. And she didn't come out. Might not be true, though. Can't trust everything you hear around here, you know?"

"Can I get in there?"

"You don't want to go in there. That simple enough for you?"

I got up from my chair and paced around the kitchen. It was too much to take. Vincent was evasive, speaking in riddles, not being straight with me. Both my hands were resting on the top of my head like I was gathering my breath after a sprint, and I turned to face Vincent.

"Is Willow dead?" I asked.

He looked away. "I don't know," he muttered.

It was a blow to the chest. The answer was supposed to be *no.*

Hell no, actually.

But *I don't know?*

What did that mean?

I felt woozy, my knees about to buckle. I collapsed in my chair at the kitchen table. Willow being dead was a possibility I hadn't truly prepared myself for. Missing, sure. Hiding out alone, craving space, needing time? Absolutely.

But *dead?*

I looked up at Vincent, who took a seat in front of me.

"Please," I said, my voice cracking. "Just tell me what's happening on this island. Tell me what happened to my sister."

Vincent thought for a moment, then scooted his chair backward and held up his shirt. Five long scratch marks ran across his chest in a diagonal direction. The marks looked deep, and fresh. He dropped his shirt and scooted forward. "That was from a few days ago. A nice Christmas present from the wife." He chuckled to himself. "There are things on this island, Harper. Dead things. That's what we are up against, that and a greater evil so powerful it can't even be fathomed. That's *what's happening* on this island."

"Is that what happened to Willow?" I gestured over at his shirt.

"Like I said, I don't know what happened to your sister. I do know that she'd grown wise to what was happening on this island, and she was going to help my daughter tell the whole world all of our secrets."

He leaned forward and shook his finger at me.

"And they were going to get *your* help to do it."

33

WILLOW

Nine Days until Her Disappearance

Dear Dominic,

I'm not sure if this even counts as a letter anymore. It's more like a diary or a journal at this point. But I need to keep writing them, and I need to keep writing them *to you*—even if I'm not sending them—because I think they help me keep whatever sanity I have left. They help me feel connected to you, Dom, even if you're not reading them at all. I know it's hard to understand. But for now, I'm going to keep writing and then just cram these letters into a drawer, and maybe I'll send them all at once and you'll get a big batch of them out of the blue one day.

Just try to read them in order, I guess.

I don't know what to say anymore. It's just . . . I feel so alone here. When I'm not at the church or at youth group meetings, I'm combing the island looking for our boy. People think I'm hiking, when in reality I'm scouring every square inch of this island, trudging up and down roads and through dark forests. He could be anywhere, you know? I keep thinking I'll see him behind every tree or just over the next ridge. I even visited the island cemetery—it was this interesting mix of headstones and markers, some ancient and crumbling, some garish while others were simple and had nothing etched on them at all—and I read every single name.

Andersen. Olsen. Hansen. Ruckert. Millar. Erickson. Dozens and dozens more.

The Clifford Sickness graves were there, which was interesting to see. And I wasn't expecting to see Jacob's name or anything, but I just felt compelled to explore.

He wasn't there, obviously.

Nor is he anywhere else.

I continuously go back to the same stores and buildings downtown, thinking maybe I missed something, but Jacob's never there. The one constant is the boombox man, whom I've run into numerous times, who keeps blasting "Livin' on the Edge." That tune feels like my theme song at this point, and it makes me feel like I'll live every single day on Clifford, on repeat, forever. I actually approached the man today, and I asked him why he played the song so often. I was nice about it, but I asked him. He paused the boombox and kind of shrugged.

"Makes me feel good," he said.

Fair enough, moving on.

I sometimes walk the beaches at night in the shivering cold, humming that song, thinking that could be the magic hour and place. There is no real reason for Jacob to be on the beach—I think I just enjoy the waves rolling into the shore and receding into the lake. It clears my head, brings me a measure of peace, of hope. But he hasn't come back to me. Not since that night. I've even tried saying the words: *I just want my boy back.* No luck. It's like the sorcery that occurred that one night has evaporated. And it wasn't just a dream, Dom. I'm not certifiable. Not yet, anyway.

My near breaking point was seeing a group of children playing in a front yard. Two of them were tossing a baseball around, and one of the kids' mitts looked like Jacob's mitt. I sprinted up to him and just about ripped it off the poor boy's hand to check if it had the *J.S.* initials on the back. God, I'm sure I looked positively deranged. This younger girl, the boy's sister, I'm sure—who'd been nearby playing with one of those pink Skip It toys—had this look of utter confusion on her face.

It wasn't Jacob's glove, of course. I'm sure you have it. But if the kid's mom didn't see this happen from the window, I'm sure she was told about it minutes later. Dollars to doughnuts I'm on some sort of a list now. *Crazy lady who attempts to steal baseball gloves.* These people may tie me to a boat and light it on fire like some Viking funeral.

I don't know who to talk to about all of this island stuff. I unloaded on Lily from the youth group tonight. The other members had left, and here I am just pestering poor Lily with questions, all about the island and the absence of current technology around here. She listened to everything I had to say about Clifford, but she was mostly mum and her answer was "That's the way things are around here." She compared the island to a cult or commune, saying adults just like things a certain way. But she wasn't a fan of any of it, she told me. The kid can't wait to go to college and "peace the hell out of here." Her words, not mine, and I don't blame her.

Lily asked me a lot of questions, too, about my life back in Illinois and my family. We talked about this stuff in youth group before, but that was more the CliffsNotes version. I waded into the details this time. I told her about Harper and him being a sports reporter, and she kind of perked up at that, you know, she's an athlete and all that. She wanted to know all about him and what he does: the circulation of his newspaper, if he was famous, if he'd ever written anything super popular. I wish I knew more about his career, honestly, and I answered the best I could.

I told her the story of how we met in college, our marriage, Jacob's accident, how I stumbled across a job opening up here. She just really wanted to know about my life before this, what drove me up to this place.

Why would anyone come here? she asked me.

I couldn't help but laugh.

I didn't tell her about the words on Jacob's floor, but I told her this really long story about when I knew I needed a change. It was around April, I think, during my last year in the classroom, and one of my students popped into my classroom during my free period to ask me a question. I'd had this student all year long—so, like, seven months at this point. She was applying for a local scholarship, and she wanted me to write her a recommendation letter. I told her I'd be happy to, and I blew off grading that night to write her a real good one. It was a mini-mission of mine to get it right. Just *really* help this one kid, because, I guess, I didn't have our own to help anymore.

I wrote the letter. It was glowing and perfect. She came back to me the next day, and I handed it to her, and I asked her to quickly scan it to see if she needed anything changed or added. I watched her read the letter, standing in front of my desk, and her face just melted right in front of me. She just looked positively mortified.

I ask her, "Something wrong, Avery?"

The kid handed me the letter and said, "I'm not Avery. You wrote this about someone else."

I mixed her up with another kid in class. Like I said, she'd been in my class for almost two whole semesters.

I was an absolute monster.

That's when I knew, I told Lily, that I was done. That I needed something new in my life. It wasn't the accident, it wasn't the crumbling relationship between you and me, it was getting it wrong on that scholarship letter. I think I told my principal that very day that I was leaving the profession at the end of the school year. I think about that student a lot—her name is Paige, not Avery—and I wonder, is she all right? Will she always doubt herself with teachers and professors moving forward? Maybe I'm giving myself too much weight.

When I eventually leave this place, I'm going to look Paige up and tell her how dreadfully sorry I am about everything. That I still think about her, every day. That might be the first thing I do, actually. You get into teaching to help as many kids as possible, but it's been so long now and I'm so royally messed up, that I think maybe if I can just help *one* kid right now it will help makes things right.

Maybe that kid is Lily.

I didn't tell her all that, but I did tell her the Paige story. More stuff about my life, about Jacob, about you and me and going our separate ways. My last few weeks before heading up here. Again, I left out the part about *Clifford Island* being written on Jacob's floor, and I certainly didn't tell her about our boy visiting me the other night. I was vulnerable, but not vulnerable enough to spill my deepest secrets to a teenager I'd known for only about three weeks. Lily still doesn't know why I'm really on Clifford or the things I've seen. That I've seen *him*. I think it's for the best right now, even if she seems trustworthy. I did ask her if we could keep all of this between us, and she swore that she would.

Lily is just a really good kid, Dom. She has this way about her where she makes really good eye contact with you when you're speaking. Bright, personable, funny. God, I just hope she makes it, you know? Follows her hoop dreams, all that stuff. She deserves it.

And here's something else interesting about this kid: her father is the city clerk on Clifford. Has been for years. I asked Lily if she'd heard anything about someone named Gloria dying on the island, and she told me that she hadn't. She seemed sincere about it, too. I don't think she was lying.

But her father would have records, or something, right? Of anyone on the island who has died?

Maybe.

I'm going to find out.

Willow

34

WILLOW

Nine Days until Her Disappearance

There's someone outside my cottage. And it's not Jacob. I can just feel it. It's someone else, maybe someone from the island checking up on me. Watching me. Maybe it's the person from the woods that night after the game, the Peeping Tom, back for another look. But that had been an accident—the guy was mortified about that, according to Rita, so I don't think so. Or perhaps Lily told someone about the things I told her, that I was fishing for information about Gloria, and now they're here. Her dad, a neighbor, a friend. Word got around. But she *wouldn't* have told anyone, right? Maybe someone was listening? I just don't know.

This anxiety is chipping away at me. I've drawn the shades. The lights are out. I barricaded the door with my nightstand. I'm terrified someone will come barreling through at any moment. It feels like my nightmare, but I know it's not a monster with red hair. It's probably an islander who thinks I'm trouble and am disrupting their perfect society. I just need dawn to come. Light always scatters the bad men back to their homes.

They can scare me, but they can't drive me away. My son is some-where on this island, and I'm not going away until I see him again.

Footsteps. They're all around the cottage now, crunching in the snow. A few pairs of them, maybe more.

I won't leave.

I won't.

CLIFFORD ISLAND

EXCERPT OF KAYLA ELLIOT INTERVIEW WITH RITA HIGGINS

KAYLA: I want to talk about ghosts.

RITA: Ghosts, sweetie?

KAYLA: Yeah.

RITA: And this is for a school project?

KAYLA: It's for Ms. Stone.

RITA: Ms. Stone wants you to interview me about ghosts?

KAYLA: No. I mean, not that I know of. We are doing an island history project for youth group.

RITA: This project was Ms. Stone's idea?

KAYLA: Yeah. She brought it up at our meeting the other night.

RITA: This isn't something that you or Lily or one of the other kids came up with?

KAYLA: Lily was there, but it's Ms. Stone's project. She really wants us to do it. Is that okay?

RITA: Of course it is, honey. I think there's a lot of misconceptions out there about ghosts, as you call them. I'm happy to talk with you.

KAYLA: And is it okay that I'm recording this?

RITA: That's fine.

KAYLA: Really?

RITA: I trust you, dear. As long as you're comfortable.

KAYLA: Okay, great. Well, thanks for talking to me. My name is Kayla Elliot . . . you know that. Sorry, I've, like, never really interviewed someone before.

RITA: Oh, it's fine, I'll help. So, Ms. Elliot, what would you like to know about ghosts?

KAYLA: Where do they come from?

RITA: Well, different people tend to believe different things. But your idea of a ghost, the kind you've read about in books or seen in a film, is probably very different than what they actually are.

KAYLA: Okay.

RITA: Let's call them what they are. They are dead things.

KAYLA: Okay, dead things.

RITA: Because a ghost doesn't really exist, honey. This idea of a loved one returning to impart a message, or folks haunting the place where they died, is simply not possible.

KAYLA: Why not?

RITA: Because the Bible says so, from God's mouth to our ears, it's the truth. Once a person dies and their soul moves on, that's it. There's no coming back, sweetie. The Good Lord would simply not allow it.

KAYLA: But what about—

RITA: This place?

KAYLA: Yeah.

RITA: Clifford Island. You want to know why people here see what they see.

KAYLA: Yeah.

RITA: What have you seen?

KAYLA: You want to know if I've seen a gho— I mean, a dead thing?

RITA: Have you?

KAYLA: Well . . .

RITA: Honey, it's okay if you have. There are reasons why these dead things appear. And the better understanding you have, the less scary it is.

KAYLA: I know.

RITA: Tell me what you've seen.

KAYLA: My grandmother.

RITA: What does she say to you?

KAYLA: She doesn't say anything. I don't think she can.

RITA: Why not?

KAYLA: Because her body is all torn apart. She's just kind of heaving and huffing. And there's blood, everywhere. She's covered in it.

RITA: What happened to your grandmother?

KAYLA: You don't know?

RITA: I want to know what you know.

KAYLA: I only know what my mom and dad told me.

RITA: What did they tell you?

KAYLA: That she was sucked under a boat.

RITA: And how did that happen?

KAYLA: It was an accident. When I was little, my grandparents had a fishing boat, and they liked to take me on rides around the island. My grandfather usually did the steering and stuff like that, getting the boat ready, handling all of the controls, I guess. And, one day when I was four or five, I went out there with just my grandmother.

RITA: She wasn't as experienced?

KAYLA: I don't think so. Someone on the shore saw it happen. My grandmother and I were on the boat, and we were stuck in shallow water. She hopped into the water to push us, and the motor was still running. She got sucked underwater, and the propellors ripped her arm off. Her body was just . . . I guess it was pretty gruesome. They rushed her to the doctor, but it didn't matter. She lost so much blood. It was too late.

RITA: Are you still scarred by this?

KAYLA: Maybe I've blocked it out, or whatever, but I don't remember any of this. I don't even remember my grandmother. Well, the living grandmother. I've only seen her . . . how she looks now. She comes out of the woods sometimes. At night. I'm not sure why at night, but it's only then. And she's all torn up. Kind of stumbling around. The last time she showed up she wasn't even walking anymore. She was on her hands and knees, crawling. Well, *hand*, I guess. She's still missing her arm. And there's blood everywhere.

RITA: Does anyone else know about this? That you see this thing coming out of the woods?

KAYLA: My dad knows. And my mom. I've told them. I don't talk about it with my friends.

RITA: Why not?

KAYLA: I don't want them to make fun of me, I guess. Lily doesn't believe in any of this.

RITA: Have you ever followed her? This dead thing, that is?

KAYLA: No. But I want to. Almost like I can't stop myself. Is that normal?

RITA: Same thing happens to a lot of folks around here. They feel . . . compelled, to follow those things. It's one of the tricks they play, the dead things. It's what they do. But that thing in your backyard is not your grandmother, always remember that. It's a trick. It's a manifestation. A demon has made that thing come back, and it feeds off of the love you feel for the person who died. And you loved your grandmother, I expect?

KAYLA: I probably did. And maybe . . . I don't know. But when I see her, when she comes back, I just feel this intense feeling of . . . guilt.

RITA: You feel responsible for her death?

KAYLA: I do, in a weird way. Like, why did she take me out on that boat alone? Was I bugging her to take me for a ride, even though she wasn't comfortable? I feel this . . . *urge*, I guess, when she comes back. This burning sensation running throughout my body, to go to her, to tell her that I'm sorry. I'm sorry for making her take me out onto the water that day.

RITA: This dead thing knows how you feel, too. It's feeding off this guilt, your love for Grandma, and it's hoping you'll slip up. Follow it to your own death. It's playing games with you, honey. And you must never, ever follow this thing. Shut your curtains, shut your eyes, pull those covers up over your head. This dead thing will go away.

KAYLA: Do you ever see them?

RITA: I do. Heavens yes, I do.

KAYLA: Are they your family?

RITA: Sometimes they are, yes.

KAYLA: Your dad died in an accident, too, didn't he? When you were a girl? I remember you saying something in a sermon about that.

RITA: My daddy had an accident, a long, long time ago. Fell off a horse, is what happened. He didn't die, praise the Lord, not from the accident. Jesus didn't call him home until he was very old.

KAYLA: But he was hurt pretty badly?

RITA: Couldn't walk anymore, after he fell. I took care of him after that—dressing, feeding, bathing, and the like. My daddy was a good man. Didn't deserve what happened to him, being in that wheelchair, legs not working. But that's how life goes sometimes.

KAYLA: Is he one of the things that comes back? Pastor Rita?

RITA: Haven't seen my daddy since the day he died.

KAYLA: Because you don't break any rules, right?

RITA: I do my best, sweetie. Just like everyone else here.

KAYLA: But why am I seeing my grandma at all? I'm not breaking any rules. I don't have any rituals. I wasn't even alive when, you know, the thing with the—I know we don't really talk about it—when *it* happened on the island. Shouldn't that make me, I don't know, exempt?

RITA: You know all about the Clifford Sickness, don't you? Learned about it in school?

KAYLA: We did.

RITA: Some of the people that died saw the dead things then, too, before they were taken. And there were no rituals back then, no rules to break. But those dead things came all the same. They're harbingers, sweetie, do you know what that means?

KAYLA: I don't.

RITA: They announce something, like a clap of thunder before the downpour. And these dead things are harbingers, all right. If they come for you, that means you're supposed to die.

KAYLA: Wait, because I'm seeing my grandmother, I'm supposed to die? Pastor Rita, I—

RITA: Honey, we are *all* supposed to die. Every single person on this island should've died a very long time ago. We are cheating death, every single day. That's why you are seeing one of those things, why I have, why so many other people have. It's not just the rule breakers, but boy howdy, that'll make those creepy things come out of the woodwork, for sure.

KAYLA: Lily hasn't.

RITA: What's that?

KAYLA: Lily hasn't seen a dead thing. Does that mean she's safe?

RITA: Not all of the Clifford Sickness folks saw the dead things, either, and they were taken all the same.

KAYLA: What about the . . . the old pastor? And the kids.

RITA: No one knows what they saw before they were taken, but I expect some of them might've seen a dead thing that night. You have to believe in these sorts of things to see them, sweetie.

KAYLA: Like, believe in ghosts?

RITA: Well, sure, if you want to put it that way. That's what we've found over the years; that seems to be the pattern. The islanders who haven't seen one of these things seem to fall more on the skeptical side, have a less open-minded view of the world we live in. About spirits, the supernatural, whatever you want to call it. But that won't stop the evil on this island from taking them if we slip up, that's for darn sure.

KAYLA: So, I'm a believer, then.

RITA: Honey, you're more than a believer. You're a fighter, one of the best fighters we've got. We need you, Kayla. We need you to help keep everyone safe. People have vanished on this island before. Lots of people. It's happened in the very homes we live in, and it's happened on other islands, too. I know that you know this.

KAYLA: I do.

RITA: You know our history, and you know what will happen to all of us if we let our guard down.

KAYLA: I've heard the stories my whole life.

RITA: It's so much more than stories, Kayla. Strange things have happened on these islands for hundreds of years.

KAYLA: Then why didn't people figure out how to fight it sooner? Why have we let all these terrible things happen to us?

RITA: That's a difficult question, but a fair one. It's something I've thought about for decades and decades, dear. The best I can come up with is, it's sort of like a belief in God, a belief in Jesus. We are all born with the capacity to believe, but at some point, we have to open up our hearts and let it in. And sometimes it takes a single moment to do that. I think that's what happened on that terrible night. You know the one I mean.

KAYLA: Like, people knew, but they needed to see it?

RITA: Unfortunately, yes. But I could be wrong. I don't have all the answers, darling. But I do intend on keeping everyone here safe. You trust me when I say that, right?

KAYLA: I do.

RITA: What happened on the other islands won't happen here. Not if we stick together and follow the rules. We share a common purpose. You, me, everyone here. You are a soldier, child. We all are. Now, repeat after me: I am a soldier.

KAYLA: I am a soldier.

RITA: Good. That's very good. Now, is there anything else you'd like to talk to me about?

KAYLA: Can I . . . can we . . .

RITA: Yes, dear?

KAYLA: Never mind.

CLIFFORD ISLAND

Seven Days until Willow's Disappearance

TEXT MESSAGES BETWEEN LILY BECKER AND CONNOR HUDSON

CONNOR: Hey I'm sending you something

You there?

I found a journal article about the islands up here

And all the strange stuff

It doesn't mention dead things

But it gets into the other stuff

About people vanishing

On Lake Michigan

It might be more than legend

The article lays out the patterns

Really weird things have happened on the other islands

Shilling and Wallin

Groups of people disappear sporadically over a
one-hundred-year span

Until eventually it takes everyone

And the island is empty

Just no one left

Lily what if it's all true?

You say it's myths and legends but what if it isn't?

Sorry that was dramatic

Sending now

You around?

Lily?

Read the article ASAP

What if the wackos are right?

Willis, S. W. "A Short History of the Islands Surrounding the Door
   County Peninsula." *Journal of Lake Michigan Research* 17, no. 3
   (2003): 112–13.

Of particular note is the mystery surrounding the disappearances of
missionaries and settlers on the islands of Shilling and Wallin. While
no consensus can be reached among Great Lakes scholars, it is likely
that the vanishings of the populations of people can be traced to a
combination of incidents of disease, displacement, assimilation, ac-
cidents, and abandonment.

   In the 1700s, Shilling Island served as a settlement for French
Jesuit missionaries, and excavations of the island revealed the remains of a chapel and numerous small cabins. Few primary accounts
exist regarding activities on Shilling Island, but according to a letter
written by missionary Julien Laurent dated October 12, 1788, a
handful of missionaries on the island "unfortunately disappeared"
sometime early in the century, and while he was not on the island
when this occurred, "their disappearance is still a matter of much

debate among the missionaries, and their names are invoked often" (Castille 1953, 162). Laurent did not elaborate on the matter in his letter, and there are no corroborations of his account. Laurent was expected back in France in 1790, but his Shilling traveling party never arrived, their fate ultimately left unknown. A visiting missionary reported in 1799 that "the island is completely devoid of life, and it looks to have been that way for some time" (163).

In the nineteenth century, nearby Wallin Island also experienced disappearances of groups of people, according to primary documents from the time period. Paul and Louis Pierre set up a fishing operation on the island in 1815, and it is believed that between one and two hundred French fishermen and Potawatomi lived on the island temporarily during the fishing season, which ran from August through November. A disappearance occurred in 1822, when it was reported that ten fishermen were discovered missing from their beds in the early morning. In a letter to his wife, Paul Pierre wrote, "The men vanished sometime in the night. Some believe they ventured out after dusk and became mired in the fog, as it was particularly heavy during the evening hours and into the dawn. But no boats were missing and the men's belongings were left behind, which is particularly vexing" (Leonard 2001, 378). According to Pierre, a few of the men had experienced "hallucinations" before their disappearances, which Pierre hoped "would not spread amongst the entirety of the island" (378). Pierre speculated that "perhaps a sickness overtook the men and they wandered into the waters, for there was no discernable reason for them to have traveled together late into the evening. I long for answers and clarity on the matter, but I'm finding there are little. My heart hopes they simply wished to flee the island for reasons unknown to me, and perhaps they were picked up by another fishing party, and I very much hope this is the case, as many of the men had wives and families. I pray for their souls; God willing they are alive" (378). There is no record of the fishermen being seen again.

Another disappearance occurred in 1887 when thirteen fishermen vanished from the island on an October morning, similar in circumstances to the 1822 incident. According to journal writings at the time, some of the fishermen were experiencing "delusions," perhaps due to ingesting "tainted meat brought by canoe" (380). One fisherman who'd vanished "insisted his son was visiting him in the night, only the boy had perished from disease the previous winter" (380). The fishery continued to operate until sometime in the 1890s, at which point the camp was suddenly abandoned. The exact year of the abandonment is unknown, although some researchers point to a maritime journal entry as their best clue.

In 1896, the SS *Fortune*, a wooden-hulled steamship, was traveling across Lake Michigan near the Door County islands. In a journal entry dated November 24 of that year, sailor Jonas Carlson wrote, "In the late morning, we discovered an old man adrift in a small boat. He was badly malnourished. I do not know his origin, nor if he had family. All the man said was, 'Wallin' and 'The evil has descended.' He repeated this phrase many times, which the crew found curious and quite macabre. He is being treated below, but I fear he will not survive" (Stafford 1998, 122). It is not known with certainty whether the man found adrift had in fact originated from Wallin Island, nor why the island was ultimately abandoned. DNA tests suggest that some of the French fishermen may have assimilated into Indian tribes in the Ontario region, and an excavation of Wallin Island revealed various fishing relics and the remains of a small stone cottage (Murray et al. 1949, 74).

There have been discussions in the last two decades, primarily among urban legend enthusiasts and conspiracy theorists, pointing out that the vanishings of peoples on Wallin and Shilling Islands follow a similar, century-long trajectory: a group of people go missing early in the century, then another sizable group vanishes later in the century, and then every person on the island vanishes before the century concludes. The Wallin Island disappearances paint the clearest picture, with vanishings of people in 1822 and 1887, followed by the complete abandonment of the island in the 1890s. Although the trajectory is comparable on Shilling Island during the 1700s, it is difficult to argue conclusively that any person actually vanished on the island, as Julien Laurent's letters are the only primary reference to potential disappearances from the time period.

Nevertheless, while an argument can be made that the disappearances and/or deaths of people on Wallin and Shilling Islands do follow an identifiable pattern, the most likely scenario is that this is simply a coincidental combination of events, such as disease and desertion, common to the region during those times.

WILLOW

Five Days until Her Disappearance

Dominic,

I have a name. Gloria Henderson.

Want to know how I got it? Good, old-fashioned espionage.

I invited myself over to Lily's place for dinner. Told her I wanted to get to know the families of the youth group students, and she said it was cool. At the time, I was a little surprised she didn't see right through my plan.

I got there around six. Average house, two stories, quaint. Little dated, but isn't everything around here? It was my first time formally meeting her father, Vincent. I'd been intimidated by the guy before. Once at a basketball game, and again a few weeks back when I was convinced that he and Rita were having some hushed conversation about me in her office. Thankfully, when I walked into his home, he was nothing but friendly and cordial.

We sit down for dinner, and the whole time I'm being pleasant and talkative, but I'm really just wondering where Vincent's office is. You know, Mr. City Clerk? And then, thank my lucky stars, it turned out his office was in the same hallway as the bathroom. I saw him go in and out a few times. Too easy, right?

So, it's getting a little later in the night, and I feign a bit of a stomach issue. Lily and Vincent stay at the kitchen table, and I head to the bathroom, but instead I detour right into Dad's office. I'm not sure what made me so brazen, but I did it. Just crept right in there. Typical dad zone: guy is a big sports fan. The place is overflowing with vintage Michael Jordan photos and Chicago Bulls championship paraphernalia. Framed posters, pennants, a signed basketball. I spot his desk, and he has one of those really old, fat white computer monitors. I jab at the power button, thinking I might find some important file or something, and the entire monitor slides a few inches on the desk. The thing moves like it's featherlight. I slide it back, pick the whole thing up, and then I figure it out.

It's fake. It's made of plastic. Like one of those props you see at IKEA.

What the hell is going on?

I poke at the keyboard. That's fake, too. I riffle through a few drawers. Notebooks and pens. A Rolodex. Bills and such. Nothing of particular interest.

I scan the room again. There's a television sitting on a nightstand, and underneath the TV is a VCR. But I look closer, and I realize it's just the front of a VCR. It's been glued or screwed onto the outside of a drawer, like he wanted it to *look like* a VCR was there. Why would he do that? I open the drawer with the attached VCR head, and there's a DVD player inside. First I've seen on the island, but he's obviously keeping it hidden.

Just so darn peculiar, you know?

I move to the bookshelf. Nada. My eyes are flickering around the room, and I spot a box underneath his desk that I missed before. Bingo. Inside are more files and papers, and I ransack it. Frantically searching, hoping. Then I find it. A death certificate. Gloria Henderson. She died at the age of eighty-seven, just a few weeks before I showed up on the island. This has to be the Gloria, right? Died of natural causes, the certificate reads. But there's a little yellow note attached to the death certificate that has a few bullet points written on it.

Those read: *nightgown?; Esther, neighbor.*

I stare at it, thinking for a bit. I have no idea what it means. No clue. But I have a name, and Gloria's address. Maybe that's all I need. I look at my watch.

Crap.

I've been in the office for ten minutes. I put everything back as it was, and I return to the kitchen. Lily and Vincent are still sitting there. Neither came to check on me, and neither asked me any questions when I got back. I'm the luckiest person on Earth, right?

It wasn't luck. Lily walks me out not long after that, and she tells me, "I just saved your ass." Yep, she knew what I was up to. She had to make up some story to her dad about me having irritable bowel syndrome (!) and being too embarrassed to talk about it. She told him I'd be mortified if anyone checked on me, and that it would make me feel so much better if he stayed at the table and shut up about it. Clever kid.

She asked me, "Did you find what you were looking for? This is the Gloria thing, right?"

"I did find something," I told her.

And she just nodded. "I hope it helps. And tell me next time before you do something like that, for real. That shit wasn't cool."

I asked her about the office. The props and all that. She said something about her old man working in real estate and keeping all of the old staging stuff. Really? I wondered what type of real estate market there ever was on Clifford Island, but I didn't press. Then the kid asked me something that came out of left field:

"Hey, your brother, Harper, right? He has connections and all that, yeah?"

It took me a moment to recall how she actually knew about him, before remembering I'd told her my family history in a therapy session the other day. Still, I didn't know what she meant. Like, connections to athletes? Publishing, editors, something like that?

She didn't have time to clarify. Vincent was watching us from the window, and I really needed to bail. But it looks like I have an honest-to-God ally in this. I can't believe it. I really can't. It's hard to explain, but when Lily and I were speaking outside her house, it was like we shared this unspoken, common understanding. Almost like this current passed through both of us, that we both had secrets that we wanted to share but we just couldn't.

I just had this *feeling* that Lily and I were on the same wavelength, that we were both thinking: *Something is happening on this island, and you and I are in this together.*

I'm hoping she felt it, too, because I really need to know.

Can this kid be trusted?

Willow

CLIFFORD ISLAND

Five Days until Willow's Disappearance

TEXT MESSAGES BETWEEN LILY BECKER AND CONNOR HUDSON

LILY: Hey

Talk to me Hudson

CONNOR: What's up?

LILY: There's a new person on my island

My youth group director

And I think she might be undercover or something

Or doing an investigation

CONNOR: You serious?

LILY: She snuck into my dad's office

Wanted someone's death certificate

It was REAL sneaky

CONNOR: Wow

Did you talk to her about it?

LILY: Kind of

She didn't tell me what she was up to

But I had another thought

CONNOR: Okay

LILY: Her brother is a reporter

CONNOR: Cool

Like for TV?

LILY: Sports reporter

For a newspaper

CONNOR: Okay

What are you thinking?

LILY: What if we teamed up with her

In a way

Maybe her brother could help publish our stuff

I don't know

Maybe reach a wider audience?

And stuff in a newspaper can't be erased

You know

Just thinking out loud

CONNOR: Do you think that's what she was doing?

Investigating for a newspaper

Or with her brother or something

Looking to expose Clifford like us?

LILY: I don't know

Maybe?

CONNOR: Do you trust her?

LILY: I think so?

She seems cool

But it's hard to say

Everyone around here has secrets

You know?

CONNOR: I haven't told anyone about our secret

Just letting you know

LILY: I know

CONNOR: Did you get the article I sent you?

The journal thing

LILY: Yep

It's good ammo

How did you find it?

CONNOR: Used my dad's access to a bunch of academic sites

It's good stuff

LILY: He's a teacher right?

CONNOR: Professor

Yeah

LILY: Cool

CONNOR: You read it right?

LILY: Yep

CONNOR: And it didn't give you pause?

About all this stuff?

LILY: Not really

CONNOR: Lily

The article says the disappearances are all true

That people up here have just vanished

For hundreds of years

Like back in the 1700s and 1800s

So that whole pattern of vanishings

It's a real thing

LILY: Okay

I mean that stuff is normal

CONNOR: Normal?

LILY: Settlers got diseases and stuff all the time

This isn't a conspiracy

CONNOR: I'm just saying

Maybe the things people say on Clifford aren't
so crazy

Maybe the vanishings actually happened?

LILY: Oh come on

Connor

We are just trying to expose everything

Don't start believing in this stuff

CONNOR: Oh

Well

You definitely won't like the next part

LILY: Oh boy

What are you going to tell me

CONNOR: Okay

So you know my friend Eric?

LILY: Point guard right?

JIMMY JULIANO

CONNOR: Yeah good dude

We took my dad's boat for a ride the other day

Went fishing

LILY: Okay

CONNOR: We rode by the other two islands

Wallin and Shilling

Where the disappearances happened

I wanted to check them out

Because I was curious you know?

LILY: They are just normal boring islands

Nothing but trees and rocks

CONNOR: Okay

But then we rode by Clifford

And Eric saw something

I didn't see it

But he did

LILY: What?

CONNOR: He saw a baby

Crawling on the beach

By the shore

LILY: Wait what?

Like a human baby?

CONNOR: Kind of

More like a fetus

LILY: Dude

What are you talking about?

CONNOR: I know I know

It sounds crazy

I didn't see it

But Eric just screams out

PENELOPE

And he literally jumps off the boat

He's thrashing around in the water

And he's hysterical

LILY: Connor

What is going on

CONNOR: I had to throw him a life jacket

And jump in after him

I'm pretty sure I saved his life

It was like he was in a trance

I've never seen him like that

Crazy

LILY: What was it actually?

Turtle?

Because he didn't see a baby

Excuse me

A fetus

On the shore

CONNOR: I don't know

Lily

LILY: Yes

CONNOR: Before Eric was born

His mom had a miscarriage

Real late in the pregnancy

LILY: Where are you going with this?

CONNOR: She was going to name the baby Penelope

Penelope!

They have a tombstone for the baby and everything

I've seen it

What if

LILY: ???

CONNOR: What if Eric saw his dead sister?

LILY: I don't know what to say

It's creepy I know

He was probably just fooling around

CONNOR: He wouldn't fool around

Not about that

LILY: Someone put him up to it?

Maybe it was a prank

He knows you're into this urban legend stuff

CONNOR: I don't know

I don't think he would do that

He hasn't responded to my texts

I even called the guy

He totally ghosted me

I think he's legit traumatized

LILY: It just can't be true Connor

It's not possible

CONNOR: You think in no way it's possible?

That the stories are true

LILY: How can they be?

CONNOR: It's like what you told me on the phone

People see dead things

The things that try to lure you away

LILY: Oh stop it

CONNOR: You don't think it's in the realm of possibility?

That the evil cursed your island

And then people see things

Like what Eric saw

Lily

These vanishings and the dead things could be all related

It just makes sense

LILY: You've got to be joking

CONNOR: You've never seen one?

A dead thing?

LILY: OMG STOP IT

I told you before

I've lived here my whole life and NO

I've never seen a dead thing

It's all made up

These are lies and stories to make us live a certain way

Just like the Oga stuff

Just like other stories they fed us as kids

Don't believe it

You just can't

Out of all people you can't believe in this stuff

I'm begging you

CONNOR: Okay

I'm sorry

I'll stop

LILY: Our mission is not to believe

It's to expose everyone on Clifford for the looneys they are

And you can't be one too

Why are you so into this?

CONNOR: It's interesting?

I don't know

I've always liked this kind of stuff

Urban legends and scary stories

LILY: Oh crap

I just realized

Is that why you like me?

Because I'm some freak from Clifford Island?

CONNOR: No no no no

Lily

That's not it

LILY: If that's the way it is just tell me

Because everyone else in my life is batshit crazy

And YOU were supposed to be the normal one

You can't be one of them Connor

You just can't

JIMMY JULIANO

CONNOR: I know I know

LILY: You don't know what it's like on this island

To feel hopeless

And to know you can't step out of line

You have it so good

It's like you live in a different world

The better one

The normal one

I need you okay?

CONNOR: I'm sorry

I really am

I swear

I want to help you

LILY: You don't get it

It's not just me

You can help ALL of us Connor

Everyone

My friends on the island

Steven and Kayla

Those who know better and those who don't

My dad wants me to live here forever

All of the other parents think that way too

They want us to waste our lives in this terrible place

To grow up and work some boring job right here

And then have babies of our own

And pass down to them the same crap we were told

Feed them the same lies about Clifford

Lather rinse repeat

Forever

And I just won't accept that

CONNOR: I know

I know

LILY: So we need to do this

For everyone here

And I need to know that you're with me

CONNOR: You can count on me

I swear

You can

LILY: Good

So let's do this then

Do you have anything else?

CONNOR: What do you mean?

LILY: For the expose

What about the message boards?

Where you read about Seminary House?

More there?

CONNOR: It's gone

Well the post is gone

I can't find it

LILY: Ugh

Really?

CONNOR: Yes

Maybe it was erased

Like you said

People on the outside

LILY: Damnit

We need more

CONNOR: Well we have the journal article

I can do a write-up of what Eric saw

Hallucinated

Whatever

Add it to our small collection

Expose the looneys

Right?

LILY: Right

Okay

CONNOR: Did you find anything?

From your dad?

LILY: I'm still poking around

Oh

I found a church bulletin from last summer

From a service

My dad kept it for some reason

CONNOR: What does it say?

LILY: Not much

But it's like the only item I've ever seen

That actually mentions the thing

CONNOR: The thing?

LILY: God I am so programmed

Even I feel weird saying it

But it says at the top

"It's been twenty-five years since our children left"

CONNOR: Cryptic

LILY: Subtle but it's evidence

Right?

But OH

I almost forgot

CONNOR: Yes?

LILY: I have another idea

CONNOR: Okay

LILY: You have a portable projector right?

And speakers?

CONNOR: Yeah

Why?

LILY: I'm going to take things up a notch

Have a little fun

CONNOR: Okay . . .

LILY: You remember island rule 1?

No modern technology?

CONNOR: Sure yeah

Why?

LILY: Want to mess with people up here a bit?

40

HARPER

I sat slumped in my chair in Vincent's kitchen, absolutely gobsmacked.

I wanted to press pause on our conversation and take a step back, just, evaluate the situation like I was making sense of a movie. We were talking about ghosts and horrible things returning from the dead, and Vincent had the tenor of a guy dictating a grocery list. I wanted to think that he was simply a superb actor, and this was just some big *gotcha* scenario. But it all felt so authentic.

Vincent had me convinced.

Willow had been on this island for weeks, the islander had told me. Then my sister, along with Vincent's daughter, was going to enlist *my help* to publish something about all the crazy things going on up here.

Dead things, evil, earthquakes.

The note Willow had left me was starting to make sense.

Run to your mother.

Don't follow them.

I assumed my sister had seen some serious shit. And yet, I wasn't convinced she was dead. Even Vincent wasn't sure. I was pushing him for more clarity, and he seemed to be doing his absolute best to explain just how these dead things operated.

Because I certainly needed more clarity before going to that house. *Seminary House.*

If that's where she was taken, then that's where I was going, ghosts and evil be damned. I knew that's where my journey was leading.

But I still needed to know more.

"These dead things used to be calmer," Vincent was currently explaining to me. "Hell, there wasn't that much of a reason to be afraid, outside of seeing your dead loved one come back from the grave. Yeah, they'd tell you awful things, make you feel bad about yourself, but they couldn't hurt you. Not physically, anyway. It was more mental warfare. Just don't listen, you know? Close your eyes. Don't give in. But now? What I'm saying is that these things are getting more powerful. No more mental torture, although that ain't no picnic, either. They've somehow learned to make physical contact." He patted his chest. "And I'm not the only one with one of these. Other islanders have gotten hurt when these things show up."

My thoughts flashed to the bar. The locking of the doors, the seemingly forbidden singalong.

"Did you . . ." I searched for the right words. "Summon? Your wife? At the bar, earlier? By playing that song?"

He smiled. "Now you're catching on."

"But how? Why?"

"There are certain rules we all follow on Clifford Island. And if you break these rules, the dead things come out. They try to lure you away."

He had more to say, but I put my hands up in the air, stopping him. "So you're saying that listening to a song that's not classic rock makes a ghost appear? Because that's what happened, right?"

"Sort of, I s'pose. It's hard to say."

"That's not a good enough answer for me."

Vincent sighed. "I wish this was more black-and-white. How do I put this . . . There's something in the air around here. Something we can't see. But it moves around, and it's looking for things that are different. It likes order; it likes routine. But when it senses something is different, it's angry. The dead things come out, and they try to coax you away."

He lifted his cigarette to his mouth. Another long drag. His gaze looked past me; his words carried an undeniable heaviness.

The man was as serious as a heart attack.

"Like I said," he continued, inhaling deeply and then exhaling, "they didn't used to be so dangerous or come out as frequently as they do. But the more time that passes, the more of these things seem to come out of the woodwork. Hell, you don't even have to break a routine for them to show up. Ain't no guarantees around here, not anymore. But if you *do* break a routine, oh boy, watch your back, son. It's definitely coming for you, and it's pissed off."

"Does everyone see these things?" I asked. "Or hear them?"

Vincent shook his head. "Only the believers, seems to be the case."

"Believers? Like in ghosts?"

"Pretty much, yeah."

"So you were the only one at the bar who believes in ghosts?"

He shook his head. "Like I said, I wish this was cut-and-dry. If you see one of these dead things, it's just for you. No one else can see it, no one else can hear it. Unless it breaks a window or throws something across the room, well, you'd bet your ass someone else would notice that. But the way they look, the moaning, the screaming, the awful things it tells you . . . it's your own personal nightmare."

The islander looked off, formulating his thoughts.

"And Leota," he finally said, "well, the last few months or so, nightmare's getting worse. Doors haven't stopped her, hiding does nothing. Every time Leota has come back she's been stronger."

"Does your daughter know?"

"About my wife?"

"Yeah."

"Yes and no," he said. "She knows I've seen her, but she doesn't know about the violence, about her getting physical. Last few times Leota has shown up I've made myself gone in a hurry. I won't be around Lily when that happens, because I don't want anything to happen to her. Kid still doesn't believe, so she still hasn't seen a dead thing." He chuckled. "I used to want her to believe. Not anymore, though. Not with what these things can do now."

"Then why did you summon her tonight?" I asked. "If she could've killed you? I mean, come on. No one likes Billie Eilish *that much*."

Vincent leaned forward in his chair. "Because *you* needed to see. You need to learn about what's happening around here."

"What, for the article I'm supposed to write about this place?"

He shook his head. "That article ain't happening. No one can know about what goes on up here. It's too dangerous, for everyone."

"Then why tell me?"

"Because it's the right thing to do. We may have our secrets, but we are good, decent people on this island. At least I am, for what it's worth. And the decent thing to do is to tell you the truth about your sister, every piece of it."

He thought for a moment, and his eyes darkened. "And the more you know about this place—the gravity of what we are actually doing— the more likely you are to keep its secrets. And when you leave this island, God willing, we're gonna need you to keep our secrets, and I strongly suspect you will."

Vincent's features softened. "And in return, I need your help."

I straightened up in my chair. "My help?"

Vincent nodded and stubbed out his cigarette on a paper plate.

"I need you to look after my daughter," he said. "She needs to leave the island forever. And I want you to help her do it."

I didn't know what to say.

Vincent rose from his chair, and he opened a cupboard door above him. The inside was dotted with Polaroid pictures.

"That's Lily with Leota," Vincent said, pointing at a picture of his wife pushing their young daughter on a tree swing. "Radiant, aren't they? The first time Leota came back to me after she died, she looked like that. Beautiful, not a scratch on her. Just a perfect re-creation. That was what . . . fifteen years ago?"

I zoned in on the photo, and I couldn't disagree with him. The pair were glowing, happy. Leota in a sundress, Lily in overalls. The lake shimmered and sparkled in the background.

"Now when she comes back," Vincent continued, "her body is all mangled, mud caked in her hair. Bones broken. She likes to scream at me; she gets a real kick out of that. But her screams are all garbled because her mouth is full of dirt and worms, like she just crawled out of the grave. And there's this fire in her eyes, this intense hatred. For me. And I don't blame her for it. I really don't. Leota was a free spirit, like Lily. My wife was never meant for this place."

He paused.

"Neither is my daughter," he added. "I won't let this place poison her any longer. I won't let her stay here."

"I'm sorry."

It was all I could think to say, and my condolences seemed to mean nothing to him.

Vincent closed the cupboard and grabbed the dwindling pack of Marlboros from the table, fishing out a fresh smoke and sparking it up. "Lily needs to leave this place. For many reasons. I won't let her get hurt. I won't let her end up like Leota. I see that now." He nodded over toward the staircase in the hallway. "She is quitting basketball because of me."

The kid with one of the smoothest shots I'd ever seen, and I'd covered a lot of games. I didn't know Lily at all, but it didn't seem right.

"For years I pushed her to quit," Vincent continued, "to not invest her energy into something that ultimately didn't matter, because back then I believed that what really mattered was *this* place, *this* mission. I was horrified at the thought that I'd someday lose her, she'd get recruited to go play basketball and she'd leave, and Clifford would lose her . . . and then when she actually quit after they took your sister to that house . . . to see my only child broken like that, turning her back on something she had worked so hard for . . . it shattered me."

I remembered the way Lily had spoken about Willow. There was both affection and remorse there.

I wondered, did she feel responsible?

Again, I didn't know her. But quitting didn't seem like something that was in her nature. In the few minutes I'd spoken with Lily, she'd seemed like the type of kid who would fight back.

A wisp of smoke escaped from Vincent's mouth. "I was wrong, Harper. Ain't two ways about this. And I won't go to my own grave with regrets, that my daughter got hurt or gave up what she loved because her old man was stubborn and selfish, and he thought he knew what was best for her. No, this island will be fine without her. It will tick on, it will—" Vincent paused for a moment, searching for words. "You've got to protect what you love most. I lost sight of that."

The man looked at me square in the eye.

"Will you help her?"

I didn't know what to say, because I didn't know what he meant.

Did Vincent want me to smuggle the kid off the island? Stash her on a boat? Charter a helicopter?

Could she really not leave?

My eyebrows rose a bit as I considered his request.

"Why me?" I finally asked.

His answer came swiftly and firmly. "Because you aren't an islander. You have no connections to this place. Every single person in my life is associated with Clifford, and I don't trust a single one. Lily trusted your sister, and I think that means I can trust you, too."

I still wasn't quite sure how to respond. I barely knew Vincent, had known the man all of a few hours. But his willingness to trust in me seemed genuine, and knowing what I knew about his past, I understood his trepidation about other islanders. The people who might've murdered his wife, he thought. I understood why I, an outsider, might seem so compelling.

Vincent's eyes were pleading.

I still hadn't responded.

"There are documents," he said.

"Documents?"

He nodded. "Haven't read them, but I've seen them. Your sister was writing letters up here, to her husband, I think, but they never made it off the island."

"Wait, never made it? What do you mean?"

"She dropped them in the mailbox downtown, and someone fished them out before they went on their way."

"Who took them? Rita?"

Vincent shrugged. "Does it matter? Willow was growing wise to what was happening up here, and she was writing all about it, is what Rita said. And I suspect she *also* grew wise to the fact that her letters were being monitored and snatched up, because at some point Willow just quit writing."

Out of everything Vincent had told me over the course of the evening, these mail revelations, for some reason, set me off.

"This is crazy," I said sharply. "The things you are telling me, what you did to her. Monitoring her, stealing her letters. You know this, right?"

"Like I said before, no one can know about this place. We do what we gotta do. But I can *get you* those letters that were never sent. They're on this island somewhere, most likely with the good pastor. And there are other documents, too—about your sister, things from her past—and some recordings about the things going on up here. They might be enough to tell Willow's story. Give you the answers you deserve. Fill in the gaps. You help Lily, and I'll help you get those documents, help you get those recordings."

I calmed down a bit, intrigued at Vincent's offer, but still confused.

"Vincent," I began, "I appreciate you helping me. Truly, I do. But with all due respect, I don't want documents or recordings right now. I'm here to find my sister. And the only thing you seem to know that's an absolute certainty is that Willow was taken to that house."

And might be alive, I thought.

I was still holding out hope.

"You want to go there," Vincent said.

"I do. I'm not settling for anything else."

"I'm going to kindly dissuade you from doing that." His eyes lit up a bit, as if he just remembered something and was keen to tell me. "I still haven't told you what's in there, have I?"

I shook my head.

Vincent took a deep breath.

"You better buckle up."

41

WILLOW

Four Days until Her Disappearance

Dominic,

I went to the address this afternoon. It was down a country road I'd been before, but I'd never actually gone up to the houses. Gloria's house was a simple country farmhouse. White siding, blue shutters, green picket fence with cracked paint. I knocked first, and there was no answer. I realized that I didn't know if Gloria had lived alone. Did she have a husband? I peered inside through a window, and the place looked spotless. Formal furniture, place mats and doilies still out on the dining room table. Fine china resting on shelves. I kept looking for flashes of movement, but there was nothing inside.

Did this place have anything to do with Jacob? I thought back to pictures he used to draw, thinking maybe he'd drawn this house before or something. My memory came up empty.

There was another house across the street. It was the only other place within eyeshot—this had to be Esther's, no? The woman from the sticky note?

The house looked very similar to Gloria's. I knocked a few times, and this delicate old lady answered the door. We recognized each other from church, but I'd never actually learned her name.

It was the woman.

Esther.

She invited me inside for coffee, and we chatted for quite some time. She was just the sweetest thing on the planet, her white perm bobbing up and down as she spoke. It was like speaking to my own grandmother. Esther told me that she is the last of her family on the island. Outlived them all, even her own kids. There was something so profoundly sad about that.

I asked about her neighbor. Esther put down her tea and went to the window, gazing across the road. She told me her neighbor's name was Gloria, and I started prying and prying. Did she live alone? Widow, huh? What was her last name? Oh, I think I knew her! Did Gloria ever mention having family in Illinois? No? Never mentioned a Willow or Jacob Stone? How about a Dominic? Huh, I thought maybe she knew us or something. How did she die? Really, went just like that?

I felt more and more frustrated, like, I'd come here and I'd thought I would learn something important but I hadn't, so finally I blurted out, "I heard something about a nightgown?" I had a feeling that I wasn't supposed to know that piece of information, and it was so freaking rude of me to just accost her with it.

Esther didn't respond. There was this uncomfortable silence between us. It felt like she wanted to tell me more, but she couldn't for some reason. The air in her house suddenly felt thick with secrets. I can't explain it. And then this alarm started buzzing. Esther turned it off, and she walked out of the room. She returned with this white nightgown that smelled of fresh linen.

"I sewed this," she told me.

"The pastor took the original, the one Gloria wore.

"This looks just like it.

"Just a little less wear and tear."

She laughed to herself after that last part. Esther then told me that she and Gloria had a routine where the two of them checked their mailboxes at the same time, every day, and that they hadn't missed a day for decades. Until she died, of course. Esther wanted to relive the experience one more time in Gloria's memory, so she asked me to wear the nightgown and pretend to be Gloria checking the mail. It was an unusual request, to say the least. But Esther was just so sincere and emotional about the whole thing.

I couldn't say no.

I slipped on the nightgown and walked across the street to Gloria's front stoop. Then I circled back down the driveway and pretended to check the mail. The wind was gusting, and I'm getting blasted in the face with swirling snow. I'm standing at this dead woman's mailbox performing some morbid ritual, and then it hit me.

I knew.

I knew what this place was. What was happening at Clifford Island.

Clifford Island is me. I am Clifford Island.

The old televisions and cars, the clothing, Pogs and Skip Its, all of it. People here are living in the past, like I was back home. I kept Jacob's room looking exactly as it did the morning of the accident. His dresser, his bed. The posters he hung slightly off-kilter that I never dreamed of leveling. Everything. If you walked in his room, it was like entering a time portal. And that's what this place is.

Clifford Island is a memorial. Something tragic happened, and the people never moved on.

Just like me.

I guess . . . maybe this is why I came here. Those words on Jacob's bedroom floor—*Clifford Island*—maybe you were right about them. Maybe they were never there, and I imagined them, and I've been imagining them the whole time. And I subconsciously knew this place existed and came here because I wanted to *be* one of the islanders, to live in this tight-knit support group they've built for themselves. These people will stay here forever, and that's what I would've done back home. I would've withered away in that house until my heart gave out and my lungs dried up, tending to Jacob's bedroom every single day, pretending that no time had passed, because it made me feel good, you know?

And I know it was all an illusion, one that I created. You can only pull the wool over your eyes so long before reality tears its way inside. I was living in fantasyland in Illinois, and you had every right to walk away. I see that now. It took living on an island that was a mirror of myself to see it. And maybe I could go home and sell the house, suck it up and put a few of Jacob's things in boxes and donate the rest—the thought of it nearly makes me hyperventilate, but I could do it, I swear I could do it—and you and I can start fresh. Be stronger for each other, which is what we should have done all along.

Only, I can't. Because while back home it was all a fantasy, up here, this is real. Those words *were* on Jacob's floor, and I was supposed to find them and see our son again, and then find out what it all means. I've been wrestling so much with wanting to be happy and wanting to honor our son, and I never dreamed I could have both.

But maybe I can?

On Clifford, I can be my best self and still carry hope, every day, that our son will be standing at my bedside, and maybe, just maybe, I can cradle him in my arms again. And it's all because of this place, because of *these people*. Something is happening. Something willed our boy back to me, and maybe it's what the islanders are doing. Maybe they are magicians waving some truly demented magic wands. Because it's more than just old technology. It's more than just Esther and Gloria checking their mail.

Quite frankly, it's madness.

There are more people like me up here, except they've taken it further. I just hadn't noticed. Well, I *had* noticed, but I hadn't fully processed any of it. Like my brain wasn't tuned to the correct frequency. Do you remember that part in *Halloween* when Jamie Lee Curtis knows something is up, so she searches the neighbor's house and finds the bodies of all of her friends? That's what I did, except, the island was the house, and the bodies were all of the things and people I've seen during my few weeks here.

You won't believe this, but here goes.

After my revelation at Gloria's mailbox, I went back to Larry's house. You know, the guy who I think was maybe abducted by the islanders? I hung back in the trees, and I watched his wife, cordless phone to her ear, slogging through the snow in her backyard to hang her laundry on the line. It was the same time I'd been at the house before. She was doing *exactly* the same thing, beat for beat, clothespins in the exact same spots.

Downtown was my next stop. I knew the guy would be there, I just knew it. And then he showed up. That man in his mid-fifties, boombox perched on his shoulder, blaring "Livin' on the Edge" for the whole island to hear. How had I not realized he was doing this at the *same time* every single day without fail?

I tried to remember where I saw the family watching the O.J. chase on TV a few weeks ago. It clicked, and I checked out the house when the sun went down. Crept up to their window like some burglar and peered through the narrow crack in their drapes, and sure enough, there they were, parked on sofas in the living room, eyes glued to the TV as the Ford Bronco roared down the expressway.

Same deal at the pub. Same old guy from before, drinking alone at the bar, O.J. on the tube. For God's sake, this is it, Dom. There are people on this island doing the same thing over and over again. Every single day. They are doing what I did back home, but they are taking it to places I didn't know were humanly possible. Like, Jacob's bedroom times one million. Good Lord, to go *that far* with a coping mechanism. This island should be swarming with scientists in white lab coats. It's lunacy.

Or not. Maybe people are doing these things and living this way for a reason. Perhaps these routines are somehow willing Jacob back to me, creating some cosmic hiccup where things that shouldn't exist actually do. And maybe it brings others back, too. Are there *more* like Jacob? Why did I not consider that before?

But why did the islanders choose that one point in time to relive? What in God's name happened up here? It had to have happened in the early or mid-'90s. That seems to be the "freeze point" or whatever. When was the O.J. stuff? 1994? '95? I feel like I should know that. I can't believe it took me this long to figure out. And I am *right*, right?

Before I left Esther's place to go on my Jamie Lee Curtis exploration, I flat-out asked the old woman, "Did something really bad happen on this island? Like twenty-five years ago?" She clammed up. I took one final glance around her sitting room, and I spotted it. A VHS tape tucked into a bookshelf. Scribbled on the white label were the words: *O.J. Chase/ News Coverage.* Are these tapes everywhere?

I'm *this* close, Dom. So, so close. Twenty-five years ago, something happened here. Something people won't talk about. And when I find out exactly what that thing is, everything will change. It's why I'm here.

I'm almost there.

Willow

CLIFFORD ISLAND

EXCERPT OF STEVEN OLSEN INTERVIEW WITH SHERIFF ROY DONOVAN

STEVEN: What can you tell me about the Clifford Sickness?

DONOVAN: Hold on a second. What is this for exactly? School?

STEVEN: Ms. Stone wants us to do an oral history project about Clifford Island.

DONOVAN: Ms. Stone?

STEVEN: Yeah, for church.

DONOVAN: Does Pastor Rita know about this?

STEVEN: I think so. We're doing interviews.

DONOVAN: If I gave the good pastor a call right now, she'd give this her blessing?

STEVEN: I mean, yeah, I guess. We're doing this for youth group.

DONOVAN: Fine. What would you like to know? I only have a few minutes.

STEVEN: What do you know about the Clifford Sickness?

DONOVAN: What about it?

STEVEN: What happened, I guess.

DONOVAN: Well, a lot of islanders got sick right around the same time, and some people died.

STEVEN: When was this?

DONOVAN: Back in the 1920s. You can check the plaque, if you like.

STEVEN: And how did they get sick?

DONOVAN: No one knows for sure. Just one of those things.

STEVEN: What were their symptoms?

DONOVAN: From what I understand, it was a combination of things. High fevers. Hallucinations. Convulsions. Stuff like that.

STEVEN: How many people died?

DONOVAN: Nine, if my memory serves.

STEVEN: And this was the first time?

DONOVAN: I'm afraid I don't understand the question. First time for what?

STEVEN: The first time anything bad happened here.

DONOVAN: What do you mean by that?

STEVEN: I just mean that nine people dying really sucks, and I was curious if you knew of any more incidents on Clifford Island before that? Or on an island around us? Like, on Shilling or Wallin?

DONOVAN: Incidents?

STEVEN: You know, lots of people dying at once.

DONOVAN: It's okay that we're recording this? The pastor said this is okay?

STEVEN: Yeah, it's fine.

DONOVAN: Who's going to listen to this?

STEVEN: I don't know. Ms. Stone didn't say.

DONOVAN: Hmm. What was the question again?

STEVEN: I was wondering if you knew of other incidents of people disappearing or dying on the islands.

DONOVAN: Not that I'm aware of, no.

STEVEN: What about the missionaries?

DONOVAN: The missionaries?

STEVEN: You know, on Shilling, I think. They were some of the first people that lived on the islands.

DONOVAN: What is this, gotcha journalism?

STEVEN: What? No. I heard about it in history class. I just wanted to know the department's official position on it. For the project.

DONOVAN: Officially, I have no damn clue what you're talking about.

STEVEN: Oh. Well, it's not much. Just that some French missionaries used to live up here, and then they were just, kind of, gone, I guess.

DONOVAN: Well, you might want to find a historian to talk about that. I'm no help there.

STEVEN: You did know about the Clifford Sickness, so I just thought—

DONOVAN: Well, there's that damn commemorative bronze plate I drive by every day, so it's kind of hard not to know about the Clifford Sickness.

STEVEN: Okay, well—

DONOVAN: Is that it?

STEVEN: Can we go off the record for a minute?

DONOVAN: Off the record? You've been watching too many TV shows.

STEVEN: I guess I have one more question.

DONOVAN: Fine. Go ahead.

STEVEN: Can we talk about the kids?

DONOVAN: The who?

STEVEN: You know, from '94. The dead eleven.

DONOVAN: You shut that damn thing off right now.

43

Swanson, J. "11 People Found Dead; Carbon Monoxide Suspected."
Sturgeon Bay Gazette, June 21, 1994, p. A1.

A youth pastor and ten children were found dead Saturday morning, their bodies discovered inside a house on Prince of Peace Church property on Clifford Island. Local police said the people died sometime Friday night after a furnace malfunction in the house caused a carbon monoxide leak.

Authorities said the furnace was switched on during the night during the church's annual youth lock-in sleepover event. A cracked heat exchanger inside the furnace is the suspected cause of the leak. The sleepover attendees were found in their sleeping bags in the living room of Seminary House.

"I'm without words," said Clifford Island Sheriff Roy Donovan. "This is an unspeakable tragedy. We only ask to be left alone so the families and every person on this island can mourn the loss of the deceased."

The lock-in event was a yearly sleepover hosted by the church. When the youth pastor, Tim Burkweiler, and the children did not emerge from the house in the morning, local islanders entered the property and discovered the bodies, notifying authorities shortly thereafter.

Local police identified the victims as Tim Burkweiler, 34, and youth members of the church Paul Bailey, 11; Michael Bell, 13; Samantha Bell, 9; Anna Saunders, 8; Cody Harris, 11; Olivia Joiner, 15; Shane Richardson, 9; Patricia Simmons, 14; Heather Turner, 11; and Kimberly Walker, 12.

"The lock-in is a cherished summertime event," said Prince of Peace Pastor Rita Higgins, who discovered the bodies a little before eight o'clock on Saturday morning. "It's a way to build communion and community amongst the youth on the island. For this to happen at a church function? I can't comprehend what the families are feeling right now. If it's any consolation, the children didn't feel any pain. They weren't panicking. They all passed peacefully. God bless them."

The furnace was serviced in November 1993 as part of routine maintenance, Higgins said. It's yet unknown how the furnace got switched on, as the low temperature on Clifford Island early Saturday morning was sixty-two degrees, with temperatures climbing into the low eighties during the day on Friday. Seminary House is typically very warm in the summer months, Higgins said, and she theorized that perhaps one of the lock-in attendees attempted to turn on the air-conditioning in the middle of the night but turned on the furnace by mistake.

"Anything we can do to provide comfort to the families of the deceased is our priority right now," said Sheriff Donovan.

The incident remains under investigation.

44

RITA

June 19, 1994

The room felt more cluttered than usual. Rita had been down there before, of course, but never with such panicked intention. She'd really only used the archive room for storage—it was the church's equivalent of the underside of a child's bed. When Rita or other church employees needed an item to go away, into the archive room it went. The room was littered with folding chairs, an old coffeemaker, table dressings, candleholders, stained vestments—on and on the list went.

Behind that hodgepodge, somewhere, was information that Rita desperately needed to find. At least, that's what the pastor was banking on. The town meeting was in a few hours, and Rita needed *something*. She wasn't sure what she was looking for down in the church archives. Rita had no specific document in mind, only a goal:

The people of Clifford Island demanded answers, and she would find them.

Eleven people had been taken—ten of them children. *Taken.*

Many islanders had refused to believe it at first. The nearby shores and cliffs were thoroughly searched, in case the group of children and young pastor had decided to venture off for a hike in the wee hours of the night. Nothing in the Clifford forests seemed amiss. Every square inch of the island was combed; no boats were missing from the dock, and nothing pointed to a youth pastor absconding with a group of children—and besides, he wasn't *that type of guy*, the islanders agreed.

But everyone knew this had happened before. The legends of the evil that resided in the Great Lakes region had existed for centuries, and every islander knew them, chapter and verse. Rita had been fascinated by the stories as a child—but she'd eventually decided they were just that: stories. Men wandering off into a deep fog, never to return. An entire fishing camp abandoned suddenly, its residents never heard from again. But it had all happened so long ago. Was there any way to prove what had really happened to those people? The myths suggested something sinister had transpired.

Whispers of an ancient evil.

And *dead things*.

But grown-up Rita had never believed it. And then there was the Clifford Sickness. Those disappearances happened right here on her own island, her *home*, a mere seventy-five years prior. But the only islanders who were old enough to have been alive at the time had been infants or toddlers when that happened. And time has a way of dulling the blade; truth turning into legend; facts morphing into ghost stories.

We should've known, the pastor thought.

I should've known.

We could've done something.

Rita looked through the jumbled mess in the church archive room once more. *I'm a leader here, dagnabbit, I should've known better. Why didn't I think the legends were actually real?*

She'd asked that question of herself plenty the past few days, and she didn't have a satisfactory answer. Rita didn't suspect she ever would, and she expected to go to her grave still asking herself that very same thing, the puzzling question being perhaps the last thought she'd ever have before death gripped her and the lights went out. All she could do now was turn the tide, to try to give the people of Clifford answers to *why* such a horrific thing could befall their very children, and perhaps stop it from happening again.

The archives were her last-ditch effort to find those answers. Rita was kicking herself for not remembering the room sooner, but she hadn't had much time for rumination over the past thirty-six hours. She'd spent seemingly every waking moment with the parents of those poor kids, holding hands and passing tissues, listening with a heavy heart, providing words of wisdom—and those words were falling flat, the pastor thought. She hadn't had answers for them. How could she? This evil was unfathomable, its intentions ungodly, operating outside the comforting idea of a divine, grand plan. Since the eleven had disappeared, Rita needed more than two hands to count the number of times she'd heard an islander ask:

How would God allow this?

Even Rita didn't know.

She'd prayed for answers, but the answers didn't come. The pastor flipped through her cherished leather-bound personal Bible, but where before she'd always found inspiration without fail, she now found nothing. The pastor was frustrated. She didn't have an answer for why God allowed this evil to fester and then feast on the island's most innocent and vulnerable. Doubt and anger began to corrupt her usually optimistic thoughts. She felt powerless.

How can anyone explain any of this? Rita thought.

Where could I possibly find an answer to this madness?

Alone and mere hours before the town meeting, it finally occurred to her that the answer about Clifford's future and an answer to the question *How would God allow this?* might be connected somehow—and that shared answer might come from the past. Might there be a record or writing, something that shed light on the evil that lived on the island? A compass of sorts, a guidepost that might help the pastor in shepherding her flock? Maybe words from a former Clifford pastor, or perhaps from a religious text? Rita had exhausted her own ideas and had already paged through all the books from her own collection—but maybe what the islanders needed was already on the island, waiting to be discovered in the forgotten church archives.

It was a Hail Mary, that was for sure.

Rita sighed and looked at her watch—never did it seem to tick so quickly. The town meeting was commencing soon, and if she didn't have answers by then, she didn't know what the islanders would do. All sorts of options were on the table: abandon the island; just stick it out and carry on; find the damn thing and kill it; maybe even figure out a way to bring those kids and the youth pastor *back*, if something that daft was even possible. Not everyone was on the same page, and Rita couldn't blame them. This evil could not be understood, and the grief was clouding everyone's judgment. No one was really thinking clearly, not even the pastor herself. And she needed to be. This was her job, after all: to provide comfort and answers when they couldn't be found anywhere else.

The pastor peered through the mess that seemed to spill out of the room. The collection of spiritual texts and pastoral writings was still safe and sound, perched upon the bookshelves along the walls. Decades upon decades of church records filled plastic crates and containers, some stacked to the ceiling. She figured it would take days or weeks to properly examine and sort through those materials alone, but there was even more to explore.

Before Rita's time, the Prince of Peace archive had served as a repository of historical documents related to the surrounding islands, and those were *also* in the room and scattered about, sitting haphazardly in piles on the bookshelves or crammed into cardboard boxes. Many of those documents were from the personal collections of Clifford pastors and island history buffs of yore—this wasn't an *official* archive; there was no inventory or organization system—and Rita wasn't sure exactly what she'd find. She wasn't even sure where to start.

Seeing everything shoved into the room so carelessly, Rita's heart sank, and it made her again feel responsible for what had happened. *But I might be ten feet away from an answer right now*, Rita thought, and this filled her with optimism, and she wondered in what form the answer would be delivered.

Misplaced and bygone scripture.

Pastoral literature.

Long-forgotten journals and diaries.

Religious scrolls.

Heck, it could be written on a napkin, and that'd be all right with me, Rita thought.

She began her search.

Rita tore through the pastoral writings and religious books first, scanning pages quickly, shaking them out when she was done in case a loose piece of paper was wedged tightly between the pages. Satisfied the text was of no help, she'd toss it to the other side of the room, content to clean up and rearrange later. There was no time for that right now.

The clock was ticking.

She skimmed at a frantic pace, looking for underlined words, circled paragraphs, phrases that might stand out like a blinking neon sign on an otherwise dark highway. Most of the former pastors' writings were dull, boring. Outlines for sermons, ruminations on mortality, baptismal messages. There was simply so much to sift through, including the old Bibles—there were dozens and dozens of these—many of them marked up with notes in the margins and scribbles in the footnotes, resembling well-read college textbooks passed down from student to student. And there were not only the personal Bibles of the Clifford ministers from the last century but also *additional* Bibles from their own collections, accumulated over the years from their own travels, gifts from their own spiritual mentors. It was a sea of religious texts, and Rita was wading into it without a life vest, bobbing up and down, struggling for air. She was quite certain Clifford Island wasn't specifically mentioned in the original words of the Good Book, but the evil that dwelled here certainly could be.

It was ancient, the legends said. Billions of years old, as old as the earth itself, somehow sneaking into God's creation of the planet, worming its way inside. It lingered unseen, like a virus buried deep in a computer code, lying in wait for the right opportunity to show itself. According to the legends, of course. No one knew why this evil chose the Great Lakes region—but all forms of evil were random and unpredictable, Rita always thought. Clifford was no more or less special than anywhere else in the world. It was just a spin of the wheel that the evil resided here, a roll of the dice.

But maybe we are all on this island for a reason, Rita thought as she chucked another dusty book across the room. *Maybe we are equipped to handle it somehow.* The island was small, the fraternity tight. The islanders' roots ran deep, and they were all intertwined. Perhaps they were strong enough to shoulder this burden of evil.

If only I knew what to do.

If only I knew more than just the basics of the legend.

The pastor had often pondered the origins of the tale—speculating on just *where* these stories came from—and she never came to a satisfying conclusion. Rumors of evil lurking in the Great Lakes region had been passed down from islander to islander over the centuries—that much was known, and Rita was fascinated by them in her youth, dazzled by the almost forbidden nature of the stories. But where and when did they start? Rita theorized that the stories had perhaps originated on Shilling Island, the former home of the French Jesuit missionaries. Perhaps one of the missionaries had a vision of sorts, the pastor thought— maybe God gave the missionary a glimpse of the evil that dwelled in the Great Lakes, burdening this man with knowledge of the evil's unholy intentions—and the missionary shared what he saw, the game of telephone starting there. Or maybe an account of the evil existed in an early religious text, its origins outlined perhaps centuries ago. Then the book or scripture was lost, and all that was left were the oral retellings, the details changing a bit every time the story was told.

Or maybe it wasn't that way at all. Maybe nothing was ever written down or seen in a vision from God. Perhaps it began as a campfire tale to explain the mysterious disappearances, the myth twisting and turning a bit over time, and now . . .

It doesn't matter now, the pastor thought, stopping herself.

It's real enough, and it's here.

She dispensed with a row of texts, then another, and then another.

Scan, shake, toss.

Sift, flip, throw.

The pile of books and journals and Bibles on the opposite side of the room was growing, and the pastor's time was running out.

Two hours until the town meeting.

Ninety minutes.

Sixty minutes.

Rita's head ached. Her eyes burned. Her lower back was stiff; she hadn't sat down the entire time. Still, she was feeding off the adrenaline. It raced through her body, beseeching her to continue. She'd never read so quickly in her entire life, never devoured so much information in such a short amount of time. It was information overload, and she wondered at one point how many of these details she would retain, before quickly dismissing the thought. It didn't matter. She was only hoping to learn about *one* thing; the rest of the information wasn't important. She'd go back at a later date, God willing, and really absorb the texts. Respect her history, as she should've done years ago.

Thirty minutes.

Twenty-five.

She ransacked the folders and envelopes stacked on the bookshelves, discovering census records, family histories, deeds, soldiers' accounts from World War I, letters from islanders in the region over the centuries. Roughly one dozen of the Door County islands had been represented in the hundreds if not thousands of documents she'd combed through, but she'd read nothing concerning Shilling or Wallin Island, nothing referencing ungodly evil or disappearances of groups of people.

Rita's hands shook like she'd guzzled four cups of coffee, although she hadn't had a drop of caffeine the entire day. A stress lump emerged in her neck; it felt like someone had jammed a walnut down her throat, and now it was stuck there. She was biting her lip, grinding her teeth. But there was no time to take a step back; if she closed her eyes and counted to ten to gather herself, that would be ten seconds lost. Rita couldn't afford that. She kept going.

Twenty minutes.

She flipped through a binder three inches thick that consisted solely of maps and atlases, scouring the pages for footnotes and markings. Nothing.

Rita yanked a slim text from the shelf. It was an old comic book from the 1970s, its faded cover reading *The Most Spectacular Stories Ever Told from the Bible*. Emblazoned under the title was an illustration of a stone-faced Moses wielding a staff and clutching the Ten Commandments tablet, and the pastor paused, examining the comic wistfully.

She was short on time, but she couldn't help it. Memories charged through her—Rita recalled days long gone, being a young girl and reading comics with her father. The pair would read together into the darkest hours of the night, the young Rita caressing her father's hand, leaning into his broken and wheelchair-bound body, sometimes fiddling with the brim of his brown Stetson hat.

The memories made her miss him terribly, and it made her long for the comics of her youth. She could still remember her macabre collection: *Adventures into the Unknown. Spook. Skeleton Hand. Forbidden Worlds.*

Rita's eyes sparkled.

My goodness, life was simple back then, she thought. *I had my cowboy, and horror stories were just stories.*

Alone in the church archive room, Rita wished to smell her daddy's

Old Spice aftershave just once more, to feel his hand tousle her hair, and—

She snapped out of her spell.

There wasn't time for this.

Rita quickly ripped through the Moses comic, finding nothing important, and moving on.

Fifteen minutes.

The pastor began tearing through boxes, starting with the ones that appeared to be the oldest. Rita flung documents behind her at an exceptional rate, a flurry of papers flying into the air as if they'd been lifted by a windstorm. Records of all sorts from all eras—mainly from Clifford, but also related to other islands. Nothing seemed to be in any discernible order, by date or by category. It was a nightmare of file mismanagement.

One box down.

Two.

Five.

The documents kept coming. Receipts, articles of incorporation, tax letters, budget reports, meeting minutes.

She kept going.

And then she found something.

Nestled between a Clifford building report from 1937 and a list of committee duties from 1958 were four pieces of paper folded together into three sections. Rita unfolded the papers, and she first studied how they looked. The paper was thin and old, the ink faded and inconsistent, written by quill pen, Rita immediately assumed.

She scanned the contents.

Her eyes were immediately drawn to two words written in cursive near the top of the first page:

Wallin Island.

Rita quickly devoured the paper's contents. Her eyes were aglow, and her lips quivered.

She knew it wasn't by chance she'd found this.

She was *meant* to find this.

In a flash, the pastor was out the door.

"I say we burn the house to the damn ground," muttered Emery Knudsen, a Clifford islander since his birth in 1927. The vein in his forehead could be seen from across the theater. "It's the only way to be sure."

Smatters of applause and shouting emerged from the crowd. Other islanders sat stoically in their seats, arms folded, staring straight ahead. Every parent of the ten children was there, some of them in tears, most of them looking utterly lost. The youth pastor's widow was there, too, a snotty, balled-up tissue clutched in her hand. Rita was impressed they'd all come to the town meeting—everyone grieves on their own terms, the pastor thought, and that's quite all right. The Lord provides comfort in different ways. But the fact they were all *here* right now told Rita something about their devotion to the island.

The pastor sat in the front row of the cozy auditorium, newly discovered papers from the archive in hand. She'd arrived just as the meeting started, her heart racing, her chest pounding. Rita felt heads turn to look at her as she flopped into her seat—*I must be quite the sight*, she thought. She assumed she looked terrible, and judging by the expression on Sheriff Donovan's face when he glanced down at her from the stage, her suspicions were confirmed.

Donovan raised his eyebrows at Rita—*Everything all right?* they asked.

Rita nodded.

Everything's just fine.

She had what she needed, and she was eager to share what she'd found. But it didn't feel like the right moment.

Let's give these people a little time, she thought. *Time to blow off some steam. The grievers and the pitchfork bearers.*

"Okay, okay, let's just back it up a bit," Sheriff Donovan implored from the stage, motioning with his arms for people to settle down. The slim officer had bags under his eyes, and his shirt was partially untucked. Rita thought he looked like he'd aged ten years in the past two days. "We still don't know what we're dealing with here," the sheriff continued, "and let's not do anything rash. We still might find them."

There were a few audible groans and sharp sobs from the assembled crowd of about three hundred people. The community center theater was so full that islanders were sitting in the aisles and standing in the back. It was the largest single collection of people Rita had ever seen on Clifford. Some of these people she'd *never* even seen, not even in church. The pastor noticed the sweaty armpits of many of them, and she hoped the heat wouldn't lead to rash and quick thinking. She'd given sermons before when the air conditioner was broken, and she knew firsthand how impatient people could get. The tapping of the feet, the loosening of the top buttons. The *just finish already* faces.

The islanders certainly needed their wits about them, and a few of them didn't seem to have them—at least, Emery did not.

"*Might* find them?" the man yelled. He stood up and pointed his finger at Donovan. "You—we—know damn well what took those kids, and this is your fault!"

Rita considered chiming in to defend the sheriff—blaming Donovan for this was absolute nonsense; Emery had to know that—but she stopped herself. She knew Emery didn't mean it. This was cathartic for him, she reasoned. The pastor slid her thumb back and forth across the papers in her hand.

This is the answer.

Emery will understand; everyone will understand.

But it wasn't time yet.

And so, she waited.

"Let's everyone calm down," a voice said. Rita turned her head, and she saw Vincent Becker stand up. "This is all so terrible, and I think we need to give everyone a chance to speak who wants to. But we need to do it calmly and not let our emotions get the better of us, okay?" He looked down and locked eyes with his wife, Leota, who patted Vincent's arm. Rita tried to read her face. Leota looked bemused and somewhat detached, which wasn't surprising—the woman was seemingly always the outsider, no matter the occasion. It made perfect sense to Rita that Leota might be puzzled right now; Leota was an island transplant, and Clifford's history must be hard to accept.

Still, Rita thought. *At least she came. That says a lot.*

Donovan shoved the loose part of his shirt into his brown pants and nodded toward Vincent. "Thank you, Vince. I think it's important to hear from all sides to figure out what to do next, to make sure we are all on the same page. Emery, I hear your frustration, and maybe lighting fire to the house might be something we decide to do, but we need to come to an agreement first before anyone does a damn thing, you get me?"

Emery folded his arms and sat back down, and the islanders went silent.

Just wait until it's time, Rita thought. *Let these people settle down, and then you can convince them. You have a plan. God has a plan. They'll see.*

"Now," Donovan continued, "I want to say that whatever we discuss here is not meant to disparage any of the families. We don't mean to disrespect anyone, but we do need to talk through some difficult things. Right here, right now. All options are on the table, and we're open to suggestions. But point of fact, there are many here who believe the clock is ticking on this island, so time is of the essence."

Rita felt the silence in the room. There was no objection to that last point.

"Can I?" A hand rose from somewhere in the middle of the crowd. Peter Elliot rose to his feet. "I know that everyone knows the stories and legends and . . . well, I knew them. And I took them seriously, like I think everyone here did, but I never took them seriously enough. I never thought this would actually happen, but it did. I wasn't here that night, so I didn't hear or feel anything strange, but I firmly believe that this was the second culling, and I'm here to confess my culpability in not thinking this would actually happen." Peter paused to collect his thoughts. The guidance counselor was a man of a reason; Rita knew his words would go a long way with the islanders.

"Peter's right," a soft voice piped up. The woman did not stand, and Rita raised herself out of her chair to get a better look. It was Gloria Henderson, an island lifer in her early sixties. "I couldn't sleep that night; I was up all night thinking. I went for a long walk to clear my head. Something just didn't feel right. I think in my bones, I knew something was amiss. I was near the church around ten thirty, and I felt this dip in the temperature. For, I don't know, close to a minute, it must've been ten, twenty degrees. It was like finding a cold spot in a lake. I saw my breath in the air. Then the temperature suddenly shot back up. And that's not normal, it's . . . not possible. Something happened. Something unnatural and evil. May God look after those children, bless their hearts."

This elicited murmurs in the crowd.

"I think we should all leave," Peter said, still standing. "Right now. Each and every one of us. Pack up and leave this place before it takes us all. Because it will. Every single person in this room."

Oh, dear Peter, Rita thought. *God bless you, but that's not the right thing to do. You know it isn't. This island saved you, and now you want to abandon it?*

The guidance counselor took his seat, and the chattering in the crowd came to a halt. Rita felt an undercurrent of fear run through her, as she imagined it ran through everyone else. She knew the tragedy at Seminary House must be Clifford's second culling, the second time a disappearance of islanders had occurred. The Clifford Sickness had been the first. Everyone knew the legends, knew where this story was leading, and Rita interpreted the silence in the crowd as an understanding, a meditation on their own personal fates.

If this evil operated like it had on the other two nearby islands, then there would be a third and final culling, and soon. And this time everyone on Clifford would be taken. Perhaps in a few years, maybe a couple of weeks, heck, even this very night. This great and unbearable evil could pounce *at this very moment*, if it chose, in this theater, suffocating the life from the islanders and gobbling them up to a fate unknown. Not a single person would be spared, and the sustained silence in the theater confirmed to the pastor that the islanders were keenly aware of this grisly fact.

But they still hadn't heard from Rita.

They didn't know it yet, but their fates were not etched in stone.

"None of this is your fault, Pete," Donovan said.

Donovan is right, she thought. *It's my fault. If only I'd explored that archive earlier, I could've prevented this.*

She tapped her thigh impatiently with the pieces of paper.

"Enough of this *horseshit*," Emery shouted, rising to his feet. The old guy finally boiled over. "We all knew the stories, and *you* and *you*"—he jabbed his finger toward Donovan and Rita—"pretended like everything was fine. We put our faith in you, and now look what happened!"

Emery raged on, and Rita felt her moment coming.

"You all do what you please," Emery growled, "but I tell you where I'll be tonight if anyone wants to join me."

Almost.

"I'll be taking a barrel of gasoline and a torch to that damn house—"

Not quite.

"—and giving these poor families—"

Wait.

"—the justice they deserve!"

Now.

"You want justice, Emery?" Rita stood from her seat in the front row, and she turned to face the theater. "Only the good Lord can deliver the justice our children so rightfully deserve. And making embers out of that house will mean our children died in vain, because that is not what God has intended for this island, no sirree, Bob."

Emery's face was beet red, and he looked like he wanted to interject. But he'd never interrupted Rita before—not in conversation, not during one of Rita's sermons—and the pastor didn't think he was going to start right now. He took his seat somewhat sheepishly, and the islanders sat at attention like it was Sunday morning at Prince of Peace.

"This weekend, I've felt the most excruciating pain I've ever felt in my life," Rita said calmly. She moved along the front row to the aisle and began slowly walking toward the back of the theater. "And I know my pain is but a single drop compared to the ocean's worth of grief the families of our children are feeling."

She paused, collecting her thoughts. "I didn't know what I'd be saying here tonight. Didn't know until a few minutes ago, actually. And it won't come easy for any of us here. But I'll tell all of you this, right from the start. The Lord has selected us—you, me, everyone here on Clifford Island—as his soldiers, to do his bidding, and to keep the world safe from the evil that resides here."

She hadn't planned to say that word. *Soldiers.* But she liked how it sounded, and she noticed how the islanders perked up when she said it. Emery. Gloria. The whole lot of them. Rita raised her right hand, brandishing the papers to the crowd. It only felt a little wrong to hold a text aloft that wasn't a Bible, but the point needed to be made.

"I did some exploring in the church archives before this meeting, and I found something. Something very interesting. We aren't the first ones to experience tragedy up here, but we might be the last."

She sensed a charge in the crowd, running through every person—whatever the islanders seemed to be expecting, it certainly wasn't this.

"We all know the stories about the disappearances on Shilling, the disappearances on Wallin," Rita continued, lowering the papers. "But what you don't know is that someone actually survived the wipeout on Wallin—that island's great vanishing—and the proof is right here in the pudding." She carefully unfolded the papers and faced them toward the crowd. "What I have here are the dying words of a man found adrift in the lake after he was spared."

Rita paused.

"Let me say that again in a different way. This man *survived* the evil. He was not taken in the wipeout. And I have his story, right here."

The pastor turned the letter inward and began reading.

"*To those that read this: please know that some terrible and unholy force exists on Wallin Island, and I do not know its origin nor if it plans to stay or travel someplace else, only that I am the sole survivor of its madness. I left the island by canoe and I've been lost and adrift for eight days by my recollection— no food for five of them, no water for three, and I feel my sanity and life slipping away from me.*

"*I departed Wallin Island after every last man was taken, their screams hanging in the air, the evil seeming to descend on everything all at once. It swirled amongst the men and then down like a cloud, truly a suffocating and terrible force, so much so that it seemed to linger days after it happened, at which point I felt compelled to leave the island, as I did not feel I could stomach its crushing presence much longer, as if I was living on cursed ground destined to sink into the lake, creating some unholy abyss.*"

The islanders were spellbound. This was no different from one of Rita's sermons in church, and she had them at rapt attention again.

The pastor continued.

"*I do not know why I was spared from this calamity, yet I will share my story just the same, as I've led something of an unconventional life. I have lived on Wallin Island since I was a boy and experienced many tragedies, the first being the vanishing of my younger brother, Thomas, lost some seventy years ago. When he was very young Thomas disappeared into the night, never to return, along with some Frenchmen and members of the Potawatomi tribe. My brother was very close to me, and the incident left me with paralyzing pain and remorse, so much so that I could not move on from this tragic event.*

And so I remained settled into the solitary hut we shared, mourning his loss for the years and decades that followed, leaving his items in the same locations they resided the night he vanished. I did not so much as move Thomas's tools, plates, or bedding a single inch. Dust and grime collected around my brother's few belongings, yet I did not disturb them, as they brought me feelings of peace and comfort.

"'Still, the punishing grief of losing Thomas has never left me and stings me to this very day, perhaps buoyed by the undisturbed collection of his be-longings, of which I consider a fair balance for the solace they also provide. I know not for certain why my brother and the others vanished all those decades ago, nor why a number of men on the island also vanished just a few years prior, nor why some unexplainable force descended and took every living soul save me just days ago. I only know that Wallin Island is a place of tragedy, and I could not remain.'"

Rita paused for effect and surveyed the crowd. Emery had finally calmed down. The parents were no longer crying. Leota no longer ap-peared detached; she looked like one of the islanders, like she finally belonged.

Every eye in the theater was trained on Rita. She had them.

This was it.

"'I am quite old yet still retain my capacities, although I'm not sure for how much longer this will be the case. I feel my time here growing short, and I very much look forward to expunging this evil's stench that seems to stick to my soul, and to reuniting with Thomas soon.'"

Rita folded the papers and brought them to her side. She expected the naysayers to leap out at her, but there were none. The feeling in the theater was palpable.

The letter was legit.

"When I tore through that church archive just a few hours ago like a hurricane, I wasn't sure what I would find," Rita said. "Only what I wanted to find. Something that might bring all of us comfort, answers to the questions we all have about what happened, about *why* our children were taken. But I found *more* than that."

She waited a few seconds before continuing. The eyes in the crowd remained fixed on her.

"I found *hope*," the pastor said. "The Lord led me right to it. He commanded that I, that *we*, all of us in this theater right now, not abandon this island in the hour of our greatest pain. Instead, he is commanding us to stay. He has handed us the key to stopping this unspeakable evil that took our children." She again held out the papers for effect, shaking them a few times as she spoke. "This is the answer. It's right here, clear as a bell, you heard the poor man's words." Rita opened the letter again and reread a single passage: "*The punishing grief of losing Thomas has never left me and stings me to this very day, perhaps buoyed by the undisturbed collection of his belongings, of which I consider a fair balance for the solace they also provide.*'"

She brought the papers back down and noticed heads nodding in the crowd.

Rita felt the buzz.

They were getting it.

"It's right here on the page," the pastor continued. "If we honor these children and our youth pastor forever—if we do what the man in the hut did—the evil will spare us."

Her tone grew grave.

"And if we don't act, the evil will take all of us that remain here, just like it did on Wallin Island. And then it will move to the mainland, and it will eventually take everyone."

Rita sincerely meant every word. She believed she was *meant* to find that letter, that the letter was *meant* to find its way to Clifford Island somehow, perhaps falling out of a minister's Bible decades or even a century ago, or perhaps it was brought to the island among a trove of other documents and simply got lost in the jumble. Heck, it could've been a message in a bottle, or maybe God materialized the letter himself.

Did it matter?

Not one person in the theater doubted its legitimacy.

That's what mattered.

Rita returned to the front of the theater, and she felt the eyes of each and every islander following her. She turned around to face her flock.

"I know many of you want to leave this place, and I understand that, Lord knows I do. But I believe God has selected us—you, me, all of us in this theater right now—to be his soldiers, to stop this evil in its tracks, and make darn sure it never takes another person ever again. Now, what I'm going to propose isn't going to be easy, but I believe it's our best chance. Our only chance, my friends. To many of you this will sound radical, ridiculous, while to others it might feel like a stab to the heart. An eternal jabbing of the wounds you've developed over the past two days. And to those folks I sincerely apologize, because you don't deserve for your pain to continue. But I ask all of you to hear me out, and to keep an open mind."

A few heads nodded, and someone in the back blew their nose. But there were no objections. Not yet.

"What if we kept everything, right here on Clifford Island, the same, forever? What if we pretended that everything is as it was that terrible, unspeakable night, just like the man in the cottage did a few centuries ago? What happened to Pastor Tim and our children *was* the second culling—I think we can all agree on that—but what if when the evil wakes up a third time to terrorize and consume every person, it is confused? It looks around, smells the air, and it thinks—no, this is wrong. Something is not right. It will think, huh, the second culling just happened. It will think, my belly is still full. It is not yet time for the wipeout. So the evil goes back to sleep. And if it ever wakes up again—be it five years, ten years, fifty years, God willing—it will again be confused. Every time. Its belly is still full. The second culling occurred moments ago. It's not time yet. And the evil retreats back into its slumber."

It was a lot to take in; Rita knew that. She spotted eyes quivering, people processing and thinking. But no one told her she was a loon; she was not heckled out of the room. The pastor almost couldn't quite believe it, but she knew she had backup. She felt *the Lord* speaking through her, and she could nearly see his power floating through the air as if it were a small jet stream, weaving this way and that, entering every single islander in the theater and electrifying their bodies and souls with the Holy Spirit, convincing them.

Yes, this is the path we must take.

This is the only way.

"This won't be a walk in the park," Rita continued. "Grief fades over time. It just does, and that is a comfort provided to us from our protector up above, thank you, Jesus. But we have to keep that grief fresh. It must be done. Because the evil will know when it fades. It will know immediately, and then it will be time. For all of us, my friends. Here and on the peninsula, and only the Lord knows where next."

More nodding. No objections.

"We will honor our children, no doubt about that. They will always be with us, an integral part of our community, forever. But you, me, all of us—we must remain in June 17, 1994, for all time. This whole island can be just like the hut of the griever from Wallin, the man from the letter. And if we do that, if, let's say, if our homes don't change, our cars don't change, our clothes don't change—and I'm just spitballing right now; I haven't thought all of this through yet—but if we pretend our dear children passed on only moments ago, then our grief will remain. And the evil will rest once again."

It would take more convincing; she knew that. But the foundation had been laid. Seminary House wouldn't be destroyed; the island wouldn't be abandoned. Rita would need to further discuss her vision with Donovan and the island hierarchy, and even though her potential "rules" for Clifford sounded outlandish, she knew everyone would come around, if they hadn't already. Rita already had other brainstorms percolating for the island, more ideas she hadn't yet announced to the islanders.

No ferries.

No hotels or motels.

No renting houses or properties to outsiders.

A ban on music, movies, or TV shows released after the night the eleven were taken.

A 1994 fashion stop date.

She also imagined they would need a cover story for the rest of the world to make this work. An accident that explained the deaths of the children, something tragic but more human and ordinary, a tragedy that someone would hear about and think, *Oh, how awful*, but then move on with their day. Perhaps a fire, a poisoning, maybe a gas leak. Rita still wasn't sure. But they'd have to keep out the people asking questions: investigative reporters, paranormal researchers, tourists, wackos— every single one. A single person could blow the whole thing, dooming everyone, and Rita would not let that happen.

This would be hard, no doubt, especially fabricating a reason why their children perished. But the islanders were *strong*, and it could be done.

These were just the pastor's initial thoughts, and she knew they would have to fine-tune the details, reexamine the Clifford rules as times changed. Who knew what the future held, how different technology would look? Different laws would have to be proposed and amended, adaptations made. That was a no-brainer. But Rita was certain that the islanders could do what she asked—what the Lord demanded of them— and not necessarily just because it was their duty.

But because it would make it feel like those kids were still with them.

And that would lift everyone up.

Rita had the islanders in the palm of her hand, and she was confident that it would always be this way. But as she looked out over the crowd of her admirers and disciples, she knew many of them were not long for this world. No one was. At some point, Rita knew, they would have to find more islanders to carry on the mission. These people sitting before her would eventually die off; that was an inevitability. It seemed silly to worry about something that wouldn't occur for decades when the initial plan hadn't even been *enacted* yet, but Rita couldn't help herself.

Isn't that partially why we are in this mess right now? the pastor thought.

Due to a lack of foresight?

Her thoughts ran wild with possibilities, both for that very night and for years into the future. She had to account for every scenario. It was the only way this would work.

Yes, everyone in this theater will one day be gone.

But it won't be at the hands of the evil.

She wasn't sure when, but eventually, that day would come. And that was the only thing that filled the pastor with unease. It was the one part of God's plan that Rita hadn't quite figured out.

How would she find these people?

45

JENNIFER LARSON-QUINT

Fifty-Five Days until Willow's Disappearance

Jennifer Larson-Quint sat in her car on a quiet, leafy suburban street in Wildwood, Illinois, gawking at the two men in the van outside Willow's house.

The van was white with the words BILL'S BLUE STAR PLUMBING emblazoned on the sliding door in a striking blue font. There were two men sitting inside, and their outfits gave Jennifer pause. One was sporting a striped polo—the kind someone would wear while golfing—and the other was dressed in a patterned long-sleeve dress shirt.

Odd outfits for plumbers, Jennifer thought.

The men appeared to be watching Willow's house—casing the place, it looked like—and she spotted a pair of binoculars sitting on the dash inside the van. Perhaps Jennifer had seen too many movies, but she wondered if those guys didn't actually work for a plumbing company.

Is that . . . a surveillance van?

She wasn't entirely sure.

But if it was, those men inside were here because of her.

———————

Jennifer had met Willow some four years earlier, shortly after she'd been hired to teach advanced algebra and calculus at Wildwood High School. The women taught in different departments—Willow in English, Jennifer in math—and the departments didn't collaborate a whole lot. The two teachers mainly crossed paths at faculty meetings or in the cafeteria, where they shared polite hellos. Jennifer didn't have much time for chitchat, not being a first-year teacher, anyway. There was simply too much to grade, too many new lessons to plan, too much lay of the land to learn. Education was Jennifer's second career, and she desperately wanted to prove to herself that she'd made the right call.

She wasn't there to make friends—she was there to *teach*.

But that all changed when Jennifer read the October 2015 edition of *The Wild Times*, the Wildwood High School student newspaper. She'd enjoyed reading the first couple of editions of the newspaper that fall—it provided some nice insight into the pulse of the school, which she thought could help her make inroads on the path to tenure. When Jennifer read the October edition, she wasn't looking for anything other than to learn more about her school and maybe crack a smile or two, but then she flipped to page eight. She read the interview with Willow, started to turn the page, and then stopped. She thought for a bit, and then read the article again.

Contributing something to the greater good.

Ghosts.

Monsters.

There might be more to the world than just what we see.

Jennifer had a stack of quizzes to grade, but she knew those would have to wait. She had to make a call, had to tell someone about what she'd found. It wasn't clear-cut and wasn't a sure thing, but Jennifer thought it was a decent-enough lead to pass along the news.

I might've found someone, she needed to share.

Jennifer and Willow became friends not long after. Jennifer timed her walk out of the school one day to coincide with Willow's walk to her car. The two chatted, and a playdate was soon arranged between Willow's son and Jennifer's two kids. A friendship between the two teachers blossomed from there.

The women were open books with each other, save for a couple of important details. Jennifer never mentioned her connections to a place up north called Clifford Island. Her grandmother lived there, and Jennifer had visited the island as a child. She hadn't been there in some time, but she and her grandmother were still close. Certainly close enough for Jennifer to know all about the island's history—the stories, the legends, the mission. Jennifer was a believer, and she wanted to do her part.

Her part was to find others, and then, when the time was right, those others might be recruited to become a part of Clifford's true purpose.

The more Jennifer got to know Willow, the more she couldn't believe her luck in finding this person. Willow was simple, loving, had a good heart. The woman adored her son, adored her husband. But Willow's husband—he just wasn't a Clifford candidate, Jennifer thought. Dominic was a former psychologist who'd abruptly quit the profession in 2012. He wouldn't share too many details, but Jennifer was able to wrestle a few juicy tidbits out of him. He'd gotten close to many clients over the years—people suffering from night terrors, sleep paralysis, stuff like that. A few specific details really intrigued Jennifer. The first was something one of Dominic's patients referred to as "the skeleton man," a floating collection of bones that would hover over the patient at night, inches from the man's face. The other was something Dominic had seen in a few patients: finding words or phrases written in odd locations around the house and believing they were written by supernatural forces. It was Dominic's job to cure people from situations like these, to convince them that they weren't real.

But he just wasn't good enough to help them, Dominic lamented.

He even tried a different tactic, he said—giving his patients the benefit of the doubt, longing to see things from their points of view, trying to actively *believe* in the supernatural. That also failed. His natural skepticism would always bubble to the surface.

Those poor souls, Dominic told Jennifer, *they just couldn't realize that their own minds were creating their demons. And those patients finding the writing in their houses, they'd written those words themselves. They just couldn't realize it.*

He looked profoundly sad when he told Jennifer this, but she also thought she detected a bit of a smirk.

How anyone could believe in such things . . . he said, before trailing off.

Dominic's experiences were enough for him to quit psychology altogether, and he started a second career as a floor manager at a plastic-cup shipping facility.

It was probably for the best, Jennifer thought.

She was sure to never press more than she needed to, to not look like she was actively digging for information to report back to someone, which, of course, she was. For years, Jennifer and her husband were close with the Stones. The kids played; the couples went out to dinner every now and then. Jennifer and Willow commiserated about changes at the school—new leadership, those annoying evaluations the teachers were put through. Jennifer learned about Dominic's guilty pleasure of Walt Disney World—Willow enjoyed ragging on her husband about him being a "Disney Adult"; they'd visited with Jacob a few times, and Dominic seemed to enjoy himself even more than their son. *We would be able to afford to send Jacob to college one day*, Willow joked, *if not for Dominic's collection of souvenir resort mugs.* Dominic often openly fantasized about moving the family down to Orlando near his brother, and they could start new lives closer to the Most Magical Place on Earth with fresh ANNUAL PASSHOLDER stickers on their cars. Willow would just roll her eyes, and Jennifer found it funny. She *liked* Willow and Dominic, and she actually hoped nothing bad would ever happen to them and that they would simply remain potential Clifford recruits forever.

But then tragedy struck.

Jennifer sometimes wondered if it was cosmic. Whether the fact that she had seen Willow's interview and become close to her was the reason that Willow's son was hit by the car. It kept her up at night wondering. She eventually decided it was not cosmic but simply fortuitous for Clifford Island. One of these people had to work out at some point—as far as Jennifer knew, no identified candidate had ever actually come to Clifford Island. Willow would be the inaugural new recruit, the first of this grand Clifford experiment. And, if it hadn't been for Jennifer's legwork, no one might have ever found Willow. She would've been just another griever with a dead kid and a broken marriage, of which there were many, but not all of them were right for Clifford. Jennifer wouldn't let feelings of guilt strip her of her years of work. She was a Clifford soldier, and soldiers deserved to be celebrated for their bravery on the battlefield.

Jennifer and Willow didn't talk much after the accident. Willow retreated into her shell and quit teaching. Jennifer never saw it herself, but she heard about Jacob's bedroom.

Willow's shrine to her son, someone had described it. *Frozen in time.*

Jennifer found it morbid but perfect, the absolute cherry on top.

She'd also heard through the grapevine that Willow and Dominic were having problems, the husband considering moving to Florida. Jennifer pictured Dominic finally buying that annual pass to Disney World, spending his days at the Magic Kingdom or EPCOT, eating churros and taking artsy photos of Space Mountain or Spaceship Earth, always trying to capture that perfect angle.

And if he *did* do that, Jennifer found the whole scenario kind of fitting, Dominic retreating to his own fantasyland, a place where he could plug his ears and pretend that the outside world didn't exist.

His own Clifford Island.

No matter.

She had Willow, and she was definitely the one.

Now it was only a matter of time.

Jennifer was running errands on a Sunday morning about a week before Willow found the words *Clifford Island* written on her son's floor. Driving about town, Jennifer found herself near Willow's place. Curiosity got the better of her, and she turned into Willow's neighborhood.

She pulled off near Willow's home and gazed at the house, missing her old friend yet excited at the prospect of helping the Clifford Island mission at the same time. Willow's car was in the driveway, and Jennifer considered getting out and knocking on Willow's door, just to say hello. Her stare wandered to an upstairs window—Jacob's window, she remembered from her times visiting with Willow and her family—and Jennifer shuddered and looked away.

That's when she noticed the van.

The plumbing van with the two well-dressed men inside.

Binoculars on the dash.

Jennifer still wasn't sure if the men inside were surveilling Willow.

Could they be?

She considered the thought for a moment, deciding it was too peculiar a thing to actually find on a suburban street, before remembering that what was currently happening on Clifford Island might be the most peculiar thing to *ever* occur, anywhere, so why wouldn't there be a surveillance vehicle keeping tabs on Willow, the potential new island recruit? After Jennifer had reported to her island contacts that she'd found the perfect Clifford candidate, she had wondered how they would get Willow to the island.

Surely they can't just tell this stranger about what is going on up there, Jennifer had thought. *You can't just let slip this massive secret, a secret that's been kept for twenty-five years.*

What if Willow blew the whole thing?

They'd have to watch her, to learn more.

Maybe convince her to come to Clifford in some other way than just flat out inviting her.

She really didn't know, and that wasn't her job anyway.

The guys in the van—maybe it's their job.

Jennifer studied the men in the van for a few more moments. She couldn't explain it, but she could see it. They seemed to radiate with a divine purpose. As Jennifer's car passed the van, she solemnly nodded at the two men, and the men nodded back.

It was then she knew it was true.

They were soldiers, like her.

46

WILLOW

Two Days until Her Disappearance

Dom,

I'm upping the ante. I've got what I think is a pretty good plan. You remember the Great Depression oral history book I used to teach in my class? I met with the youth group kids tonight, and I proposed we do an oral history of Clifford Island. Each of them finds someone from the island and asks them to tell their story. Conduct an interview, record it, and now we have personal slices of Clifford Island history. I told the kids it would build community and all that. That sounds like something a youth group would do, right? It'd be the next step in my investigation. A way to learn a lot without putting myself out there. God, I'm using my youth group kids as my bulletproof vest now.

I mustered the best teacher enthusiasm I had, and I pitched this idea to the three kids who actually showed up to youth group today. And you know what I got in return?

Silence. Total and absolute silence. I was expecting maybe some groans or another form of teenage apathy, like an eye roll or whatever.

But I got nothing at all. And I felt like I'd been kicked in the gut. Look, this was a pretty reasonable idea. A church youth group should be doing community outreach, no? And every single person who ascended through the American public school system did the "interview a grandparent" assignment in middle school. So what the heck was so wrong with my idea? Why were these kids behaving like I'd asked them to drive a getaway car or help me bury a body? Steven's hands looked clammy, and he rubbed the thumb and index finger of his right hand together over and over again. Kayla's eyes shifted to the ceiling, and Lily just looked at the floor. And I've told this kid some pretty personal things, and now she chose to look away. If anyone would have had my back, I figured it would be Lily. That girl was supposed to be my ally in this. I thought we shared this unspoken connection, and now she was quiet. But her jaw trembled, almost like she wanted to say something but couldn't quite form the words.

I didn't say anything for a moment, that old teacher trick called "wait time." Just let the students sit there and ponder whatever question you posed to them. Give them time to think, to process. No need to fill the dead space with endless jabber like so many bad teachers tend to do. I used to receive high marks on my evaluations for my wait-time techniques during my lessons. But that was then. My other life. Now I just wanted to blurt something, anything at these kids.

So I did.

I let them have it. Well, not them, but I unloaded about all of the twisted things I'd seen on the island. The outdated technology, the thrift store clothing, how every car is shitty and old, the lunatics doing the exact same things every single day. Yeah, I've noticed that stuff, I told them. Only a fool wouldn't see it, blah blah blah. This only made them more uncomfortable. Steven fidgeted in his seat, and Kayla looked toward the exit like she was worried someone was on the outside holding a cup to the door, listening in. Lily looked like she was still lost in her own thoughts.

The moment my rant ended, I regretted it. These kids didn't want to hear that stuff from me. They lived it, every day. It wasn't a revelation. It was an attack on their way of life. And I'm telling you, Dom, there are weird things happening on this island that I can't fully comprehend, and maybe these kids feel complicit. Lily did call this place a "cult." Maybe they're scared or angry, or maybe they just won't help someone like me because they aren't supposed to. Right then, standing there in front of those three quiet teenagers, I'd never felt like more of an outsider and a pest.

And then I cracked.

Just, finally and utterly split open. I'd spent nearly five weeks on this strange and mysterious island, keeping my mission all to myself, not sure of whom I could trust. I still wasn't sure I could trust these kids sitting before me. How could I? But there is just something so genuine and beautiful about youth. Like the world hasn't corrupted you yet. I hoped it was true of these three kiddos. That maybe, just maybe, Clifford Island hadn't sunk its claws so deep into these kids that there was no turning back. I didn't want to imagine Steven, Kayla, and Lily—especially Lily— evolving into the other kooks on this island. I didn't want them to become what the other people had become. Headcases. Recluses. Lifers. Whatever the case, these kids were all I had.

So I told them the truth.

Well, pieces of it.

"I think this island might have something to do with the death of my son. And I just want to know why. I need your help."

I did the wait-time thing, for real. The old teacher in me. We sat there for I'm not sure how long. It had to have been one of my finest efforts. Lily eventually broke the ice.

"We will help you, Ms. Stone," the kid said. She looked to the others. "We will do the interviews. Right, guys?"

I had them, Dom. I finally had them. First it was me who cracked, and then it was them. Mainly Lily and Steven. Kayla only nodded along. A mixture of: *Of course this place is weird, Ms. Stone. We live a certain way because it's our culture. It's been passed down to us. No, thrust upon us. We don't have a choice. And you shouldn't be on this island. Strangers aren't allowed here. We aren't sure why you are here, but we want to help you.*

And if the floodgates weren't already opened enough, Lily decided to open up even further.

"I'm planning on taking this whole place down," she announced. She kind of blurted it out, like she'd been keeping it to herself so long and couldn't hold on any longer. The kid was practically bouncing in her chair.

Steven and Kayla were pretty speechless. I was, too. Lily told us that she and her mainland boyfriend were gathering as many documents as they could about Clifford and were hoping to publish an exposé of sorts. Be island stool pigeons, in a way. She wasn't sure what it would all look like yet, but that's where I would come in, she said.

"Ms. Stone, do you think your brother could help with this? Like, he could help us get it published?"

There it was. The reason Lily had been so interested in Harper's job. I told her that I wasn't sure, but probably. Obviously this wasn't something that belonged in the prep sports section, but he could be of guidance, at the very least. And yeah, he could point them in the right direction, or help them write it up.

He's a good writer, I told them.

Lily's eyes were buzzing with possibilities. She could add the interviews to her exposé, and that would really be the kicker, she said. But the other kids weren't so sure. Helping Ms. Stone with an oral history project was one thing, Steven said, but this was really hard-core. But the more Lily talked about it, the more Steven warmed up to it. He got excited, too. Kayla, though . . . the kiddo just looked a little shell-shocked. Lots of *I don't know about this* and *This might be a really bad idea.*

I thought back to her crying on my shoulder, telling me all about her teacher who she thought was missing . . . and, for a moment, I wanted to take everything back. This ball was rolling downhill *really fast*, and I hadn't totally considered what the oral history project might do to Kayla's psyche. And now, with Lily's thing, I was worried Kayla would completely crack.

Lily sensed it, too. She told Kayla something like:

"You don't have to be a part of this. I'll take the fall. Just do the thing for Ms. Stone, and I'll act like I took the recordings and made them a part of my exposé on my own, cool?"

That seemed to do the trick, and Kayla slowly calmed down after that. It's a pattern I've seen before. Kayla will always come around to Lily's side. Whether it's something as simple as what music to listen to during youth group, what bag of chips to open, what movie is better than another one—Kayla has an opinion, but she eventually rolls over and shows her belly to Lily. It's not the biggest surprise; I'd seen plenty of girls like Kayla throughout my years in the classroom.

It's just that . . . this seems like a *really* big deal. Bigger than Fritos vs. Doritos, obviously. I hope I'm doing the right thing. I hope Lily is doing the right thing.

But man, Dom, I wish you would have been there for this. It was almost like a group of rebels planning a revolution. I really hope these kids get out of here; this island has done a number on them. They were all letting out their lifelong frustrations, but it was in these hushed and whispered voices, continuously glancing toward the door, mindful of their cover being blown. And it was a good thing, too, because Pastor Rita popped in to say hello during our vent session. The three kids stiffened up immediately, and it was like nothing had happened. Just another normal, boring youth group meeting.

We dispersed soon after that. I chatted with Rita a bit on my way out, and I didn't mention the interviews. I probably *should have*, because she's certainly going to hear about it when the kids are gallivanting around town with microphones at my insistence.

I don't know, Dom.

I really hope I'm doing the right thing.

Later, bucko.
Willow

47

WILLOW

The Night of Her Disappearance

Dom,

Holy crap, it was pandemonium tonight. I was at a Saturday evening church service. We do these sometimes. And there's probably sixty or seventy people inside, and then this guy runs in screaming about the kids, and that everyone needs to come quick. The church starts to empty, slowly at first, but then faster and faster. No one quite knows what's going on. I go outside and follow the crowd up the path and through the trees a bit, and then I see it. Everyone sees it. Over by Seminary House.

A group of kids in camping chairs sitting around a laptop, some speakers, and a projector. They're projecting a movie onto the side of the house. Some superhero movie, I'm not sure which one. I see Iron Man and Spider-Man zipping around, and the kids are just hanging out like it's no big deal. Just enjoying the show. I recognize some of them. I spot Steven, Kayla, Lily, and Lily's boyfriend is there, too. I'm not sure of his name, but Lily's head was resting on the boy's shoulder.

Time kind of stands still. Everyone is just gawking at them.

Then, all hell breaks loose. Yelling, screaming. *Turn it off! What are they doing? Stop them, stop them!* The projector gets flipped over, the laptop slammed shut. Kayla's dad yanks her so hard that she slips and falls in the snow, and all of the kids are escorted toward the church like they are criminals. Lily's boyfriend follows her, and then Lily's father quickly turns and starts barking something at the poor kid. Lily is just smirking the whole time, kind of a *Yeah, what are you gonna do about this?* type look.

Most of us are still by Seminary House kind of stunned and getting it together, and I hear the cars speed away. I figure maybe everything is over, but then, I swear to God, the ground underneath us *shook*, like, literally shook. It was a small thing—as if earthquakes could be small, but you know what I mean—but it happened, and it was over before it even started. Everyone noticed and was looking around like, *Did you feel that?*

Did that actually happen?

I'm standing in this crowd of people, and they are all staring at Seminary House with bated breath. Almost like they are expecting someone to walk out. But the place is all boarded up, so I'm not quite sure what they are thinking is going to happen. Finally, Rita tells everyone to go on home, and everyone does just that.

This was an hour ago. I'm in my cottage, and every now and then I look outside. I can't quite see Seminary House from here, but it's so close. It's like I'm waiting for something to happen, but I don't know what.

I'll write more later.

Willow

CLIFFORD ISLAND

The Night of Willow's Disappearance

AUDIO RECORDINGS OF WILLOW STONE AND LILY BECKER

WILLOW: Are you sure you should be here right now?

LILY: What do you mean?

WILLOW: I thought you'd be on house arrest after what you guys did.

LILY: Oh, the movie? Just some harmless fun.

WILLOW: Really? Your parents looked like they wanted to murder you guys.

LILY: They wouldn't dream of doing anything to us.

WILLOW: It's just that . . .

LILY: What?

WILLOW: I'm nervous. Talking to you. And you're recording this, and—

LILY: Should I not? I have the other interviews, and I thought you would be the perfect last one. The "tell all" interview, or whatever, me and you. For the exposé. The grand finale.

WILLOW: I'm just feeling, what's the word, unsettled?

LILY: Why?

WILLOW: Can we . . . hold on. Let me close these.

LILY: If I'd known you were this nervous, I would have brought my clamps.

WILLOW: Your what?

LILY: Never mind. Look, Ms. Stone, I think it's fine. No one saw me come over here.

WILLOW: Are you sure?

LILY: Why are you freaking out right now?

WILLOW: I don't know . . . it feels like everything is coming to a head. This interview project, your movie at Seminary House, the earthquake after the—

LILY: What are you talking about?

WILLOW: After you guys left the church. There was a literal earthquake. Like, the ground literally shook.

LILY: Really? Like, an honest-to-God earthquake?

WILLOW: Yes. You guys might have already driven away, but I definitely felt it.

LILY: I mean, if you say so. Are you sure?

WILLOW: Lily, just—I'm sorry. I guess I have a lot of things on my mind. A lot of . . . questions?

LILY: Then it's the perfect time for an interview! We'll get some meaty stuff for the exposé. Some really emotional reactions. It'll be fine. Stop worrying.

WILLOW: Okay. You're right. I'll stop worrying.

LILY: You still do want to know, right? About what this place really is?

WILLOW: I do. Everything, yes. Everything.

LILY: Well, then, let me officially start by saying that I'm sorry.

WILLOW: For what?

LILY: For being a liar. We are all liars here. No one ever tells the truth about Clifford. But it's time that you know. If we are going to do this thing together, then you have to know.

WILLOW: Okay. That was pretty serious, but okay.

LILY: So, Clifford Island is . . . you know what? I don't know where to start. I told Connor and it took a while for . . . actually, hold up. Let me play you the other interviews first. That might help ease you in a little.

WILLOW: If you think they will help.

LILY: Yeah, a little freshman orientation, Clifford style. Okay, hold on, let me just—

RECORDING STOPS

NEW RECORDING

LILY: And, we're back!

WILLOW: Okay. I'm . . . getting it together here.

LILY: What do you want to know? Maybe it's better if I answer your questions.

WILLOW: Wow, I . . . okay, well—

LILY: Wait!

WILLOW: What?

LILY: Hold on . . . read this. For context. It's an article from 1994. So you know the real origin, that something actually happened here.

WILLOW: Where did you get this?

LILY: It's my dad's copy. I found it stashed away.

RECORDING STOPS

NEW RECORDING

LILY: Ready?

WILLOW: It's just so heartbreaking. How come I didn't hear about this? Why isn't this on the internet? I googled Clifford Island like crazy before I came here.

LILY: Things about the island are suppressed online. Like, deleted or hidden. It's crazy. I've seen it happen.

WILLOW: Are you serious?

LILY: I wish I wasn't.

WILLOW: How would you even do that? And eleven people dying? Ten kids? It's kind of a big deal. There's no way there'd be no trace of something like that.

LILY: It was a long time ago.

WILLOW: It wasn't that long ago.

LILY: We are a small island. And it was the same night as the O.J. stuff, so the media was kind of fixated on that. We got kind of lucky, in a weird way. There was probably not a lot written about it in the first place.

WILLOW: I guess, but—

LILY: There's a lot of people out there covering for this place. That's what I've heard. Like, all over. Making sure we stay a secret.

WILLOW: Lily, just give it to me straight. What is really happening here?

LILY: Okay, stay with me now. Because this is, like, really nuts.

WILLOW: Okay.

LILY: There's a curse, or a legend, I guess, about the islands up here. About Clifford. That before people ever came to the islands, something else lived up here first. Something ancient. Like a biblical terror. A demon. Most people call it "the evil" or "the First One."

WILLOW: The First One?

LILY: Because it was on these islands before anyone else, just kind of buried in the ground for billions of years. And then a few hundred years ago it emerged from a sinkhole or some kind of a hole, I guess, on Shilling Island. That's just the lore. You still with me?

WILLOW: Yes.

LILY: And this thing, this First One or demon or whatever it is, it needs to feed. It needs to eat. It lived on Shilling Island, then on Wallin, and now it lives here. It takes people, kind of in a pattern.

WILLOW: A pattern?

LILY: One sec. I downloaded this thing somewhere. Where do these things go? Files? Got it. Here, read this one now.

WILLOW: What is this?

LILY: It's a journal article Connor sent me. About the disappearances up here.

WILLOW: Okay.

LILY: Take your time.

RECORDING STOPS

NEW RECORDING

LILY: I'm not saying I believe in this stuff, but do you see the pattern?

WILLOW: I guess so.

LILY: A handful of people on an island vanish at the beginning of a century, then more people vanish about sixty or seventy years later, and then, poof, literally every person on the island is gone. Disappear completely. A total wipeout in the last decade of a century.

WILLOW: And this happened twice before. On the other two islands.

LILY: Yeah. Well, according to the legends.

WILLOW: And what you're telling me is, people think that this evil thing is here now? On Clifford Island?

LILY: Can I draw on that?

WILLOW: Hmm?

LILY: That piece of paper.

WILLOW: Oh, sure.

LILY: Here's my Clifford Island crib sheet of what people believe up here. Okay. Here's Shilling, Wallin, and Clifford. It's a straight line from Shilling to the mainland. The demon started at Shilling, stopped off at Wallin for a century, and now it's here. Last stop before Wisconsin. It takes some people, it takes some more, then it takes everyone, then it moves on to the next place. It always follows the same pattern.

WILLOW: Just so we're on the same page, people think the Clifford Sickness thing and the people in Seminary House dying are the same things that happened on the other islands? The vanishings leading up to a total wipeout?

LILY: We call them cullings.

WILLOW: Cullings?

LILY: You know, when animals are selected to be slaughtered. People around here call them cullings. When people vanish in big groups.

WILLOW: But those people in the house didn't vanish. It was carbon monoxide.

LILY: Again, I don't believe in any of this stuff, but people up here say the carbon monoxide thing was a cover. For the papers and the mainland, you know? Apparently, the coffins are empty. The kids and the pastor just disappeared from Seminary House. Like, there was nobody in the house that morning. No bodies. The First One took them. It was the second culling. The Clifford Sickness came first. But no one actually got sick. Those people just vanished, too. That was the first culling. Ms. Stone?

WILLOW: I'm sorry. This is just a lot to take in.

LILY: I know. I feel like I'm bombarding you right now.

WILLOW: Just . . . keep going.

LILY: But if other people found out about the demon that lives up here, it would cause a ton of annoying tourists and occult-obsessed weirdos to descend on our island and ruin our way of life, which would, I guess, jeopardize literally everyone. I don't know. That's the story around here, anyway. And they are lunatics, every last one of them. Ms. Stone? You have that *look* again.

WILLOW: Just, spacing out.

LILY: You don't believe me. And that's cool, because you absolutely shouldn't.

WILLOW: So, it's not just some really demented coping mechanism?

LILY: What?

WILLOW: I guess I thought maybe people just couldn't mentally move on. Like, something really terrible happened, and this is how people cope. That the kids dying in 1994 just kind of broke everyone. So nothing ever changed and people just lost their minds, and . . . oh, God.

LILY: What is it?

WILLOW: I just realized it. I think I've met some of these people. Some of the parents of those kids. I'm trying to remember . . . a man with a son who loved trains, Clarence and his daughter, I think . . . how come I didn't see it?

LILY: What do you mean?

WILLOW: They told me about their dead children, but the way they talked about them . . . it was like they died a week ago, a day ago, even. The tragedy up here, it just seemed so fresh to them. The wounds, you know? Time is supposed to heal them—heal *all* wounds, I guess—but these people . . . it's like no time has passed at all up here. Like they haven't recovered at all. How did I not realize this?

LILY: All those people dying, the kids—it's everywhere, but it's hidden, too. It's hard to explain. You have to kind of look closely to really realize it. People here still mourn, but we can't let the world know our secret at the same time. You know, because of the curse, the legend and all that.

WILLOW: But I have seen the names.

LILY: You have?

WILLOW: Hand me the article again.

LILY: Here.

WILLOW: I've seen these names before. Olivia. Shane, too. On that old schoolhouse with all the graffiti. They were painted all over the sides. Is that whole schoolhouse covered with the names of those dead kids? The pastor? They are, aren't they?

LILY: You have a keen eye. It's a little memorial, I guess. That thing you said a second ago, about it seeming like those kids died yesterday, it's—

WILLOW: Wait, wait, wait. I think I got it.

LILY: You do?

WILLOW: You are all pretending it's 1994, like, all the time. You are trying to trick the First One, this demon, to make it believe that no time has passed since the second culling. Then the total wipeout won't happen. So if it poked its head out of the ground and took a look around, the demon will always think it's the early '90s.

LILY: Holy crap, you said that, like, so intensely. Yeah, that's pretty much it. We're living in 1994-land up here.

WILLOW: Jesus.

LILY: I know, right?

WILLOW: The lack of technology, the—your dad's fake computer monitor in his office. He didn't used to work in real estate, I take it?

LILY: Yeah, no, I lied about that one. Again, I'm really sorry. The props are a thing, yeah. They are out in the wild here and there. They help with the '94 vibe.

WILLOW: He had a hidden DVD player.

LILY: You saw that? That was my mom's when she was alive, but my dad still uses it. He puts on a good show for everyone, but he skirts the island rules with the best of them. Not that he would let anyone know it. Funny how normal I'm making this sound, when it's anything but normal. It used to be weird to me, too, but I guess I'm just so used to it now.

WILLOW: I guess if you're raised that way. You grow up a certain way and people tell you what to—

LILY: That's why we have such bizarro rules up here. The clothes, the cell phones, the—

WILLOW: God, the cell phones. Some old guy broke mine on the first day.

LILY: Lucky you. If it wasn't him, it would've been someone else. But they don't really work up here anyway, so there's no real point.

WILLOW: You have one. You know, you're the only person I've seen with one, actually.

LILY: That's because I'm a total baller, Ms. Stone. I only use it at home, all covert-like. We are the lucky house with one bar of reception. It's my dad's concession to me so I won't full-on revolt from the Waco lifestyle. I wouldn't flash this thing in public. I break it out in youth group because that's pretty chill, but you know what I mean.

WILLOW: I'm sorry if I'm being weird. I'm still processing.

LILY: Take your time. It's a lot.

WILLOW: It's just . . . I get it. It makes sense.

LILY: Oh my God, stop it, you're freaking me out! I told you, I don't believe any of this demon crap. You shouldn't, either. It's just what most people think. And most people around here have lost their minds.

WILLOW: What does it look like?

LILY: What does what look like?

WILLOW: The First One. The demon. Allegedly, I guess.

LILY: I have no idea. I heard stories as a kid that it kind of looked like . . . oh my God, what are we doing right now! It's not real! We live in crazy town. Capital *C*. I'm serious, it's not—

WILLOW: Stop.

LILY: What?

WILLOW: Just . . . quiet. I think I heard something outside. Turn that off for a second.

RECORDING STOPS

NEW RECORDING

LILY: We good?

WILLOW: Sorry, I'm a bit edgy, I guess.

LILY: It's cool.

WILLOW: What about the *Groundhog Day* stuff?

LILY: What about it?

WILLOW: I've just seen a bunch of different people do the same things over and over. Like, watch the O.J. chase on TV, or take a walk downtown with a boombox at the same time every day.

LILY: Oh, the boombox guy! That's Dick. Super-nice guy, actually.

WILLOW: But why does he . . . do that?

LILY: Some people take it to extremes. Kind of weird, right? Even for this place.

WILLOW: Not everyone does it?

LILY: Nah. Mainly older people. People who were here when it happened.

WILLOW: So they're doing something they did the day the kids vanished? June . . . what was it?

LILY: Seventeenth. Yeah, pretty much. It's their gift to the First One. Their own offering of insanity. It's so normal to me now I don't even notice.

WILLOW: Like, are they told by someone to do it? You do this, you do that. A schedule or something? A script?

LILY: There's no real manual, I guess. And really, I can't explain why people think any of this works. I think it's more of the vibe people create by reliving things. You feel the vibe, right?

WILLOW: It's there, yeah.

LILY: People up here are doing their jobs well, I guess. I'll make sure to pass that along.

WILLOW: But some people think they should be doing *Groundhog Day* stuff. Or it helps them cope with what happened?

LILY: Different strokes. Most people just do the living-history thing, and they think that's enough. That it helps stop the demon. The monster, or, whatever. If someone wants to watch O.J. every night and think it stops the evil from killing people, well, more power to them. Whatever helps them sleep at night. I really don't think watching 1994 news footage over and over again helps anything, or that watching a movie made in the last ten years would set a creature loose on the island. Does the demon have IMDb? I mean, it's just so stupid. You agree with me, right, Ms. Stone?

WILLOW: I guess so.

LILY: It's just that, it's not about the monster at all, really. It's about people. No one wants to be the one to do things differently, because this is just life up here. It's our culture. And us kids go along with it, because this is the world we live in. And we've been warned our whole lives to keep our mouths freaking shut. You saw what happened tonight. When we watched an Avengers movie? Oh my God, Kayla's dad lost it. I thought the man was going to have a stroke.

WILLOW: She's fine, right? Kayla?

LILY: Slap on the wrist at worst. What are they going to do? Feed her to a demon? I mean, come on.

WILLOW: Well, this guy on the island—Larry, I don't know his last name—told me something he shouldn't have, and I think someone may have shut him up.

LILY: Really?

WILLOW: I think so.

LILY: I mean . . . anything's possible. But I've never heard of that happening before. Islanders usually take care of other islanders up here. Except me. People don't mind screwing over my future.

WILLOW: What do you mean?

LILY: I . . . It doesn't matter. Look, it's just, I dunno, so sucky up here. What us kids live with. We are raised to not know any different. Play along, or something bad might happen. Look at how we dress, for God's sake. Yeah, it's retro, and I think I look pretty cool, all things considered, but I don't have a choice in the matter.

WILLOW: Wait.

LILY: What?

WILLOW: Did you hear that?

LILY: I—

WILLOW: Hold on.

RECORDING STOPS

NEW RECORDING

WILLOW: I'll relax, I swear.

LILY: Really, it's fine. I just told you a lot of really strange stuff, so I don't blame you for being a bit uneasy.

WILLOW: What about the ghosts? Rita said they're unholy? Or not ghosts? I can't remember exactly what she called them.

LILY: Dead things.

WILLOW: Dead things. Do people do things to bring them back? Like, on purpose?

LILY: You think?

WILLOW: I guess I have no idea. I thought maybe people would like seeing their dead relatives. Like it would comfort them?

LILY: I don't know. I've always thought of them as unwanted demon by-product. You know, like industrial waste? We're supposed to be scared of them.

WILLOW: Right.

LILY: It's just something else we've been fed since we were little kids. That the demon can create illusions of dead people.

WILLOW: That's . . . interesting.

LILY: That's one way of putting it. And on Clifford, if you see a ghost—a dead thing, whatever—it wants you to follow it. It's like bait for the First One. To lure you in, you know? Play with your emotions. They supposedly know things from your life. Things that add to the allure, make you want to go after it. And if you follow it, then, sayonara. But I guess they are getting worse over the years, at least that's what I've heard. Like, the further we get from '94, the further we get from the wipeout that didn't happen, the dead things just get more erratic. The more they come back, the more messed up they are.

WILLOW: Wow.

LILY: It's just a classic ghost story, you know? That's supposed to teach you a lesson? Don't go exploring in places you shouldn't be. Don't wander away at night. Blah, blah, blah. We've been fed this crap since we were five years old. Have you heard about Mother Oga?

WILLOW: Mother Oga?

LILY: Yeah, it's some scary story we were told as kids. Just to groom us into thinking a certain way. It was never real, just kind of an indoctrination to the Clifford mentality, I guess. Never let go of old things in your life. Always hold on to the past.

WILLOW: Oh my God. I saw this children's book in the school. The message was the same, about respecting the past, never letting go. Mary and . . . God, what was it called?

LILY: *Mary and Patches!* A Clifford Island classic. More Brainwashing 101. Can you believe I grew up with this stuff and didn't wind up totally broken? It's a miracle my brain doesn't think it sees dead things. Ms. Stone?

WILLOW: Yeah?

LILY: You're doing that thing again. Where you are thinking really hard.

WILLOW: Oh, just, still processing.

LILY: Wait, you haven't seen anything, right?

WILLOW: Anything?

LILY: Like a demon or a dead thing. Ms. Stone?

WILLOW: No, I haven't.

LILY: Okay, thank God. You freaked me out for a second. I can't have another person in my life that sees these things.

WILLOW: Kayla?

LILY: I really hope she's lying, just to see what Pastor Rita would say. She's never told me about a dead-thing grandmother. I hope she isn't screwed up, you know? In the head, from everything we've grown up with.

WILLOW: Kayla is very . . . She seems fragile to me.

LILY: That's one way of putting it.

WILLOW: You probably don't know this, but she broke down in front of me a few weeks ago. She was worried about your history teacher.

LILY: Mr. Gordon?

WILLOW: He's . . . fine, right?

LILY: Oh, I don't know. I'm sure he's fine. We heard his brother got sick or something.

WILLOW: That's what Pastor Rita told me.

LILY: See, fine and dandy! Not that I'd trust anything the pastor says, you know, considering we've been lied to since we came out the womb. You mind?

WILLOW: The notebook?

LILY: Yeah. And can I bring that trash can in here? Shoot hoops? Sorry, I get a little restless sometimes.

WILLOW: Go crazy.

LILY: Ms. Stone, I'm just telling you what people believe. No one talks about this stuff, because you'd get in trouble. It's one big secret. But people are catching on. Mainly urban legend junkies. Hell, Connor was sort of clued in before I told him everything. If you lurk in the right corners of the internet, it's there. Swish! Two points.

WILLOW: Nice shot.

LILY: Thanks. It's just, I'm fed up. Others are, too. We're ready to move on from this place. Boom. Nothing but net.

WILLOW: I'm sorry I'm asking so many questions.

LILY: It's cool. Better for the exposé. Between this and the other interviews, I will have quite the collection. The shocking truth about Clifford Island finally revealed! Story at nine! Do you think your brother . . . What's his name again?

WILLOW: Harper.

LILY: Do you think he can really help us?

WILLOW: This is all just so wild. Even if it's not true—

LILY: It's *not* true.

WILLOW: Sorry. Even *though* it's not true, it's really, I don't know, interesting? You know, the things people say, the lives they lead up here. It's a pretty compelling human-interest story. I'm sure Harper can help you guys do something with it. Publish it in his newspaper, maybe a different one.

LILY: A magazine?

WILLOW: Yeah, maybe.

LILY: But you can give everything to him, right?

WILLOW: I haven't seen him in . . . gosh, it's been a really long time.

LILY: But you have his address, right? And you could just call him?

WILLOW: Do you want me to do that? From everything you've told me, and the things I've seen up here . . . I don't know, Lily. I'd just be really worried about you guys. It sounds like you'd make a lot of people really upset.

LILY: I'm flattered, Ms. Stone. Really, I am, but no one is going to hurt me. Trust me.

WILLOW: This will sound really cheesy, but—

LILY: Oh man, here we go—

WILLOW: Just let me finish! I want to see you guys get out of here and make something of yourselves. You deserve it. You've been through so much. I can't even imagine.

LILY: Well, thanks, Ms. Stone. That wasn't too cheesy, I guess. Just . . . give me a little more time. We have a few articles, the recordings—let me see what else I can get. Then you'll call your brother?

WILLOW: I will.

LILY: I'm just . . . so ready. Everyone here is a liar or totally brainwashed. My dad, Pastor Rita, everyone. I've had it. They want me to stay forever. They even sabotaged my chances at a basketball scholarship. But I won't let that stop me. Ten for ten!

WILLOW: Where are you going?

LILY: Anywhere that will let me play ball. I just have to work harder now. Play better. Send letters to schools. I don't know. I'll think of something.

WILLOW: And you're sure they'll let you leave? Even after you expose everything?

LILY: They better. Like I said, islanders take care of islanders. I think in the end they'll let me go. Most people don't go anywhere. Most people stay here until they die. And I get it, you know? This is our island. Our home. Our families are here and will always be here. Our parents don't want us to go to college. They flat out tell us that. So islanders grow up and never leave, everyone keeps their mouths shut about all the weird stuff up here, and life goes on. It's super messed up but super normal at the same time. Does that make sense?

WILLOW: Why don't people leave? If this demon, this thing, needs to be fed and might kill everyone at any moment, why don't people leave?

LILY: Take a look at the map. You know what's to the bottom left of Clifford, right? What the arrow is pointing to next?

WILLOW: The peninsula. The mainland.

LILY: Yep. No one really talks about any of this much. We just don't. But I think people are worried about the First One getting to the peninsula. You know, hitting up Wisconsin. Pastor Rita said it in her interview, didn't she? Like, what would happen then? If it took everyone here and moved on, what would happen to the rest of the world? That's what my dad told me once, when I was younger. I think people feel like it's their job to stay. Saving the world, I guess. They are soldiers. Like what Pastor Rita told Kayla.

WILLOW: *I am a soldier.*

LILY: Bingo. And the soldiers' duty, or whatever, is to honor the dead eleven forever and pretend that no time has passed. Then maybe the First One will spare everyone and never leave. The wipeout won't ever happen. We'll confuse it. Stop it. Stop the evil, you know? Maybe it will lie dormant forever. Ms. Stone?

WILLOW: Yes?

LILY: Does any of this help *you* at all? With your son?

WILLOW: I don't know yet. It's just so much, you know? I think it will?

LILY: Then I'm glad. This was the right thing to do.

WILLOW: Lily?

LILY: Hmm?

WILLOW: What is inside Seminary House? Where all those kids were that night. It's just still . . . there.

LILY: The house?

WILLOW: Yeah. I remember Rita saying something about water damage? Mold, I think?

LILY: I don't know. I've never been inside.

WILLOW: Huh.

LILY: Dang it, missed one. We're good, right?

WILLOW: What's that?

LILY: The recording. I think I covered it all.

WILLOW: Oh.

LILY: Just hit the—

49

KAYLA

The Night of Willow's Disappearance

Her parents looked pissed, but they hadn't yelled. Kayla was a bit surprised. They weren't the shouting types, but this seemed like the perfect moment for some raised parental voices. After the movie incident outside Seminary House, the Elliots merely escorted Kayla to the car, and the family drove home in silence. Kayla sat in the back seat with her younger brother, Kyle, who perched both of his arms on the armrest of the door, his forehead on the window, the trees rolling by quickly as the family minivan accelerated through the darkness. Kayla wasn't sure if Kyle was smirking—*my sister is in big trouble and I'm not, sucks to be her*—but she imagined he might be.

And he'd be right, she thought.

Only, when they got home, their parents immediately left the house. Kayla assumed there would be an immediate lecture or a "family meeting"—it was never a good sign when those two words were uttered—but the Elliots merely dumped the kids and hit the road again.

"Back in a bit," Peter Elliot muttered.

This must be really bad, Kayla thought.

Kyle went to his room and shut the door, and Kayla nervously paced the house. Her thoughts began to run away from her, which was maybe what her parents wanted to happen. Better than a lecture, perhaps. A self-learned lesson.

Why did I let Lily drag me to that movie?

God, why do I always listen to her?

We could've unleashed the First One tonight.

It could've been a slaughter.

The wipeout.

All because I'm too scared to stand up to Lily?

Really?

I'm pathetic.

Kayla walked inside her bedroom, and she studied her belongings and the decor like she was looking at them for the first time.

She'd been *so good*.

The Trapper Keeper that still held together. The peach-and-seafoam-colored Kaboodle where she'd kept her cosmetics since her parents allowed her to wear makeup. The transparent telephone with the orange, curly cord. The lava lamp. The *Rolling Stone* covers pinned to her closet door: Winona Ryder in overalls; a shirtless Anthony Kiedis; Courtney Love in a black dress; Blind Melon sans any clothing whatsoever. And the posters, *so many posters*—the album covers for Pearl Jam's *Ten* and U2's *The Joshua Tree*; the cast of *Beverly Hills, 90210*; a Nirvana group shot; *Jurassic Park*; *Edward Scissorhands*—and this was only the area directly above her headboard.

Kayla's gaze traveled to the corkboard hanging above her desk. It was sprinkled with Polaroids of Kayla and her friends—Lily was in just about every photo. Smiling at a church barbecue. Arms around each other on the basketball court. Some of the photos were from when they were small children—playing with toys in kindergarten, clutching stuffed animals at their first sleepover.

Kayla looked to her bed, and she smiled. There sat Eddy, her stuffed brown hedgehog she'd had since she was a toddler. Eddy was stained;

his stitching torn too many times to count; the strands of thick black yarn running across the hedgehog's back and head ratty and matted. Eddy was much plumper in the old photos—his stuffing had flattened over the years; he wasn't much of a stuffed animal anymore. More like a limp rag doll now.

But Kayla loved him just the same.

And it wasn't just because she'd been trained to love Eddy. Sure, she could recite the *Mary and Patches* storybook by heart, and there was a time as a kid when she'd believed the Mother Oga legend, which was what the island elders wanted.

Take care of your old things. Never let go. Or something really bad will come for you.

No, Kayla cherished Eddy for reasons more than that. It wasn't because she was brainwashed or someone had told her to love him or tricked her into holding on.

It was simply the right thing to do.

Even if no one had told her to grip the beloved thing from her past tightly and never let go, she would've done it anyway. She just loved the little guy, and she'd never once had an urge to get a new one.

This was her choice.

This was who she was.

Kayla turned back toward the corkboard, and she smiled at the picture of the Eddy of old. He'd clocked some city miles the past fifteen years—soda spills, drops in muddy puddles, lost at the beach for a few days—but he'd made it through okay.

The girl's smile faded. She noticed Lily's stuffed animal in the photo—a black Labrador that Lily had named Cindry. Kayla remembered the games they'd play with Eddy and Cindry, how the girls pretended the two animals were best friends who would eventually get married and have some sort of hybrid hedgehog/canine offspring. That never happened, of course, and not only because they were stuffed animals and that simply wasn't possible.

Lily had thrown out Cindry years ago. Just tossed him into a garbage can without a second thought. Kayla had been there when Lily had done it, and she hadn't said a word.

Kayla's eyes narrowed, and she bit down on her lower lip.

I'd say something now, she thought.

I swear to God I would.

A moan from outside caught Kayla's attention. It was a familiar sound; the girl knew exactly what was making it. The moan turned to coughing, to spitting, to choking. The sounds grew louder and closer.

Kayla wasn't scared this time. She'd been frightened before and had hidden under her covers, or sometimes under her bed. When those hideous noises arrived, she would grip Eddy tighter and tighter, praying that her love of things that were old and ancient would ward off the evil ghosts of the night.

No, Kayla thought. *These aren't ghosts at all. What did Pastor Rita call them?*

Dead things.

That's right.

Ghosts don't exist.

These are spirits sent by the demon that dwells here.

The girl walked confidently to the window and threw open the curtains. She saw what she'd expected to see, only it was worse than the last time.

It was always worse than the time before.

That's what these things *did*.

She saw a creature that looked like her dead grandmother, sprawled out on the ground on its belly, grabbing clumps of snow and pulling itself forward through the backyard with its one remaining arm. The dead thing grunted painfully with each movement, blood spilling out of its mouth and running down its ripped and torn overalls—*its body looks more shredded each visit*, Kayla thought. The dead thing's eyes were crazed, locked on to Kayla's, imploring her to come outside and say hello.

KAYLLAAAAAAAAAA, it moaned.

The thing had never managed to actually say Kayla's name before. Not in any of its other visits. But it could this time, and there was malice in her voice.

KAYLLAAAAAAAAAA.

It choked on its own blood again and rolled onto its back, watching Kayla with upside-down eyes, its gray, tangled hair splayed across the snow. The girl in the window didn't budge. She felt the familiar urge in her belly begin to spread, that feeling of absolute guilt, that it was *her fault* her grandmother had been shredded and killed by that boat propellor. But this time, she didn't want to go to her. Kayla didn't long to follow the dead thing into the night. She fought the urge with everything she had, and replaced it with anger and rage. She *hated* what type of person she'd grown into, despised herself for being so meek and allowing others to make choices for her.

No, Kayla wouldn't hypnotically follow her grandmother, and she'd no longer let Lily make decisions she was capable of making herself. She took a deep breath, and the bout of fury dissipated. Kayla suddenly felt at peace. She watched her grandmother now almost detachedly, and the dead thing's jaw clenched shut and it gritted its teeth.

It looked irritated.

It knows, Kayla thought. *It knows how confident I am now.*

It knows I've changed.

It can't affect me.

The dead thing's arm reached into its chest and clawed around inside its own mangled body—a sight that would have once sent Kayla diving under the bed—and it pulled out its own heart, holding it aloft for Kayla to see. The organ dripped blood onto the dead thing's face, and it greedily lapped up the falling droplets with its tongue. Then the dead thing started *laughing*, spurts of blood misting out of its mouth and spraying the white canvas of snow all around it.

Is that blood really there? Kayla wondered. *Is it all an illusion?*

She wasn't sure. All she knew was that this was the worst it had ever been, and she decided that she was to blame. That stupid movie on Seminary House—her refusing to stand up to Lily, yet again—had caused this. The First One was close, she thought. Coiled, ready to strike. It was almost ready to take them all. And it was her fault.

Somehow, she had to set this right.

The door to Kayla's bedroom squeaked open, and Kayla yanked the curtains closed. Peter Elliot stood in the doorway and looked at his daughter, and he didn't appear mad or disappointed. On the contrary. The man looked calm, determined. He didn't seem to notice the gurgling and hysterical laughter from the demon's spawn in the backyard. Either he didn't hear it or he couldn't hear it—Kayla still wasn't sure how these dead things actually operated.

Her eyes shifted to the floor and then back up at her father. Their eyes met, and Kayla nodded. Peter nodded back. No words were necessary.

Peter moved to the side, and Pastor Rita appeared. She took a step into Kayla's bedroom and opened her mouth to speak, but Kayla spoke first.

"Pastor Rita," Kayla said. "There's things I have to tell you."

"Yes, honey?" the pastor replied.

There was so much to tell.

Mr. Gordon. The real purpose of the interviews. Lily's plan. Willow's brother.

And Kayla was ready to tell it all.

50

HARPER AND LILY

The clock on the Beckers' mantel read 2:57.

Vincent had retired to his bedroom around two thirty, leaving me alone in the living room downstairs. I turned over on the sofa again and again, trying to get comfortable, trying to decide what to do next.

A sliver of moonlight crept in through the drawn curtains, casting a soft light on my duffel bag on the floor next to me. I imagined leaving the island with a pile of documents and audio recordings stuffed inside the bag—things Vincent wanted me to have, the trade for helping his daughter. But I didn't want those things. I wasn't looking for *evidence* or whatever Vincent was offering me. I wanted Willow.

Because my sister might be on this island, alive.

The idea was compelling, and the more I spun the thought around, the more I believed it. Vincent didn't know for sure what had happened. She'd just been taken to the house, he'd told me. But the way his eyes dropped and looked away when he'd said the words, how his voice cracked and trailed off—it was clear what he thought the end result was.

He knew what was inside that house.

The evil that stirred within.

The *demon*.

Before I'd crashed on the sofa, Vincent explained the entire sordid history of Clifford Island and the other islands just off the Door County peninsula. The cullings, how the demon eventually takes everyone. And that thing currently slumbered inside Seminary House, the place where Willow was last seen. It was madness—every last word of it—but the sheer audacity of what Vincent laid out for me was dulled by my singular motivation of finding my sister. Because, despite mass disappearances and an ancient evil that dwelled on Clifford, Vincent didn't know Willow's true fate. That's what I clung to.

And so, Seminary House beckoned.

It was close—probably a twenty-minute walk from Vincent's house—and I'd pressed Vincent to help me get inside, but the man wouldn't budge. He wouldn't even entertain the *thought* of it, even as I hypothesized different ideas for sidestepping the sheriff and prying off the plywood that covered the front door. Vincent stared blankly ahead, absently nodding now and then, and it felt like he wasn't really listening to me. I was simply a chatterbox child to him, tugging on his shirt and jabbering on and on about something unimportant, and his nods and noncommittal "uh-huhs" were the best he could muster to make me feel heard.

I suggested a diversion of sorts—like fireworks or a car alarm, something like that—something to draw the sheriff away from Seminary House, and it was then that Vincent reached his breaking point. He actually threw back his head in laughter before telling me:

"Aren't you getting this? Donovan is the least of your concerns. We can tie him in a sack and toss him in my trunk. Won't make a lick of difference. That evil inside is what you should be concerned about, and sure as you're born, you aren't leaving that house after you step inside."

Pastor Rita was the only one who ever went inside, he'd told me. Presenting offerings to the damn thing. Little gifts from the islanders.

"Guess it likes that." He'd shrugged. "But no one else who goes into that place comes out again."

I wondered why Vincent was so concerned for my safety, before re-membering that he *needed* me alive, to eventually leave Clifford and be his daughter's protector of sorts.

It still wasn't crystallized—what that arrangement would look like. Vincent didn't need me to smuggle the kid off the island—there were boats everywhere, and people could physically leave at any time; noth-ing was stopping Lily herself from taking off at a moment's notice—Vincent simply wanted me to *be there* for her when she eventually chose to leave Clifford, which he was absolutely positive she would do one day soon. He wanted me to stay in touch with his daughter, keep tabs, en-sure she was safe from the "people on the outside." There was quite the Clifford network out there, he said, people who would do anything to keep the secrets of the island safe.

"And my daughter is a threat," he'd explained. "I can't trust a single one of them. And I can't be there to help her."

Vincent was staying here, he told me, forever. He was a lifer, com-mitted to the island, entrusted with keeping its secrets and continuing its mission. He'd mentioned the exposé again that Lily had been plot-ting, and how we couldn't let Lily go through with that—in no way, shape, or form. I was to talk her out of that in any way necessary, and she would listen to me, he hoped, because I was Willow's brother, be-cause I was an outsider, someone not from Clifford.

"She's never listened to a single thing anyone has ever said here," he'd joked. "But maybe she'd listen to you."

I assured him that I would help his daughter, and I even shook Vin-cent's hand, sealing the arrangement. There was certainly more to dis-cuss, but Vincent told me he needed some damn sleep and we'd regroup in the morning.

And that was that.

I'd flopped onto a lumpy sofa in the Becker living room, the house quiet, dawn approaching quickly.

I felt like I was running out of time.

Lily sat on her bed, her right leg shaking, her heel rhythmically tapping the carpet.

The girl was antsy, anxious.

She felt she needed to act.

It's put-up-or-shut-up time, Lily thought.

The girl had heard everything. She'd tiptoed downstairs when her father had arrived home with Harper, and she'd stood on the second-to-bottom step for their entire conversation, bracing herself against the wall, listening intently.

She'd imagined her father would be disappointed she was doing this. Lily had told her father that she was done with everything. Done snooping around, done with the pranks, done with stirring up trouble. Heck, she was even done with basketball, the thing she loved most. This whole island, it was all too much for her. Everything was tainted.

She still didn't know what really happened to Willow.

A demon in a house can't take people.

It just can't.

For weeks, Lily had wondered if Willow had been murdered and if she was responsible for that, the guilt heavy on her mind, sleep only coming a few hours a night. No one talked about Willow anymore. It was like the woman never came here, never existed. All Kayla had said was:

She went inside the house. And she didn't come out.

It gave Lily butterflies.

Still, Lily assumed it was all lies, all brainwashing. She couldn't believe anything anyone said around here. A person had done something to Willow, Lily thought, something unimaginable. It wasn't a demon.

But then she listened to her father talk to Harper.

She heard all about the mother she couldn't remember, and she listened closely as her father told the story. He had never talked *that way* to Lily before, not about things on Clifford. His wavering voice, his yearning to actually leave and to protect her—this was new. Lily had always felt loved, no doubt about that, but she'd always felt that her father's love for her was equal to his love for Clifford. He was devoted to the people, committed to the mission. Lily had always figured that when the chips were down, her father would somehow find a way to keep her on the island forever.

But that wasn't true at all.

Her father was choosing her.

Her happiness.

He would stay, but he wanted her to leave.

And he wanted Harper to help keep her safe.

Lily opened up the drawer to her nightstand, and she lifted out the false bottom. It was where she kept the letters. There were a handful of them, unmailed letters written from Willow to Dominic, and Lily was the only person who knew they existed, the girl assumed.

The night Willow vanished, Rita had come by Lily's house and told her the jig was up—Kayla had told her everything, the pastor said—and she demanded that Lily give her the interview tapes she'd played for Willow that night, including the girl's interview with Willow for the exposé that never came to be.

Kayla, Lily thought, *that turncoat.*

Lily handed over the tapes, and she was never sure what the pastor did with them. Destroyed them, she guessed.

But Lily never told Rita or anyone else about the unmailed letters.

The girl had found them in Willow's nightstand. Hours after the surprise visit from the pastor—and a very long, tense conversation with her father—Lily had snuck out in the middle of the night to warn Willow that she might be in trouble, but the cottage was empty. Willow was gone. Lily poked around and found the letters in Willow's nightstand, a whole stack of them, never mailed. Their contents surprised even Lily, especially one detail.

Willow had seen a dead thing.

Her son.

Sitting on her bed, letters in her hand, Lily still didn't know what to think, what to believe. So many people in her life seemed to think it was all true.

Kayla.

Her father.

And now Willow.

Lily had never considered that even a single iota of what people said about Clifford was true. She'd erected a mental block so strong and so thick that it was impenetrable.

But for the first time in her young life, the girl was having doubts. Before Willow, the island was all lifers. Born and raised Cliffordites. Emerge from the womb and the indoctrination begins. Then Ms. Stone arrived. An outsider, oblivious to the islanders' ways, uncorrupted by a lifetime supply of the Clifford poison.

And she *saw* a dead thing.

It was right there in the woman's letters. She hadn't told Lily this—in fact, she'd told Lily to her face that she *hadn't* seen a dead thing—but the letters seemed so personal, almost like confessionals. Willow did not want this fact known, but she still needed to unburden herself all the same. Lily didn't know why. It didn't really matter.

All that mattered were the seeds of doubt that had been sown in the girl's mind, and she'd been trying to sweep them away, refusing to let them take root. But they were starting to grow, and Lily was having trouble stopping them. She felt that mental block—that wall she'd built in her head, brick by brick—beginning to topple.

Lily tossed the letters back into the drawer, then secured the false bottom into place, shoving the drawer closed when she was done.

She couldn't believe in this stuff.

Wouldn't couldn't shouldn't.

Any idea to the contrary needed to be strangled in the cradle.

Lily dropped her head and massaged her temples with her fingers. This was all too much, and she needed that wall in her head rebuilt, to recapture the fire and intense hatred she'd had for Clifford for as long as she could remember. She needed to become the Lily of old, the rebel, the troublemaker. She wouldn't let the islanders win. No way.

Fuck that.

She had to act. Lily grabbed her cell phone off her nightstand—she had not placed it in the safe that night, and her father had been, well, busy—and the girl dialed Connor. It was extremely late, but she knew he'd answer. He did, very groggily.

"Lily?" Connor said, the sleep dripping from his voice. "What's going on?"

Lily's response was strong and measured.

"How quickly can you get here?"

51

WILLOW

The Night of Her Disappearance

Willow didn't know what to do with the information she'd received. She needed to process everything first. After Lily left, Willow sprawled out on her dingy sofa. Willow wholeheartedly believed she had seen Jacob's spirit here and she was open-minded about the existence of the supernatural, but this was really too much to take in. Saving the world? The truth was paralyzing, and doing nothing seemed like an appropriate response for the moment.

Still, it wasn't the fate of the planet that consumed Willow's thoughts.

It was how she'd lied to Lily. On the matter of dead things, she'd been crystal clear:

She hadn't seen one.

Willow wondered why she'd lied so easily to Lily when the kid was pouring her heart out, spilling the beans on decades of Clifford secrets.

Do I still not trust her? she considered.

What is wrong with me?

It had somehow felt like the right thing to do in that moment, and she'd just rolled with it. She needed Lily to trust her, and she knew Lily didn't believe in that kind of thing.

What would the kid think of her?

It was all making her head hurt, and Willow fidgeted on the sofa. She closed her eyes and then pinched them open. She did it again and again. Each time she opened them, Willow wished she'd been magically transported back to Illinois, back to Jacob's bedroom. She craved her old rituals more than anything. Just one more time dusting the dresser. Mopping the floor, burying herself in her boy's sheets. She yearned to clean Jacob's windows and breathe in the scent of glass cleaner. God, that sweet ammonia. She wanted to huff the damn stuff.

Just take me there. Just one more time.

It would help her think more clearly, give her clarity. Because at the moment, she had none.

Eyes closed, eyes open.

Still there.

Still at the cottage.

This isn't working.

Thoughts zoomed by. Willow didn't have much time to contemplate each one before the next whizzed into the frame.

Am I going to be killed by a monster?

God, these poor, poor kids.

Why didn't I tell Lily the truth about the things I've seen?

I've seen my son.

Oh my God. I'm just as crazy as the lot of them.

A gentle knock on the door interrupted Willow's thoughts. It didn't sound like Rita's knock. Willow had grown to recognize that one. And it was late. Too late. Had Lily returned? She tiptoed to the door and touched the handle.

"Hello?" Willow said through the door.

No response.

She pushed open the blinds and looked outside. Standing about thirty feet away, in the snow and in the moonlight, was Jacob. The boy didn't look pristine anymore. The road rash on his face was raw, and his jeans were bloodied and torn. His right arm hung lower than the left, just kind of dangling there, limp and broken.

He'd come back.

Actually, not he, Willow thought.

It.

Emotions ripped through Willow, and her whole body shuddered.

Snowflakes swirled around the creature, and it simply stood there, as still as stone, like it had found peace in the eye of a small, snowy hurricane. Then it turned and staggered away.

Willow froze.

She remembered what Lily and Rita had said about the First One and the dead things. How the demon used illusions to trick you, how they toyed with your emotions, goading you into following them. How they always came back worse than before.

More messed up, Lily had said.

This wasn't her son hobbling away into the night. Willow felt quite sure of that. It was just one of the dead things. The first time Jacob returned to her, her boy was himself, uttering the *I'm sorry* Jacob-ism, going right for Willow's heartstrings. But that version of her son had disappeared right before Willow's eyes; it had changed into something else entirely. Her boy would never utter those cursed words, *Run to your mother*. Jacob had never even known about that dark chapter of Willow's past. But, somehow, the First One knew. It had burrowed its way into Willow's head and merrily sliced away at that old wound, because that's just what the demon did. It *knew things* about your life. Then it sent a dead thing to torment you, to throw those nightmare words back in your face solely to twist the knife just a little bit more. And now that dead thing was lumbering away in the snow, imploring Willow to follow it, which she was absolutely certain that she should not do.

"He's not real, he's not real," Willow said to herself. The words came gasping out. She was moments from retreating to her bedroom and burying herself under a mountain of blankets, content with hiding from whatever tricks the demon had up its sleeve.

But then her conversation with Lily came back. The girl was so certain it was all a lie. There was no demon, no First One. Just brainwashed people who would stop at nothing to hold on to their traditions. This lost and hurt boy outside her door, her own *child*, must be here for another reason. Willow wasn't sure if it was her own psychosis or if there was something else, perhaps something magical and different about Clifford Island that made her see the things she saw. In that moment, her lips trembling and her breath fogging the windowpane, she decided it didn't matter. For God's sake, this was her son outside. Her everything. The entire reason for her existence. She had spent nearly two years mourning Jacob and keeping his bedroom as her personal shrine to him, then upended her life and moved to this mystifying speck of land to chase a wisp of a clue he might have left behind for her.

And now, this was it. Do-or-die time. The answers Willow needed were mere steps away, and if she let Jacob just disappear into the wilderness, she might lose him forever.

How could she not go to him?

Willow frantically looked around the cottage. There was so much to consider, and she had precious little time to consider any of it. One thought, though, stuck out from the bunch.

I might never come back here.

And someone has to know what happened to me.

It was a dreadful thought, but Willow knew it was true.

But what to write, and to whom?

How can I leave a message to someone that no one else will find?

Willow felt her heart racing. Her fingers twitched; she nearly bounced up and down as her eyes hurriedly scanned the room.

Kitchen, drawers, silverware, sofa, television, painting . . .

An idea popped into her head.

Good enough.

Willow dashed to the coffee table and ripped a page of paper from the notebook. She desperately began to write:

Dear Harper,

There are things I need to tell you about

No. There wasn't time for this.

Jacob was outside.

Heck, she might've already lost him.

She needed to summarize everything quickly and concisely.

Words and sentences hurtled by inside her head, and then she wrote:

Run to your mother.

Don't follow them.

It was the best she could think of in the moment, the time slipping away, her *son* perhaps slipping away, and hopefully Harper could decipher this somewhat coded message.

There are monsters that live here, and you should not follow them.

Like I'm about to do, she thought.

She knew it was wrong, but she just couldn't help herself.

Couldn't *stop* herself.

Willow raced to the kitchen and yanked out an envelope from a drawer. She scribbled *Harper* on the outside, jammed the paper inside, and shoved the envelope into the backside of a picture frame on the wall, tilting the painting ever so slightly, just like when they were kids playing that secret agent game.

He will come to look for me.

He will know what it means.

He will know to look here.

Please God, if something happens to me, let him look here.

Willow grabbed a flashlight from the junk drawer, and she bolted out the front door to find her son.

A blast of snow and wind to the face greeted Willow as she hurried outside. The Christmas lights she'd hung on the cottage twinkled. Her eyes quivered as she examined the forest and the path cutting through it, and Willow wondered if she'd taken too long, if that forty-five-second head start she'd given Jacob meant that she'd now lost him forever.

The boy was waiting for her.

He was just off the path, looking back at Willow from about twenty-five yards away, and when their eyes locked, the boy staggered away.

She followed him.

HARPER AND LILY

A hand jostling my shoulder woke me up.

Everything felt strange. The pillow, the cushions. Even the air smelled different. It wasn't my apartment; I knew that immediately.

Where am I?

I shot upright, acclimating myself to my surroundings, trying to shake off the confusion. I finally regained my bearings.

Clifford Island.

The Beckers' sofa.

And I'd fallen asleep.

I certainly was not asleep anymore, and I found myself face-to-face with Vincent, who looked panicked.

"Where is she?" he asked frantically. "Did you see her leave?"

I blinked a few times, the grogginess still with me. It was still dark, not yet dawn.

"I, uh," I stammered. "Lily? Um, no, I was—"

"Wait," Vincent interrupted. "Do you hear that?"

I focused in. I *did* hear something. It was faint and in the distance, but it was there.

Rhythmic. Steady. A clanging.

A bell.

Vincent and I shared a look. Even in the dimly lit room, I saw terror in the man's eyes.

I didn't know how far away this bell was or how much time I had, but I knew it was my best chance. If we could hear it, so could the sheriff. So could everyone on this island, I imagined.

Vincent bolted for the door. He knew where he was going.

And I knew where I was going.

Lily pulled down on the rope again and again.

It was heavier than she'd thought, and when she'd begun, she was worried that it was so old that the rope would simply snap off, or perhaps the bell would tumble down from its perch at the peak of the steeple. She'd never heard the schoolhouse bell ring before, and she wondered when it had last been rung.

Not since '94, that's for sure, the girl thought.

But the rope held firm, and the bolts securing the iron bell to the tower held tight.

And now this sucker was *ringing*, and Lily instinctively pinched her eyes together and hunched her shoulders to brace herself against the noise. It was *loud*. She figured it would be, but it still caught her off guard all the same.

Lily kept pulling and pulling, getting lost in the groove of the cadence she'd created, wondering how far the sound was traveling.

Certainly from end to end of this tiny island, she thought.

Heck, I bet someone might hear this thing in Gills Rock or Sister Bay.

And you know what?

Good.

I hope the whole damn peninsula knows what I'm doing.

When she was satisfied that she'd caused enough of a disturbance—

Rita, the sheriff, and her father would soon be here to investigate the ruckus, she knew—Lily released the rope from her hand. The bell rang again, followed by a much lighter clang as its speed slowed, and then the ringing ceased. Lily found herself alone in the darkness, savoring the moment, relishing her return to form.

This would *really* piss people off, she knew.

And now all that was left was hope.

Hope that this diversion would work, that Harper would be able to find a way inside Seminary House, that Connor would be there to help him escape the island. Her boyfriend said he needed ninety minutes to sneak out, hitch up his dad's boat, drive to the dock, and make it to Clifford. It would be tight, Connor told Lily, but he'd be able to do it.

It's gonna be really freaking cold on that lake, he added, *but you can count on me.*

Connor was the security net, Lily figured. She'd assumed if this plan all worked out, Harper would find something in that house— something linking the islanders to Ms. Stone's death, maybe even Ms. Stone's body, Lily thought—and then he'd have to get out of there, *fast*. These islanders wouldn't let him leave with that knowledge, that evidence. Connor could then hustle Harper off the island.

As long as he makes it on time, Lily thought.

There was no way of knowing. There was no cell reception at the schoolhouse—all she had was Connor's word that he could make it on time and locate Seminary House.

And so, she waited for the cavalry to arrive.

Lily sat down on the floor of the schoolhouse and wrapped her arms around her torso, rocking back and forth a little bit, warming herself from the cold. She wondered if she should have told Harper her plan—given him a heads-up of sorts—but she'd deemed that too risky. He might've asked her not to do it, deferring to her father's judgment. Heck, her father might've overheard their conversation himself. She couldn't risk that. Lily had had to go full stealth mode, leaving her house quickly and quietly.

Harper had to have heard the bell, she thought.

I know this worked; I just know it.

Sitting cross-legged on the cold schoolhouse floor, Lily's thoughts began to wander. She began contemplating the gravity of her decision, what it actually meant for the island, just how spectacularly she'd broken the Clifford rules. If anyone else had done such a brash and forbidden thing, they'd be terrified of the repercussions.

Supernatural repercussions.

What would Ms. Stone think of me doing this? she thought.

Her thoughts kept running, speeding forward, faster and faster, and Lily was unable to stop where they were going. They charged ahead, landing again on Willow's unmailed letters, the ones dictating how Willow had seen her dead son on the island, how she had become a Clifford believer. Lily didn't *want* to think about those things, but her thoughts landed there just the same. She again felt the mental wall she'd built inside her head cracking, the bricks tumbling, the gaps widening.

And then she heard something.

Inside the schoolhouse.

Footsteps from behind her, near the front of the schoolhouse where there was no door.

No, I've been alone this whole time, Lily thought.

I'm imagining this.

She closed her eyes anyway.

The footsteps shuffled toward her, and Lily rocked faster and faster on the floor. The footsteps were closer now, and Lily felt a presence behind her.

This isn't real.

I'm tricking myself.

This is what the people here want.

This is how it happens.

It's just mind games.

That's all it is.

Lily stopped rocking.

The girl felt a tickle on the back of her neck.

It was like someone gently breathing on her.

I won't let them win.

No.

NO.

A fingertip.

Tracing her neck near her hairline.

STOP.

IT'S NOT REAL.

Lily ducked her head between her knees and screamed. The sound bounced around the walls of the schoolhouse, and then the silence returned.

She lifted her head.

The girl felt totally alone.

Then she heard another noise. The sound of an approaching car.

It was coming, fast.

She saw the headlights through the open door of the schoolhouse, and they were joined by more.

Then another set arrived.

The cavalry was here.

Lily smiled.

WILLOW

The Night of Her Disappearance

Willow knew where her son was leading her.

There was no other place.

It was where those kids vanished all those years ago.

That strange, cursed antebellum house.

Everything flowed from there.

She hadn't known that until tonight, but now she knew.

The board that once covered the front door had been torn off. It was lying on the front porch. The front door was wide open, and Jacob slipped inside.

Willow felt her chest tightening, a lump in her throat forming—but she didn't give her nerves a second thought. She didn't know what her future held, what she might do the next morning or the day after. She didn't know where she would go or whom she would be with a week from now. Maybe she would catch a flight to Florida and knock on Dominic's door. Maybe they would work it out. She just didn't know.

All she knew was, this was it.

This could be the last time I ever see my son.

Any parent would do what I'm about to do.

She went inside.

The dampness nearly overwhelmed Willow, and moonlight crept in wherever it could.

"Jacob?" she called out.

Her voice echoed around the large home, and her call was not returned.

Willow shined the flashlight back and forth, taking careful stock of her surroundings. To her left was a formal sitting room. Red couches, glass coffee tables, spiderwebs. An open book sat draped across the arm of an easy chair, as if someone had just put it down moments before she walked inside. Two empty and grimy drinking glasses sat on a wooden end table. A small art easel stood in the center of the room, and a piece of paper littered with ticktacktoe games hung from the long clamp along the top. One of the games was unfinished, and two crayons lay on the floor beneath the easel as if they'd been carelessly dropped and never picked up. To Willow's right was an office with an open door. She spied a desk and large bookshelves, everything covered in cobwebs. Willow breathed in and immediately covered her mouth. The place smelled like an old library book.

But where is all the water damage? Willow thought. *The black mold? This place was supposed to be unsalvageable, and it doesn't look that way at all.*

She wasn't surprised that it was all a lie.

The island was full of them.

Willow heard a rustling ahead, and she pointed the flashlight in that direction. Willow caught a glimpse of something, just a blur, dashing down the hallway and around the corner.

She followed the movement, the narrow beam of the flashlight penetrating the darkness. Willow crept through the hallway and into the kitchen. She bumped into the kitchen table, and porcelain rattled. Plates were laid out on place mats; table settings surrounded the dishes. Empty pitchers sat in the center of the table.

Has this been here for twenty-five years? Willow wondered.

She pressed forward.

Willow entered the living room. Her foot caught on something, and she stooped down. It was a sleeping bag, and it was caked in muck and dust. It looked like it'd been there for decades, but the bag was partially unzipped as if someone had just laid it out that night.

She stood, and the flashlight threw a shaky beam on the objects in the room. Pillows. Backpacks, some half-opened with clothes hanging out. More sleeping bags. About ten of them, she figured. Willow stepped between them, and she accidentally trampled over a Monopoly game board. Cards and game pieces scattered around the room.

Her mind flashed to her son's bedroom in Wildwood. She thought of the time she had spent keeping it pristine. Mopping. Dusting. Changing the sheets. Keeping it exactly the same as it had been the day of Jacob's accident. If someone had torn through his room, Willow would be beside herself.

She dropped to her knees and hastily gathered up the game pieces and cards, but she abruptly stopped. Willow spotted an object across the room, and her eyes zeroed in. Even through the darkness she could make out the colors and the precise features. Blue-and-red design, embroidered logo along the bottom, leather pocket with the intricate lacing.

It can't be, Willow thought.

But she knew that it was.

Willow stood up and, like she was in a trance, shambled over and picked up the small item, which was sitting on a table along with other objects. She flipped the item over and looked at the back side. There, near the bottom of the baseball mitt, were the initials written in black permanent marker.

J.S.

Jacob's baseball mitt.

It had been resting next to a host of other items, and Willow examined them as she clutched the glove in her hand. A brown cowboy hat.

A white teapot with pink flowers. A pair of aviator sunglasses. A model ship. Military medals, a watercolor palette, gardening shears. More and more and more.

Nothing seemed to go together, and nothing seemed to *belong* in this house—they couldn't have been there during the children's sleepover, Willow decided. Everything seemed to have been placed there more recently; the arrangement of the items reminded Willow of a memorial table at a wake or funeral.

And then she spotted it at the back corner of the table. A tattered white garment, folded neatly. Willow placed the glove back down and unfolded the piece of clothing. It was a nightgown. Just like the one Willow had donned outside Esther's home.

Gloria's nightgown.

The original one, she immediately knew, the one taken by Pastor Rita.

Willow recoiled a bit, thinking that she shouldn't be touching it—that it was wrong, in some way—and she quickly refolded the nightgown and placed it back where she'd found it. She picked up the baseball mitt again and buried her nose in the pocket. The woodsy leather aroma reminded her of shuttling Jacob back and forth to baseball practice, of doing mom things, of her boy simply being *her boy*, of the blissful simplicity of her previous life in Wildwood with her family.

And then she knew.

At that moment, in the creepy old house filled with memorial items and the relics of a terrible, wretched night long ago, Willow knew with absolute certainty why she had come to Clifford Island. Why she had felt compelled to live up north, what she truly had in common with the islanders tucked away from society. It was all so glaringly obvious now.

I was chosen by these people, Willow thought. *To be one of them.*

She had felt it before at Gloria's mailbox, but she really felt it now.

God, I do exactly what the islanders do. I am one of these people.

I grieve like they do.

That's why she was here.

I'm the perfect new recruit for their cult.

She'd been singled out.

Chosen.

The words on Jacob's floor. That job posting appearing, *poof*, in her inbox. It had all happened so fast.

These people had found her.

Her son had not been keeping secrets from her. There was no divine calling to visit Clifford Island. Willow had been duped, plain and simple. Her mission was not her mission.

It was someone else's.

She had been *selected* to live with the islanders forever and ever, because she believed what they believed. That living in the past was just a better way to live. Jacob's bedroom was her personal, miniature Clifford Island. Her pilgrimage to this place and grieving much like the islanders did was no coincidence. Her arrival was by design.

These cultists brought me here.

But why did they take my boy's baseball mitt and put it inside this horrible time capsule along with those other things?

Then the whopper of all horrifying thoughts struck Willow.

Did they arrange my son's accident?

Willow didn't have time to weigh the consequences of that thought. At that moment, she just wanted to find every single Monopoly piece and put them back exactly where they'd been. House here, thimble there, hotel right here, stack of cards there. It was the right thing to do. Only, she would do it wrong. She knew every inch of her son's bedroom, but she didn't know where these pieces went. She cursed herself, cursed her intrusion. Willow felt like she was desecrating a mausoleum.

And now Willow *truly* began to believe. She believed what the islanders believed. That this 1994 fantasy was actually working. And it was *this* house. The kitchen, the sleeping bag, the game board. This was what made it all work. It all stemmed from this place. They had pulled the wool over the evil's eyes. The island had a system in place, and she was disrupting it. Her actions were putting others in danger.

A sound nearby interrupted her thoughts.

Giggling.

She heard *giggling*, from a doorway. She knew her son's voice, and this wasn't it.

"Hello?" Willow said. "Who's there?"

The baseball mitt dangling from her left hand and flashlight aiming forward with her right, Willow approached the doorway. The ancient hinges creaked as she pushed it open. She saw stairs leading to a basement.

Willow poked her head inside. A cold draft pelted her face. Basements were always cold, but this one felt much colder. She shined the light down the stairs, but she saw nothing.

"Mom?" a shaky voice called out from below.

It was him.

It was her son, and he sounded scared. He needed his mother. The flashlight beam shook quickly. Willow couldn't hold it straight.

"Jacob?" she whispered. She didn't mean to whisper it. But it was all that would come out.

"It's me," Jacob called from the darkness. "I'm hurt, Mom. Can you help me?"

His meek voice almost shattered Willow completely. Her knees were wobbly and her arms felt like jelly, but Willow mustered whatever strength and courage she had left. Still holding her son's baseball mitt, she moved to go downstairs. But then she heard more voices. More giggling. A few voices shushing the others.

It sounded mischievous. It sounded to Willow like they were using Jacob to goad her down there. Willow figured these were the illusions; these were the tricks that Lily had warned her about.

This was the First One's doing, calling her downstairs.

She hadn't felt it earlier, but she certainly felt it now.

Willow felt in danger.

The giggling turned into words. All the voices—children, she decided—began saying the same thing, in unison, led by her son.

"Run to your mother! Run to your mother!"

She instantly regretted everything. Regretted following her son. Coming into this house. Not fully recognizing the danger of Clifford Island earlier.

"Run to your mother! Run to your mother!"

She regretted ever taking this godforsaken job to begin with. She wished she was back in Wildwood, squeegeeing Jacob's bedroom windows again and again.

There, she'd be safe.

Here, there was an ancient demon in the basement using her son as bait.

"Run to your mother! Run to your mother! Run to your mother! Run to your mother!"

She ran. Willow bolted through the living room, past the game board, over the sleeping bags. She was through the kitchen, down a hallway, and back in the foyer.

Only, the front door was shut.

And there was pounding from outside.

It sounded like something was being *nailed* to the house.

Willow dropped the flashlight and threw open the door, finding a large sheet of plywood covering the entry. She flung her body into the board, but it gave way very little.

Pound. Pound. Pound.

She heard the hammering coming from different places. There were numerous people outside nailing the entry shut. She could tell. Willow screamed and yelled and pleaded. She hurled herself against the board, again and again. Each time it gave way less and less.

When she realized she was trapped, she collapsed onto the floor.

The baseball mitt fell from her hand to her side. She thought she knew what was about to happen, and she wouldn't cry. Willow wouldn't give them the satisfaction.

The pounding stopped. She heard several pairs of footsteps walk away down the porch steps, but she still felt someone's presence on the other side of the plywood.

"I know it's you," Willow said, her back to the board.

The person didn't respond.

"I just want to know one thing," Willow said.

Silence.

"Did you kill my son?"

The person on the other side of the board cleared her throat.

"Heavens no," Pastor Rita said. "I'm offended you would even *think* such a thing. We are opportunists, not monsters. We wanted you, sweetie."

Willow felt only the slightest bit of relief. It wasn't much of a feeling, but it was there. But then she realized what was about to happen to her, and that relief quickly dissipated. "Were you always planning on killing me?" she asked.

"That was never the plan. We were hoping you'd be an asset in our fight."

"Because I was perfect for this place?"

Rita chuckled. "Almost, dearie, almost. It took us a long time to find you. It wasn't easy. Not everyone is capable of believing in the magic of this island. Circumstances need to be just right. And we were this close. You were this close to joining us and helping us carry this forward. Why did you have to ask so many questions and get those kids all riled up?"

A rumbling. Downstairs, below. Something unnatural was stirring. Willow heard it, and she felt it. It was coming.

"Did you really think I'd see all of these crazy things and just keep my mouth shut?" Willow asked.

"Quite frankly, yes," Rita said. "That was the plan. Call it what you will. Misguided? Foolhardy? I'm still working on it. I expected hiccups, but not like this."

"Hiccups?"

"Your nosiness, for lack of a better word. I was hoping you'd slowly accept this island for what it is, that you'd find comfort and peace. Most people would go running for the hills—and, trust me, if you even float the idea of what this place is to an ordinary person, you lose them from the first syllable—but you aren't most people, Willow. I thought there was something special about you, something that made you different from the rest. I thought you'd want to live on this island and respect our mission. That seeing your son again would be so extraordinary that you'd not take it for granted. And we never told you anything because . . ."

Rita paused for a moment. "You've seen *Beauty and the Beast*, I'm sure, right?" she asked.

Willow didn't know how to respond. "I mean, yes, but, what does that have to do with—"

"Have you ever wondered why the candle and the clock never told Belle the reason behind the curse? About the spell on the castle? Because if Belle had known she had to fall in love with the Beast to lift the curse, it never would've happened. It had to remain a secret. That love had to blossom organically. That's what we wanted to happen with you. And when you discovered our little secrets, you could've talked to me about what you saw at any time. That might have been your final step to acceptance, and I was honestly expecting you would, dear, but you didn't. Or you could've kept your mouth shut and carried on, honoring your boy's memory and helping everyone here who copes and grieves, people just like you. But instead, you enlisted the help of our precious children. You tried to blow the whistle on us, planning on taking everything to your brother. To the *press*. Did you honestly think you could get away with that, that we would let you do that?"

How does she know? Willow thought.

There were so many possibilities, and Willow couldn't latch on to one.

Her taped conversation with Lily from hours earlier . . .

Perhaps an eavesdropper had been outside her cottage . . .

Maybe Rita overheard the kids hatching their plan at the church . . .

It didn't matter.

All that mattered was that Rita was right. Willow had been planning to help Lily with her exposé, planning to blow the whistle—spilling the island's secrets hadn't been her first inclination when she'd seen her dead son, or when she'd had her epiphany on the road across from Esther's place. But upon Lily's insistence, she was going to do it. She'd been planning to call Harper, to assist the kids in getting their exposé published.

Rita's right to be pissed.

Her desire for revenge, it's justified.

"I was wrong about you, Willow," the pastor continued, the irritation and anger dripping from her voice. "There will be no island coronation for you. Only this. I wish I'd never found you."

"How did you find me?" Willow squeaked out.

"We have people on the outside," Rita said, almost disinterestedly. "They research and send us leads."

"Leads?"

"We look for grievers, first and foremost. People who have lost everything. But they have to feel like they came here on their own. That something called them here, otherwise it's just too crazy to believe. So, we create *callings*, if you will."

"He didn't write *Clifford Island* on the floor," Willow said. "I know that now."

"You're right. We put that there."

Willow considered when this could've happened. She'd been home *a lot* in the year and a half following Jacob's death, but someone could have snuck in at any time, maybe when she was sleeping. Willow remembered hearing noises in the middle of the night and mistaking them for her son, *convincing* herself that it was her son, that his tragedy had never occurred.

The footsteps in the hallway, Willow thought.

Seeing a figure in the dark outside my bedroom door.

That wasn't my mind playing tricks on me.

That was an intruder.

"Our people are very, very good at what they do," the pastor continued. "The fact that you had nightmares as a child and believed in monsters made you the perfect candidate. You know, that red-haired creature you mentioned in that interview from college? Our people dug that up."

"How did you find that?" Willow asked.

"As I said before, our people are very good," Rita said. "It's such a shame, really. You could have grown old here. Had more babies. Helped us keep this train rolling down the tracks."

Willow slid farther down the plywood. She had been duped about everything. Her son having secrets, the Clifford Island connection scribbled on Jacob's bedroom floor, the red-haired monster having any significance whatsoever. None of it was true. She was the perfect mark, and she'd fallen for it. Hook, line, and sinker.

"Does it really work?" Willow asked. "The 1994 illusion?"

"Clifford Island is a special place," Rita said. "We do things a certain way around here. People want it this way. They want to pretend those kids are still alive, you understand? You know what that's like."

Of course Willow knew what that was like. It had consumed her entire life for nearly two years. But she wouldn't admit that to the woman holding her captive, so Willow said nothing.

"To be honest," Rita continued, "I don't think the world is that different than it was twenty-five years ago. The VCRs, the old cars, those junky computers. Those are very minor things. It's window dressing. They help people believe, but it's not the secret sauce. Do you know what is?"

"No," Willow whispered absently.

"It's grief, honey. It hangs in the air around here. It gives this place a certain scent. Maybe that's what the First One really craves. What it truly desires."

Willow picked up Jacob's baseball mitt, and she turned it over in her hands a few times. She brought it up to her nose, and she breathed deep.

Leather.

Oily conditioner.

And, yes, grief.

She felt the aroma travel deep down to her core. Willow knew why the glove had been placed in the room among the children's sleeping bags and games, even if it truly didn't belong. It was just another sacrifice to the monster underneath the house, something that might keep the evil from ravaging everything and everyone around it. If it inhaled that grief each and every day, it might be too happy and numb to do anything else.

She didn't have to ask the pastor about the other items on that makeshift memorial table. She could put two and two together. They were treasured items of people who had died on the island.

Things that smelled of grief.

Willow clutched the mitt to her chest.

"What you do works," she said. "It does. You should all be dead."

"Thank you for saying that," Rita replied. "Yes, we should all be dead. Erased from this tiny little island. And it should've happened a long time ago. Can you believe it?"

"I take it you aren't letting me out of here," Willow said. She meant for the words to sound sarcastic and defiant, but they kind of crackled out of her. She wouldn't cry, though. She wouldn't let this vile woman hear her sobs.

"You know I can't," Rita said.

"You can."

"I wish I could. You're just too much trouble. I'm not a bad person, Willow. We're not bad people."

"You are. You're sacrificing me, and you sacrificed Larry. Locked him up inside this house like you're doing to me. I heard him scream that night."

Rita chuckled. "You better check your facts, dearie. We take care of each other on this island. Larry is doing just fine now. He just needed to get back on the wagon, a polite little kick in the rear." Her tone grew more irritated. "I would never, ever hurt one of our own. We need everyone here. Every man, woman, and child. This entire island should've been taken by the First One decades ago. Then it would've moved on. Only the Lord knows what it would do to the peninsula, to the mainland. We are saving the entire world, Willow. You understand this, don't you?"

Willow did. It was madness, but she understood.

"You're a smart cookie," Rita continued. "You've figured it out. You listened to the interviews, your little project."

"How did you—"

"Do you really think you haven't been watched since the moment you arrived? Lily played you those interviews just a few hours ago. You heard them. So you know what we do takes courage. It takes commitment. And we ask for nothing in return."

The realizations were making Willow's head spin. *Walking home from the basketball game, the footprints outside her cottage in the snow.* Those tracks weren't made by some embarrassed or curious hunter. No, she was being watched, plain and simple. Followed, tracked, stalked, all of the above. These people were checking in on her like they'd done many other times, for sure.

Her own gullibility in all this was making her throat thick, her chest hurt.

Another rumble. The house shook.

"This island is overdue," Rita said. "Long overdue, actually. That ticking clock stopped ticking a long time ago, but we're all still here. And now we need people like you to grow old on Clifford and carry our torch. Everyone here will die, eventually. Not by the First One, God willing. But we need people to keep this going."

"Soldiers," Willow said absently. It was what Lily had told her.

They are soldiers.

"That's right," Rita said. "And you were perfect, honey. Oh, you were so perfect."

Willow didn't respond. She knew Rita was right. A grieving mother with an estranged husband, looking for an escape, looking for answers. Seeking comfort and peace. She was the perfect candidate to live out her days on Clifford, wallowing in grief with everyone else. Living in the past, forever.

Goddamn it, she was right about me, Willow thought.

But she wouldn't admit it in the end. She was a fighter. She wouldn't concede.

"Willow?" Rita said.

"Yes?" Her voice was barely above a whisper now.

"I just want you to know that I'm sorry. I like you, Willow. Everyone likes you. But you stirred up all those kids, made them crazy. The interviews. Projecting a movie on this cursed house. Your willingness to hand everything over to the press. That's never happened before."

It's not just me, Willow thought. *Lily's boyfriend got her all riled up. He knows what's going on here. There has to be more. The world shrinks every day. More people will find out about this place and what's going on.*

She thought about telling this to the pastor, but she didn't. There was no point.

Willow clutched the mitt tighter to her chest. The house rattled again, and Willow felt the goose bumps run up and down her body.

"Everything was working until you showed up," Rita continued. "Now there's more of these little earthquakes, the kids are acting out, doing things they've never done before. Stirring up trouble, playing pranks on unsuspecting island folk. Randy Gordon, God rest his soul."

Randy Gordon.

Willow scanned her memory, and she remembered her conversation with Kayla after a youth group meeting.

"The . . . teacher?" Willow asked.

"One and the same," Rita said. "Kayla was real torn up about it. She told me that *whole* story and a few juicy tidbits about you just a little bit ago—poured her heart out to me, the sweet kid. Growing up is hard, isn't it? Especially in a place like this. But she's one of the reasons you and I are speaking so frankly right now, why you're in there, and why I'm out here."

Kayla had broken.

Ratted her out.

Willow wasn't surprised. And she wasn't angry, either.

It all just made sense.

Everything made sense.

"Don't think these kids will be acting out again," Rita continued. "Poor Randy, didn't deserve what came to him. Those kids learned a valuable lesson, though, I'll give you that much. Maybe it's for the best in the long run. Maybe they'll want to stick around and make things right. Feels wrong to say that, but I've always been a bit of an optimist, you know? We've worked so hard and come so far. We can't ruin this thing now. You know this. That's why we're going to leave you in there and leave the rest up to the good Lord."

"This won't work forever," Willow said.

"What's that?"

"Your experiment. Your plan. The kids will leave, the rest will die. It'll end."

Rumble. And footsteps climbing the basement steps.

"There will always be more out there," Rita said. "More people like you. And next time I'll get it right. Next time, I'll find someone who wants to stay with us forever."

Forever. Willow couldn't help but wonder whether she could've hopped on a boat at any time and taken off. She'd never truly considered it, and she supposed it didn't matter now. Still, she wondered.

"Could I have ever left this place?" Willow choked out.

The footsteps from below drew closer. It was almost time.

"We didn't think you'd want to, dear," Rita replied.

Willow heard the squeak of the porch steps as the pastor left her there.

She thought about hiding, but she figured it wouldn't matter. The First One would find her. And even though her dire situation was simply too twisted for any rational person to believe, Willow found that it actually made perfect sense. She even saw a glimmer of hope: Maybe, just maybe, her death would satiate the creature for decades, possibly centuries. Even forever. Maybe all the creature needed was *her*, that it had lived on these islands for billions of years just waiting for Willow Stone to arrive. Perhaps there was the tiniest possibility that her sacrifice could save the kids on Clifford, save Lily.

That's why I didn't tell Lily about seeing my son, Willow thought.

Because if I had told her that, she might have believed me. Then she might have stayed here, forever, with the rest of them.

Maybe Lily will now leave this horrible place.

The demon that would undoubtedly feast upon her would soon emerge from the basement staircase, but Willow still cracked a smile. She had helped guide a young person up here after all, and she felt like a teacher again. Everything came flooding back to her. Willow remembered the family barbecues and carpools, inside jokes and bear hugs, bedtime stories and sweet dreams—before each and every horrid domino in her life began to fall.

For just an instant, Willow was her old self.

But then the First One came for her, and it brought Willow's limping son with it. Her fantasy was over. Willow reached out to touch her son's shoulder, but as her hand got closer, the boy vanished.

Just, gone.

The ancient thing now loomed over her, and Willow craned her head to look at it. She was crying now, and her eyes stung. Strangely, Willow found herself wishing that the demon before her would resemble the red-haired monster from her dreams, perched on two impossibly long arms, mouth open, saliva dripping from razor-sharp teeth, ready to feed. If it did resemble that nightmare creature, then this entire journey would all have come full circle, beginning with her childhood and ending here, in this dank and harrowing house. Perhaps Willow was actually here for some cosmic reason. Maybe she wasn't just tricked by some rubes from a backwoods island she'd never heard of. Maybe she was meant to come here.

But it wasn't the creature from her dreams.

Willow struggled to make out what this demon before her looked like, and it wasn't just the tears in her eyes obscuring her vision. Her senses were assaulting her with a ferocity she'd never felt before, and she was having trouble making sense of what they were telling her. She smelled rotting garlic, mountains and mountains of the stuff, and the odor was so sour and pungent that it felt like it would pervade her pores and cause her skin to melt right off her bones. Willow's chest seemed to cave in upon itself, as though the force of this evil thing before her needed the space to breathe, to continue to grow, and any living thing in its path would be squeezed out. It didn't have eyes—not really; Willow couldn't spot them—but she felt them all the same. Felt them coveting her. She had the feeling this demon knew her every thought— it understood her past, her present, and even her future. She'd always imagined Jacob growing up and she rocking her grandbaby on her knee, and she swore that the thought materialized before her and was gobbled up by this primitive monster, and she knew then that she would never be capable of thinking that thought ever again. It didn't belong to her anymore—it had been stolen, consumed by this creature advancing slowly toward its feeble meal shaking on the floor. Her mouth went dry, and then she tasted blood. It was sweet, for a moment. She liked that. But more came, and she wasn't sure why it was there, why it seemed to fill her mouth, faster and faster.

Willow thought, *Even my blood is trying to escape what's coming.*

Her thoughts flashed to her childhood nightmares—the demon

allowed her to think this; it wanted her to, she thought—of lying in her bed, a monster heaving and huffing outside her bedroom door, waiting for a young Willow to let it inside. Willow had once feared that she'd willed an evil thing into existence, and others would pay the price. But now, in her final moments, she didn't feel the shame and fear she'd felt as a girl.

Instead, she was filled with a strange sense of relief.

Of purpose.

A real monster had finally come, but now it was here for Willow, and only her. She'd have no more secrets to keep. No humiliation. No grief.

Only her death.

Willow closed her eyes. Despite the madness enveloping her, she was able to hear Rita's voice again, reciting some kind of prayer or invocation outside the house, but she didn't try to home in on the pastor's muffled words. She instead thought of Paige, the student from her final year of teaching. The girl with the scholarship-letter request. Willow lamented the fact that she'd never know how Paige ended up, if she was okay. Willow desperately hoped she was, and she regretted not making that right before she came to Clifford Island.

And then she thought of Lily, and how maybe their connection would balance things out, just a little.

Leave this island, Willow thought.

Lily, just—

The baseball mitt fell from Willow's hands, and the ancient thing came down upon her.

54

KAYLA

The Night of Willow's Disappearance

The screaming finally ceased. Kayla thought it had sounded like the shrieks had been snuffed out—snatched out of the air, *just like that*, as if they'd never existed at all. The girl felt the heaviness behind the doorway, could sense the demon's presence, and it made her recoil and almost drop the hammer from her hand.

She was still holding it, standing at the foot of the Seminary House steps next to her father and Steven. Kayla had hammered four nails into the plywood, her father helping her with the first one, and then she'd figured out how to do it alone. It surprised her to find she was so deft at wielding a hammer—she'd never swung one before—and she'd smiled while she did it, her pride for Clifford Island growing with each swing and smack of the nail.

Peter Elliot had wanted her and Steven *to see*.

And did those kids see, all right.

They watched and listened as Pastor Rita had her final conversation with Willow, before the woman was consumed by the evil creature inside the house. If they'd had any doubts at all about what dwelled on Clifford Island, those had been erased completely.

Trembling in the cold outside, Kayla wondered what it looked like in the foyer—just what was left of Ms. Stone—and then she decided she didn't want to think about that. The girl instead turned toward her father and buried her head in his jacket.

That's when the tears came. Kayla began to sob, and Peter put his arm around his daughter, assuring her that everything was going to be okay, that they did what had to be done.

She didn't need reassuring.

Her tears were not of sadness, but of joy.

The girl finally belonged.

55

HARPER

Seminary House stood before me, the place these islanders had taken my sister.

I looked at the hammer in my right hand—the one I'd hurriedly snatched from a workbench in the Becker garage—and I dropped it on the ground. I wouldn't be needing it. The front door was wide open, and the plywood sheet that had once covered the entry lay on the porch. It appeared it had been ripped off. *Or maybe blown off*, I thought. Perhaps by a similar force to the one that had nearly blasted its way into the pub earlier in the night.

If I didn't know any better, I would think the house was expecting my arrival.

I fished my phone from my pocket and activated the flashlight. It was nearly dawn now, the gray twilight soon approaching. The guard was nowhere to be seen. Lily's ruse had worked, and I imagined her father was none too pleased with the stunt she'd pulled. Still, it had given me the time I needed.

But how much time I actually had was a matter for debate.

My feet planted to the snowy ground, I was still clinging to the notion that Willow might be inside the house just a few feet away—maybe tied to a chair, chained to a wall, locked in a bedroom—and the idea of her still being *alive* was causing my adrenaline to spike, my heart to race. I listened for her cries from inside, but I heard nothing but silence. I worried that the islanders had expected my arrival and had removed Willow from the house, perhaps just moments earlier.

Or, on the contrary, maybe Willow had just escaped.

I shined the light all around me, seeing the sheriff's footprints in the snow, and they made a well-trodden path of sorts around the house. I examined the area for more footprints, perhaps leading from the house somewhere else, but I didn't see any. The sheriff's footprints were consistent—he'd followed the same route, back and forth, over and over again, and those footprints then led to the path back toward the church.

There were no more footprints in the snow, save mine.

If my sister had escaped, or if someone had snatched her from the house, there would have been another set of prints, unless they'd followed the sheriff's steps precisely. It didn't seem likely. I felt a tingle of hope.

She is in that house.

And I knew what I had to do.

I took one last gander at the antebellum mansion—the stunning white columns and siding contrasted with the brown plywood nailed across the windows—thinking it was somewhat poetic that I was here, right now, staring down the same house my sister had faced weeks earlier, perhaps from the exact same spot she had stood.

Did Willow know what she was walking into? I thought.

Did she know what was inside?

And for the umpteenth time since I'd arrived on the island, I again questioned my own beliefs. If someone had asked me a week earlier if I believed in ghosts and spirits, I would have replied, resoundingly, no. And even though I still hadn't *seen* a supernatural being myself, the evidence was slapping me in the face. But it was more than Vincent's words, the startling details he'd shared with me.

It was his absolute, unwavering conviction. His desire to see a safe life for his daughter, free of a lingering evil and malevolent force. The jaw-dropped reactions of those islanders at the pub.

How could this not all be true?

How could monsters and demons not be real?

I swallowed hard, and I ascended the front steps of Seminary House, ready to find my sister.

I closed the door behind me after I stepped inside.

I pointed my phone's flashlight around the entryway, examining the rooms to my left and right. Couches. Bookshelves. An open book on an easy chair. An art easel with an unfinished game on the board. If it wasn't for the cobwebs, dust, and grime covering everything, it almost looked like people had been in this house earlier in the day. Then I remembered what Vincent had told me about the house.

It's the same as it was that terrible night.

June 17, 1994.

I shined the beam on the stairs, aiming the phone at the top step, then moving the light back down.

"Willow?" I called out. My voice echoed around the house, but I received no response. I called out again, and nothing. It was deathly quiet inside, and I blinked hard a few times, fighting the tiredness that was attempting to overtake me. I moved farther into the house, down the hallway. The kitchen lay ahead, and I was about to enter and turn the corner when I heard the voice.

"Harper?" it said.

It was Willow. Unmistakably.

My heart leapt into my chest, and I bounded into the kitchen, skidding to a stop. I desperately pointed the light left and right.

"Willow?" I blurted. "Where are you? Tell me where you are!"

Then I gasped.

Crouched over a sleeping bag in the adjacent living room was my sister.

She wasn't chained or tied up.

She looked peaceful.

Willow was wearing shorts and a hooded sweatshirt, and she appeared to be caressing one of the many sleeping bags that lay spread out on the floor. She stood up, and she smiled. Her features were soft, radiant. And she was *healthy*. The last time I'd seen her she had dark bags under her eyes, and her cheeks had appeared gaunt.

I couldn't speak.

Couldn't move.

I wanted to run over and sweep my sister into my arms, but something was stopping me. My hand trembled as the light illuminated her.

"You came for me," Willow said.

"I did."

"You found my letter?"

I absently nodded.

"I knew you'd find it," Willow said. "You were always such a good brother." She took a step toward me.

"Wait," I said.

Willow stopped, and her eyes narrowed. "What's the matter?"

I was trying to pinpoint what was holding me back. I had worried about my sister's well-being ever since her neighbor in Wildwood contacted me, and now, here I was, the puzzle pieces snapped together, her secret letter to me delivered, her location found, and I was mere *feet* away from the moment I'd imagined since I arrived on Clifford Island.

But something seemed off.

She didn't appear like a hostage. It was her calmness. Her posture. She was too relaxed. It carried an air of cockiness, like she had an agenda. I couldn't comprehend it.

"Don't come any closer," I snapped. The words just came out; I hadn't planned on saying them. I think my brain just *knew*.

"Why not?" she asked, surprised.

"I know what you are," I told her, my voice cracking.

She grimaced at this, tilting her head to the side. "What do you mean?"

"You're one of those things."

Vincent's words came back to me. Stories of dead things, who sees them, and why they see them. The man had seen his wife, and now I was seeing my sister.

Because they were both dead.

And because he and I both *believed*.

Vincent had laid the groundwork, and over the course of just one day on Clifford Island, I'd become a believer.

The look of confusion did not leave Willow's face. "Harper, they locked me in here weeks ago. Someone's been sending me food, shoving it into the house like I'm some prisoner in a jail cell."

"I don't think that's true," I said haltingly.

"It is. I was going to help the kids here, tell everyone the island's secrets, give those kids a chance at a better life. Then Rita found out, and she . . ." Willow's head turned down, and she sniffled. When she looked back up at me, there were tears in her eyes. "She locked me in here. Everyone on this island is crazy, Harper, don't you realize that? All of these stories, all of these myths and legends, nothing is true. People are just pretending. It's just one big show to keep the kids in line, to live the way they want to live. And now they've locked me in here, and you have to help me!"

Willow put her head in her hands, and she began to weep.

I again felt the urge to wrap my arms around my sister and carry her out of this haunted house, leaving this cursed island forever.

I stopped myself.

She almost had me.

I knew none of what she said was true, but it broke my heart just the same. The world seemed to be spinning around me, and I longed for

Willow to be crying on my shoulder right now. I felt an invisible rope around my waist, pulling me in Willow's direction, and I made a point to steady myself, tensing my muscles, making darn sure I wasn't going to move.

"Willow," I said, "if you're in there, I want you to know that I'm sorry. I'm sorry I was such a terrible brother. I'm sorry we lost touch, I'm sorry about Jacob, I'm sorry about everything. I should have been there for you. Maybe you would never have come here. I don't know if this means anything to you right now. It probably doesn't. But I had to say it."

Her crying grew more manic. I'd never seen a person so broken and weak.

Then, on a dime, her cries ceased.

For a second, I thought my confession had affected her, that I was able to reason with one of these things. All this time, all we needed to do was appeal to their humanity, to not fear them, but to love them like we had when they were alive. I'd discovered the secret, and all it took was one conversation.

Of course, I was deathly wrong.

My sister looked up at me, flashing a mischievous grin. The tears were gone from her eyes. "You were always a shitty brother."

I took a step back, and the dead thing took a step forward.

"*Mr. Big-Time Writer Man*," the dead thing mocked, "too busy writing stupid high school box scores to actually come visit his sister, you know, the one whose kid freaking died? You're a terrible, terrible person, Harper. One of the absolute worst."

Another step forward.

"Jacob never even liked you," she hissed. "He *despised you*. He told me so, all the time. The few times you did visit, he would cry before you walked inside. Absolutely wail. *Please. Mommy, please, I just hate him so much*. I had to drag him out of his bedroom, bribe him just to spend any time with you. That's how much he loathed your very presence."

I knew they were lies.

It was what these dead things did.

But her words cut deep all the same.

I took another step backward, the light from my phone not leaving the dead thing's face.

My sister smiled devilishly. "One of those bribes was a new scooter, which was the same one he was riding when that car ran him down. How does that make you feel?"

That can't be true, I thought.

It just can't.

I felt physically nauseous, about to double over from the pain swelling in my stomach, and my sister noticed my discomfort, causing her smile to widen.

And then, my sister started to change right before my eyes.

The dead thing's skin turned blotchy, the heavy bags under its eyes returned. Its frame slowly became more spindly, more emaciated, and the shorts hung looser off its body. Willow's full, reddish-brown hair turned darker and scraggly, the veins on her neck pronounced. The sister I knew was gone. The resemblance remained, but the being before me was an imposter, something truly inhuman. I noticed the thing's wild eyes, its fingers dancing at its waist, as if it was raring to strike me, to claw me, and it absolutely couldn't wait to do so.

The creature took another step, and then it lunged for me.

I jumped to my left and dodged its grasp.

The dead thing pounced toward me again. I again eluded its clutches, dashing into the living room and stumbling into a small table, sending a handful of items on its surface tumbling to the floor.

The thing abruptly stopped its pursuit.

It straightened up.

The creature's fury was gone, replaced with a look of shock and concern. The dead thing gaped at what had fallen from the table, and I swung my phone in that direction. An assortment of objects had plunged onto the floor. Military medals, a pair of gardening shears, a

cowboy hat, a teapot. I swiveled the light toward the dead thing, th
back toward the items, wondering why the creature was so affected b
the disturbance.

I remembered what Vincent had told me. That there were more than
just things from the 1994 sleepover in this house. There was also a place
where Rita brought items.

Offerings to the demon.

If this was indeed some sort of altar, I'd just desecrated it—and the
dead thing was aghast at what I'd done. I scrambled to pick up the objects, and my hands came across a small overturned box. I flipped it
upright, and underneath, spilled out on the carpet, was an assortment
of documents and cassette tapes.

Vincent, I thought.

This is what he wanted to give me.

I scanned the items with my light.

Letters written by Willow. A newspaper article from the high
school where she'd taught. A transcript of an interview conducted by
Dominic from when they were in college.

Vincent was right.

But why are they here?

It didn't matter. I shoved the documents and tapes back into the box
and rose to my feet, oddly surprised to find that I was again staring
down a dead thing—in my amazement at this treasure trove of evidence
relating to my sister's death, I'd somehow forgotten her vengeful spirit
was still in the house with me. It still seemed to be frozen just outside
the kitchen.

I saw my opening.

I was planning on sidestepping the creature and walking right out
of the house, hoping the thing was still so appalled at my violation of
the sacred Seminary House that it would just dumbfoundedly let me
stroll away.

I wasn't that lucky.

g charged toward me and lashed out with its right
ted this time, the nails clawing deep into the side of my
sed onto the ground, and I could feel my cheek just *hanging*
d been partially torn off. The creature stayed on top of me,
ing and grabbing, and I mindlessly brought one arm upward to
ect myself, the other still clutching the box to my chest.

Warm blood ran down my neck.

The fire inside spread.

I was only dimly aware of the fact that it was my dead sister doing these things to me. It simply felt like a flurry of movements, a cacophony of pain.

The creature stopped.

I rose weakly to one knee, still clasping the box.

The dead thing was walking away from me, gracefully, toward a doorway across the room. It looked back at me and softly smiled, and I forgot completely about the grisly assault and the injuries it had just inflicted upon me. The pain running through my body was fierce, but the dead thing's movements carried a certain calmness—there was a peacefulness to its demeanor, a strange healthiness juxtaposed with its skeletal frame that I desperately wished to possess.

A longing engulfed me. Something was telling me that I could be healed, that my burning agony could immediately be extinguished. I ached to be beside the creature, to feel what it appeared to be feeling—confidence, tranquility, contentedness. I could experience those things, too, but only if I followed it.

Follow.

Words flashed in my mind, Willow's warning to me:

Don't follow them.

A small part of me knew that this dead thing had cast its spell, that I was in some sort of trance.

That recognition vanished, and I ignored Willow's warning completely.

I managed to rise to both feet, limping slightly, noticing the tears on my pants and the gashes running down both legs. I brought a trembling hand up to my face to feel what was left of it—I felt warm blood and soft tissue, and it made my entire body shudder. The dead thing looked back once more before disappearing into the doorway, and I hobbled in that direction, each step more excruciating than the last, still clenching the box at my side.

I clutched the doorframe for support when I arrived there, and my eyes adjusted. Through the doorway was a staircase, leading downward. I caught a final glimpse of the dead thing as it disappeared out of sight into the basement below, and I was hit by a blast of cold air that was both stinging and utterly refreshing at the same time. The impulse to follow the creature was overwhelming, but I wasn't sure if I could do it—I could feel the consciousness beginning to slip away, my legs about to completely give out from underneath me.

Healing and redemption were mere steps away, if only I could make it downstairs to be with Willow. She wasn't some horrible dead thing—she was *my sister*. And she'd take back the nasty things she said about me, would nurse me back to health. I could endear myself to her, prove that I wasn't her deadbeat sibling but someone whom she'd be proud to call her brother.

I knew I wouldn't make it. One step and I'd trip and stumble down the steps, the fall perhaps doing me in completely, but *damn it*, I was going to try. I noticed my own labored breath, felt the blood trickling off my body, hearing it drip on the top step of the staircase. The darkness was almost overtaking me, my consciousness almost completely lost, but I managed to tilt forward anyway, prepared to tumble head over heels toward my salvation.

I closed my eyes.

Then I felt something.

A hand on my shoulder, pulling me back.

It was then the blackness finally came.

HARPER

My eyes fluttered open, and they were met with pain.

The daylight was blinding. More pain. Burning and intense. My cheek, my chest. I wiggled my legs, and the pain shot lower.

My eyes adjusted. The room was airy, bright.

A hospital room.

Then a voice.

"How are you feeling, sweetie?"

I knew that voice. Warm, yet condescending.

Pastor Rita.

I turned my head to face her, and the pain traveled up my neck and back to my cheek. My eyes adjusted, and they met the pastor's.

"That was quite a deer goring you survived," she said, her voice dripping with sarcasm.

Deer goring?

My memory was hazy, and I tried to remember what had happened to me.

There was the house, a dead thing.

That's right.

Then, pain, so much pain.

The creature tried to lure me away, somewhere down below the house.

And then . . . someone grabbed me?

It was extra foggy from there. But I had glimpses of a dock, a boat. The roar of an engine. Cold water sprinkling my face. And then I was here.

"Where," I started saying, before grimacing from the aching in my jaw. "Where am I?"

"Mainland hospital," Rita answered. "Someone saved your life, that's for sure. Dragged you from that car after you hit that buck. Twelve-pointer, real beauty. It got stuck in your windshield, don't you remember? Gave you quite a goring, one of the worst I've ever seen. But some kind soul pulled you from that vehicle and got you here, thank your lucky stars. Doctors say you are going to be just fine."

I had an urge to wring her neck, but I didn't have the strength. My eyes looked past Rita. The door was closed, and we appeared to be alone. She noticed my gaze.

"Yes, honey, it's just us," she said.

"You killed my sister," I said slowly, still struggling through the pain. "You sacrificed her."

The pastor nodded slowly. "I don't blame you for thinking that. Not one bit. But we aren't some crazy blood cult. Your sister was a fine person, and locking her inside that house was never the plan. I was forced into something I didn't want to do, and I don't expect it to happen again. You have my word on that."

I could still taste the blood in my mouth, and Rita noticed me grimace. She pulled a handkerchief from her pocket and blotted the inside of my lips.

"Now," she said, shoving the handkerchief back into her pocket, "you know a lot of special things about our little home. Lots of secrets you shouldn't know. I think you came across some letters and tapes, didn't you?"

Rita's words jogged my memory.

The box.

Willow's letters, the cassette tapes. Other documents.

My eyes frantically scanned the room and I turned my head, sending another searing blast of pain to my neck.

"They're not here," Rita said. "I'm gonna have to assume the boy has them, or maybe he did something with them. We're working on that. Just don't know."

The boy? Was that the person who pulled me away? I still didn't know the identity of my savior. Maybe I should have known, but I still wasn't thinking clearly. It didn't really matter right now, I supposed, so I wasn't going to press. There was something else I wanted to know.

"The letters," I said. "The tapes. What were they doing in the house? Why didn't you destroy them?"

The pastor thought for a moment. "We place special things in that house. Things that remind us of the people we love who have been lost. I think you saw a cowboy hat in there, didn't you?"

Rita paused, her eyes drifting downward, before snapping back and meeting mine. Her tone abruptly changed then, becoming inquisitive and soft. "What did that thing look like, when it came for you?" she asked.

For the first time since I'd met her, it suddenly felt like she wasn't in control of the conversation.

The pastor seemed shaky.

Fragile.

It seemed to me that she wanted to know just *to know*, not so she could tuck my answer away and wield it as a weapon later on.

I didn't want to think about seeing the dead thing masquerading as my sister, but the pastor's question jogged my memory just the same. The ratty hair, the gangly frame, the sullen and sunken eyes. Its violent and cocky posture.

I hoped to never see the creature again.

"It wasn't Willow," I finally said. "If that's what you want to know."

I thought back to what had triggered her question to me. "Whoever owned that hat wouldn't come back the same, either."

I sensed a gleam of remembrance in Rita's eyes. "It belonged to my daddy, way back when," she told me. "Sometimes at night, I hear his horse whinnying outside, and the smell of the old barn and the fields comes wafting in my window. And I can almost sense my daddy's presence; he's close to me, I know he is, just outside my front door, standing on two legs again. And he's got this big smile on his face, waiting for me to welcome him inside. And I know it's wrong—oh, dearie, do I know it's wrong—but I've opened that door before, and he's not there. Praise God, my cowboy's not there, because I'm not sure what I'd do if he was."

She looked off, her thoughts continuing, and then her eyes returned to mine, her focus back on the situation at hand. "I grieve for my father, and you might not believe me, but I also grieve for your sister. Every day I do since it happened. And those letters and tapes, well, they remind me of Willow. I couldn't bring myself to destroy them. That's why they were in that house next to my father's hat. There's a quality about them the First One might like. A scent, if I can be so bold to say."

That laser-intensity focus in Rita's eyes returned. She was back on familiar ground, speaking of keeping the evil at bay, saving the world. I noticed Rita's hand hovering near her pocket, and I considered for a second whether she might be about to remove the handkerchief again and this time shove it down my throat, finishing me off once and for all.

She's in control again, I thought.

Her one moment of weakness had passed, and I was just an injured and broken man lying before her, completely at her mercy.

She picked up on my fearful gaze, and she laughed heartily. "Oh, relax, I'm not gonna hurt you. I told you before, we are good people. Don't want to hurt anybody. And I get the feeling that you don't want to hurt anybody, either, which is why you are going to keep our secrets all to yourself."

The pastor looked up and down my body—I must have been quite a sight. "You know better than anyone what would happen if people found out about us. If that evil was allowed to leave. You know it's all real, based upon you getting gored by that deer, and all."

I knew.

The dead thing that nearly thrashed me apart. How she hypnotized me and tried to lead me to something unspeakably unholy and evil downstairs. The totality of those memories was still bubbling to the surface.

But I knew.

"I think you'll keep your mouth shut," she said. "I know it, actually. But we'll be watching you, all the same."

It finally struck me that I shouldn't have been alone with her.

Where is the doctor or nurses?

Why didn't I see them first?

Why was I allowed to wake up with this person at my side?

"How did you get in here?" I asked.

Rita shrugged. "I'm friends with the administrator here. We have people everywhere, Harper."

It was a threat, and not a very coded one at that.

The pastor winked and left me alone.

SIX
MONTHS
LATER

57

HARPER

If you're reading this right now, I'm not sure how.

Maybe Lily passed it along to someone and now it's out in the wild. It's certainly possible my email or computer was hacked, and the file containing my Clifford Island project was snared in the intrusion. It wouldn't be the most insidious thing ever done by someone connected to the island.

It's been six months since I went to Clifford Island, and I haven't been back since. I've spent most of my time working on this manuscript or traveling to high school gymnasiums and baseball diamonds back home in Indiana, writing game recaps for *The Noblesville Gazette*.

When I'm not looking over my shoulder, that is.

I haven't been approached by anyone connected to Clifford Island, but that hasn't stopped me from thinking they are never far away. Coffee shops, the bleachers at a basketball game—I've felt the stares, the dodgy glances. I've even experienced a few Jennifer Larson-Quint scenarios where I've been convinced a car in the neighborhood near my apartment is some sort of surveillance vehicle.

But no one has spoken to me about Clifford, and I haven't been threatened.

Not yet, anyway.

If I ever decide to actually do something with this manuscript, I'm sure the Clifford network will make itself known in full force. But as it stands, I'm still not sure what I'm going to do with the project.

It just felt right to put it together. I promised Vincent that I would stop his daughter from ever releasing an exposé about Clifford Island, but I couldn't stop myself from starting one of my own. I simply have so much evidence about what happened to Willow on Clifford. I have all the letters she wrote on the island—everything arrived by mail, addressed to me at the offices of *The Noblesville Gazette*, postmarked from Sturgeon Bay. The letters were only one part of a package that included the other documents I'd found in Seminary House, along with the audio interviews and printouts of text messages between Connor and Lily.

Not even Rita can control everything.

Vincent arranged getting everything sent to me, fulfilling the promise he made in his kitchen on that cold December night. I know he feels the same way I do: my sister deserves justice in some form, even if it's only her brother knowing the full truth.

Officially, it is not known what happened to Willow. She was eventually reported missing, and the authorities looked into it. They talked to me, and I told them what I knew, which was nothing at all.

I hadn't spoken with her in months, I said.

It turned my stomach when I told the lie, but I said it just the same.

Her disappearance never turned into a national news story, and thus I was never scrutinized, nor was Willow's husband. I spoke with Dominic once sometime in February when she was officially reported missing—I think by him, but I'm not entirely sure—and I told him the same thing I told the one police officer who called me. I'm not sure if Dominic ever traveled to Clifford Island himself to ask questions, but I don't think he did—I probably would've heard about that from Vincent or Lily.

After recovering from the events that occurred in late December, I kept in touch with both of them. I still hadn't forgotten my promise to Vincent—to keep tabs on his daughter—and I intended to keep it. Over the phone, Vincent explained more and more about the history of Clifford and the people who lived there, allowing me to fill in the blanks about the island's history and what was going on behind the scenes with certain individuals. Esther, Gloria, Rita. Vincent's knowledge was the basis for my reconstructions in those chapters of the manuscript.

The man loves to talk, and he wants me to know more and more.

I keep listening, and I keep learning.

I learned that after I was attacked by a dead thing and nearly lured away to a demon, it was Lily's boyfriend, Connor, who came to my rescue. Apparently, I'd clutched that box of documents and tapes to my chest and refused to let go, even as the kid dragged me from Seminary House to his dad's boat, which had been docked near the church. Connor still has no idea how I didn't drop it. He took the box with him after I was transported to a mainland hospital after my unfortunate "deer goring," and he eventually gave it to Vincent, who mailed its contents to my office. As for what Connor saw or sensed inside that house, I'm not sure. He refuses to talk about that part, and he broke up with Lily soon after. I don't know if someone connected to Clifford *strongly suggested* to him that he stop seeing her, but I think it's certainly possible. Gun to my head, I'd say the kid is likely being watched, just like me. But I'm not positive about that, which jives with everything I know about the island. Certain things are speculated upon, then shared here and there, passed down from this person to that person. Kind of like this project, I guess.

I still don't know what will become of this.

I'm desperate to tell Willow's story, and I stand by what I told the pastor in that hospital room after I'd nearly been torn apart.

You killed my sister.

Yes, it was an ancient creature as old as our planet that did the deed, but it didn't have to be that way. I remain angry and vengeful, but I can't bring myself to actually do anything about it. Perhaps putting this whole thing together is just my weird therapy, and I know deep down that I won't actually share this with the world, despite teasing myself with the possibility.

I look no further than Vincent, and I realize I've become him, in a way. He believes his wife was murdered by the islanders, yet he remains on Clifford with the people responsible because he feels an obligation to keep the world safe. That's his therapy. That, and telling me everything he knows—maybe that makes him feel a bit better, too.

And he wouldn't be doing that if he thought I would spill the beans.

He knows that I won't, because the more I know about Clifford, the less likely I am to do anything about it. I *know* the danger of that place. I experienced the horrors of Clifford Island firsthand. If the secrets of Clifford Island ever get loose, the islanders might not be able to live the way they live. And that evil that lives there might take everyone.

I believe it.

I feel the same obligation that Vincent feels.

I am now a soldier, in my own way.

And so, this manuscript sits in a folder on my computer desktop, and it will never see the light of day. But it felt good to put it together, and hopefully its mere existence in the universe helps Willow somehow, maybe repairs our relationship.

I still haven't forgotten the things she told me in that house. About being a useless brother, a terrible uncle. And I know the rules of dead things perhaps better than anyone, so I know that they are lies meant to get into my head.

But it doesn't stop the nightmares.

A decomposed Willow often invades my dreams, gleefully outlining my shortcomings as a brother and uncle, laughing at my ineptitude, despising my very existence. And every time I have one of these nightmares I wake up in horror, unable to fall back asleep, my mind fixated on Clifford Island for hours on end. I simply lie in bed and dwell on the events I experienced while on the island, wondering what life is like there now.

I wonder about Steven and Kayla, curious about the people they will grow up to be.

I wonder about Kayla's dad, Peter Elliot, and I picture him with headphones over his ears late at night, nodding along to the band playing that show from the Eagles Ballroom the night that *it* happened, and I wonder if there will ever be a day when the music stops for him.

I wonder about the families of the dead eleven.

I wonder about Rita and her incredible responsibility, curious about what she would do if her cowboy was ever standing on her doorstep.

But mostly, I wonder about Lily.

I kept my word to Vincent, and I've been checking in with her. Lily and I don't live particularly close, but we exchange messages. I let her know that I'm here if she wants to talk, and she took me up on the offer not too long ago.

We chatted for a few minutes on the phone, and the topic turned to Clifford. Talking about the island is difficult for her, but she did it anyway. Maybe she felt an obligation to Willow. I'm not really sure.

I jokingly asked her if she'd recently watched the white Bronco car chase. She laughed, and then used colorful language to explain what she'd do to any and all VHS tapes featuring O. J. Simpson.

She paused, and I sensed something in that silence.

Lily had more to share.

And after that conversation I was left wondering:

Will the kid ever be okay?

58

LILY

The boat engine rumbled, and the propellers turned. The small vessel moved backward through the water before spinning around, pointing toward the peninsula, which was five miles to the west. Lily sat on a padded seat near the cockpit, bags at her feet, and she turned to face the island she'd called home for the first eighteen years of her life.

She was finally leaving, and she couldn't wait to put Clifford behind her.

The boat accelerated, and the bow kicked up a bit. Lily watched the island closely, the June sun beating down on her face. She wished to relish the view of the trees receding, the shoreline disappearing from her vision.

Lily was counting on it being the last time she'd see any of it.

She thought back on her life over the past year. Quitting the team, then rejoining it after the events at the schoolhouse, the fire in her belly reignited. The girl had poured herself into the game, spending every free moment at the school gymnasium firing jump shots, fine-tuning her post moves, and sprinting from baseline to baseline until her lungs burned.

It paid off. In her last game of the season in mid-February, Lily scored twenty-nine points and recorded a triple-double, the ninth of her high school career. A scout from Marquette University was at the game, and that was that. Lily landed a basketball scholarship, and she was now heading to campus for summer conditioning.

Her basketball memories were the only ones she wanted to keep. The rest could go. She'd shared everything she knew about Clifford with Harper, and that was the last time she planned to relive any of it.

Mr. Gordon. The exposé. The schoolhouse.

She'd tried to forget about the schoolhouse incident soon after it happened. Lily had gotten pretty good at building mental walls during her life on Clifford, and she assumed that what happened to her in the schoolhouse would be no different. Still, she often found herself re-membering, and she'd shove the thoughts back down, hoping that would be the last time they emerged.

But now, as the boat sped through the water with Lily aboard, the thoughts again resurfaced, and the girl could do nothing to stop them. She remembered the presence in the cold schoolhouse, the warm breath on her neck, the finger tracing her hairline. The thoughts lingered there as the island continued to shrink. Lily was so close now. So close to putting that world behind her, so close to the myths and tales of the island never belonging to her ever again.

Lily spied the woods, and she thought about how it might be the last time she ever laid her eyes upon them.

Clifford Island, her home.

But then she saw her. A person, strolling out of the woods onto the stony shore. She was dressed in shorts and a gray hooded sweatshirt, the same thing she'd been wearing the night she was fed to the ancient be-ing inside Seminary House, the same thing she'd been wearing when Lily told her everything. There was no mistaking her.

Only, Lily sensed that something was off about this person. No, this wasn't a person at all. It was something else. An alluring feeling spread inside Lily's belly, and she fought the sudden and powerful urge to go back to the island. She'd spent her whole life not believing in the legends and whispers, but on the cusp of leaving forever, Lily understood that she'd been wrong. She knew what it was standing there. Or what it wasn't, actually.

It wasn't Willow. It was one of the dead things.

It beckoned Lily back home, and the girl wanted to give in. She almost yelled for the driver to turn back, but she buried her scream deep down inside, biting her lip so hard that she drew blood. Lily stared hard at the dead thing, which was now looming motionless at the water's edge, and the dead thing stared right back. The feeling in Lily's belly diminished, and then it vanished completely. The engine roared, and the boat picked up speed. Sprays of water dampened Lily's face, but the girl didn't notice. The thing that was once Willow and the island both grew smaller, and eventually they were nothing but dots in the distance.

The dead thing turned and walked into the woods.

Acknowledgments

From the seed of an idea to this book in your hands, it took the efforts of many remarkable people to make it happen. First and foremost, I thank my wife and partner-in-everything, Sheryl. She believed in this thing before there was even a word on the page. I could not have written this novel without her encouragement, suggestions, and flexibility with her time and talents. Sheryl, from the bottom of my heart, thank you for everything.

Endless thanks to my brilliant editor at Dutton, Lindsey Rose, who enthusiastically encouraged my best instincts and steered me from my worst ones with patience and kindness. Lindsey, this novel is immensely better with your expert guidance, and I am forever grateful. Many thanks are also in order to the entire Dutton team, especially Charlotte Peters, Kristin del Rosario, Jason Booher, LeeAnn Pemberton, Susan Schwartz, Nicole Jarvis, Ryan Richardson, Gaelyn Galbreath, and Jamie Knapp. Endless gratitude to Alex Robbins for the evocative and awesomely creepy cover design. Special thanks to my copy editor, Eileen Chetti, for going in the weeds and adding a layer of shine, and to my amazing proofreader, Erica Ferguson.

My manager, Josh Dove, saw this idea through from short story to novella to novel. Josh, your guidance and notes along the way were pivotal. Honestly, this wouldn't have happened without you.

ACKNOWLEDGMENTS

To my absolute titan of a literary agent, Liz Parker: within minutes of meeting, I knew you were the perfect person to take *Dead Eleven* out into the world. You simply *got* what I was trying to do with this book, and I really feel that I have the best dang lit agent on the planet. No joke. Parker Davis and Chris Lupo deserve shout-outs as well. Being a client at Verve has been nothing short of a dream.

Thank you to Foster Driver and Zoë Kent for seeing the adaptation potential in *Dead Eleven*. Your enthusiasm for this book and this world is so sincere, and I've truly found the ideal partners in taking this story to the screen. Of course, thank you to Tom Lerner and A+E Studios. It's been such a cool ride already, and I can't wait to see where it winds up. Molly Fenton has been extraordinarily helpful throughout all of this as well.

My family—especially my mom—has cheered my creative side since I was a child, and it continues to this day. Thanks, Mom!

Finally, to my daughter, Isla. Thank you for inspiring me every single day—to be a better person, to be a better father, to be a better storyteller. I hope you follow your dreams as passionately as you inspire me to follow mine.

About the Author

Jimmy Juliano is a writer and high school educator. Several of his stories have gone viral on the Reddit "NoSleep" forum. *Dead Eleven* is his debut novel, and is currently in development at A+E Studios. He lives outside Chicago with his wife, daughter, and miniature goldendoodle.